PRAISE FOR
ERICA FERENCIK'S BOOKS

Into the Jungle

"Erica Ferencik paints a picture of a jungle ripe with the amorality of nature, where dropping one's guard or losing focus means death from any number of sources. . . . As the greenery flowers and bursts and rots from within so, too, does the prose."

—*The New York Times Book Review*

"Gripping, breathtaking, and exquisitely told, *Into the Jungle* pulls you into another world, returning you forever transformed."

—*USA Today* bestselling author Wendy Walker

"The action is nonstop, the characters unforgettable, and Erica Ferencik's prose dazzles. I couldn't put it down!"

—National Book Award finalist Sy Montgomery

"[A] ferocious fever dream of a thriller . . . Ferencik delivers an alternately terrifying and exhilarating tale."

—*Publishers Weekly* (starred review)

"Relentless and frightening, *Into the Jungle* . . . [is a] torturous coming-of-age in the unforgiving Amazon wilderness. A nail-biter."

—*USA Today* bestselling author A. J. Banner

"I was lured in, caught off guard, and ensnared. I spent hours hunched over every word, deliciously creeped out, and finally out for blood. You won't want to miss one thrilling detail."

—Susan Bernhard

"A death-defying Bolivian adventure in the primordial forest . . . Thrilling, bloody, and ferocious."

—*Kirkus Reviews*

The River at Night

ALSO BY ERICA FERENCIK

The River at Night

INTO THE JUNGLE

ERICA FERENCIK

SCOUT PRESS

New York   London   Toronto   Sydney   New Delhi

Scout Press
An Imprint of Simon & Schuster, Inc.
1230 Avenue of the Americas
New York, NY 10020

First Scout Press trade paperback edition March 2020

SCOUT PRESS and colophon are registered trademarks of Simon & Schuster, Inc.

For information about special discounts for bulk purchases,
please contact Simon & Schuster Special Sales at 1-866-506-1949
or business@simonandschuster.com.

The Simon & Schuster Speakers Bureau can bring authors
to your live event. For more information or to book an event,
contact the Simon & Schuster Speakers Bureau at 1-866-248-3049
or visit our website at www.simonspeakers.com.

Interior design by Michelle Marchese

Manufactured in the United States of America

1   3   5   7   9   10   8   6   4   2

The Library of Congress has cataloged the hardcover edition as follows:

Names: Ferencik, Erica, author.
Title: Into the jungle / Erica Ferencik.
Description: First Scout Press hardcover edition. | New York : Scout Press, 2019.
Identifiers: LCCN 2018047677 | ISBN 9781501168925 (hardcover) | ISBN
9781501168949 (trade paper) | ISBN 9781501168932 (ebook)
Subjects: | GSAFD: Suspense fiction.
Classification: LCC PS3606.E68 I58 2019 | DDC 813/.6—dc23
LC record available at https://lccn.loc.gov/2018047677

ISBN 978-1-5011-6892-5
ISBN 978-1-5011-6894-9 (pbk)
ISBN 978-1-5011-6893-2 (ebook)

For George

A shaman is not a shaman until she brings back her gifts.

—*Source unknown*

PROLOGUE

It was past midnight, some lonely, small hour of the morning. Naked, I dropped to my knees at the shore. Moonlight glowed on the mist that roamed and drifted just above the glistening black river. I lifted a gourd full of river water and poured it over my hugely pregnant body, not caring what—or who—was watching or crawling toward me from the steaming jungle that loomed behind me. I would have done anything—*was* doing anything—for relief from the heat that was driving me half out of my mind, crushing me like a giant hand. I took bites of hot, sharp air. Waited for any sort of breeze. Filled the gourd again and again, drenched myself, gasping.

But the moment the water flowed off my flesh, I stippled again with sweat. My breasts glowed golden in the starlight, my nipples like sprung plugs, belly swollen drum tight, unrecognizable as my own. I squeezed my eyes shut—even my eyelids were sweating—trying to picture the beloved face of this child's father, Omar, out hunting for game so we could survive. All around me night creatures—insects, frogs, birds—hummed, croaked, and chattered, their calls breaking off now and then as they listened for their predators' approach.

Throwing the calabash aside, I pushed myself to my feet, stumbling up the short walk on hardened dirt to our hut. It had been three weeks since Omar and the rest of the hunters had been gone, weeks in which my belly exploded with growth. I felt the jungle wanting life, life craving more life, and I felt just one more obscene part of it; like the strangler figs choking the trees, this baby was taking me over, tapping every ounce of my strength.

Back in the gloom of the hut, I lifted the mosquito netting that draped our thin mattress, making sure the metal cans the legs of the bed stood in were brimming with kerosene. On the one night I hadn't filled them, I woke to a five-inch translucent-green scorpion on the back of my hand, its spiral tail quivering and stuttering. My screams brought the Ayacheran women in, rubbing their eyes and laughing at me as they batted it off with a broom. Afterward they wandered back to their huts, slurring in sleepy Spanish, their children scuffing back to their beds.

I crawled onto my back on the thin mat, inhaling the smell of burning cecropia wood that sifted through the grates of our clay oven, picturing the stone-gray scales of half a dozen armored catfish, their long whiskers sizzling in the embers.

Lying so very still, I thought about the delicacy of everything that lives, how this fine mesh suspended over me—so easily torn—was the only thing between me and every vicious flying insect, every creeping beast. I thought of the parts of America I missed: Dairy Queen, the movies, candy bars, Cheerios, malls, scented soap, libraries, fall leaves, snow; things Omar had never seen, had no interest in seeing.

To calm myself, I closed my eyes and conjured a blizzard. In my mind, snow swirled down a mountain pass, sugaring the pines until the winds picked up and piles drifted against houses and barns, painting everything with the same white brush. I cracked open my mouth to taste the cold flakes on my lips and tongue; I swear the thought cooled me. I fell off into this heaven until I felt a presence near my feet.

Something silky slid across my ankles, followed by a heavy, heated weight over my toes. Solid warmth oozed under my calves.

Still half-asleep, I got to my elbows and looked down my body at the wide, trapezoidal head of an anaconda, neon green with flecks of yellow around her cleft mouth. As if suspended by some mad puppet maker, she hovered at eye level, swaying hypnotically. My eyes followed hers back and forth, my head doing this little dip along with her. I didn't scream because even as I watched, I wasn't sure what I was seeing.

I couldn't tell if she was real.

She encircled my ankles. Pellet eyes locked on mine, her head made its way up the length of my body as she languidly wreathed herself around my legs and oh dear God—why, I don't know—but I didn't feel like struggling. She had me. I could feel her eggs, solid lumps just under the satin of her white belly. The meat of her was soft and blood warm; I couldn't take my eyes off the grace of her as she coiled her ever thicker body around my knees now, wrapped herself around my thighs, pelvis, groin. Head swinging, unsupported, she opened her mouth. Her vermilion tongue snapped out, forked end flickering. She blew her sultry breath on me and said *aahhhhhhhhh*.

Each time I exhaled, she cinched tighter; she knew me. It was intimate, sensual; she melted into me, compressed me, made me smaller. I could feel her reading my muscles, mapping the suck and hush of blood in my veins; planning every bone she would snap and crush, the iridescent diamonds of her flesh whisper-dry, and I didn't care if she kept going, it just felt so good, but one more turn and she would encase my belly.

I need to do something now, I thought. *Now*. This is my baby; if I can't care about myself, I must care for this child. Omar's child.

Her breath singed my face with all the sweetness of decay, as I thought, *Come on, Lily, this is happening, do something*. I remembered Omar telling me snakes smell their prey with their tongue; hers snapped in and out, ever faster, sniffing my fecundity. My ripeness seemed to enrage her. Quickly she looped herself once more around my belly, squeezing tight as if to pop me like a balloon, head raised in ecstasy.

I woke the next morning—the first day of the fourth week Omar had been gone—to the shrieks of macaws, their cries so heart-wrenching it felt like the end of the world every single day. Of course it had all been a dream; still, I couldn't explain why my body ached, or the bruises that throbbed on my thighs. From the doorway of our hut I watched a vulture swing up and down over the river, a deathly black cutout against the pale blue sky.

I was beginning to give up.

And then I heard his voice.

The relief was chemical; his voice among the others down by the boats made something break and re-form in my chest. I was desperate to run to the shore, but dizziness overwhelmed me and I had to sit and wait for it to pass.

He crashed into the hut, arms and chest still streaked with mud and blood from the hunt. He threw his arms around me and pulled me to my feet, stroking my hair, crying. *Why was he crying?*

"Lily, you're alive. Thank God, thank God," he sobbed. "Are you all right? Tell me you are, tell me the baby's okay." His wide, strong hands read my belly.

Stunned with relief, I couldn't speak as parts of myself glued back together with the knowledge he was alive.

"I killed an anaconda last night," he said. "I had to. He was hunting me."

His eyes searched my face like there was something I should know about this.

"Lily, they mate for life. They come after your mate when you kill theirs. They hold grudges. It's a spirit thing, they travel in other worlds."

I told him about her crushing weight, her breathtaking power, the bright green scales hissing across my flesh, the wonder and terror of her visit. He listened closely, nodding, serious, his handsome face a map of exhaustion and relief. As the words tumbled out of my mouth, I felt myself giving in; believing, finally, that everything in this place was magical and connected, that nothing here was happenstance. That my child's life depended on opening my eyes and heart to this new world.

ONE

"What do you mean, you don't know how to steal?" I asked my two new besties who sat next to me on the hard plastic seat of the ancient, shock-less bus.

For me, thieving was a life skill, like lying my way out of a jam, or taking off at the first sign of trouble. Most nineteen-year-olds bum around Europe a month or two, then scoot back home to college like good boys and girls. Well, fuck that. I was a half-starved, high-strung wild child who lived out of a backpack, homeless since I was thirteen, obsessed with Spanish-speaking countries, animals, and the jungle. I was also a desperately lonely, cocky-yet-petrified infant. In the space of a minute I could drown in self-pity for what I thought I'd missed—a real family—then toss that aside to satisfy a rabid curiosity for the world and everything in it. That second part may have been what saved me in the end.

On my right, seventeen-year-old Britta from Austria gazed out the open window, taciturn, dreamy, dark hair blowing back from her pale face. "I stole something once," she said. "Mints. From a restaurant."

Molly, a tall, talky American from Seattle, grinned and leaned in to her with a bony shoulder. "News flash: those are free." A ghost of a pedicure clung to her dusty feet in beat-up sandals, just flecks of red polish on every other toenail.

Britta shrugged. "I took more than one."

Molly and I howled with laughter. "Mint stealer! They're gonna lock you up, girl."

Below us, the narrow one-way street buzzed with lawless vitality and frenetic energy. Small European cars blew past stop signs with only a warning honk, pausing barely long enough for a withered Bolivian woman to yank a stubborn llama across the cobblestones. Young men on motorcycles cut between cars, even zoomed across sidewalks. These weren't the downtown Boston streets I knew that zipped up at night with crusty Brahmin efficiency; this was raw, stinky chaos, life out loud with all its mess, sprawl, and noise, and I couldn't get enough of it.

We three groaned each time we slammed into a pothole, tailbones bruised and aching. Laughing with fear and exhilaration, we clung to the windowsills, the seats in front of us, or each other as the cigar-chomping driver took every turn too hard and too fast. Pop music blared from the bus's tinny speakers. Diesel gassed us through the open windows. Chickens squawked and scattered across the road as we blasted by.

We bulleted around one last corner, the bus practically coasting on its left side wheels as we turned onto a flagstone courtyard. I relished the feel of my switchblade cool against my thigh, nestled in the long pockets of my baggy shorts, my beloved backpack clutched under one bony arm. With a last belch of black smoke, the bus ground to a stop near a small *farmacia* tucked between rows of vegetable stands.

"This is it," I said, jumping to my feet. "Let's go."

"Okay, *chiquita*," Molly said, tumbling out her side of the seat. "We're going, we're going."

We squinted into the afternoon sun's last rays as they sliced across the plaza, the towers of a looming seventeenth-century church casting cold black shadows across us. We wove our way past shopkeepers hawking jewelry, clothing, blankets, and cheap knickknacks, their stores squeezed into impossibly thin corridors between crumbling stone buildings. The usual stew of fear, pride, and excitement that preceded a heist—big or small—churned in my stomach. Everywhere the sweetish whiff of rotting vegetables mixed with a low note of sizzling meat, a smell that—those days—only ratcheted up the pain in my gut.

Britta pulled up short at a stall where a young girl was flipping fried corn cakes filled with melting cheese. She scouted around in her bag for some change.

"Come on, Brit," I said. "Later." *Never rob a store on a full stomach*: seriously, did I really need to explain this?

"But I'm starving."

"Not now."

"Oh, for God's sake. Just because *you* never eat."

I tugged the straps of my backpack tighter across my shoulders. Pitiful as the contents were, I always had food, whether stolen or bought. Ziplock bags of dusty peanuts, half-melted candy bars, sad old apples, stale M&M's, anything I could get my hands on. The truth was, I was always hungry; it was just a matter of degree. Growing up with seven other foster kids had me well acquainted with a chronic emptiness in my gut.

I glanced around nervously. "We'll get something after, okay?" As used to copping things as I was, it had only just occurred to me that the punishment here might be a lot less lenient than in the States. Would it be actual jail time? Hard labor? And how in fuck would I get myself out with barely a boliviano to my name?

Grumbling, Britta zipped her sweatshirt to her chin with a shiver and joined Molly and me as we huddled outside the pharmacy. "So, Molly, you've stolen things before?" she asked.

Molly gave me a sly look. "Of course."

"What's the biggest thing you've ever stolen?"

"A boyfriend."

"Good to know." Britta laughed, then turned to me. "Lily? Biggest thing?"

"As in size? Or worth?"

"Size."

"A turkey. For Thanksgiving."

"Did you get caught?"

"Nope."

Molly whistled, impressed, but back on task as she glanced apprehensively at the drugstore. "So, how is this going to go—?"

"We go in," I said. "We're super friendly. Smile and say *hola*. You know that much Spanish, right?" I pulled out a beat-up map from my backpack and handed it to Molly. "Just do what we talked about. We'll be fine."

Molly's head knocked into a little cowbell that hung over the door, announcing our entrance more than I would have liked. She giggled as she approached a solemn-faced woman who slouched behind a cash register staring out a narrow lead-paned window. Molly and Britta stood near her to block her view of me. I cased the aisles quickly: the place was dirty, everything looked old and beat. Pawed-over packets of Band-Aids, dusty bottles of American shampoo, toothpaste, deodorant. We honestly could have used all of it, but I had to concentrate on what we came for. Even before they had unfolded the map and began to ask the proprietor in stumbling Spanish the best way to get to La Paz by bus, I had lifted a roll of rubbers, three boxes of tampons, three small bags of rough-cut tobacco, and rolling papers.

"Hey, Molly," I called out. This was the signal that I was done, and they could step apart. The woman peered down at me as I picked through some dry goods. "You wanted cornmeal, right, Molls?" The absolute cheapest thing in the store, at twenty-five centavos a half kilo.

"Sure, yeah."

I grabbed a small package and took it to the counter. A glass bowl of wrapped mints sat near the old-fashioned crank register. I took three and laid them next to the cornmeal. "How much?" I asked in Spanish, counting out a few coins.

"The mints?" she said with a gap-toothed smile. "Those are free."

Molly burst out laughing and couldn't stop. Britta fought to contain herself and was unsuccessful, turning crimson as she folded the map. The woman's smile soured as she watched us, folding her arms across her sparrow chest. She looked me dead in the eye and said, "Show me what is in your backpack."

"Why?"

Her face grew stone-hard. "My son is outside. He's a big man. He'll open it for me."

Feigning offense, I counted out twenty-five centavos and stuffed the cornmeal in my bag. "*Buenos días, señora.*"

I took a big stride toward the door, but she cut me off and ran past us into the square, shouting, "Diego! Diego! They robbed me, Diego!" We sprinted past her toward the bus that had just fired up its engine, leaping aboard as it lurched into motion. In seconds, the square receded behind us and we were climbing the steep hills back to the city center.

Screaming and laughing, high from our theft, we burst into the Hostel Versailles Cochabamba—a hilariously named fleabag where we all worked for room and board—and raced down to the basement, our roach-infested "staff apartment," which was just a moldy bunk room the size of a jail cell, complete with cold, always-damp cement walls. I dumped the contents of my backpack onto a broken-down couch squeezed between the cots.

All the stolen goodies tumbled out, along with a beat-up copy of a book I'd lifted from my last group home in Boston. Reddening, I reached for it, but Molly grabbed the book and turned it over, while

Britta nabbed a pouch of tobacco and rolling papers and bolted up the stairs.

"*Charlotte's Web*?" Molly said, examining me. "I remember this book from when I was a kid. Can't remember reading much since, if you want to know the truth."

At the time, I had no explanation for why this little pig's life saved by the efforts of the spider who really loved him tore my guts out. I only knew that the story had gotten to me, made me cry, but also gave me hope that I could—someday—overcome my wordless sorrow.

"I keep some old photos in it."

As Molly flipped the pages, one fell out, all dog-eared and scratched. "Is this your foster mom?"

I took the photo from her. "Yeah, that's Tia." As I gazed at the picture, I was struck by the resemblance between the proprietor of the store I'd just robbed and Tia, my Bolivian foster mom who had died of cancer when I was twelve. Same age, same tight expression of defensiveness against great odds. Ashamed tears backed up behind my eyes, but I held them off.

"She has a kind face."

"She did the best she could with eight of us running around," I said, eyes downcast as I stuffed the book back in my bag, embarrassed to be seen reading anything other than the Jack Kerouac or Charles Bukowski from the ragtag hostel library, not that Molly or Britta would have been impressed by that sort of thing. Of course, I looked nothing like Tia; I don't look like anyone. Well, I guess I did look like a miniature version of my real mom, who I'd never known. Same curly red hair, blue eyes, but I lacked her glamorous length of bone; she stood six feet in flats, while I was just five one. Small and small boned. A social worker once told me my mom—who overdosed when I was a baby—had been a poet; in my fantasies she was a brilliant one, too brilliant to live, like Sylvia Plath.

Molly sorted the condoms from the pile and stashed them in her pants pocket. "Thanks for doing this. Mark'll be here in a few days. He never has anything."

"No problem," I said, slinging my bag over my shoulder. "But I've got to go." Thirty-four beds needed a change of sheets.

"Me too. Britta's alone at check-in. Bad idea." We grinned at each other. Britta rarely stopped flirting long enough to write down reservations and keep the beds from being double-booked. A nightmare when dozens of exhausted international travelers flooded in nightly, all of them desperate for food and sleep, none with the cash for a real hotel.

Halfway up the stairs, I turned back to look at Molly, to find her gazing after me. "A turkey, really?" she said.

"Yeah. I wore a big coat. Pretended I was pregnant. Worked like a dream."

None of us ever had enough cash. Evenings off, we made spare change washing dishes alongside laughing toothless grandmothers in local cantinas. On the best days, we nailed the occasional gig teaching English to the sons and daughters of rich families in parts of the city with dreamy names like Cala Cala or El Mirador. We were picked up in big, noiseless town cars to spend an hour or two with their precious babies in vast rooms with balconies featuring jaw-dropping views of the city and mountains beyond, then taken back to the Versailles, to our damp room with floors that glittered with silverfish. Otherwise, we worked constantly at the hostel— booking rooms, cleaning floors, washing linens, and cutting onions and potatoes for enormous pots of stew till our fingers bled.

All of us were running away from something. I'd been suckered down that January to teach English at a school that didn't exist. Stole the money—over time at a shit job in an appliance store—for plane fare, got here, no one met my plane or answered my calls. I had maybe five dollars on me, which got me a cab to the Versailles. I begged my way in, then stayed, too broke to go home.

Molly had dough, even though she swore she didn't. How could you travel the world to get over a guy, à la *Eat Pray Love*, sans cash? Still, there was something else wrong that kept her from going home, I could feel it. Britta had been traveling nonstop for a year with no idea what to do next. *Anything but Vienna*, she'd quip between deep inhales of her hash pipe—*anything but that*. Something about her father. She didn't elaborate, but that was fine. I never did either. It didn't matter.

I loved these girls with all the passionate intensity and conviction and delusion of my not-yet-twenty-year-old self. The damage in me honored the damage in them, and as far as I was concerned, that was the sum total of truth in the world. Ignoring the fact that we didn't have much in common, that Britta had a mean side and Molly lied probably more than me—which was saying something—I told myself we'd be friends forever.

But my gut knew that we were all lost children pretending we were A-OK with our clove cigarettes and our fuck-everything, we're-never-going-home attitudes. None of us had any idea what we were doing; all of us were devastated inside. There were reasons we'd ended up there, trying to sleep in noisy bunk rooms with doors that didn't lock, a new boss every other week who leered and leched at each of us. But it was as if we were stuck there, like food caught in a drain. If anyone had asked us, *What makes you tick? Where are you going? Why are you here? Why can't you get through the day without crying? What do you want from your life?* We would have been stumped for any answers at all.

As I whipped the thin sheets off rows of narrow cots, grimacing at the occasional period stain or worse, I tried to feel happy for Molly, but the truth was, this new fragile family of lost girls was falling apart, bit by bit. Did it matter who would be the first to leave? For all of us, it was just a matter of time. Soon, I would have to face life after the Versailles, a fate I dreaded—exhaustion, filth, and roaches be damned.

Nine years later, I wish I could wrap my arms around my younger, stupider self and tell her to hold on tight, because flying to Bolivia on a scam was the least of a series of bad decisions I was about to make.

TWO

With Molly leaving soon to travel with Mark, the three of us decided to blow out after our shifts one night. Just to smoke and drink and laugh, feel alive and be together. Arm in arm, we strolled along the Eastern Promenade, a bright string of nightlife packed with markets, where every imaginable fruit seemed blown up to two, three, five times its normal size: huge, creamy Brazil nuts; tart guavas; bittersweet *maracujas*, or passionfruit. Baby toucans sold as pets squawked in their bamboo cages under shelves groaning with wallets and purses made of anaconda hide. Two-foot-tall, stuffed baby black caiman—alligators that grew to over twenty feet long in the slow-moving waters of the Amazon, what I wouldn't have given to see them in real life!—had been posed on their hind feet dressed in pink tutus and carrying matching parasols. A sign propped under them said in Spanish: PERFECT TO FIT IN YOUR LUGGAGE!

Under a hand-scrawled poster that read *chamánicos*, or "shamanic," a wizened man in a vermilion poncho puffed on a fat cigarette. He sat at a low table; two stuffed and mounted jaguar heads snarling at each elbow. Across from him, a young woman held a baby whose top lip indented toward its little nose, exposing a wedge of pink gum. A thousand lines working in his face, yellowed eyes on the child, the man chanted as he waved his gnarled hands over its swaddled form.

We meandered through the cloud of tobacco smoke surrounding the woman and her baby, the droning incantations of the shaman low and constant. I stopped to watch, even as Britta nudged me away. "Come on, Lily, what are you doing? Thirty-five centavos to cure a cleft palate? I don't think so," she said with a sneer, trying to catch sight of Molly, who'd been whining about getting wasted since early that morning and was probably already at the bar.

I waved her on, but she put her hands on her hips and squared off with me. "You're really interested in this hocus-pocus bullshit? Like, abracadabra, your face is all better? Give me a break."

"Look, Britta, I'll catch up, okay?"

She rolled her eyes and strolled away, shaking her head as she went.

Of course his sorcery wouldn't work. I knew that, and maybe the mother did, too; still, I couldn't take my eyes off her—she was rapt, spellbound, lit from within. I felt a stab of sadness, even jealousy; how comforting to believe in a magical world, one where things could actually change for the better. Nothing anchored me anywhere.

I joined my friends at a café under a broken neon sign on the Prado. Around us, couples sat nuzzling; at other tables, tight knots of men played cards in tense silence. Encircled by mountains that jutted up into the night, I had the comforting sensation of sitting at the base of a vast, jagged-edged bowl. Far from the city center, ours was the last bar on a dead-end street that dissolved into a copse of trees, their branches interlocking thickly above us. To be in the city yet at the jungle's door; this element of Cochabamba never ceased to astound me.

"Lily," Molly said, getting to her feet. "Nice of you to show up. What're you drinking?"

"Tequila."

She made the sign for *loco* before heading for the bar.

Britta swept up her gorgeous hair in a messy bun, fully conscious of the men's turning heads. "You crazy American bitch," she said with a smile. "Did I tell you what I did the last time I drank tequila?"

"Fucked someone you shouldn't have? Again?"

"Have you been reading my diary? Again?"

We had a good laugh and I loved her anew. She took a swig of her beer and glanced around. A few men at a table not far away laughed with one another as they ogled us, as if daring each other to go first.

"Ugh, here we go." Molly slid between us with two tequilas.

"Easy for you to say, Little Miss I'm-Outta-Here," I said, checking out the men on the sly.

"Don't tell me you *like* Bolivian guys."

"What's wrong with them?"

"They're all macho, drug-dealing assholes."

"Maybe she likes macho, drug-dealing assholes," Britta said. "At least they have cash."

Working at the hostel afforded us our pick of single male travelers: the long-limbed Germans and Swedes; the gung-ho Americans; the big, brawling Australians. An international all-you-can-eat buffet walked through the doors of the Versailles every single evening. Still, in my three months at the hostel, only one backpacker had ever really appealed to me, this sweet French guy who read Camus and smoked continually, but after hanging out for a few weeks, he just took off one morning—bed perfectly made—and I never saw him again. In the end, most of the guys seemed sanitized and self-important, or privileged and full of shit, on their way to Machu Picchu in their high-end hiking gear, on the phone with their girlfriends back home in between lame pickup attempts.

"Tonight," Molly said, setting her shot glass down with a thud, "I'm celebrating being an expat. We're the coolest, am I right, ladies?"

"Absolutely," I said. "Fuck McDonald's. Fuck Burger King."

"Fuck all the Burger Kings in Austria," Britta said with a little beer burp. "You know we have those, right?"

"Fuck *malls*," I said. "In fact, fuck *America*, that place is so screwed up, pulleeze!! I don't care if I *never* go back!" I knocked back my drink with a wince and thought: *I am not a child anymore. Friends will have to do.* I slammed my glass down. "Fuck everywhere we've lived before here, and everyone we ever knew before us. And fuck guys, too, right, Britta?"

She winked and smiled and said, "Anytime."

I glanced up at a nearby circle of men gathered around a card game. They stubbed out glowing cigarettes in overflowing ashtrays, countless empty beer bottles scattered around their table. One of them seemed utterly disinterested in the game. He sat tilted back in his cheap plastic chair, arms crossed behind his head, a smile playing at his mouth as he stared at me through a pair of horn-rimmed glasses. I squared my shoulders and looked away, kept talking shit about America and how we were going to be intellectuals and artists and save the world from its asinine self. All the while, hot embarrassment at being watched licked up my neck.

Something clammy and small groped my forearm: a little boy's brown hand, fingernails ringed with dirt. I pulled away, but he stood his ground, staring up at me with thickly lashed eyes. With his other hand, he thrust at me a sweaty bunch of heavy-headed purple and crimson flowers. After I accepted them, he turned and hurried back to the man who'd been staring at me, and was slipped a coin or two before sprinting off down shadowy streets.

Britta's eyes grew wide. "Fuuuck. Lily, somebody *likes* you!"

Molly narrowed her eyes and sucked hard on her fat, hand-rolled cigarette, blowing smoke out both nostrils like a dragon. "Lily, you have to return the flowers, otherwise that means *yes*!"

But I was already smelling them; inhaling traces of tuberose, white lily, plus a spice, like clove mixed with grass. "Yes to what?"

Molly rolled her eyes. "What do you *think*? These guys are not subtle . . ."

I felt him before I saw him. This push of air, a cool shadow over us where he blocked the brash overhead lights that ticked and swayed in the breeze. A flame of self-consciousness, of awareness of beautiful male, zipped up my spine. All this, and I hadn't even looked up from my stranglehold on the bouquet. A long-legged black insect emerged from the throat of one of the fluted flowers, tending one of its delicate limbs into the scented night air. My friends shrank back into their chairs, stared holes into me, breathless for me to say something.

"Here," I said, thrusting the flowers in his direction. "I can't accept these."

That's when I finally looked at him. A gymnast's build, a bit taller than me, inhabiting his clothes—short-sleeved shirt a size too big and unbuttoned over the universal white wife-beater, baggy American shorts cinched with a colorful woven belt—like he wasn't aware of them. Thick black hair cut short, missing the usual pomade Bolivian men used to slick it back or spike it up. Under the blocky glasses, carved, high cheekbones shadowed a wide, full mouth. Around his neck hung a black cord strung with the incisors of a peccary, a wild hog deadly in herds; lots of guys wore them, but on him it looked right. Cheap American sandals, the $1.99 type, wide feet, beaten and dusty looking on the sides; they looked unused to being in shoes of any kind.

His fierce brown eyes, magnified by the lenses, lasered into me like he'd found something he'd been looking for, and who was I to stop him? Like what was wrong with me for not remembering who he was. Of the three of us, Britta was the knockout, hands down, so I couldn't stop wondering, *Why me, dude?* And what was with the Clark Kent glasses? Bolivian men, many of them slick and preening, often acted like they were doing you a favor offering to bed you down; *this guy*, handsome as he was, looked like he got dressed, cut his own hair, and combed it in the dark without a mirror.

"Where are you from?" he said in Spanish. He made no move to take the flowers.

"I said, I don't want them." I carefully laid out the flowers on the table as if I was showing my losing hand in a card game. I kept my eyes on the heavy velvet petals as my fingers lingered there.

Britta took a swallow of her tequila and head gestured at me. "She's from the land of strip malls and Burger Kings. Ever been there?"

"No," he said. His eyes burned into me. "My name is Omar," he added in heavily accented English.

Molly snorted into her drink. "I don't remember anyone asking you."

I squirmed in my seat, swirled the dregs of tequila in my glass. Had no choice but to look up at him again. He gave me a quizzical look, like we'd had this appointment to chat and I was ignoring him. Clearly, he had no intention of going anywhere. I reddened as a flush of heat shot up the back of my neck. I felt *chosen* in a way that flooded me with joy. Nothing like this had ever happened to me before.

"What's your name?" he asked in Spanish.

I told him, also in Spanish. Introduced Britta and Molly, who afforded him a desultory wave or small nod, tittering into their hands.

Britta said, "She doesn't want to talk to you, okay? Get it?"

I gave her a wilting look.

"Okay, Lily," he said. "So you don't care about flowers. Do you like animals better?"

I looked up at him and smiled. "Absolutely." I thought of the kitten I'd stolen from a shelter years ago, then hidden in my room at my group home. It curled onto my chest nightly, the motor of its purr setting me off into the deepest sleep I'd ever known. One of the other kids ratted me out and I had to take it back, but I never forgot the joy of being in the company of a creature not freighted with being human.

Molly couldn't hold it in. "Lily, what are you *doing*?"

Britta just shook her head and smoked, casually cruising the other men at his table. Maybe she was pissed he hadn't picked her—she was really used to that.

Omar ignored them both. They were fading into the background for me as well, with their sneers and snide comments and I-know-who-you-like-better-than-you-do attitudes.

"Come with me, Lily. It's close," he said. "Something a lot better than flowers."

He pointed to the dark outskirts of the bar, past the blinking string of Christmas lights, toward a cluster of trees and a dense mat of branches with arrow-shaped leaves that drooped down almost to the leaf-littered earth. "I saw something back there. I think you'll be amazed." He took a step back as if I were already on my feet and following him. "Just give me a minute. That's all. Then you can go back to your friends."

My brain sputtered as to what to do next. I flushed and folded my arms. Sure my friends could be bitchy, but it was a cattiness I knew inside out and could handle in my sleep. They were my fellow warriors at the Versailles; after all, they covered my ass when I overslept or put aside a bowl of stew for me if I missed a meal. But how could I shove this guy in the trash heap of Bolivian men as they saw them? How could they know he had nothing to teach me? Didn't they wonder what it was he was trying to show me—*weren't they the least bit curious?*

Just beyond the lights of the bar, the tangled knot of green and black pulsated in the hovering gloom. I sensed the dark heart of something there. The desire to know what huddled nearby pulled at me, but more than that—to say yes to his delicious urgency to show me, and *only* me, something that thrilled him—found me slipping the strap of my backpack over one shoulder. Among the pouts and sighs of my girlfriends, I felt myself getting to my feet.

Omar, in fact, stood a few inches taller than me, but was even more powerfully built than he had seemed from my chair. "I'm glad you decided to give me a few minutes," he said, his face blooming with a smile that lit small fires in his eyes.

I followed his shirt, which glowed white in the dimness down the three stairs from the stone patio to a shadowy stretch of high grass, stopping near the delicate branches of a eucalyptus tree. A soft night wind rustled the silver leaves as a full moon watched from behind feathery clouds.

He pointed into the nest of branches. "See? It's looking right at you."

I peered but saw nothing. Just fluttering leaves. As I inhaled the clean, bright smell of the tree my heart sped up—*Is this a trick?* I took a step closer and stopped short. Three feet from my face, a creature with thickly furred arms and legs hung suspended like a slack green hammock from a branch, five-inch curved claws locking it in place, its bandit-eyed face staring out at me. A much smaller, fluffier version, kitten-sized, peered from its hideaway on its mother's stomach; same eyes, low forehead, rubbery grin. A mother sloth and her baby, something I'd seen only in photos before that moment.

I took a step backward.

"Don't worry, they're slow. They sleep all their life, sometimes they die in their sleep. That's why algae grows in their fur, see the green? But watch out for their hands, their claws. Never let them get you in their grip, they'll rip you up." Magnified by the lenses, his eyes examined me. "Are you afraid?"

"No." But I was, a little.

"Good." He grinned. "They're not very smart."

As if to prove him right, the sloth lifted up one heavy arm—ever so slowly—toward a branch so slender it wouldn't have supported her infant, curled her black claws around it, and tried to swing. She came crashing down with a thump; the infant rolled away down a short hill in a terrified ball of fur. Blinking, her eerie smile stretching wider across her face, the mother sloth lifted her head from the earth and swung it side to side with a soft bleating sound. She pushed herself to her belly, dragging her torso along like a creature not meant to be on the ground, slowly swimming herself among the long grasses toward her mewling infant.

Omar sprinted down the hill, scooped up the ball of fluff, and ran back to me. "Open your hands," he said.

Insanely soft, the baby sloth rolled into my cupped hands. Its tiny eyes blinked against the light, its arms falling back as in a silent fit of laughter before curling forward in a ball. It breathed hotly into my palm before drifting back asleep as if drugged. Maybe even snored there. Omar took it from me and ran to the mother, who had only moved a yard or so, her version of top speed, unbearably clumsy as she scrabbled forward with outstretched arms. He placed the baby sloth in the grass next to her. With infinite tenderness, she found her infant, nudging her snub-nosed snout into its fur. The baby sloth woke and crawl-rolled, whimpering and snuffling, onto her back.

"Was I right? Are you amazed?" Omar said.

"I am."

"You have a boyfriend, Lily?"

We stood too close to each other for me to breathe. The trees shadowed then revealed his face as the winds gently moved the leaves. "I don't want a boyfriend," I choked out.

He nodded and smiled. "How do you speak Spanish so well?"

"Studied it in school."

"What do you think about teaching me English? Are you an English teacher here?"

I shrugged, reddening as I recalled my shame at the airport when

I realized no one was going to meet me and sweep me away to some fabulous teaching job. "Sometimes. Nothing steady."

The sloth had made it a yard or so up the trunk of the tree to the lowest branch; she swung from one arm and one leg, smiling her enigmatic sloth smile under her low forehead, her twin in miniature clinging to her chest.

"Let's start tomorrow. Okay, Lily?"

I laughed and looked at him. Who *was* this guy? What did he really want? Then again, couldn't he actually be who he appeared to be—somebody decent? Britta and Molly singsonged my name, motioning for me to return to our table. I didn't wave back.

"What's your number?" He reached in his shirt pocket and took out a book of matches and a stubby little pencil.

"I don't have a phone."

"Where do you live? I'll be there at two o'clock sharp."

I finally met his eye. "I don't want to teach you English."

He raised an eyebrow and laughed. "No? Then maybe we'll just take a motorcycle ride. Have a picnic in the Beni."

"No way will I get on one of those things."

He looked confused, borderline hurt. Two parallel scars just above his right eye deepened momentarily. "I'm the best driver out there, the safest in Bolivia, like a magic carpet ride. You'll be fine, I swear. I won't let anything bad happen to you."

I thought about what Molly had said when I'd remarked that all the guys drove their bikes like maniacs through the streets of Cochabamba. She'd brushed that away. *Those jungle guys, they can ride a motorcycle in their sleep. They're hard-core.* Even Molly had to grant Bolivian men this much grace. But more than that, the man had offered to take me on a picnic! Had any man ever proposed such a romantic and gentlemanly date? So a few beds would be left unmade at the Versailles. *Fuck it.* What did I have to lose?

"Lily," he said, like he knew me, all my disappointments, my desperate longings. Then he said it again. In his throat, the word thrummed down my spine, jellied my legs. "How can you be scared? That's not possible. It's my life, my motorcycle. It's my horse, my city horse." He handed me the matchbook. "Write down your address. Two o'clock."

I wrote the address and handed it to him, thinking, *Well, this is humiliating. I'll never see this guy again.* But I was dead wrong. Those few words and numbers scribbled on a scrap of matchbook cover changed my life forever.

THREE

At two o'clock the next day, Omar walked through the doors of the Versailles and to the front desk where I sat with Britta. Just a simple promise kept, but it gleamed and sparkled on the trash heap of broken promises that seemed to have made up my life thus far.

It took only minutes to leave the stink and noise of the city behind. We buzzed through the hill towns of the Beni, a heaven of green valleys and low, wide, sleepy rivers, of endless farmland nestled in a shallow bowl wrapped in the arms of the Andes. It was like Shangri-La. And I wasn't scared for one second. I felt liberated. I hugged him from behind, his scent of tobacco, machine oil, and sweat blowing back at me.

At a village market, we bought fruit and enchiladas for our picnic lunch. On a windswept plain near a stream, cows grazing nearby, we settled on a soft woven blanket, drinking sugary wine. He asked me question after question about myself. All the while, my anxiety grew. I thought, *The minute I give him a hint of how lost I am, he'll just take the fuck off . . .*

"Back home I go to Harvard," I lied breezily. "It's a university in Cambridge, in Massachusetts."

He lay back, resting on one elbow, watching me. "That's where you learned Spanish?"

I sat up straight and reached for the wine. "Yes, but I'm thinking about veterinary school. Maybe becoming a large-animal vet."

"What's that?"

"You, you know, work with horses and cows and stuff. There's a big demand for it now in the States."

He looked at me with intentionality, a focus. "Why are you here if you need to study?"

"I'm taking a year off to travel. Just to clear my head." I reddened. Sweat bloomed on my brow. Usually I was so much better at this. Problem was, most people I lied to didn't seem so vested in the truth.

"Do you have any brothers or sisters?"

"Just me. I grew up in this big old house on the ocean with four fireplaces."

"Is that a lot of fireplaces for houses in America?"

"More than a lot of people have." I reached for a piece of cheese, stuffed it in my mouth. It was like he was looking *through* me. I bumbled on. "My parents, they're both doctors, both surgeons. They're really amazing people; they're really worried about me coming down here by myself and all; they call me constantly and I tell them I'm fine—"

"But you don't have a phone."

I gulped the wine and shrugged my shoulders. "I tossed it. Sick of dealing with them all the time." With what I hoped was an appealing sort of spunkiness, I tucked my hair behind my ears and met his eye. "So much for me. What about you?"

He held out one hand, then turned it. "I fix motorcycles." His fingernails were ringed with black. Permanent-looking oil stains mapped the lines in his palm, his knuckles. "Show me any bike, and I can take it apart and put it back together, fix any sort of motor. Most cars, too. For ten years—since I was seventeen—I've worked in a repair shop, just around the corner from the Versailles. I used to think that was all I wanted to do."

He pushed himself up to a seated position, slapped the crumbs off his hands, fixed me with his intense gaze. "I grew up in the jungle, a few hundred kilometers from here, in a village called Ayachero, along a branch of the Amazon. It's five days by water from the closest village, no roads, the last outpost before the jungle. My two brothers—Panchito and Franz—they still live there, so does my mother.

"I miss it, Lily. I miss everything about it—my family, hunting, the animals, the air, the sounds. I'm seventh-generation Amazonian. My father and grandfather were famous jaguar hunters."

"*Jaguar hunters?*" Holy crap—*was there really such a thing?* If so, I wanted to know everything . . . then again, was he bullshitting *me* now?

He shrugged. "Sure, I didn't like killing them, but we had to sometimes. Once a jaguar comes and kills one of our cows or pigs, it won't stop. They've got the taste in their mouth; they remember where their last meal came from. And they'll keep coming back until they take everything—chickens, dogs—so we have to take them out. It's us or them. Understand?"

I nodded. I understood *us or them* perfectly.

"So, Lily, listen. What I really want now is to be a jungle guide. This British guy came into the shop a few months ago—I fixed his bike—he's got a lodge near Iquitos, in Peru. He told me, if you know the jungle like you say you do, just learn English. You'll have a job with me."

"You can get in touch with him?"

"I kept his card. And I have friends who do it. They've all learned English; they make a good living. So what do you think, Lily, will you give me an assignment so I can get started?"

I laughed. "You're really serious about this."

"Absolutely."

"Okay . . . all right. Your first assignment is to write about why you want to be a jungle guide."

He perked up, eyes blazing. "When's it due?"

I laughed again. "Whenever you—"

"I can have it for you by the end of the week." He picked up a short-handled knife and began to peel a brilliant red *aguaje*, slicing me a section of mustard-yellow fruit. The taste was subtle—a tart saffron. I wanted more.

"So that's how I know how to live: motorcycles, or the jungle life, hunting tapir for food and fighting jaguars." Sad and serious, his face in partial shadow from a passing cloud, he took a deep breath, then let it out slowly. "This is who I am. The truth, okay? What about you? The truth."

My stomach tightened down. I wasn't roaming the Boston streets with my backpack, blowing off school and feeling sorry for myself. I was facing a grown man who had taken the time to tell me about himself, to be respectful, to show a genuine interest in me. Plus, he was beautiful.

Panic. "What do you mean?"

"The truth. About you."

I flushed, a headache surging in, the wine buzz already turning. "I already told you."

"Yes, the big house. The surgeons. Harvard."

I found my sweatshirt and put it on. I wasn't cold, just stalling. "There's nothing else to tell."

He smiled, and I crumpled inside.

Why am I such an ass?

He took my hand and held it between his warm ones. "Come on, Lily, it's all right. I'm not going to run away."

I took my hand back, swirled the sugary wine in my tin cup. "I don't get it, Omar. My girlfriends are pretty. Why'd you choose me?"

He cupped my face gently in his hands, did his laser-focus thing on me until I almost couldn't bear the sweetness of it. Before that moment, I was convinced that lust was something I was already done with. I'd had my share of encounters, at least the kind where you look up at the zitty high school boy sweating above you and leave your body. Sex was nothing, or it was a violence, a currency; love a ruse. My heart—a flinty thing, bloodless, shriveled up—was stored in a tiny box in a locked room for which I believed there was no key. But it was my own dead heart, and I guarded it fiercely.

He said, "I was behind you when you three were walking through the market. I saw you stop and watch the shaman. Your friends didn't. You want to know about magic, about the jungle, don't you?"

I shivered with pleasure, with the thrill of being seen, observed, appreciated; especially since the best pickup lines from the Patagonia-clad boy trekkers had been no better than, "So, you're American?" or, "When's breakfast?"

I held Omar's gaze. "Are they the same thing?"

"Sometimes."

"Have you ever met a real shaman?" I wanted to ask, *Could one cure me of myself?*

"There was one in Ayachero while I was growing up. She was called Beya."

"Tell me about her."

"A shaman's bag is sacred, like all their tools. She used to carry this little cloth one that was always moving. She kept it filled with scorpions and small, poisonous snakes."

"Jesus, why?"

"Nobody was really sure. Maybe to scare us away. Maybe she used them somehow."

"For what?"

He smiled again, and I almost wept with desire. "I've said enough about her, and about me. It's your turn."

Those eyes, those words, anyone would have broken down and talked, even me. So I spilled about being a foster kid with seven others in a tiny house in Western Massachusetts, where I really had learned Spanish. About how I loved Tia, my Bolivian foster mom who worked in a dry cleaning store as a seamstress, how she taught me to sew, how I adored her even though she was tough, how at twelve I took care of the other kids while she was dying. How for years after her death I bounced from group home to group home, convinced there was no such thing as family for me ever again.

Evening came on fast, and we packed up to leave. As I wrapped my arms around him on the motorcycle, shame and embarrassment about my lies mixed with exhilaration at telling the truth, or as much of it as I could bear. I shivered in the chill breeze whisking down from the mountains, but soon my skin warmed, amber from the sunset's glow, my bare thighs tight against his.

We tooted along the outskirts of a dusty town, the last before the city's glowing lights. Suddenly he braked hard, fishtailing in a circle and dragging his sandaled foot in the dirt. We putt-putted toward a cluster of adobe homes, smoke rising from outdoor ovens. He got off the bike, the front of my body cold where he had been, a lick of fear trembling my hands that clutched my knees.

"What are you doing?"

He ignored the question as he rooted around in one of his saddlebags, pulling out a ball of twine. "Stay on the bike."

A scatter of chickens pecked at the dust, their heads jerking as they hunted down stray nubs of corn. A rooster stood chained by one leg with a wire tight to the base of a twisted palm, no lead at all, not one inch to move around, his ball-bearing eyes bugging and half-mad. Omar crouched down and snatched it up, binding its regal red comb under one arm, so with all its yowling and kicking it couldn't peck at him. He unwound the wire from the rooster's leg where it had worn away rubbery flesh to gristly bone. Still holding him fast, he wrapped a length of twine loosely but firmly around the bird's other leg, then tied it to the same tree, this time allowing it a generous lead.

Head drooping, the rooster haltingly lifted its formerly chained leg, stopping short in midair as if expecting the usual agony, then—quivering—extended the ravaged limb and took a step, then another, and another, before running around the full length of its lead, flapping its bright orange wings. Red wattles shaking in joy, it strutted and crowed at the top of its lungs.

Looking back, that was the moment when the door opened for me. My dried-up heart took on warmth, acknowledged this flash of sunshine and expanded, as much as I tried to stuff it back and away. The thing I swore I would never let happen was happening, had happened. I was a goner. My mouth was dry. I hugged myself warm again; I couldn't look away.

He wrapped the spare twine back into a ball as he smiled at me. He knew.

He circled the tree the rooster was tied to, his fingers lightly tracing the bark. "Poor thing. Look at this." A cement cistern had been cruelly dug deep into the tree's root system. Dead leaves curled along its withered branches.

He cast a wary glance at the shack just yards from us; its door hanging off its hinges, a feed sack for a curtain billowing in the one small window. "You can know a person by how they love their trees. Their animals."

I was only half listening to his words, because he sounded like a kind of music.

I had no idea who he was yet, really, even this side of him, the sweet side. All I could do then was spend every waking moment with him—and every sleeping one—in his tiny flat near the clock tower in the main square, on the second floor over a store that sold cheap plastic shoes. From then on, I would associate the reek of rubber and glue with sexual ecstasy, with longing, with the abject terror of letting go.

FOUR

– APRIL –

We met at dawn on the mornings I worked the night shift at the Versailles and couldn't stay with him. Just to have a few minutes together before the work and grind of the day. Steps from his shop was an outdoor breakfast hole-in-the-wall that served vegetable truckers and farmers bringing their animals through town for the morning markets. A grungy, impossibly dusty place where the owners would call back to the cooks when we arrived, to say, simply, *los amantes están aquí*—the lovers are here—and in moments our coffees and pastry would arrive, the waiter all smiles and winks.

One bright cool morning, Omar shuffled to our table with a book bag slung over his shoulder, a pleased grin on his face.

"Sorry this is late," he said, sliding in next to me. "But you keep me pretty busy, you know." He tore some sheets from a notebook and handed them to me.

I swept the papers around to have a look. Omar in English. I couldn't even picture it, but there they were, pages of his words in blocky capital letters.

"It was harder than I thought, Lily. I had to use the dictionary for almost every word. Okay," he said with a smile. "Every word."

I laughed, glancing it over. "This is really good, Omar."

"So you're giving me an A for 'excellent'?"

I slid the papers back to him. "Not until you read it aloud to me."

"*What?* No." He shook his head. "That wasn't part of the assignment." He glanced around at the rough men who filled the place, as many of them drinking cerveza as coffee before eight in the morning.

"So you're just going to hand out written notes when you're a guide?"

"Come on, it'll sound like a five-year-old wrote it."

I smiled. "Omar, no one is listening but me."

He snatched the papers up. Sighing heavily, black bangs badly in need of a trim sweeping across one eye, he pulled his battered reading glasses from his bag and slipped them on. "Okay, Señorita Lily Bushwold. Here it is: 'Why I Want to Be a Jungle Guide,' by Omar Mathias Alvarez." He spoke in a low voice, his eyes glued to mine when he wasn't reading from the page.

I nodded, elated to play teacher with him.

"'I love the jungle. It is my home. I leave the jungle to make money repairing many motorcycles. I think, this is why I am on earth. Motors and wheels. But when I leave Ayachero and try the city I am unhappy. I am surprised.'" He rolled his eyes. "Well, the Cochabamba story is another story," he added in Spanish.

"Go on. English."

"'I am angry about roads coming in the jungle, about poachers who kill rare game, mahogany prospectors, narcos, ranchers who burn the forests. I know, I am part of this problem, maybe, because I kill animals in the jungle, but only for saving people or to have food for the villagers. These men destroy my paradise, the paradise that belongs to the world. I call these men *los hombres de oportunidad*. In English, "men of opportunity." Maybe they drive a barge that leaves poison chemicals, mercury, in ten kilometers of river to pull only ten grams of gold from the mud. Everything dies. Maybe they kill the giant pregnant mother tortoise for her shell, the baby caiman to make stupid dolls. Maybe they look for big mahogany. They don't care what they destroy, they want the money, the money, the money.

"'One of these men is Fat Carlos. His friend is Dutchie. These are men of opportunity. Five men are with them when I live there, always they kill the rare game. When I am fifteen or sixteen my belief is to fight them, fight all of them. With my hands, with guns or knives. I have violence inside. But now I am older, and I know I am one man only. What can I do?'"

Enamored with his story and him, I reached out for his hand; he gave me a nervous smile and continued.

"'It is maybe a contra-dic-shun, but now I believe the only way to save the jungle is bringing people from all over the world to see it. Next they love it. Next they want to save it. How else to teach about jaguar, anaconda, giant river otter who is two meters long, the hilarious bird that looks insane with spikes on his head and smells bad and can barely fly, this bird is called *hoatzin*. How else to teach about spider monkey, titi monkey, or howler monkey you can hear from ten kilometers, about white-lipped peccary who can attack you but taste delicious, about plants that give you fresh water from their bodies, plants that heal your skin, that heal your belly, heal your mind? This is why I want to be a jungle guide.'" He tossed the paper on the table. "The end."

Not caring if anyone was watching, I pulled him in for a long kiss.

"Pretty bad, huh," he said, slipping his glasses off. "Was that a pity kiss?"

"Don't be insane. That was incredible. You get an A plus. Are the river otters really that big? Can you really drink from the plants?"

"Yes about the plants, and we call the river otters river wolves. It's not safe to be in the water with them, but when they play together, there's nothing more fun to watch."

"Now, Ohms, I want you to tell me a secret. About you, or the jungle." His incredible story had only whetted my appetite for more.

He folded his arms, considering me. "Why?"

"Well . . . I've told you some things about myself I've never told anyone. It's only fair . . ."

He pushed aside his assignment and we leaned in close to each other. His face grew serious, his voice almost a whisper.

"You promise to keep my secrets?"

"I promise."

"All right." He took my hands in his. "There's a huge grove of mahogany, several hectares, a rare thing because there are very few groves of anything in the jungle. There's a tribe that lives two days into the jungle from Ayachero, called the Tatinga. Only the Tatinga know where it is. When I was a kid, I hunted with them, and one day we found the grove. If the wrong people find it, like Fat Carlos, everything in that part of the jungle will be destroyed. Roads, machinery, destruction. It'll be the end of Ayachero, the end of the Tatinga. This is sacred knowledge, Lily, and I'm trusting you with it."

FIVE

I skipped up the stairs to the raised patio of the cantina where we met each Friday at eight. We loved this place because of the band that played slow songs; we'd dance a few before heading off into the night, drunk with each other. The evening was cool and calm, the sky rang with bright stars. I took off my backpack and had a look around. No Omar. For the first time ever, I had beat him to our usual table.

In minutes a man approached me, open shirted, big gutted, flirting hard until I slapped back with some real nasty fuck-you Spanish Omar had taught me. His face screwed up in a lemon-sucking grimace and I was rid of him. It was 8:23 by the Mickey Mouse watch I'd found on the street.

My mind raced. Maybe he was still at the shop, cranking on a busted engine he'd promised some friend would be fixed by the end of the day; he was always doing that, staying as long as it took to get the job done. Or maybe I got it wrong, and we were supposed to meet at his place first . . .

8:45. Impossible to sit there one more second. I paid for my cerveza and sprinted from the place, bounding down all the shortcuts and alleys, rats snacking on garbage lumbering out of my way as I ran. I flew up the rattling fire escape—his "private" entrance.

Knocked hard. No answer. Called his name, my voice wretched in the night. Hands shaking, I got out my key and let myself in, locking the door behind me.

The overhead bulb swung back and forth, casting monstrous shadows. Suddenly cold, I opened his closet, grabbed his warmest shirt, and slipped it on. I scouted out the bottle of tequila we'd tapped the night before, took a big gulp, and sat on the bed, rocking and humming the theme song to a forgotten television show from my childhood. A few flights up, a man and woman argued loudly, their baby chiming in with its own high-pitched misery.

Half an hour crawled by. Plenty of time to listen to the scratchings of whatever lived in his wall, plenty of time to imagine terrible things, plenty of time to finally get that I was crazy about this guy, to have no concept of how I could go on without him in my life. To feel gutted like a gourd by the prospect of being without him.

He had to be at the shop. I bolted down the rickety stairs. Head down, shoulders drawn tight, face flushed with an old shame—a chronic fear of being deceived—I jogged down the crowded streets, parting the waves of Friday night revelers, the tourists, the hustlers. *Had he decided to leave me, just like that?* Just get to Omar, I told myself. Then everything will be all right.

I turned the corner to the motorcycle shop. Even from a block away, I could see it was dark and shuttered, the wide garage doorway closed and chain-locked, all the display bikes rolled in for the night. Still, I banged at the window, resting my hot forehead on the cold metal of the door, searching for the calm core of myself that did not exist.

I lifted my head. A light in the back of the shop, dim, flickering. I beat at the glass, pausing only to rub a spot clean with the palm of my hand. The sound of boots on concrete. Tumblers turned in the lock, a metal finality. The heavy door creaked open. Pride long gone, I threw myself at Omar. He wrapped his arms around me, dipped his head in my hair and breathed me in.

"Where were you?" I cried.

He held me for another moment, then took me by the shoulders and pulled me away. I glanced behind him. The shadow of a person sat at a table in the back of the room. "I'm sorry, Lily. There was an emergency, and you don't have a phone, so I couldn't—"

"You could have come and gotten me, why didn't you—"

"I went to the restaurant. You'd already left. Then the Versailles."

"I went to your place, Omar. Where else would I—"

"Calm down." He drew me to him, obviously unnerved and surprised by how upset I was. "Try to calm yourself."

I shuddered into him a few extra seconds before he took my hand with a firm grip. I followed him past rows of bikes leaning low into their stands like dozing animals, to a shadowy alcove in the back of the store.

A heavyset man sat at a card table nursing a beer and a smoke. He wore a filthy madras shirt and ragged cutoffs. His eyes were slits in his chubby face, clipped black hair slicked back. One foot wore a rope and leather sandal, the other leg was missing from the knee down; a complex system of straps and clasps held a roughly carved wooden prosthetic. His belly was a perfectly round ball straining the two remaining buttons of the shirt.

He pushed himself to standing and held out his hand for me to shake.

"Lily, this is my brother Panchito."

"*Encantado*," he said. He smiled briefly, his eyes disappearing in puffy cheeks.

"Panchito came from Ayachero to tell me some bad news." Omar sat heavily in a blown-out armchair, rubbing his face with his hands. "Have a seat, Lily."

The weight of exhaustion and sorrow in the room mixed with the reek of crankcase oil, rubber, and gasoline. I pulled out a rickety stool and tried to get comfortable on it, while Panchito awkwardly took his seat again, setting his leg at right angles to his knee under the table with his hands.

"A jaguar has killed our brother Franz's son, Benicio," Omar said. "He was only four years old."

Panchito stubbed out his cigarette in the overflowing tray. "We saw jaguar prints at the far end of the Tortoise Beach. Way down past all the boats. We think he wandered off to play with the baby tortoises. Or maybe to gather some eggs for dinner to surprise his mother. It was Anna's birthday. He was always trying to help. He looked a lot like you, Omar, everyone said."

He handed Omar a beat-up photo. Omar gazed at it, then handed it to me. A little-boy version of Omar straddled an overturned canoe, grinning as he held an enormous fish to the camera.

"I'm sorry," I said.

"We haven't found a body. No clothing, nothing. But we're sure. The way his prints went, and then the jaguar's . . ."

"No one heard anything?" Omar leaned forward in his chair, shoulders rigid, strong hands hanging down loosely from his wrists. Harsh overhead light carved dark circles under his eyes as he focused on some distant point on the floor. Fear flipped my heart; I knew him, but not well enough to know how this would touch him.

"The men were hunting," Panchito continued. "The women— mostly they were in the manioc fields. The Frannies were down from their camp teaching the older kids, but they do that in the longhouse. It's hard to hear from up there."

"The Frannies are two American missionaries," Omar said, eyes still glazed over. "Both named Frances. I'm amazed they're still around."

Panchito crossed his arms high over his belly. "It's not like it was. So many men have left, Omar, so many young families, off to San

Solidad, then La Paz. We're down to maybe a hundred now, lots of old people, lots of kids. Maybe half a dozen guys who can still hunt. You leaving . . . It gave everyone ideas."

Omar hunched his shoulders. "How's Mother?"

Panchito smiled a little, running a thick paw through his slicked hair. "She's tough, you know, she can handle a lot. But this one hit her real hard. Her little grandson, you know. She wants you to come home, Omar. Everybody does."

Later that night, we sat across from each other at a rickety table in his tiny kitchen alcove, the bottle of tequila between us.

"Let me come with you."

"You don't know what you're talking about."

He grabbed the bottle and got up, leaning against the sill of the open window as he drank, stars glittering in the night sky behind him. Fuck, he was beautiful. His rugged jawline, that direct stare, his utter lack of self-doubt. This power he had. I felt a dropping sensation in the deep space of my pelvis, telling me what it wanted, yet again; I had a premonition of the beginning of a bad habit, a brand-new one for me—child that I was—but the part of me that should have been afraid—Jaguars! Snakes! Tarantulas!—was obliterated by the strongest pull of all, sweeter and darker and delicious. And who can argue with the body and biology, the thing that keeps the world spinning on its axis? I wasn't the first in line for that.

The yellow liquid in the bottle swished like nausea in his grip, the blind tequila worm twisting in the dregs. He took another drink, wiping his mouth with the back of his hand. Suddenly he looked a decade older than his twenty-seven years.

I got up and snatched the bottle from him, took a gulp, my head already warm and runny and spinny after two sips. "I'm coming with you."

All information to the contrary, I had begun to conjure some fairy-tale magical life under the stars in "nature," away from the filth and noise of the city; just us in a hut making love endlessly for the rest our lives. He would kill the jaguar, and all would be well. His family would welcome me with open arms. Fruited trees would drop their bounty on us; the fields of manioc—whatever that was—would provide.

Everything I knew about the jungle then came from *The Jungle Book*. Surely a kind and wise panther animated by some baritone-voiced actor would guide me through the not-very-scary cartoon perils of a green and mysterious world.

"No electricity. No running water. No fancy restaurants, no roads, no stores, nothing. You live in a hut made of palm and bamboo."

Stores? Really, I couldn't care less. And fancy restaurants? Wasn't that where rich people went to celebrate with their families? "I'm fine with that."

"Have you ever fired a gun?"

"No, but I've seen plenty of—"

"Movies? Do you know how to use a bow and arrow?"

I shook my head.

He began to pace. "A slingshot? Blowgun? Spear? You afraid of blood? You're a vegetarian, for crying out loud, you'll be freaked out every second of every day. Everybody eats meat there, fish. Not from some market where it comes wrapped up all pretty, understand? Catch it yourself, clean it yourself, cook it yourself."

"You're not going to talk me out of it."

He laughed and shook his head. "You wouldn't survive. You'd be begging me to leave in a week."

"Bullshit, Omar. I can handle it."

"You can handle insects, and heat, and floods? Me being gone on hunts for days and days?"

I folded my arms hard over my chest. "Why don't you think I can hack this? You think I can't learn new things, I'm soft or something? You think I've never had to fight for my life?"

He couldn't suppress a warm little smile. "Tell me about that."

"This girl in a group home I was living in. She hated me, no idea why, still don't know. She was in some kind of gang. I woke up one morning and she'd hacked off most of my hair while I was sleeping. She said, 'Meet me outside tonight, six o'clock, all my girls will be there to beat the shit out of you.'"

"What'd you do?"

"I showed up."

"Did you have your switchblade?"

It was my turn to pace. "Yes. But in the end I just used my fists. They made me fight this big girl, not the one who'd cut my hair. This one was twice my size, a monster. The rest of them stood back. Made bets. Cheered her on."

"What happened?"

"She wasn't as angry as I was. And no way was she as scared. She was just big. Slow." Could never forget the look of surprise on her face as I jammed my knee in her back, her cheek grinding into the gravel. "My foster brothers showed me a bunch of tricks, because I was so small."

"You're very brave."

"Maybe I'm just stupid." I huffed back to my seat and plopped down, miserable in my stew of love and desperation. "Begging to go fight jaguars with you."

"I love you, Lily. That's why I'm telling you how hard it is."

We were both quiet a moment, his declaration of love seeping into me like syrup into a cake.

"What the fuck, Omar?" I said more softly now. "What about learning English? What about being a guide? Don't you want that anymore?"

"Course I do. But I want you safe and happy more."

"I'm safe and happy with you. Only with you."

He put the bottle down and rubbed his eyes. "You'd go to the jungle with some grease jockey you've known for two months?"

I nodded. "You love the jungle. Every day you tell me that. You want to try to save it. Why can't I be a part of where you love, if you love me?"

He stared at me for several seconds, as if seeing me clearly for the first time. His face softened. "Will you take the time to learn about my home? Will you be patient? It's hard physical work, lots of cooking and hauling water and working in the fields."

"Please. You know the hours I put in at the Versailles. I've had a job since I was twelve."

"Will you do everything I tell you to do if we go to Ayachero? Every last thing?"

"Yes."

"It's life or death, this promise you're making. *Your* life or death. These aren't just words. Don't just say them to please me."

"I'm not. I promise to do everything you tell me to do."

He nodded, and I went to him; he held me like family. "We won't stay there forever. I need to make sure everyone is safe," he mumbled into my hair. "Then we can move on." He took me by the hand and led me to his bed; we sat down side by side. He watched me for a long minute, then reached over and took my hand.

"Lily, what's your biggest sorrow?"

No one had ever asked me anything like that before. The question felt so personal and painful I tried to pull my hand away, but he wouldn't let me. "Why don't you tell me yours?"

He looked at me as if to ask, *Do you really want to know?* I put my hand over his to show I did. "The loss of my good feeling. The loss of my jungle life. Leaving my family, especially as the oldest son. Everything that I've killed inside myself to live here. This big, dirty city. There's something else, I don't have the words for what it is. Maybe the loss of *Pachamama*, what's that in English? She's a goddess of fertility, but it means Mother Earth, trees, water, animals, rain, plants. I thought I was done with that somehow, didn't need it anymore. Crazy."

"I think I know what you mean."

"Really? Do you?" His eyes glittered with tears. "It's good to talk to you, Liliana." We lay down on his creaking bed on our sides, facing each other. His small buzzy lamp bathed us in a warm orange glow.

"Omar, that first time we went out, how did you know I was lying about Boston and my parents being doctors and all that?"

He stroked my face with his rough hand. "I've never seen anyone eat like you before."

Shame flooded me. "What's wrong with the way I eat?"

"You don't eat much, but you eat so fast, like you've never seen food before. No one has ever told you?"

"No."

"And the way you wrap your arm around your plate, like someone's going to take it from you. You're not a regular spoiled American *chica*."

I pouted a little. "Speaking of that, why not go with some rich American *chica*?"

He sputtered out a laugh. "To them I'm just a dirty bike mechanic. I don't even speak English. They look down at me. You've never done that. Why should I care about them?"

"So you don't wish I were like them?"

"Lily Bushwold, don't you see your own loveliness?" He stroked my hair, my cheek. "And you loved that sloth, didn't you? We're more the same than you think. You in your jungle, me in mine."

I kissed him then, as long as I wanted to, touched him where I wanted to. I felt him watching me so closely, waiting for us to be in sync, as if he refused to go one step past me on the path, determined to ride the sweet wave together.

This felt like love to me, the closest I had ever come, like something I would do anything not to lose. Omar slept turned away from me with his arms around his pillow, one knee drawn up as he dreamed his jungle dreams. I stroked his shining black hair, pulled my body close to his. Why couldn't we always stay like this, cocooned, motionless?

I lay there dreaming, wide awake, enjoying the peace before the tinny radios, the screaming babies, the clang and bluster of the market below his window, right up until the moment the night sky in the window blushed pink, soft and delicate, and I couldn't help but feel a flicker of hope for the world.

Omar was my home. I had no other.

By the end of the week, we had sorted through everything we owned—a task that took minutes for me, a day for him—to fit in the small bush plane we would fly to Ayachero. We bought cheap tin "wedding" rings at the market; he'd convinced me it was best to be considered a married couple where we were going. He sweetly explained all this to me, slipping my ring on my finger with words of love and commitment made up on the fly next to a stall where whole chickens roasted on a spit. I didn't explain that I couldn't care less about marriage—at the time I saw it as some bizarre ritual actual adults took part in, in lives marked by college degrees, full-time jobs, health insurance, and other foreign concepts. The approximation of a vow felt familiar and comfortable to me; perhaps at some profound level I felt I didn't deserve the real thing. But none of that mattered to me then. If I needed a ring to smooth things over in his hometown, so be it.

I rushed to meet Molly and Britta for a goodbye beer at our favorite place, the restaurant where Omar had sent the little boy to tempt me with a bouquet of flowers a couple of months previous.

Molly sat by herself, wrapped in a ratty sweater and smoking a home-rolled cigarette to the nub, her crossed leg swinging nervously back and forth at the knee. She looked exhausted.

"Where's Britta?" I asked.

"She had to work."

"Seriously? She couldn't even come to say goodbye—"

"She had a fucking date, okay?"

I felt sucker punched. My worthlessness reinforced in a way I never felt with Omar.

Molly wrapped her hands around her sweating beer and gave me her sternest look. "You don't have to do this, Lily. Who is this guy, anyway, some motorcycle repair dude who can't even speak English? And what the fuck is this Ayachero place? I've asked around. Nobody's heard of it; it's not on any maps."

"It's where he's from. It must exist."

"But I mean, come on, Lily, the jungle? *Really?* What do you know about living in the jungle?" She shook her head, knowing it was useless, I could see it on her face. And I hadn't even told her about the jaguar. "You're fucking nuts, okay, you're fucking crazy," she said quite seriously.

Even though a niggling part of me agreed with her, all I could do was smile.

"You can still change your mind, you know. He'll get over it. You're just another girl to him. Just walk away, come back to the Versailles."

I pictured the South American–sized roaches scuttling in the sink; my hands chafed and bleeding from cooking and cleaning; my terrible loneliness, even with my friends. Omar was a new planet in my orbit, changing my gravitational pull.

Molly knocked back the dregs of her warm beer. "Can't you just fuck him and leave it at that?"

"I love him, Molly."

"Oh, please." She rolled her eyes. "That is some shit I don't want to hear about right now."

I struggled to answer; Mark had broken up with her the minute they returned from their week away together. I sat up straight. "Sorry if you don't understand."

She picked at the label with her ragged fingernail. "Okay, I get it," she sighed. "You found real love, and fuck me, maybe that's just not going to happen for me."

"Don't be ridiculous."

She waved me away. "Just remember, that top bunk will always have your name on it." She got up and hugged me hard but fast. "Good luck."

I started down the steps toward the street. Her face stayed hard and unsmiling as I turned to wave goodbye, but my joy could not, would not be diminished. No force on earth could have kept me from going to Omar on that sunny, windswept afternoon.

The jagged line of mountains that encircled me seemed to murmur, *Yes, he is your life*; the broken cobblestones under my feet whispered, *This is your future*; the laughing grandmas at the tamale stands nodded, *Yes, go to him*.

In return, everyone I passed got a smile from the mad-in-love teenage *gringa* on her way to her lover.

I never saw Molly or Britta again.

SIX

P assport in hand, my nose to the floor-to-ceiling windows of the Cochabamba airport terminal, I stood watching planes take off for La Paz or Santa Cruz, where passengers could connect to US flights; any of them could have taken me back home, or at least out of South America. Mentally I tried it: I flew back to Boston—to no place to live; to no one waiting for me; to a gray, rainy spring day; to rivers of pavement through forests of looming buildings; to everything good I had sabotaged.

An enormous canvas bag weighing one shoulder down, Omar stood at the far end of the terminal in a massive cargo door entryway, his lean body framed by the blue-eyed sky beyond him. He head-tilted for me to join him. That's all it took.

I followed him outside under a blazing sun to a distant corner of the tarmac, where we came to a rusted collection of metal scraps in the shape of a bush plane—the main cabin no bigger than the inside of a small car. It shuddered on the rutted tar, diesel sputtering, a farting, ancient beast. The propeller took its time to rotate, mulling flight with minimal enthusiasm. From the pilot's window, a tan arm in a torn sleeve rested across the metal edge, cigarette dangling.

I can leave, I thought. *I don't have to do this. This is possibly a very bad idea.*

Omar turned to me, read me, said, "It's okay, Lily. You'll be okay. I've done this many times before."

All of me wanted to believe him, even as pangs of fear and doubt sprung up in my gut. But it didn't matter; I was all in. Fear and doubt were old friends; ignoring them had served me pretty well so far, or at least that's what I believed. Besides, just beyond the cool glass wall, the waiting room bustled with strangers from around the world, with people who didn't give a shit about me, people busy heading to their own Omars, their own places they called home.

We walked together to the plane. After instructing me to sit next to the pilot, Omar disappeared in the back of the cramped four-seater. As he rearranged our small pile of belongings, I settled on the sun-bleached leather seat and strapped myself in, nodding at the little bush pilot: a ropey man in a T-shirt featuring a teenage Britney Spears in full pout, a Chicago Bears baseball cap worn backward, board shorts, and no shoes. He looked at me with no expression, then back out at the horizon. Behind me, I heard the sound of some-one spitting.

I glanced in the narrow rearview mirror, spider veined with cracks. A hunched figure rooted around in a canvas sack. Panchito tucked his bag in the narrow aisle, turned, and planted himself in the small bucket seat next to Omar's. He arranged his leg, sat up, grinned, and said *hola*. His cheeks bulged as he chewed coca leaf, the occasional shred falling from his mouth, his teeth stained faintly green. He tilted a flask in my direction; I nodded yes and knocked back a few burning gulps of strong pisco before handing it back to him.

The 1950s-era amphibious Cessna whined like a lawn mower as we wobbled and jounced across the rutted tarmac; every rock and stone under the wheels jangled us. The stiff breeze that swept down from the mountains tipped the wings up and down. Even strapped in, we helplessly rolled in our seats as the plane gathered speed.

The moment we ran out of runway we lifted off, something heavy and metal slamming in the hold with a thunderous boom as we did so, the tail dropping sickeningly before we took on any real altitude, finally gaining a delicate equilibrium, some primitive compromise of wind and metal and basic aerodynamics.

I gripped my armrests, leaned forward, breath steaming the pocked windshield. It felt like my prayers alone kept us aloft. My terror reflected back at me in the pilot's mirror shades; he smirked, his gold incisor flashing. Later I would learn that the banging noise had been improperly secured gasoline canisters in the cargo hold— the extra fuel the only way the plane could return from our destination to Cochabamba or anywhere else, for that matter. We had nine hours of fuel and a four-hour journey. Not a lot of play. The pilot slipped on his headphones and switched on or off a series of dials and knobs, ignoring all of us.

Below, the city's bright puzzle of streets under a greenish-yellow bowl of pollution swiftly fell away. Molly, Britta, the Versailles; all literally now in the rearview mirror. The plane struggled to rise above the first snow-crested mountain ridge. I craned my neck skyward, as if to achieve altitude with my will. We chugged over the first craggy peak—ponds beneath us glittered like dropped jewels—then the crests stretched out endlessly before us, valleys dropping into ominous shadow.

A meaty thump behind me. Panchito had crumpled to the floor of the plane. Rumbling around on the ripped canvas in search of comfort, he pillowed his arms under his head, false leg resting at an odd angle, the gears and straps loosened. In seconds he was snoring.

"Is he okay?" I called back.

"He's fine," Omar said, chewing on a toothpick as he watched the mountains parade beneath us.

A flush of something like shame washed over me, I wasn't sure why. How little I knew this man, really. "How did he lose his leg?"

Omar slipped the toothpick out the cracked open window; the wind snapped it away. He leaned toward me so I could hear him over the engine. "He was young. Twelve, maybe. He went off to hunt by himself. Stupid plan. You never go into the jungle by yourself. *Never*, okay? You're with me or someone who knows what they're doing. Understand?" His voice rose a little as if I'd already made such a featherbrained mistake.

I nodded tightly, still clutching my armrests, shoulders tensed.

"Anyway, he was drunk, I'm pretty sure. *Chicha*. Like a corn beer. He had a fight with our father. My dad hated him. I don't know why. It's like he had to pick one of us, and he chose Panchito. He beat him, told him he'd never be a hunter, which is like saying he'd never be a man. So Panchito ran off to hunt. He was determined to come back with something. I know he had his heart set on a big *anta*, a male tapir. They can get to four, five hundred pounds. Feed the village for a couple weeks. One had been seen near the village, but no one had been able to track it down." Omar shook his head. "I should have gone with him."

"Why did Panchito come to tell us about what happened to Benicio? Why didn't Franz do it?"

"Franz is a good man, but he has a lot of fears. One of them is flying."

Beneath us, jagged brown peaks rose up, the canyons between gaping into eternity. There were no trees, no roads, just emptiness on a scale I had never before witnessed. Glacial lakes turned dull green, then black, then silver each time the sun broke through the clouds. The immensity of the world, for thousands of miles around, dwarfed us in our tiny, sputtering plane.

"So, he didn't get the tapir. Instead a *shushupe*, a pit viper, bit him on the calf. Very, *very* poisonous. The silent carrier of death, it's called. You take medicine or you die. You have maybe three minutes.

He only had his machete, so he cut off his leg, chopped it off, see? Took off his belt and tied it around his thigh, tight, and crawled three kilometers back to the village."

I gaped at the jagged scar. Suddenly my childish dustups felt absurd. Would I cut my own leg off if I had to? I prayed I wouldn't have to find out.

"Maybe sleep a little, Lily. We have four hours, you know."

A silly proposition considering the rattling plane, diesel reek, and Omar's story, but also hard to keep talking over the roar of the engine, so I put my head back and closed my eyes and, maybe because he suggested it, fell asleep.

I woke to the pilot and Omar shouting. We had begun to drop down between mountainsides that felt too massive to be real. Static lightning danced across a bruised sky. Panchito gripped my seat as he maneuvered himself back into his; cursing, he scrambled with one hand to strap his leg back on. Turbulence lifted and slammed us down; our heads smacked on the ceiling as the wings jerked and shuddered. I vowed to be full of joy the next time gravity glued me to the earth; I pinched my eyes shut, picturing my dull routine cleaning toilets and making beds, in an attempt to calm myself with banality. We dropped. My eyes banged open. Some prevailing wind had changed its mind and abandoned us; only to buffet us up again as we soared over the final ridge.

Another sudden plunge—I might have screamed. When we evened out, I opened my eyes as bile rose in my throat.

As we steadily lost altitude, the valleys turned green and the drab, brown landscape of the mountains loomed behind us. Glacial rivers tumbled over rocky escarpments, their waters spiraled by ghostly mist. Sunlight flashed on a hidden stream or pond.

Seconds later, a total whiteout as we flew through low, thick clouds. Omar barked a command to the pilot. We rattled on, flying blind. The cloud smelled like sulfur, spitting on our skin through the broken window; the pilot, bouncing, jabbered on in Portuguese to Omar as he twisted the knobs and smacked at the dash.

In seconds, we broke through the dense wad of cloud. An ocean of green stretched from horizon to horizon beneath us; only the subtle smile of the earth holding it in. Banks of fog drifted among the treetops, evaporating and re-forming according to some unknown purpose or design. Brown, serpentine rivers coiled below, reflecting the light in gold or blue or green, depending on the slant of sun or whim of shadow.

We hurtled at a hundred miles an hour over broccoli treetops, the clouds now skimming the top of the plane. My teeth rattled in my head. The pilot shouted, spitting with panic as he gestured at a stretch of river coiling below, then mopped a sheen of sweat off his forehead with the back of his hand.

"What'd he say?"

"He wants to go back!" Omar shouted.

"In one minute, I turn around!" the pilot blurted in Spanish.

Omar gripped his shoulder. "Keep going, we have plenty of gas. Get to the airstrip!"

But the forest was an immense mask, hiding everything that lay beneath. The pilot wordlessly dipped toward an opening in the green where the river was widest.

"There!" Omar barked.

The pilot swooped down deeper into the trench of the river, struggling mightily to keep the wingtips between the branches as they flashed by on both sides. We were so close I could see individual leaves, purple and red bromeliads blooming from the crowns of the trees. We banked as the river turned, the pilot paling at every tight curve. Giant white birds burst from the banks at our approach.

Beneath us, a small semicircle of cleared land edged the river, just a few dozen huts, a longhouse, everything on stilts.

"Panchito!" Omar leaned forward gripping my seat, his breath heating my bare shoulder. "Where's the airstrip?"

"Grown over!" Panchito yelled into the noise of the engine. "We have to use the river."

"No, we're fucking not," the pilot said, tendons on his neck standing out in gristly cords as he hauled back on the choke, tearing a stretch of canvas on the floor of the plane. The nose yanked up and we slammed back against our seats; again, the cargo shifted. Pistons ground together, screeching; the air filled with smoke.

Omar looked at me big-eyed, grabbed my arm. "Change places with me!" Not waiting for a response, he flipped my buckle open and yanked me toward him. I rolled onto the floor and looked up at Panchito, his face pale and clammy, fear in his eyes mirroring mine.

"Pull up the wheels!" Omar commanded the pilot, who sat motionless at the controls as we sped farther and farther from the village.

"We go back to Cochabamba!" the little man shouted.

"Pull up the fucking wheels!" Omar held a knife to his throat, nicking him. Fat drops of blood bloomed, painting a red line alongside his bobbing Adam's apple. "*Do it!*"

As the pilot struggled to keep us airborne and his throat from the blade, Omar reached past him and turned a metal crank that moaned even louder than the engine. The teeth of the gear caught, grinding and clanking deep in the guts of the machine. "Now turn around and go back to Ayachero, you weak piece of shit."

We pulled up and zoomed just under the boiling belly of clouds, banking and turning so hard I slammed into Panchito's gut, pressing against him before the plane swung around again, releasing us from each other. We dipped, leaning again into the slipstream, but for an entire minute, the clearing seemed lost, eaten by the jungle. Just as I dragged myself back into my seat, the village came into view again, announced by a break in the bulwark of treetops. People spilled out of their huts and streamed out onto the bank, waving at us.

"Now!" Omar grunted, the knife still a breath away from the pilot's throat.

Grim faced, never meeting Omar's furious stare, he began our descent toward the river.

SEVEN

We dropped down from the sky tilted sideways, clipping off tree branches with a series of violent *thwap*s, until the left edge of the plane's landing gear sliced into the brown water once, then twice; only when Omar flung his weight against the right side of the plane did we level out. For a few beats we skipped across the surface like a stone before smacking down hard. Chocolate-colored water sent up white foaming waves. We hurtled toward a stretch of silt—a sandbar—that ran parallel to a mildly sloping mud beach, the thick water steadily checking our speed.

No one spoke for several seconds. Shoulders and neck rigid, arms out straight, palms flat against the bug-smashed window, the reality that we were no longer airborne filtered into my consciousness a bit more with every breath.

We had landed headlong into the current, which without delay began to nudge us back and away from the narrow cut in the jungle; the huts already disappearing from view. The pilot, his mouth a sullen line, revved the engine against the braiding water; cargo and canisters rolling and banging drunkenly until they found their new equilibrium. The propeller, late to stop as well as start, finally began to slow, taking dull slices at the still air. We coasted into a cathedral of green.

Four hours of engine roar had deafened me; my ears buzzed. I dropped my head into my hands, seeking stasis, replaying Omar holding a knife to the little pilot's throat. *Who is this man?* I thought, gripping my thighs, forcing breath back into my body, forcing myself to recall his words of love, the cherished way he made me feel, all the reasons I pushed him to bring me here. Soon, I heard the slap of the water against the floats, my own breathing rough in my lungs, the muffled sound of people talking and babies crying. The mournful whistle of a bird from one side of the river was answered by another of its kind on the opposite bank, like lovers in search of but never finding each other.

Omar stepped out onto one of the floats, a couple of paddles under one arm, a rope looped over his shoulder. As soon as the nose of the plane carved into dark wet sand, he drove the paddles deep into it, lassoing the rope around the handles and securing the plane at both ends. Head down, the pilot opened his own small, creaking door and leapt through it; wasting no time, he turned to the task of emptying the plane's cargo onto the sandbar as Panchito gathered his belongings in the back.

Lined up along the shore, a silent wall of several dozen people stood staring at us, their faces hard, eyes beetle dark. The women were in rough dress: peasant shirts and skirts or brown sack-like dresses, babies strapped across their breasts and shielded from the sun by banana leaves tied loosely over their shoulders. The men were mostly bare chested or in ragged shirts, including an occasional pajama top, and sweatpants, cutoffs, or sun-bleached polyester gym shorts and flip-flops, hair worn short and greased back and parted in the middle; long or in braids for the women.

A burnt-meat smell, the reek of stale water, and a stray sweet whiff of pig dung merged with a humid, breathless heat. Rough-hewn ladders leaned against square or round huts perched on twenty-five-foot stilts. Crowned with palm-thatched roofs, the huts dotted a wide stretch of cleared land, much larger than it had looked from the air. A few long, open-air rectangular buildings—also on stilts—sat interspersed between the smaller ones. Hammocks strung from the rafters with balsa-cord ropes hung limp in the heavy air, while hollowed gourds brimming with rainwater were lashed to roof corners. The biggest building of all, the longhouse, stretched almost the whole length of the cleared land, at the back perimeter of the settlement. The jungle loomed just beyond, its reflection in the river doubling its enormity.

Balancing on the float, Omar looked back at me quizzically. "Welcome to Ayachero."

I stepped out onto the float next to him, listening to the gentle whispers of the crowd, scanning the sad eyes that looked me up and down, searching for a glimmer of a welcoming smile. Nothing. But really, what was I expecting? A round of applause? Some random white woman shows up with the town's golden-boy hunter who'd abandoned them a decade ago—of course they were apprehensive. Of course they weren't jumping up and down with excitement, but I was too young and self-absorbed for that to occur to me.

Panchito scrambled out onto the floats and threw himself onto the sandbar, landing with stunning agility. The heat of the place rose up and wrapped itself around me like a wet woolen blanket; I had never felt anything close to it. I took a deep breath almost against my will, searing my lungs. The stink of diesel dissipated, replaced by the green vapors of countless trees mixed with cloying tropical jasmine. I climbed down onto the spit of sand.

A rush of mostly naked children—dozens of them—came galloping from between the spindly legs of the buildings, squealing as they raced toward the water. They weaved among their stone-faced parents, then hurled themselves in the river, swimming and splashing their way toward us, crossing the narrow channel to the sandbar in no time. They climbed up onto the floats and into the cabin of the plane, where they bounced on the seats, imitating the sounds of a small plane's engine, giggling as they turned the wheel and twisted the knobs. I had to laugh. They reminded me of my foster brothers and sisters when we were young, and all the crazy shit we got into; sure, there were hungry days, but there were moments of joy as well. That jolt of familiarity comforted me a bit. A few of the kids climbed onto the wings, creeping out to their very tips, where they balanced for a few thrilling seconds before somersaulting into the current, screaming with delight as they burst out of the water.

I wasn't spared either. Two little girls flung their arms around my legs and hugged them, while another leapt up to touch my hair. I bent down and let her. Once I did, she turned shy, smiling as she gently patted my head with her small hands. Her own blue-black hair shone in the intense sunshine; a braided liana vine was wound several times around her taut belly above torn red shorts; she was otherwise naked.

One rather undersized boy with a large, purplish birthmark that covered half his face and much of his neck—maybe six years old—squatted at my feet, chin in hand as he stared up at me, patiently waiting for the curious girl to go away. He wore ragged shorts held up by a rope. A necklace of black and red beads was looped several times around his slender neck. When the girl finally lost interest, he stood, reached up, and took my hand. After leading me a short distance away from the plane full of children, he asked me quite seriously in Spanish, "Will you be my mother? My mother is dead."

My gut knotted up just looking at him, his solemn, handsome face that burst into a blazing white smile as if to say, *Look, I'm friendly, this will be okay. Being my mother? Not such a big deal.* Still, he gripped my hand so tightly it hurt.

"*No sé . . .*" *I don't know.*

His smile faded. I died a little.

"But I am alone, miss. See?" He turned, pointing to his little shadow, stark on the hard mud. "I only have my shadow."

Panchito splashed across the narrow tributary toward the bank, his shirt flapping behind him. A couple of the men on the shore gave him a weak greeting, a back slap or vague hug as he made his way along the line of people toward a middle-aged woman who stood hands on hips, head cocked and lip curled, her heavy breasts under her loose shirt grazing the waist of her sun-bleached skirt. She nodded at him, a walnut-sized goiter at her neck bobbing. A machete dangled from one hand; a dead duck was draped over one shoulder, orange feet pointed down ballerina-style. I caught her looking at Omar with what might have been longing, but she glared at me until I reddened and looked away. By the time I had the courage to glance back at her, she had turned from the beach and was walking toward the center of the village, shoulders hunched and defeated looking. Panchito followed her, vanishing into the maze of huts and smoking fires.

"What's your name?" I asked the little boy, who still clutched my hand.

"Paco," he said, bursting with pride. "What's yours?"

"Lily. *Lirio*. Like the flower."

"*Te quiero*," he said. *I love you.*

I loved him already, but didn't know it and certainly couldn't handle it; his directness, his bald need. Like looking into a little mirror of my younger self.

The pilot, his T-shirt soaked through with sweat, lifted rubberized sacks almost as big as he was—of flour, lentils, farina, dried beans, sugar, and rice—from the hold, and dropped them in the water. Coated in liquid latex to keep water out, the canvas sacks bobbed a yard apart on a rope. A bag of machetes and shotguns floated by among the foodstuffs. Jumping into the waist-deep water, the pilot, with Omar's help, began to drag the supplies to shore.

Paco tugged at my hand. "I'm a *very* good boy. I work hard. I can show you things."

"Thank you, Paco. That's very sweet."

Not far from us, a little girl parted another little girl's hair, picked out something black and squirming, and bit it in half with her gleaming front teeth. I bent down to Paco and uncurled his fingers from mine, turned away to grab my backpack from the plane. Holding it over my head, I jumped down into the river. The current was stronger than it looked from the sandbar, much colder near the silty bottom that sucked at my sneakers as I pushed my way toward the bank.

Back muscles corded and straining, Omar dragged the rope knotted with the rubberized sacks, seizing my hand with his free one as we waded to the shore. Afternoon sun blazed murderously onto my back as we stood dripping on the crescent of dark sand.

Unlike my reception with the children, the adults continued staring without expression. It never occurred to me then that they might have simply felt shy. Defiantly, perhaps stupidly, I mirrored their sullenness. Even the babies had stopped crying and turned a solemn eye toward us, their mothers' glistening nipples abandoned for the moment. Three thirty-foot canoes carved out of immense logs knocked gently against one another at a small floating dock, just slabs of wood lashed over empty barrels. Two enormous fish—six, seven feet long—lay side by side on the shore, the lips of their gutted bellies red and swollen, mouths gaping open, eyes beady black coins. In the air: the stench of gas, fish, sweat, a heavy green rot.

From this relative silence, a huge pig, bleeding heavily from behind its massive head, came screaming from behind the longhouse on the hill. Its belly dragged on the dirt, short legs and hooves scraping for purchase against the grade of the slope, a braided liana leash dragging along behind. A few pink piglets tumbled squealing behind her, snouts twitching, little asses waggling. A small man wearing a pair of sagging shorts ran out after the sow, cursing, snatching at the leash as she dragged him down the hill. A few of the men ran to help wrangle the wounded animal back up the bank and out of sight.

Still, no one moved. Omar practically crushed my hand in his; I felt the bones of my fingers bending together.

A man and a woman solemnly descended the stairs of the long-house and made their way down the bank; a little girl clutching her mother's skirt. Grief informed their gaits with a broken, hurt quality; they looked old beyond their years. The man looked to be in his midtwenties, the woman a teenager, maybe younger than me. The crowd let them through with a quiet respect; some even bowed their heads, stroking the shoulders and bodies of their own children, pulling them close.

The couple and the little girl came and stood before us, the man a taller version of Omar, but thinner and with a heavy brow, cheeks cratered with acne scars, the woman quite pregnant, her smooth black hair pulled back from her wide, open face. Her eyes were pinched with sadness, but somehow I could picture a smile light-ing up her features; she carried herself like the town beauty she was. She nodded at me. Omar held his hand out to his brother, but Franz pulled him into a tight embrace, his face over Omar's shoulder, stricken. They held each other a long time, as if each second con-tained a year of missed history, before parting, both of their heads tilted at the dark mud.

"We're all so happy that you're here," Franz said.

A few smiles, nods, and exclamations of agreement brightened a face here and there, and I was almost able to exhale.

"This is my wife, Lily," Omar said. No one spoke a word. Keen embarrassment washed over me; what would happen if they knew we weren't really married? But Omar's face was serene, full of pride, and I loved him for it. He took his time making eye contact with each of the villagers in turn, securing at most a smile, at least the slightest of nods. "Please welcome her into your lives. Please help to teach her what you know, be kind to her."

"I'm Anna," the pregnant woman said. "And this is my husband,

Franz, and Claudia." She stroked her little girl's head, drew her close. "Thank you for coming here. Thank you for bringing Omar to help us. We know it's a lot to ask of both of you."

"It's good to be here," I said, injecting as much sincerity as I could.

"You speak Spanish," Franz said. "Where are you from?"

"Boston, Massachusetts."

"You have terrible snowstorms there, in the United States," Anna said, passing one hand protectively over her belly. "People must freeze to death in all the ice. I'd be so frightened to go there. You must be quite brave."

"I don't know about that." I shifted my weight, no idea how to proceed. "I'm sorry about what happened."

She dropped her gaze to the hard dirt. "So are we." Franz pulled her close to him.

Up on the hill, out of view, the pig screamed, its slaughter no doubt in full swing.

The pilot, finished with his duties, yanked at Omar's shirt. "Hey, now you pay me."

Omar handed him some wet bills from his back pocket. Without a second's hesitation, he began splashing back to his plane. *Please don't leave me here*, I thought.

We followed Franz, Anna, and Claudia as they climbed the muddy bank to the beaten earth of the village. The crowd of villagers parted and let us through. It was a relief to hear the rustling and soft chatter as they gathered themselves and made their way back to normalcy; somehow that helped break some strange spell. Still, I felt eyes darting furtively in my direction, at my parchment-white skin, my turmeric-red hair, my bright American clothes and backpack. We passed the man gutting the pig, scooping out its entrails with a halved calabash into the biggest pot I had ever seen. He stopped to stare a moment, nodded, then went back to his work. A dozen dogs, a ratty, nearly hairless, big-eared breed, lay dozing around the pot, a few with one eye on the proceedings. A pile of plantain peels sat nearby, buzzing with flies. Somewhere a tinny radio played a jangly love song Omar and I had danced to just weeks ago on the promenade in Cochabamba.

The green wall of the jungle hissed and steamed as we passed hut after hut, each with its own oven and fire, its own set of naked children running and playing, its own underfed, fly-bitten dog, until we came to the hut farthest from the river, its oven closed and dark. Franz and Anna said their goodbyes and turned back to the long-house as we approached the empty, cupcake-shaped building, the roof thatched palm, the sides bamboo. A fifteen-foot ladder led to a roughly square opening, which I supposed was the front door.

Inside the hut was a plank floor, a thin mattress on a low plat-form under mosquito netting, and nothing else. I wondered why no one was living there, but couldn't bring myself to ask; I didn't know where to begin. *This is the life I chose*, I thought—so far, Omar had described it perfectly. Already I missed Britta's sarcasm, Molly's big laugh, the bustle of the markets at Cochabamba, the purr of the mo-torcycles thumping over cobblestones, even our hideous bunk room at the Versailles. Had that been my real home and I was too stupid to know it? Here were jaguars that slaughtered children, snakes so poisonous you could die in minutes. *Where am I? And how in fuck could I get out of here if I decided to?*

Through the window—just a square cut out of the bamboo, no screen or glass—I watched the plane stutter to life on the river, its engine catching and grinding as it scuttled a tight U-turn and raced across the water, lifting up to the waiting sky. The silence afterward roared into my skull, louder than any motor, as I wondered when or if I would ever see a plane again.

EIGHT

We made love right away in the little hut, just dropped right down on that filthy mattress and fell into each other; his hands and mouth loving me as if after some tortured absence, like he was sealing me to this new place, wedding me to it. Even as I felt myself swell and open as we kissed, my thoughts raced: *There is nothing safe about this place.* But for those few moments I tamped down my terror and confusion, ignored the raucous chorus of frogs outside, the memory of the plane disappearing into low-hanging clouds. I abandoned myself to pleasure, felt him chemically change me into someone else, someone who would do anything to be near him, someone who would follow him into any jungle on earth. Afterward, staring up at the square of pulsating green outside the window—my own heavenly jail—I wondered, *What have I done?*

Hours later, we lay in spectral darkness as cicadas ground away at time, like metal scraping across stone, endlessly. Omar wrapped himself around me, his hand cupping my breast, listening to the blood rush through the chambers of my heart. I faced away from him, night blind. All I could see in my mind's eye was him holding the knife to the pilot's throat.

"Have you ever killed anyone, Omar?"

He rearranged himself, took his hand off me. I shuddered with its absence. "Where did that come from?"

"The pilot, you almost—"

"I wasn't going to hurt him."

"It sure looked that way."

He sat up, pulled the stub of a cigarette from his shorts and lit it, its sizzling glow the only light in the hut. Then he slipped on his glasses, though there was nothing to see.

"He was going to take us back to Cocha. That or crash the plane."

"But you were going to—"

"He's fine, Lily. He's already back in the city, drinking his paycheck."

I sat up, put on my clothes. "You still haven't answered my question."

"I've said all you need to know."

"*Need to know?*" I hooked my backpack over my shoulders, slipped on my sneakers, and got to my feet. "That's just bullshit. You owe me the truth, Ohms."

"Where are you going?"

Good question. I glanced at the blackness outside our window. Couldn't take off this time, couldn't hop a bus, flag a cab, run away, nothing. My breathing came ragged in my throat. He took me by the hand and I let him gently pull me down next to him.

"Why did we land on the water? Why is there no airstrip?"

"The people let it grow over. It doesn't take long. It's a good idea."

"But wouldn't it have been safer to land—"

"If we have a real airstrip, the loggers would come, the narcos, the men of opportunity, remember them? Poachers would be every-where, big machines, too. Now they have to come by river, which takes gas, but by plane it's too dangerous, since there's no *estirón*. You know what that is?"

I shook my head.

"It's slang for a stretch of straight water—with no turns—long enough for a plane to land on safely. Ayachero's on a series of bends. That's why the pilot was shitting himself, that's why I had to pay him so much."

"So even those men of opportunity think it's too dangerous to fly here."

He shrugged. "They come by boat, or through the jungle."

"But we did it."

"I did what I had to do. We did what we had to do. There was no time to fly to San Solidad. It has a small airport, but Ayachero's five days by boat from there. The funeral is tomorrow. The jaguar is out there, with the taste of human flesh in its mouth."

In the hanging green darkness, something shrieked at the top of its lungs, followed by a mewling, disintegrating sound.

I got up and stood close to the window. "Omar, what the hell—"

"That's a *mono de noche*, a night monkey," he whispered. "He has huge pink eyes, but can't see color."

Another scream, heartbreaking. I took a step back; my heel kicked the mattress.

"Something got him," he whispered. "Something's eating him now."

A menacing growl, a deep-throated *thud-thud-thud*.

"A crested owl, a *búho*, has his claws in his throat."

I looked down at him, this Tarzan in glasses. "How do you know?"

He laughed. "Because I know."

Something barked like a dog, but not a dog . . .

"What's that?"

"Bamboo rat. Very ugly. Nose like a tumor. They're in the cane, in the manioc fields."

The sounds continued, rustling, cackling volleys back and forth; snorting grunts, low trills, moans, hoots, then a rhythmic cawing that momentarily silenced everything—before the deranged symphony started up again. This was the jungle at night, a major freak show.

"It's like a kill party," he said. "Everything hunting everything, stalking each other. Or like a fucking party, you know? Everything looking for its lover or something to eat. It's like a story, too. If you listen long enough, you know who's talking."

I reached out into the darkness and found his shoulder, then eased down next to him.

"All the animals are looking for food and trying not to be the food. But on a full moon, a bright moon, it's so quiet and you think, *Where is everything?* The whole jungle shuts down because night creatures are made to see in the dark. A bright night is like day for them. We'll walk in the jungle under a full moon together, I'll show you."

As I imagined a full moon shining down with its blue glow, showing everything as it was, I hugged myself and rocked a bit, a habit an old group-home friend had once said made me look crazy. I forced myself to stop. "I'm scared to death of this place."

He laughed softly. "It's just life, Lily. You can't be afraid of life."

"Sure I can."

He pulled me to him. "Something you need to know. Whatever you're most afraid of in the jungle comes to you, you understand? Spiders, snakes, tapir, jaguars, monkeys, poison ants. They sense that you're afraid, so they come to scare you away, because you don't belong in a place where you're afraid. But if you don't have that fear, then the jungle becomes a caretaker. It teaches you. It cares for you."

"I'm having trouble with this jungle-is-magic stuff."

"Fine, but you're not in Cochabamba anymore. You're not in America, land of Ronald McDonald."

I pictured that horrific clown, the shit-food mascot of millions, and part of me was strangely ecstatic to be where I was.

"The jungle is something to learn," Omar said. "The death of your birth mother, the death of your foster mother, your life in those homes, those were lessons. And lessons never stop. You can learn to be here, Lily."

NINE

It was by chance I learned that the lepers bathed very early in the morning, before everyone else. Bladder bursting, I left Omar sleeping in the hut as I headed down to the far side of the beach where a rough-hewn shelter with three sides made of thatch covered a deep hole in the mud. In the bottom of the pit, dung beetles consumed all that came their way. Omar had laughingly assured me that in the jungle, nothing is wasted. Still, even with all the sketchy places I'd relieved myself in my life, I had to close my eyes as I squatted, blocking out the clicking sounds the insects made from deep inside the hole.

At the time, I didn't know the word for what afflicted this family; but they were a part of Ayachero no one seemed to talk about. On the sandbar, a young mother lifted a girl of about seven, her stick legs bent under her like a deer, off her back and laid her down in a shallow area, scooping river water over her head with a calabash and washing her hair with a slab of yellow soap. The girl's face, though terribly scarred, was joyous and open; she didn't take her eyes from her mother's. A teenage boy, legless, hand-walked into the water, his penis arcing against the muddy bank. He propelled himself into the water with his strong arms, flipping and landing on his back before wriggling his torso and backstroking himself deeper. A man with shriveled hands, the fingers mostly stubs, kicked off his leather sandals and strolled into the water, the mist rising around his waist as he lifted his face to the morning sun.

Nearby, an old woman stood watching the family bathe. She was bent over in a C shape, leaning on a bamboo cane for support. A waist-length gray braid hung down the back of a shapeless dress that grazed her ankles above bare feet. As if sensing me watching her, she turned, holding me fast in her gaze for several seconds. My heart thrummed as I took her in; a thousand wrinkles mapped her expressive face on which lines—like cat whiskers—had been drawn or tattooed. Jewel-colored feathers winged back from holes in her ears. A wildness emanated from her. I looked away, then started back to the hut.

The rest of the village had begun to wake; smoke rose from the ovens and twisted into the cloud-hung sky. A few of the women, scraping coal dust out the back of their ovens, eyed me warily as I walked past. To each of them I smiled and said *hola*, but mostly I got stares or narrowed eyes or shaking heads. They grabbed the hands of their swollen-bellied babies and led them away from this red-haired alien, a few barking something back at me I didn't catch. A dozen or so macaws—a family of split-tailed rainbows—perched in the trees over the longhouse. Some communal decision sent them flapping up into the sky, where they crossed the river in twos, wing-to-wing, cawing like madwomen.

The smells of cooking surrounded me—fish, meat, something toasty and sweet-smelling, like yams laced with cinnamon. Suddenly light-headed, feeling the cut of hunger, I stumbled up the hill to our hut. Smiling, Omar handed me a ceramic bowl of something hot; the source of that sweet yam smell. I climbed up the short flight of wooden steps, falling on my food like a starved cur, no doubt eating in the manner Omar had once described.

Through the open door, I watched Paco running with the other children, chasing the half dozen tiny piglets that had lost their mother the night before. He slowed each time he passed, smiling and waving up at me, until he gave up the game entirely and stood squarely in view, watching me eat. Behind him, the other children continued to scream and play, the baby pigs squealing and skidding on the muddy ground.

"Good morning, Miss Lily," Paco said softly.

I smiled. "Good morning."

Omar—shirtless, barefoot—sharpened a machete on a round stone on the ground. "You never told me what I was eating," I called out to him.

"Plaintain and yucca, some ground rice, some molasses sugar. Do you like it?"

"It's the best thing I ever tasted. It's like heaven in a bowl, it's—" A furry black tarantula as big as my hand dropped down from the ceiling into my bowl, dark and hairy and scrabbling. Screaming, I hurled the bowl of hot mash away from me. The spider leapt, turning in midair before launching itself toward the wall of the hut, where it hung on briefly before skittering down to the floor and out the door. Like a gymnast, it whirled down the stairs, leaping and spinning as if I was the most frightening thing it had ever seen.

Paco stayed where he was as Omar burst past him, leaping up the stairs and into the hut. All I could do was point, before another hairy beast dropped to my shoulder with an actual thudding weight, crawled down my arm, and jumped to the thin plywood floor. I rocketed down the stairs, skipping the last three as I leapt onto the hard ground. I rolled over and looked up. Spider after spider dropped down, a dozen or more, the whole brood skittering and crossing over one another. Omar shooed them out of the hut, cursing. They trapezed down the stairs, scattering in every direction.

"Omar, what the *fuck*!"

"Calm down, Lily, they're only spiders."

"*Only spiders!* How can you say that? They're fucking giant tarantulas falling all over me!" I almost added, *Get me out of here*, but I was too stubborn—determined to not have his words, "you'd be begging me to leave in a week," come true. Still, I sputtered and cursed, replaying the thud of them on my back and shoulders, the feel of their scratchy fur as they leapt off me. I turned in a small, tight circle, bruised knees throbbing from my rough landing. I was so hungry. I pictured my breakfast smashed against the wall.

"Were those in the ceiling all night?"

"In the walls, more likely," he said, gently kicking the rest of them out the door.

"I am never going in that hut again."

Three more dropped down behind him like special ops fighters. They skittered off into the shadows of the hut. Next to me, Paco squatted in the dirt, his slight bony back glowing bronze in the sunshine. With a short stick, he poked at the air above one of the spiders, which had stopped short in front of him. It opened and closed its hairy mandibles in a vain attempt to hook onto the stick, as two of its furred, segmented limbs lifted in exploration. Finally it caught hold of one end, and Paco lifted it, laughing as he swayed the leggy creature back and forth in the heavy morning air. A few of the children running by saw the game and started to gather their own sticks.

Defeated looking, Omar came down the stairs and put his arms around me. "I'm sorry, Lily. This happens sometimes in huts when the bamboo isn't split."

I stepped away from him and planted my hands on my hips. "It *does*?"

"They like bamboo. It's hollow, you know—"

"I know bamboo is hollow. I'm not an idiot."

Cross-legged on the ground, chin wedged under his two fists, Paco listened intently to us argue. He pushed himself to his feet, stood in front of me, and said, "Bamboo is like a little, *little* house." He held his hands cupped together as if to demonstrate a little casa for me. "Don't be mad, Miss Lily. Everybody needs a house, even spiders."

One of the children, a beautiful little girl who wore her hair in two impossibly thick and shining braids, jerked a bright green cricket—several inches long—tied to a string across the hard earth. It waved its orange filament antennae in alarm, trying to leap away on strong hairpin legs, but she snapped him back each time. One of the spiders reared up, dropped, and charged the insect, but the girl protracted the game, endlessly drawing the cricket away.

I looked around at the other huts. Ours was the only one built with bamboo that was not split, as far as I could tell. The others were thatched palm, tin, or split bamboo; there were even a few rough brick constructions, and a weird one that looked made out of recycled swimming pool tile.

"So, are you going to tell me that the spiders came because I'm afraid of them?"

He fought back a smile and shrugged as he stirred the remaining food in the pot over the fire.

"Fuck this," I said, sounding like the teenager I was. The children coaxed one of the spiders into a long bamboo tube, then turned it upside down. The spider dropped out, hit the dirt, reared back in defense, and scrambled away, vanishing under a mat of leaf litter.

"This kind of tarantula only eats insects," Omar said. "They have no interest in us. There's a kind with yellow on his back you can't play with like this, it'll jump up and bite you, it's very poisonous, but this one"—he gestured at the kids—"these are kind of sweet, right? I had one as a pet when I was a boy."

I started to cry around then. Resting the hot pan on a rock, he put his arms around me. This time I let him. A couple of women walked by loaded down with woven baskets on their backs, leather straps across their foreheads, their faces stoic with the strain. I felt like a total wuss.

"We'll have to sleep in the longhouse for a while," he said. "I'll build us our own hut. You have to be patient with me."

I wish I'd read him better then, his shame about having to sleep in the spider-filled hut since we had no other, but I was too wrapped up in myself to see it. What little cash he had he'd spent getting us there and paying off the pilot.

I wiped away my tears, pissed at myself that I'd indulged in them at all, and slipped on my backpack, a move that always comforted me. I was in a place where legions of fist-sized tarantulas falling from the ceiling was nothing to get worked up about. Maybe it was time to remember that there were man-eating jaguars out there, bamboo rats as big as dogs in the cane. Long story short: *Maybe, Dorothy, you're not in Kansas anymore, and it might be time to suck it up and learn the jungle ropes.*

TEN

I followed Omar as he wove among the huts, the brutal heat of the day like an immense hand pushing me back. A rhythmic *whoop* sounded near the river, a wild, deranged sound.

"You could have left your bag back by our oven," Omar said.

I huffed it up higher on my back, clicked the buckle at my waist. "I always have this with me," I said, in no mood to give an explanation. This backpack was in fact an upgrade; there were years I bounced from group home to group home with my belongings in a garbage bag, but one day, on a fortuitous trip to Goodwill, I'd picked up a ratty but serviceable one for a couple of bucks. I loved that bag, slept with it bundled in my arms. Each time I moved in with a new foster family, I never, ever unpacked what little I owned. It was something nobody could make me do, and besides, I never knew when I was going to have to make a run for it. I learned later that my nickname those early days in Ayachero was *Mochila*, Spanish for backpack.

Omar moved quickly across the hard-packed earth—barefoot— but with as much confidence as if he were wearing sandals. Shirt-less, his muscles rippled in his broad shoulders, which tapered to narrow hips under drawstring shorts; this slip of cloth—almost an afterthought—seemed to be his jungle outfit. He looked younger from behind, like a teenager about to jump into a quarry with a gang of high school friends, someone born to be outside, to frolic in an endless summer.

More stares on our way to the longhouse, but the children followed us, chattering and laughing as before, and that seemed to lighten the mood. We climbed a long set of stairs made from sturdy tree trunks into which treads had been sawn to the main room, which was enormous, maybe fifty feet long and several yards across. One long wall faced the jungle. Except for a series of storerooms at the far end, the structure was open on all sides, from waist-high split-bamboo walls to thatched roof. Along the side that abutted the jungle, banana leaves a dozen feet long, dull and sweating, dozed over the walls. A pig—no doubt the one from the day before—roasted on a spit over a stone oven on a deck that extended the length of the building.

In one corner of the main room, in a pile of sawdust, two chickens snuffled together, picking at stray corn, while several bare-chested men relaxed or slept in hammocks suspended from the ceiling. Sitting cross-legged on a pile of discarded burlap food bags, a young woman nursed a piglet who had contentedly fallen asleep at her nipple. She sang softly to it, rocking, stroking its pink ears, occasionally laughing as if it had delighted her in some way. I learned later that her baby had died in childbirth and she had become unhinged. Only the piglet had quieted her wailing grief.

Omar took my hand and led me to the far west end of the deck. Beneath us, huts dotted the ground all the way to the brown river ruffling the shore. "I'm going to give you a tour," he said, pointing past all the huts toward where the village ended and the jungle began. "Far down that beach are the giant tortoise nesting grounds, where Benicio was taken."

I nodded, swearing to myself I would never go there.

"Now, see that long, thin strip of wood and long, skinny roof over it? That's the Anaconda Bar."

"A real bar?"

"It's real when we have booze. The anaconda skin is over ten meters long."

"From a real anaconda?"

He looked at me like, *of course, what a question.* "At the beach is our little dock and three of our boats. Our river driver is out with the fourth one, he travels from San Solidad every two weeks with supplies. There are about forty huts, three community ones like this one, but this is the biggest one, where everybody hangs out. That square hut in the middle everyone calls the clinic. For doctors we have FrannyB, one of the missionaries from America, and Beya."

I followed him as he walked the length of the longhouse to the opposite end. "The shaman?"

"Yeah, she lives past those manioc fields, a little ways into the jungle."

"All by herself?"

He nodded. "She's Tatinga, but a long time ago she married an Ayachero man who brought her here and left her. Just took off for La Paz. But the Tatinga think of you as dead if you leave the tribe. So she couldn't go back, even though she was their most powerful shaman."

"Can't she live in the village?"

He shrugged. "The villagers are stubborn, too." He lowered his voice. "They feel superior to the tribes. I think they're afraid of her."

"Are you afraid of her?"

"When she first came here, she was pretty angry about being cut off from both communities. Word was she did some nasty stuff to people, but nobody could prove it. People are suspicious, afraid, looking to blame someone for everything bad that happens. That's the kind of thinking I didn't miss in Cochabamba, I have to tell you."

"But are you afraid of her?"

He shook his head no, but I wasn't convinced. "I'd stay away from her, Lily."

"I think I saw her this morning. Down at the beach. There was a family of people who looked like they had some bad disease."

"She must be looking after the lepers." He shook his head. "I know the Frannies wouldn't do it. No one else would do it. They don't really need that much help. They work the fields, get water, they can even fish. They just can't hunt, so Beya helps them with their traps."

"Son!" The middle-aged woman I'd seen embrace Panchito yesterday stepped up to Omar, hands on hips, long gray braids swinging behind her. She didn't look at me. I expected her to throw her arms around her eldest and welcome him home, but all she said was, "Breakfast is ready."

A corner of the main room was dedicated to cooking: ersatz pots and pans, blackened and misshapen, hung on hooks over tins of cheap cooking oil. Hovering over an oven topped by an iron grate, her face sweating with steam, she stirred a vat of long white vegetables: yucca, before sifting out a few pieces with a tin fork and sliding them on a cracked porcelain platter.

Omar took two plates and two tin forks from a wooden shelf resting on a row of nails jutting from the wall, and gestured for us to sit on a low bench.

"Lily, this is my mother, Doña Antonia."

"It's nice to meet you," I said as humbly as I could manage.

She took a seat on a stool, eyes narrowing in her flat brown face, chin stubborn and set. I tried to put an age on her: forty-five, fifty, sixty? Impossible to tell. On the railing behind her, an orange-and-green toucan with a foot-long banana-colored beak flapped its wings and barked a few times. Its perfectly round black eye observed me. With a coughing sort of call, it flapped up and away, dipping with the weight of its beak before rallying skyward as it drifted over the huts.

"And what are you going to do all day, silly American girl, while your husband is hunting? Comb your pretty hair and look in the mirror?"

She cut off a slab of meat and plopped it down on my plate.

"She doesn't eat meat," Omar said, taking the plate from me. Her brows furrowed. "*Alérgica*?" *Allergic?*

"Because I love animals," I said breathily, feeling like an asshole.

Doña Antonia threw her head back in peals of cackling laughter, her few teeth on display. "Oh, that's a funny one! You know, because we love animals, too, a lot, you see?" She took a big bite of meat, chewed as she smiled at me. "I like this girl, Omar, my boy. This one makes me laugh."

In some distant way I was hungry, starving in fact, but I couldn't bring myself to feel it as I had when we were in the hut. Omar got up and scooped out some of the yucca, adding from another pot what looked like cooked onions and garlic. I took a few bites, but that was all I could manage. The yucca tasted like air, badly in need of salt, but I forced myself to swallow.

Several of the men slipped off their hammocks and joined us, either cross-legged on the floor or on low benches. All wore the uniform of old gym shorts or cutoffs and nothing else. There were half a dozen swarthy teenagers—Omar's size or smaller, muscular, quiet; a few stole shy looks at me—and two or three much older men—ropey, sunbaked, and wizened, but tough as nails; a ragtag group of hunters.

Franz and Panchito climbed the stairs, deep in conversation. His brothers joined Omar and the other men at the impromptu meeting.

"We're grateful Omar has come," Franz said after taking a plate of food. The men nodded, mumbling their agreement. "We need to keep Ayachero strong. Strong in provisions and strong in spirit." His pitted face darkened. "Omar's been hunting since we were children. He and our father used to hunt jaguar with the Tatinga, back when we traded with one another."

One burly young man spoke up. "We're the best hunters on the river."

"You're all great hunters," Franz said, "but we all need to learn from each other. Game is scarcer now, I don't have to tell you this.

We have to go farther and farther out to hunt, stay away longer and longer. It's been hard on all of our families. Killing the sow last night was something we shouldn't have had to do. The poachers are growing in number, and they'll take anything. Now we're in competition with the Tatinga. I don't have to tell you how dangerous this is."

The men mumbled, joked uncomfortably.

"We'll need to build a platform," Omar said. "You all know how difficult it is to hunt jaguar. They always know where *you* are, but only now and then do you see signs of them, or even see one."

"I've never seen one," the burly man said. "Only prints."

"I saw one swimming once, but that was years ago," another man said.

"I wish I had easy answers for catching the one that took Benicio," Omar said.

Franz dropped his head as if physically hit by the sound of his son's name.

"Of course, we can look for scat or trees they've marked with their claws, but the best way is to take turns on the platform, waiting and watching, agreed?" Omar continued.

The men nodded, their faces serious and drawn.

"We're short of men as it is, so this will be difficult. Maybe some of the women with older children can help out. It's boring work. You're just watching, in total silence. But we all know the jaguar's not going to show up so we can kill it. We may catch this jaguar tomorrow, or next week, or never. We have to accept this. We have to be vigilant, but we have to go on."

I set down my plate of yucca, now cold and congealed in a pool of oil, as I mulled Doña Antonia's words. As I listened to the men speak, I indulged in a quick fantasy: *I* would be the one to nail the jaguar from the top of the platform. Ridiculous, of course, but I was determined to show Omar's mother I wasn't some useless, vain *gringa*. There had to be some way I could become part of this bizarre, terrifying place.

ELEVEN

B y midafternoon, most of the population of Ayachero had gathered at the foot of the longhouse in anticipation of Benicio's funeral. All of us—Omar, Panchito, the hunters, Doña Antonia, and myself—descended the stairs and joined the milling crowd of nearly a hundred. Though it was broad daylight, many carried blazing torches that licked up into the boiling air. Paco pushed his way through the crowd and took my hand. Franz and Anna were the only ones I couldn't spot in the swarm of mourners.

I followed Omar to the front of the procession, where two white women, one a head taller and fifty pounds heavier than her smaller, slighter companion, weaved among the crowd, the bigger one encouraging everyone in perfect though condescending Spanish to gather in some sort of a line. Nailed to a three-foot balsa cross braced against her shoulder was a crudely carved wooden Christ, mouth in an eternal droop, rusty tears burned into the grain. An actual crown of thorns circled his head. His pedestal was signed: FRANNYA, AYACHERO, 1998, in loopy letters.

The woman carrying the cross caught sight of me; waved, smiled, and bellowed out a cheerful hello from several yards away. I was struck by how American that gesture looked and felt; a wave of self-consciousness—*Am I that brash and loud?*—washed over me.

"Greetings," she said, reaching out to pump my hand. "You must be Lily. We're the Frannies. Not sure if you've heard of us yet. Both named Frances, so we had to, you know, differentiate." Thin gray hair pulled back in a little bun at her neck, the gaunt woman standing next to her gazed up at me through thick, round, rimless glasses, one lens cracked but somehow still holding together. The first woman continued, "She goes by FrannyA, and I'm FrannyB. For what it's worth."

Permanent sweat stains scored dark semicircles in the armpits of FrannyB's short-sleeved camo shirt. Her army pants fit snugly around generous hips and disappeared into high rubber boots. Her friend was dressed precisely the same way; on her, the clothes draped from her delicate frame, exaggerating her ethereal figure. "Sorry to meet under these circumstances," FrannyB continued. "Just a terrible, terrible thing, this loss. But that's the jungle for you, I'm afraid. Brutal place."

The crowd was once again losing its form, spreading out like a lake. Tossing her buzz-cut blond head with a melodramatic gesture—FrannyA in her wake—FrannyB threw herself back into the job of herding everyone into a procession of sorts, eventually huffing her way to the front of the line.

With a nod to Omar and me, Anna, Franz, and Claudia walked past us; the crowd parted for them. The parents carried between them a small wooden box painted white. In it were a heartbreakingly small pair of shorts and shirt neatly folded, along with a few of Benicio's possessions: a broken miniature car, a bicycle tire tube fashioned into a slingshot, some marbles, a fish hook, and a few ancient, water-warped baseball cards. Jungle flowers had been woven into a chain that graced the perimeter of the box.

Clutching a rosary to her chest, face crumpled in agony, Anna held one side of the box, Franz the other. Anna's father, a tiny man with stick legs and white hair, played a mournful tune on a ukulele as the group made its slow trek to the shore. Omar kept a strong grip on my hand as we walked; I was grateful. I thought of the nephew he had never met—would never meet—and the decisions Omar had made for that to be the case, and suddenly felt so much older than my nineteen years, as a dawning of such a thing as consequences to life decisions formed vaguely in my mind.

Anna began to cry openly now, and so too did the other women, in sympathy and terror for the random cruelty the jungle was capable of, knowing in their hearts it could have been their child, and might be their child the next day, week, year, second. Claudia and the other children, infected by the grief all around them, began to wail as well, until just about everyone, including myself, was crying for every hurt that had ever befallen them.

Together we walked the length of the village, past every hut and oven and sleeping dog, down to the narrow strip of beach where the boy was taken. Anna's father finished his song as we walked on the cinnamon-colored sand. Long, deep grooves had been gouged by the bodies of the giant tortoises who gathered there to mate and lay their eggs, their arms creating carved arcs on either side. I saw no jaguar tracks, but they could have been erased by the turtles' great, sweeping flippers. In the stultifying stillness, the arms of the jungle drooping over us, we came to a stop at an open hole dug several feet deep in the muddy bank. Franz and Anna kneeled and lay the box down next to it, pushing themselves back to their feet with great effort.

FrannyB lay the cross over the box and turned to face the silent crowd. "Oh, Lord, bless this place where the boy Benicio was taken by the forest devil in the shape of a jaguar, for the souls of the righteous are in the hands of God, and no torment will ever touch them. The Lord God has tested him and found young Benicio to be worthy of Himself, like gold in the furnace. Benicio will live in peace forever at his side . . ."

Something rustled in the forest behind her. Her sweating, pale face twitched as her voice trailed off into the drone of insects. She turned, took a step back. From the wall of green emerged a mosaic of color in the form of two men, each around five feet. Bright streaks of red stain zigzagged from mouths to earlobes; six-inch porcupine quills bristled on either side of full lips; turquoise and yellow macaw feathers dashed back from stretched earlobes. Bowl-cut ebony hair just grazed the shining foliage behind them. Except for strings of twisted fiber that reached down from around their waists to the tips of their penises, wrapping the foreskin in a small knot, they were naked.

Franz and Anna took a few steps backward, tucking Claudia between them. The ranks of the villagers shifted as the men placed themselves in front of their wives and children. Omar whispered under his breath to me, "Tatinga."

"Stay calm, everyone, stay calm." FrannyB tucked her Bible under one arm and held out a flattened hand with the other.

The taller tribesman stepped forward, pectorals bulging under his necklace of peccary incisors, lean muscle roping hips and thighs. Twin quivers packed with blowgun darts crossed his chest. Under one arm he carried a small canoe, a child-sized version of the dugouts both the villagers and tribes used.

A wave of language rippled from the men.

"What did they say?" Anna said.

FrannyB shifted to her other foot, took a rag from her pocket, and wiped her forehead. "They've brought a death canoe. They say they're here to mourn the child." She replied to the men in rapid-fire Tatinga. Their expressions—serious, grim mouthed—did not change.

"What did she say?" I whispered to Omar.

Not taking his eyes off the men, he said quietly, "'We're trying to bury our dead. We don't need your presence here.'"

The man with the canoe took a step forward, chin high as he defiantly looked into the eyes of the villagers, one by one. He said in halting Spanish, "The boy had an enemy. This is why he died. We are here to say this boy is not our enemy. Our shaman, Splitfoot, runs with the jaguar in his dreams, but he did not call this one down to the Tortoise Beach. You need to find out who is the boy's enemy, to avenge his death."

"This boy had no enemy," FrannyB answered in Spanish. "His only enemy was the jungle itself, this nest of poisons and demons and sin."

The tribesman looked with derision at the weeping Christ on the balsa wood cross. "An angry jaguar spirit affects everyone. Your rotting God cannot protect you."

The smaller tribesman, who stood closest to the jungle, took something out of a string bag. A bundle of palm thatch gathered in such a way as to look like a small child, like a doll. FrannyB waved him away, muttering a few words in Tatinga.

"She's telling him to keep his heathen idol," Omar said under his breath.

Anna took a step forward, blocking FrannyB's bluster. Her voice was low but strong. "Benicio was my child. If these people have something of comfort for us, I want to know about it."

"You're going to send your child into the everlasting fires of hell."

"Get out of my way."

With fierce disgust, FrannyB took a step back, FrannyA tight to her side.

The Tatinga man held out the doll to Anna, who took it, cradled it above her pregnant belly, and fell to her knees in the wet sand as if she had just been handed the torn and bloodied body of her son. Her convulsions over the palm-leaf child put us all in shame, reminding us that this was not our loss, and we quieted so the flowing river, the sun—weak behind a scrim of cloud—the eagle pairs huddled side by side in the trees, all could hear her lament.

The Tatinga man got to his knees and began to rock, chanting over the crumpled woman and straw child, sweeping his hands through the air above them, around them, as if sending her grief away. When she had cried herself out, he gently took the doll from her arms and laid it in the small canoe the other man had placed at the shore. He nodded toward her and Franz, who, with his wife, pushed the little canoe out into the waiting water of the Amazon. The tiny craft turned in an eddy before the main current discovered it, disappearing it around a bend in seconds. By the time I turned back to the men, they were gone.

TWELVE

Night came on as it always did in the jungle, hard and fast like a shutting door at six o'clock, exactly twelve hours from sunrise, the ruthless rotation of equatorial days. Along with the rest of the villagers, we threaded through clusters of six or seven huts arranged loosely in circles as if for safety, many of them sharing a clay oven shaped like an igloo. Trawling nets hung from trees next to rows of javelins, fishing poles, and bows and arrows.

Under a narrow, thirty-foot-long thatched roof stretched a bench of equal length rubbed smooth by countless asses. Above it, the bar: another impressive slab of termite-bitten wood, this one buffed to a well-worn sheen by a thousand elbows. Suspended over a row of fat candles, an anaconda skin as long as the bar, in variegated patterns of yellow, brown, and black triangles—over five feet at its widest—had been nailed to a plaque in short intervals. Its coloring was bright and rich, as if this creature had been alive and crawling not too long ago. Its anvil-shaped head hung down on one end in a posture of utter defeat, insect-eaten eyes leaving pinched black holes, tongue hanging down a foot or so, split, red, and stiff looking. A hand-painted sign scrawled on a thin strip of bark tacked below the fattest section of snake read: *Bienvenido a la Barra de la Anaconda*. "Welcome to the Anaconda Bar."

Omar and I settled near the tail.

A small, rotund woman dressed in a tube top and a sparkly short skirt filled glasses, pouring steadily to satisfy the milling crowd.

"You're Omar's wife?" she said with flat affect as she set out plates of tiny speckled-brown eggs—each could have fit in a teaspoon—hard-boiled quail eggs.

I nodded.

"I'm Carmelita. I'm from San Solidad," she said, as if San Solidad were the center of the universe and she was just slumming here in Ayachero. She touched her hair, which had been swept into an updo, something I hadn't seen on any of the other women, not to mention the sparkly skirt, tube top, or white plastic platform sandals.

Under the bar, three caged quails squawked in a bamboo cage, lifting their dinosaur feet and clawing at the sides, their heads crowned with a Mohawk of rainbow spikes. On the bar, a little green gecko eyed the eggs, motionless in the way only lizards can be. Carmelita brushed it away; it went flying off into the humming trees.

Omar took a few eggs, peeled them and handed some to me after he rolled them in a clay saucer of dirty-looking large-grained salt. They were delicious, still warm and dense with yolk.

"You're from the boat?" Omar gestured at what looked like a pile of junk docked at the beach. A dredge—half garbage truck, half barge—sulked under flickering torchlight. A tangle of hoses and vicious-looking metal parts hung off one side, torn canvas tented the other. A few rough-looking men in tattered shirts and shorts leaned on the metal railing, perhaps hoping for a breeze off the river.

"We just arrived," she said to Omar, leaning into him, breasts almost completely liberated from her top. "You know, we are very sorry for your loss."

Was she *flirting* with him?

With a smirk, she turned away from us, back to filling glasses and setting out plates laden with strips of meat. Nearby, skewered mouth to anus by a metal pipe, the pig hung over a fire dripping fat from its roasting flesh.

"Who's she?"

"A hooker. Some men must be coming through."

Franz and Anna approached us and accepted their glasses of sugarcane brandy. Bolivian pop tunes jangled from a boom box behind the bar, tuned to a low volume perhaps out of respect.

"We heard about the spiders in your hut," Anna said. "We need to burn that one down. Please, stay in ours until we can build you another one."

"Thank you," I said, but Omar cut me off.

"We're fine in the longhouse for now, but that's very kind of you."

In the end I was relieved we'd passed on this; their hut may have been tarantula-free, but it was tiny: just one room for them and Claudia. We would have been on top of one another. There was no privacy in the main room of the longhouse, but at least there was space.

The crowd parted as two white men blundered through. They wore ragtag camouflage gear from head to toe; heavy knives hung from leather straps at their sides, guns gleamed under belts.

A huge man, bald under his sisal hat, led the way. He was heavy in the jowls, with thick eyebrows and a mustache as bushy as a squirrel's tail. He wore the skin of a jaguar like a cape over his back, its massive head hung down over one shoulder. Flies walked stickily over its still-open eyes. The other man, gangly and gristly, wore his oily blond hair in a ponytail, exposing a badly drawn tattoo on the back of his neck of a naked woman riding a motorcycle. Whistling, he dragged a wooden cart stacked with three yellow-footed tortoises the size of garbage can lids, all bound by balsa-bark restraints. Still alive, they moved with dispirited swipes of their powerful arms. In a shadowy box jerry-rigged on top, a live infant macaw hopped and squealed, red and blue fluff flying off its body as it bounced itself off the walls of woven sugarcane. Lashed to this was a tightly wound roll of brilliant blue, red, and yellow feathers.

It unnerved me that the only other white people around—besides the Frannies—seemed to be thugs. Until that moment, I could envision a growing—perhaps painfully slow—camaraderie with the villagers. All that suddenly became a bit hazy. I shrank into myself, drank my brandy too fast, kept my head down.

The fat man waved his ham-hock hands as he knuckled his way through the crowd. Testily, the village men let him pass. "Excuse me, ladies and gentlemen, thirsty men here, coming through, coming through." The women gathered at the far reaches of the torchlight as he swung a big thigh over a stool at the end of the bar.

Bristling, Franz pulled Anna behind him as he drew closer to the big man. "When did you kill this jaguar?"

The poacher held out his hand and smiled. "Wait, wait, *wait*! A man hasn't even met these new people or had his first drink and *that's* your first question? Introduce us, Franz!"

Franz's face turned dark, taut with contained fury. "Omar, Lily, this is Fat Carlos—"

"Omar!" he said, accepting with a wink a glass of aguardiente rocketed down the bar by Carmelita. He knocked back the contents, sucking the sugar off his lips. "I remember you. The long-lost brother, the one who got away. Who went to the big city and—what—it didn't go so well? Tell me everything."

Omar got up and stood at his brother's side. "I'm here for my nephew's funeral."

"*Funeral?*" He glanced around. The crowd had afforded the men a wide berth; many were helping themselves to pig or roasted yucca. A few seemed to be actually enjoying themselves, voices rising, even laughing occasionally. The mood much different than down at the beach. "Well, I wouldn't have guessed it," he said, glancing around. "But we're surely sorry to hear that. Aren't we, Dutchie?"

The scrawny-necked man grinned and sputtered as if he'd been told a joke, his blond mustache greased with pig fat. "It's a shame when someone dies, it sure is. Who died, then, Carlos, do we know?"

Fat Carlos picked his teeth with a short knife as he eyed Franz.

"A jaguar took Benicio a week ago. Down by the Tortoise Beach," Franz said.

"Well, *that* is a tragedy. Truly. You have my condolences. I did wonder what the big spread was all about. Lovely pig. My compliments to the—"

Franz pushed in closer to the big poacher, his eyes ablaze. "When did you take this jaguar?"

"Oh, it's been a week now, hasn't it, since we've been out, Dutchie?"

"'Bout that."

"We were *way* out. West of the Tatinga. Nowhere near here. By the Black River, near that oxbow lake."

Dutchie's swimming pool–blue eyes grew wide. "She was sleeping in a tree. All sloppy-like." He did a pretend collapse in his seat, his arms falling forward, neck loose. "Like that. Got her in one shot, didn't we, Carlos?"

Franz took another step toward the big man, but Omar hissed something under his breath, seizing Franz's forearm and fastening him in place. "What was in her belly?"

Fat Carlos grinned at Franz. "You think maybe . . . oh no, oh no. Im-possible. Right, Dutch?"

Franz fumed. "What was in her belly?"

"Listen, I'm very sorry for your loss, but if you're asking what I'm thinking you're asking, well—"

"*What was in her belly?*" Franz wrenched his arm free from Omar's grip and grabbed at the tattered collar of Fat Carlos's open shirt. Dutchie freed a gleaming knife from his belt, hopping from foot to foot as if ready to pounce at his boss's command; grinning like using the blade would provide entertainment, nothing more.

"Dutchie. Enough. You're overreacting." Sheepishly, Dutchie did another dance step with the knife, dialing down the fun before cooling off completely. "We've talked about this." Carlos shrugged himself free of Franz's grip and straightened his threadbare collar with a prissy sort of care. "No need for any of this, my friends. The jaguar's belly contained—nothing like that. No boy parts. Jaguar stuff. Fish. Paca. Ocelot."

Franz gathered himself as Omar visibly relaxed. "Let me see the paws."

"Of course." Carlos got up and turned slightly toward Franz. The jaguar's long arm swayed slightly, the claws of its heavy paw scraping against the bar. With Anna just behind him, Franz picked it up and studied the three-inch claws, turned it over, examined the great soft pads ringed in black. He turned it back over, flattened it against the bar. Anna traced her forefinger around the paw, slowly, almost dreamily, then snatched it away with a yelp and covered her mouth, tears coursing down her cheeks. She turned away.

"No," Franz said, pulling her back. "No, Anna. Look, come back and look. This is a different jaguar. The prints on the beach were twice this size."

She snatched up a knife that Omar had been using to peel an *aguaje*. With a stifled scream, she stabbed the paw, attaching it to the wooden table, and stumbled off toward the longhouse. Fat Carlos pursed his lips and shook his head.

"Sorry," Franz said as he pulled out the knife and returned it to Omar. "She's not herself. She wanted this to be the one. So did I."

"It's all right." Carlos reinstalled himself in his seat next to Dutchie. "It's understandable."

Doña Antonia strode bruskly down the bar, wiping it clean, gathering plates. The place was starting to clear out, families drifting off to their huts, children held tight to their mothers' skirts. "So you're almost finished here, you two?"

Fat Carlos gave her a look. "Well, that's not very friendly of you, Doña Antonia. We were all just catching up, getting to know one another. You know, I'm remembering more about Omar, here. Didn't you tell me he hunted with the Tatinga? Omar, is that true? That's impressive. That's remarkable. You must speak Tatinga, then?"

Omar nodded, his own knife glinting from its hook on his belt.

"You must have gotten to know them pretty well. All their jungle secrets and so forth."

Omar said nothing.

"That Beya. That batshit-crazy shaman. How well do you know her?"

"As well as anyone."

"Now *she*," he said, warming to his third glass of brandy. "She scares me. Got that look in her eye, like she'd kill you and it'd be nothing. Just a day's work. Cast a spell on you, and you'd wake up with no teeth, your nose cut off and up your ass, some freaky shit like that."

Dutchie guffawed, smacking his hands together with glee. "*Nose up your ass*, you're so fucking funny, man. I love this guy."

Carlos ignored him.

"She's helped a lot of people here," Omar said.

"Maybe. Maybe she's changed. I'm sure not gonna visit her and find out."

"Men," Doña Antonia said, grabbing their glasses from them. "Leave us."

"Whoa!" Fat Carlos's hands flew up. "Okay, then. Overstayed our welcome. Clearly." Grabbing the bottle of brandy, he pushed himself to his feet, wiping greasy fingers on his many-pocketed pants. The jaguar pelt rippled in the gloom. "Dutchie, shall we?"

Tipsily, they headed off down the bank to the shore, Dutchie dragging the squeaky cart laden with the slowly struggling tortoises, Fat Carlos arm in arm with Carmelita, who tottered, loose ankled, on her platform sandals. A clot of chickens scattered in front of them; the men howled in mock surprise, pausing to take potshots. The birds exploded in little fireworks of yellow, red, and white feathers, their heads and feet flying every which way. Dutchie squealed and blasted off a few more shots up into the starlit sky for good measure.

Under the cloak of darkness, the rusted hulk of a boat strung with Christmas lights looked almost pretty reflected in the oily black river.

Doña Antonia poked at Panchito, dead asleep on folded arms at the bar. He swatted her away and turned his head, resettling like a cat. She swore a fantastic string of curses as she wiped the bar one last time, then headed up the hill, the silver in her gray braids glinting in the moonlight as she walked. Only Omar, his brothers, and I remained at the bar.

"Him and Dutchie stole that dredge," Franz said. "They were working the rig for the owner, but figured there was more in it for them with him dead. Not that *he* was some kind of angel. I mean, for years these guys poisoned a whole branch of the Beni, looking for gold. Everything's dead there now, for many, many kilometers up that river. They got the tribes killing each other for territory; hell, these two were the ones who pushed the Tatinga so close to us. Now we're competing for game like we never have before."

"What about the law?" I said. "Isn't someone going to come after these guys?"

Franz looked at me with something like pity. "Do Americans think there are laws in the jungle? Huh. Interesting." He took a contemplative swallow of his brandy. "Nobody steals canoes. That's the only law I know of."

"What about the gold? Why are they bothering with game?" Omar said.

"They hit some veins early on, but ever since they killed their boss, nothing. Not one gram. It's like they cursed themselves. So they're back here, hunting whatever they can, steering clear of the Tatinga, who'd kill them on sight."

A gust of relatively cool, wet air swept up from the river. The moon slipped behind the clouds, and in minutes a savage onslaught of tropical rain sealed us in the wall-less bar.

"It's different now, Omar," Franz continued. "Remember when we were fifteen, sixteen? Hunting trips were a day, maybe two, then we were home. And the fish! We could scoop them out of the water with our hands. Not anymore. Now, to find tapir, peccary, boar, spider monkey, anything, we have to go deep in. We're gone a week, sometimes two."

Omar peered at the shoreline; the lights of the dredge were smeared looking through the downpour. "How many men are with them?"

"I counted five this time. Sometimes he's got a dozen, more. They're animals, every one of them."

Franz woke Panchito; they took off in a trot in the rain toward the longhouse. Finally we were alone, nursing an odd quiet between us. I couldn't get the words, *we're gone a week, sometimes two*, out of my head. I took a big swallow of brandy, it burned a sweet, hot path down my throat.

"What if we took a trip together? You could take me to the mahogany grove."

He gave me a quizzical look. "You think knowing everything is good, Lily. Is that an American thing?"

"What's wrong with wanting to know everything?"

A huge beetle, maybe two inches long, landed on the bar near my glass. It lifted half its carapace and fluttered it as if to dry the shiny brown wing from its flight through the rain, rotated its antennae as if sensing us there, then lifted and shook its other wing.

"I'm protecting you," he said more softly.

I took a few more sips as a balm on the distance between us, which I didn't anticipate, then held out my empty glass. He poured me just a finger more, holding my gaze.

Above us, around us, the rain ceased as abruptly as it had begun; the jungle night steaming and hissing. I'd come to find that, even in the middle of the dry season as we were, it rained torrentially at least once a day, if only for a quarter of an hour. We listened to the sounds of water running off the thatch, chortling into thin braiding streams on muddy paths. The leaves above us dripped endlessly, creating their own rain.

"Come on, Lily," he said, taking my hand. "Let's get settled at the longhouse."

As we walked together through the hot night mist toward the glowing ovens on the hill, I tried to think of ways to lighten things between us. "Do you want to know your next assignment?"

He smiled and squeezed my hand. "Sure."

"This time, write about the Tatinga. Anything you can think of."

"Okay, Teacher, but I think I'm doing all the work here, and you just sit back and laugh at my English."

"I don't do that—" I burst out, until I saw he was kidding.

"Just trying to even things up. For every assignment I do, you tell me a Lily secret. About your American life."

"When's that due?"

"Now," he said with a laugh. "Come on. You owe me."

"All right," I said, his hand warm and alive in mine. "When I was a kid, I used to go through all the clothes that came into the shop to be dry-cleaned, and I would keep everything I found in the pockets. All the money, jewelry, buttons, anything. If anyone asked, I swore I never found anything. It got me used to this idea that stealing was kind of okay. Weird, right?"

"What's dry cleaning?"

"It's—" I had to laugh. "It's this way of cleaning fabric with chemicals."

"What's wrong with soap?"

"Nothing. It's—oh, never mind." Grinning at each other, we climbed the stairs of the longhouse. Before we entered the main room, every corner cheerfully lit by gas lamps, I pulled him around to face me. "When will you leave?"

"In a few days. As soon as we finish the platform."

"Okay," I said, pulling him toward me, trying in vain to ward off the chill that flooded me when I thought of myself alone in this place. "Okay."

THIRTEEN

In the daytime, the main room of the longhouse was a lively gathering place, with a busy kitchen and dining area, foodstuffs kept in the series of four storerooms—each with real walls, a ceiling, and a door—on the far east end of the structure. At night, it became a crash pad for the dispossessed: Paco, families in the midst of rebuilding their huts, single men, visitors from other villages passing through, anyone temporarily or even permanently homeless.

The night of the funeral, Paco slept in a hammock between Omar and me, a heavy little teardrop shape. In the corner of the room, the woman who had been nursing the piglet slept curled up with it on the floor, both of them snoring, while I lay awake. Her skirt was hitched up. I could see she wore no underwear; this made me sad and afraid, though no one else seemed to have noticed. After a time, I couldn't bear it and got up and tiptoed over to her, gently pulling her skirt down to cover her. She didn't budge.

Rain began again with no delicate warning; a crashing deluge that pounded every leaf and branch, muting the night jungle sounds. The canopy lit up like stained glass with every boom of thunder and flash of lightning. Swept in by the rain, coal-black bats swarmed over our heads, flapping and gathering in the rafters in a smutty cloud.

They hung from the wooden struts, two-foot-long draculas languidly opening and closing their wings as if to dry them.

One of the bats dropped from the ceiling to the floor just a yard away. Gleaming black against the blond balsa wood, its veined wings shuddered as the small grappling hooks at its wingtips scrabbled at the air. As if it knew it was dying, it grew calm, gazing at me peacefully with ball bearing eyes.

I woke with a mesh imprint of hemp hammock pressed deep in my cheek, shocked that I had fallen asleep at all. The hammocks were empty, the smell of fried eggs in the air. Dishes teetered in piles next to smoking ovens. The place was deserted; even the bat was gone. My mosquito netting had come loose around my head and shoulders; a cloud of them took advantage, swarming so thickly I breathed in a fistful. Coughing and waving my arms, I twisted myself into my hammock like a straitjacket until I finally got free and dropped to the floor on my elbow and hip. Embarrassed, I was relieved to see that I was alone, until I heard someone laughing shamelessly and loudly, but also very strangely. Someone's pet parrot perched swaying on Paco's deserted hammock, cackling its blue head off. I despaired of ever getting used to the crazy randomness of this place, this collision of exotica and humanity of which I was now a part.

The parrot continued to guffaw at me as I dove into my backpack and pulled out my sadly almost empty can of bug spray, in desperation blitzing the cloud of mosquitos still on the attack. I ran down the stairs—like running helped—all the way to the beach, where the women were gathered near a fire that burned under an immense metal pot. Only the three long canoes knocked gently against the dock; the poachers were gone.

"Time to go to work, Princess America who sleeps all day," Doña Antonia said. "We have to feed the dogs."

As I made my way to her, I could feel the eyes of the women watching from the bank. Most stood around the pot, tossing pieces of something into it; the others stirred its contents with a blackened tin ladle or washed off their hands in the river. Mangy-looking dogs—I counted a dozen, one with just three legs that moved with astounding agility—circled the pot, snarling and nipping at each other's heels. Doña Antonia smacked them on their asses, pushing them away from the blistering hot metal.

She motioned me over to two dead pirarucu, which meant "red fish," that had been laid out on the shore. Shaped more like some prehistoric eel than a fish, they must have weighed over two hundred pounds, each as long as a man. She handed me a serrated knife with a sharp point and gestured at the fish. "You cut out their stomachs now, okay? Cut off their heads and put them in the pot."

I looked around for Anna, for any friendly face at all. No luck. Omar was a tiny figure in the distance, busy sawing wood with the other men for the jaguar hunting platform to be installed in a tree whose massive limbs hung over the Anaconda Bar.

As I stalled, the women whispered to one another, shifting from foot to foot but making no move to help me. Even the dogs eyed my every move, panting and whining in the growing heat, their tails thumping with impatience on the hard earth. Only later did I learn that FrannyB treated more dogs than she did people, since so many of them were ravaged during the hunts and had to be sewn back together.

Sunlight had broken through a thick blanket of clouds, spiking the heat. The air boiled with humidity; water left my body at every surface, even my elbows and fingers. Heavy knife hanging from one sweaty hand, I approached one of the fish; the women parted to let me by. Its scales alternated gray and bright red; the rest of it a decaying sort of blue, the eye a hollow moon with a black center. Its square jaw drooped open in its flat triangular head; rows of pointy teeth looked ready to bite off a finger, even in death.

I dropped to my knees with the knife. I had never cut any sort of animal before, alive or dead. *It's dead already*, I thought. *You're not killing anything. Just do it.* Unable to stand the suspense, one of the dogs got up on its hind legs and lunged at another's throat; one of the women yelled and jerked him back by a rope. I hadn't realized they were all tied together.

Unfamiliar fruits from an unknown tree, orange and hairy, plunked down on the ground beside me, rolling to a stop nearby. I felt the women approach in a group, a dark wall behind me, closer and closer, each with their own knife.

I plunged my knife into the tender gills of the fish, ripping it across a line of pasty-white belly scales. As if it'd been under pressure, the flesh made a ripping sound as a mass of blue and red entrails burst out in a hot wave. Behind the guts, the big red heart still pulsed and quivered, shocking me. It kept on pumping for several seconds before sputtering to stillness. I stumbled to my feet, gagging, the loudest sound in an unearthly silence that had settled over everything. I spun around, searching the faces of the women for some shred of kindness, of pity, even humor, just: *something*. But I saw only hatred, or what I took as hatred, or gloating, or worst of all: apathy. I felt desperate to run, but knew that would seal something I couldn't unseal. And where in fuck would I go? I refused to run to Omar like a child. I straightened my shoulders, blinked the sweat out of my eyes. A strange lull followed the appalling silence, before another round of guts glugged out by my feet.

Doña Antonia stepped forward and handed me a calabash.

I took it but stood frozen as the dogs strained at their leashes and snapped at the entrails. Suddenly I became aware of the women yelling something at me: *Come on, pick them up!* I scooted the ladle under the quivering pile and heaved scoop after scoop into the boiling pot, wondering how anything could be hotter than the punishing air.

It was only then that something broke among the women. Murmuring, they withdrew their own knives from the folds of their skirts and stepped around to the other gigantic fish. Each dropped to her knees. One by one, they expertly drove the blades deep in, holding an empty calabash against the inevitable flow of guts, or sawing at a gigantic head. Cutting and scooping, cutting and scooping, we began to fill the pot.

Though the women worked in silence, efficiently, a few slipped me an encouraging nod or smile. The vat of boiling guts belched giant taut bubbles into the blistering morning air. At one point, Doña Antonia left the group, disappearing up the hill for several minutes. Huffing, she returned dragging a woven basket of bananas—her height—that had turned black and soft. Countless flies and gnats flocked to the stench. A few women ran up to help her, peeling and throwing the rotted fruit in the pot, now a thick gluey stew.

Doña Antonia tossed a dozen shallow clay bowls at a good distance from each other near the pot, then handed me the ladle. "Fill them," she grunted.

Over time I learned that we had to cook the dogs' food because eating raw flesh was a death sentence for them. Like the jaguars, once the dogs learned the taste of raw meat, they acquired a blood thirst they never forgot. Instead of circling and cornering prey so the hunters could close in, they would attack, getting themselves gored by the tusks of the wild pigs the men were trying to capture. Here, dogs weren't kept to be petted, bathed, and adored, they were kept to hunt peccary or tapir; to sniff out shyer game like tortoises and armadillos, alert families to snakes that sometimes snuck in the village at night. To show them affection was considered lunacy.

When I was done ladling, Doña Antonia macheted the liana that held the dogs. Wild-eyed, they raced for their meal, yelping and nipping at one another, each of them—in an attempt to steal the other dogs' share—wolfing their food so fast they barely swallowed their own portion. One runty mongrel with sweet brown eyes and a skunkish white stripe down her back ate far too slowly and was soon nudged aside. Whimpering, she tried her luck at the other bowls, but the three-legged dog—the most vicious of the bunch—bared her teeth in a snarl, scaring the sweet mutt witless. There wasn't a scrap of food left.

"This one, Mariposa, she pees when she sees a jaguar skin." Doña Antonia eyed the dog as it scampered up the hill, tail between her legs. "We should get rid of her."

Several of the women murmured in agreement as they collected the bowls and ambled down to the water to rinse them out. The rest of them sprinted off to corral the dogs; many had finished with their meals and had begun to wander off to find a place to shit or sleep off their full bellies. Freed from my duties for the moment, I started up the hill to find Omar. As I threaded among the huts, it hit me who Doña Antonia reminded me of—her behavior, not her appearance. A group-home manager all us kids professed to hate—we saw her as blunt, strict, a total bitch. On the other hand, we were a feral, out-of-control bunch. Maybe, like Doña Antonia hazing me and getting the dogs fed at the same time, all she was trying to do was get through the day without anybody hurt or hungry or in jail; in our beds every night, safe.

FOURTEEN

– JUNE –

Just after sunrise one morning, Omar and I sat high up on the platform that towered over the Anaconda Bar. Sounds were even louder in the matted tangle of the mid-story—the metallic rasp of insects, the screech of spider monkeys, birds whooping. Secured to a thick branch, a rope ladder dangled thirty feet to the ground below, the last rungs obscured by a cloud that dozed on the forest floor. It was thrilling to be able to see the entire village as well as most of the Tortoise Beach laid out before us, but sobering to realize how vulnerable we were. The village was only a tiny slice of cleared land in an unfathomably enormous and complex jungle. Ramshackle huts perched on spindly crane legs. I could barely imagine the rainy season, a few short months away. The river rising thirty feet, erasing the earth beneath us. Hills morphing to islands, clearings to lakes. Villagers traveling only by boat, fishing from their windows while pink dolphins swam among the trees.

"What's it like to hunt from up here?" I asked, hoping nothing would crawl or jump on the platform.

"It's really pretty boring," Omar said, lying down on his stomach and gazing out. "The hardest part about this is staying awake."

I had to admit, it all sounded so sexy: jaguar hunting, and yet, all we could really do, all any of us could do—at least in the village itself—was jaguar waiting. Anybody who could shoot a gun, blow-gun, arrow, or slingshot was to take two-hour turns at dusk and dawn guarding Ayachero from the platform.

"Tell me what it's like to see a jaguar."

He smiled, the memory lighting his face. "When they think they're not being watched, they just stumble around, like they're drunk. Three-hundred-and-fifty-pound cats. They just go here and there, they stretch and sharpen their claws on a trunk, yawn, sniff around, but the *second* they get a sense you're there, even if you make the smallest sound—*boom!*—it's electric the way they come to life. There's so much power in that instant."

"But then you have to kill them."

He stroked my hair. "Then I have to kill them. I imagine the face of the person they've killed, or the damage they've done to our animals, or what they might do to one of us, and I shoot."

We watched the men gather at the beach, loading the boats for the hunt. He pulled me toward him, kissed me quickly, chastely. "I'd better go, Lily."

I sat up, hoping to stall him. "Read me your assignment first."

"As soon as you tell me a secret about yourself."

I sighed, having momentarily forgotten our deal. "When I was living with Tia, she'd buy this cheap gallon block of ice cream, always vanilla, not because we liked vanilla so much, but because we could never all agree on a flavor. She'd cut it up in eight equal sections when she got it home. We'd sit around and watch her cut it like little wolves. If I wasn't home, one of the other kids would grab my share, and I'd come home to this empty box of ice cream on the counter. I'd open it up all the way and lick it clean. Even now when I get the chance, I eat so much ice cream I make myself sick. Okay? Is that a good enough secret?"

"Thank you," he said in English as he pulled out a ratty piece of paper.

"'Tatinga,'" he began solemnly. "'Tatinga people are a tribe that is the kind that live in one place. They do not move their houses. They make a place on the land for vegetables, for fruits, for yucca. When rubber traders come, a long time ago, they use the people as slaves, even rape, even murder them, anything to bleed rubber from the trees for American tires. Many make themselves dead to escape. The ones who live, run deep into the jungle to survive. They move and move. Now, men of opportunity come and poison rivers for gold, or kill too much game, or wrong game, or make roads to get mahogany. And game never crosses a road. So now Tatinga and other tribes are no-mad-ic.'" He looked up at me for confirmation of the word. "'They move but do not like it. Who likes to move all the time? Tatinga know how to love the jungle, so the jungle is not afraid and gives back game, fruits, plants. They do not take too many tortoise eggs, for then how are there more tortoises? They do not cut down ironwood trees, where do mother macaw put her babies then?

"'My father and I hunt with Tatinga when I am young. Then, we have the same problem with jaguars, but Ayachero works with Tatinga, like friends. We say to each other, who has seen the jaguar that steals the chickens? How to track so no one is killed? Where is the best place to build a platform? Who mans the platform, and when? The jaguar does not care if he eats an Ayachero man or a Tatinga man. Both taste delicious to him.

"'Tatinga do not name a baby for one year. They do not want to love a baby if they think it dies. Tatinga love their ancestors. The ones who die are burned. Mothers, fathers, grandmothers, grandfathers. Their bones are crushed and put in a drink and everybody drinks it every day until all is gone. Tatinga are fierce, and they kill you if they are angry and you never see them. You are just dead. They do not hate you. They want to live. They want to be alone in the jungle, but there are men of opportunity. There are Frannies. There are *ribereños*, river people, other villages like Ayachero. Everybody has an empty stomach.'" He stopped. "That's all, Lily."

My heart was close to bursting with how much I loved the way he saw the jungle and everyone in it, but I just said, "Very good, my favorite student," and kissed him slowly.

A high-pitched whine sounded from upriver. In minutes, a long-boat outfitted with a cheap motor (called a *peke peke* because of the sound it made) buzzed around a turn and headed straight toward us, the face of its driver hidden under a filthy golf cap. The sound heartened me with its whiff of civilization, a reminder of the outside world. We scrambled down the rope ladder and made our way to the shore.

I forgot the mosquitos droning in my ears as we watched the boat carve across clay-colored currents, its rear hull freighted with rubberized bags and wooden crates. The lip of the gunwale hovered just inches from the water as the boat putt-putted toward us, only the thrust from its egg-beater motor keeping the whole works from taking on water.

The driver lifted his face out from the shadow of his hat, which read, US OPEN, 1974, and smiled. His face was immediately appealing: a strong jaw, bright eyes, short hair slicked back with lots of tonka-seed oil. He wore red gym shorts and a faded Hawaiian shirt open to reveal a big tin cross on a leather cord. He was bulky in the shoulders and chest, but one of his legs looked thin and weak.

Waving and calling to Omar, he drove the boat right up onto the shore before cutting the motor. With the use of a twisted cane, he pushed himself up to his full height and stepped out of the boat. Unlike most villagers, who went around barefoot or wore cheap flip-flops, he sported plastic Colombia-made loafers with bright, gold-painted buckles, and seemed conscientious about keeping them as dry and mud-free as possible. Omar ran down to greet him, lifting him up into the air with a joyful embrace before setting him back down on the spit of sand.

"Fucking *Omar*, my man!" the man said. "Look at you! You're an old man now, over."

Omar beamed. "This is my wife, Lily."

The river driver turned to me. I couldn't guess his age; a dozen smile lines crowded his mouth and eyes; I instantly liked him just for smiling at me.

"I am called For God's Sake," the man said, reaching out to shake my hand. "You have a good husband here," he added, winking at Omar. "A great hunter. You will always be safe, never be hungry, over."

"Thanks," I said. "That's good to hear."

Omar caught my eye. "For God's Sake is the best river driver around. He worked for years in a Baptist mission in La Paz. He ran the radio operation there."

"It's true," For God's Sake said, smiling with his three teeth on top, two on the bottom. A thin mustache, carefully tended, tented his upper lip. "This is where I learn Portuguese, this is where I learn English so well. I am the radio guy, over."

Omar joined the other men who had begun to unload For God Sake's boat, which was brimming with supplies: canisters of gasoline, cooking oil, sacks of dried corn, lentils, pasta, salt, boxes of cigars and matches. For God's Sake climbed back on board and reached under his seat, extracting plastic bags of wrapped candy, which he held in the air, smiling. The kids—all who seemed to know the importance of showing up for Santa Claus—swarmed him, laughing and jumping up to grab peppermints and caramels from his hands. He good-naturedly pushed them back, making sure each child got at least one piece before tying the bags and stuffing them back under heavy sacks of rice and onions. The kids ran off and sat on the hardened mud in ecstasy as they ate their treats.

"I heard about Benicio. So sad. So terrible. I am sorry to miss the funeral. I was in La Paz. But when I heard you came back," For God's Sake said to Omar, "I rush here. The Frannies need things, too, yes. I have to come for them. But really, for you is my reason. Ten years is a long time, brother. Lots of changes, okay? And now I see I almost miss you, with your hunting, but good thing I catch you, over." His eyes twinkling, he held up one finger as in, *hold on a minute*, and clambered back in the longboat, where he wrapped his arms around a barrel keg and lifted it to one shoulder. "I think it's still cold, over."

Word spread fast. Several young men—whooping—ran down to the shore. One grabbed the keg from For God's Sake and sprinted with it—stopping midstride to dance a sort of jig before continuing up the hill to the Anaconda Bar. Someone cranked the tunes to stun, masking the sounds of cups and glasses slamming on the wooden counter. Macaws dipped and soared in the air above us, shrieking and sobbing as they landed on the muddy banks, their turquoise-and-orange wings folding like living fans.

Shrugging, the women abandoned their weaving or food preparation and headed up to the bar, their children running and playing and pulling at their skirts. Grinning like he won the lottery, Panchito moved faster than I'd ever seen him, throwing his arms around the men who, laughing, picked him up and tossed him a few feet up the hill, alcohol making fast friends of everyone.

Omar winked at me, dropping his arm over my shoulder as we followed For God's Sake up the hill to open the keg and drink every last drop of cold beer, which turned out to be Michelob ULTRA light lager. I was learning fast that the best policy in the jungle was to take whatever bounty comes to you, when it comes to you. There was something sweet about it. Pleasure was here, why wait? It was just nine o'clock in the morning.

Three hours later, the children rolled the keg down the hill to the shore, where they filled it with river water and poured it over their heads. Several of the men lay passed out snoring in hammocks or slumped over the bar. Hard to believe the beer accomplished this; no doubt some private stash of pisco had been broken out as well. The bullying heat of the day had ramped up, and most of the women had gone off into the shade to peel vegetables or skin game. Several couples had disappeared into their huts, burpy and happy and ready for love.

Meanwhile, I won a seat at the Anaconda Bar between Omar and For God's Sake.

"I am Tatinga," he said, taking a long, slow drink of his beer after I asked him about himself. "But because of this"—he glanced down at his deformed leg—"they didn't want me there. So when I was sixteen years old, I came to Ayachero. Your husband Omar here helped me, he was my good friend. He was just twelve. Can you imagine that? But he made sure I had food, he made sure I had a place to sleep. He had to fight his mother for that, right, Omar?" Both men laughed and shook their heads at the memory. "I learned Spanish, fast. I taught him Tatinga. But I can't hunt, so there was nothing for me here. I went to La Paz and found the mission. I learned English. I speak Tatinga, Spanish, English, Quechua, some Portuguese. Very helpful for communications. But the mission lost funding. I was very sad. I had a wife and two kids, one coming. I thought, what can I do? What do I *like* to do? And I think: boats, always boats. I am the best river driver, everybody knows about that. I know every branch, every creek, every lake, all the habits of the river. In my head there is a wet season map and a dry season one, and I can steer a full boat through any weather. They are my neighborhood streets. I am your river driver man." He tipped his glass at me. "So why do you come to be here, over?"

I looked at Omar and smiled.

"Yes, yes," he said with a touch of impatience, "but what is your, I don't know how to say, but in Tatinga, it means, purpose in life? Your—we call it *ca'ah*—over?" He smiled and searched my face, as if he really wanted to know. Curiosity made him handsome. "You know, Lily, there is everything that we do, and see, and talk about, but then there is *ca'ah—why* we do these things, *the reason*, what is pushing us, pulling us, what are we looking for, what makes us go, do you understand this, over?"

I gazed into my warm glass of flat beer. My gut understood it, my brain did not. "Why do they call you For God's Sake?"

"That's what they called me at the mission. Why? The answer is easy. *For God's Sake*, they said, why do you have to talk so much? Please, be quiet. *For God's Sake*, we are trying to work here, or go to sleep maybe, or get mission writing done, you know, so, *For God's Sake, shut up, will you?* So since then I am For God's Sake. I don't mind. But tell me, you know, about your *ca'ah*, over."

He looked at me with such respect and interest, as if my answer would be worth listening to, if he was only patient enough to wait for it. I reddened. The reasons for what I do—how could I know that? I seemed not to act, but only *react* to events, to lunge toward decisions—people, places, things—pulled or pushed by reasons I was barely conscious or in control of.

"I don't know. I just survive, I guess."

For God's Sake waved my silly answer away. "There has to be some *ca'ah* in you. Mostly I am confused by white man's *ca'ah*. Sometimes they are so nice they give you food, behave with fairness, speak nicely, and use respect. Sometimes—" Here he puffed out his cheeks, made a bang-bang motion with his hands, like guns going off, shaking his head. "It's like that. Mean and sad and killing. Like devils. First one thing, then the other thing, back and forth, back and forth. I don't understand *civilizado ca'ah*. What is their big purpose, their big idea? Where does their spirit live? So I keep asking everyone I meet, until I know. What do they want, can you tell me? What do you want, Lily, over?"

"Guess I'm still not sure." Those days, I'd lose myself in lofty yet vague fantasies of saving elephants and rhinos from poachers in

Africa, chimps from extinction, whales from tangled fishing ropes. Was this what he meant by *ca'ah*? "I love animals, and I like to sew."

"Ah, sewing! You can make clothes, any kind of clothes, over?"

"Any kind of clothes. I can sew linings, I can make my own patterns. I can just look at you and know what size you are."

"So someday you will make me a fine suit, a beautiful suit, that I will wear proudly to my daughter's wedding, when she has grown and found a good man, over?" For God's Sake combed his mustache with one finger thoughtfully as he spoke.

I laughed. "Of course."

Now, up close, I could put him in his midthirties, but a hard-won midthirties, leathery and sad around the eyes, even through his continual smile.

Omar pushed himself to his feet, glancing around at the men sleeping in hammocks or huddled in groups nursing the last of the beer. "The beer party's over. We need to get these men in the boat."

"Of course, of course," For God's Sake said, pushing himself to his feet that spilled out of his loafers.

"And listen, man," Omar said, taking him aside. "After you've been up to the Frannies, don't hang around. Go right back to La Paz. It's not safe for you here these days."

"So, you're talking about Fat Carlos and Dutchie and his men? I saw them on my way here from San Solidad. I heard their motor and had plenty of time to hide myself, over."

"They're not satisfied with jaguar skins anymore, understand?"

"Yes, I do, over."

"You see their boat here, you just keep on going. I'm telling you, For God's Sake, my brother."

He smiled but his eyes stayed tight. "Of course. Those are some wise words from you." He turned. "Let me help you now, get these lazy men back to work. But the beer was cold, you know? The beer is the boss when it's cold, over!" Laughing, he started off down the hill with a boisterous energy, yelling out to the men and banging on the stilts of the huts with his cane, until the still-drunk hunters stumbled out into the blistering heat, zipping their flies or combing their hands through their hair as they assembled at the shore.

I followed Omar through the crowd of men, the sharp tang of their sweat surrounding me. Some carried rifles or had longbows slung over their shoulders; others carried V-shaped contraptions wrapped with long rubber cords: slingshots that, used effectively, could kill an animal of almost any size. The hunters studiously did not look at me. I felt among men who did not want me there, who had no interest in or comfort with women except for the usual reasons. I could feel part of Omar already gone, already disappeared into the wilderness.

But no one cared about our drama, my drama. There were very few demonstrations of affection between men and women, I'd been noticing; even a hug and a kiss between mother and child seemed rare. Only later did it sink in about the villagers' profoundly different sense of privacy: want to be alone to talk? To make love? Don't get your hopes up, or perhaps get whatever it is done fast. Closed door, open door, didn't matter, people came and went at will, *mi casa es tu casa*.

All my life I'd craved privacy; here it was lacking not out of malice, but out of a shared sense of community of which I was not yet a part. These people were linked in ways I didn't yet understand. I had learned something about meals, however: everyone ate at once, or not at all. Just like when I was a kid, the food—whatever there was—was ready when it was ready and everybody showed up for it. There were no leftovers.

I stood by Omar on the bank, twirling my tin wedding ring, already loose on my finger, a fact that registered somewhere in the recesses of my mind. "Why don't you stay back this time?" I said, unable to stop the words from tumbling out.

He shifted the sack of supplies he carried to his other shoulder, examined me. "The village needs food. I want to build you a real house—"

"I don't have anyone here but you. You're my whole family now."

"Everyone in Ayachero is your family."

I scowled. He looked around, his face hardening, kindness leaking away. I estimated the total time I'd known him—it was June now—so barely three months? He scanned the shore, a bustling scene of men sorting supplies and loading the boats, their backs slick with midday sweat.

Half a dozen women packed one end of the boat with pots, knives, and a few small sacks of manioc, as the dogs circled. Some had already jumped in the canoes to claim their places; they panted, sniffed around for scraps, pausing to lick their mangy coats. The little runt Mariposa skittered along by my side.

Omar dropped his bag, pulled out a machete, and handed it to me. "Keep this with you." He was already in the jungle. I could see it.

I took it from him; the twenty-inch steel blade hung down heavily and too close to my leg. "What am I supposed to do with this?"

"Keep it in the hut. And promise me you'll stay out of the jungle. Especially dawn and dusk. Those are the worst times to be on the paths. The night animals are coming out to hunt, and the daytime animals are trying to hide. You don't want to get in their way. Are you listening? Stay in the village."

"When are you coming back?"

"We come back with food, otherwise . . ." He shrugged.

"Otherwise what?"

"Otherwise no one eats. Not you, not me, not anyone." The dog had given up on licking my hands and sat her warm ass down on my foot, staring up at me with the bottomless hope of dogs, the ridge of her bony back resting against my shin.

"But . . . the fish, can't you always catch—"

He laughed, waving me away. "This is the jungle. There is no 'always.'"

"Where's Anna? Why isn't she here to say goodbye to Franz?"

"She never does that. She thinks it's unlucky."

"Really. What will I do while I wait?" I reddened, thinking of Doña Antonia's comment about having nothing to do but stare in the mirror while he was gone.

He held me by the shoulders and looked me in the eye, as if trying to stare some strength or resolve into me. "Wait for what, *me*? Just be Lily, then everything will come to you."

He turned away and climbed into the boat with Franz and the rest of the men. The dogs sat up and wagged their tails, turning in tight circles before resettling in their strict confines. They could taste the hunt in their mouths. The current began to take interest in the boat, nudging the bow downriver.

Omar stood on the lip of the canoe, a jungle gondolier, one paddle wedged deep in the thick mud of the shore. With a powerful shove, he pushed the boat away from the bank. Perfectly spaced alongside each other, both boats—one with six men, the other with two women and several dogs—receded quickly from the bank, the river only too happy to sweep them into its narrative of currents and eddies. Villagers who had come to see the hunters off began to drift away up the hill. The bend in the river erased the canoes, as if they had never existed.

Omar never once looked back.

FIFTEEN

A breathless panic overcame me. I began to pace up and down the bank like a madwoman, from one wall of jungle to the other, all the way to the far east end of the village where the manioc fields stretched back to the barn and the leper family's hut, then the other way, past the Anaconda Bar, finding myself practically to the Tortoise Beach before stopping and gazing off into the wall of green beyond. Mosquitos followed me, circling my head, their shrill drone grinding into my brain.

The river, the color of dark mustard, flowed with its own unknowable intentions, turning and folding into itself. Ancient trees towered, trunks like columns, their intertwined crowns disappearing in vaporous clouds. Beneath the canopy seethed a boiling mess of understory vegetation. Vines hung down in coils, motionless in the still, hot air. The jungle held the village in a stranglehold on three sides; the river sealed it in. I wasn't going anywhere.

I slipped off my backpack—suddenly sick of its sweaty weight—and threw it down on the sand in a huff, stamping my feet like a frustrated child. Disturbed from their hidey-holes, hundreds of tiny, nearly transparent spiders bloomed out from the grains of sand, darted along the shore, and stepped out onto the river, skimming along the surface of the water.

I'd barely recovered from the sight when the air shattered with the screams of howler monkeys. Half a dozen big tawny ones leapt from branch to branch a hundred feet above me, freeing nuts and branches that drubbed down on my head and shoulders. I turned to run, but one of them dropped down to the earth with a thump, landing between me and the village.

Man-sized—part lion, part great ape—it came running at me, its mouth a dish-sized pink oval open in a never-ending roar. In terror, I fell back on my ass and scuttled away like a crab. So this was how I was going to die, not by the hand of some group-home skank cutting my throat, not in a plane crash, not by a jaguar lurking under our hut. A monkey's face would be the last I saw.

The creature stopped next to my pack, just a yard from me, still blaring through the echo chamber of its cavernous head; its wet fur stinking like rotted wool. Bellowing constantly, he fixed me to my spot with hooded black eyes, nostrils empty holes on his long, hairless face ringed by a thick ruff of fur. He stood up on his hind legs, his white balls pendulous between his bowlegged gait, his prehensile tail curling up and twisting crazily, as if it had a mind of its own.

The creature slipped one long arm under a strap of my backpack and lifted it up, dangling it in front of his face for long, strange seconds. Was *that* what it wanted, my bag? I scuttled back a few more feet; he paid no attention. Encouraged by the roars of his gang that swung and looped in the green chaos above us, he bugled even louder, jumping up and down, spinning the bag in the air by one strap like a lasso he was about to let fly, before bashing it over and over onto the dirt as if to kill it.

Grunting, sniffing, finally satisfied it was dead, he gripped it by the sides and stretched its main compartment over his head and face, screaming into the canvas, before slipping it by a strap over one powerful shoulder—almost like it was meant to be carried!—and launching himself into the arms of a wide-bottomed tree. His posse dangled from the branches above or squatted in the notches of trees, huffing and growling encouragingly, emitting a constant low throttle as if noise was the norm, silence an aberration, their way of saying, *I'm a howler monkey, you fuckers, and I'm here*, shitting and shaking the branches and hurling baseball-sized nuts down at me.

A good distance up the hill, Paco meandered between the huts, listlessly kicking around an empty corn-oil keg. He saw me jumping around and began to roll the can toward me. I ran to the tree that shook with monkeys, awed by their churning animal grace even as I screamed, "*Give me back my bag!*"

More nuts came raining down, followed by more branches. Grapefruit-sized yellow fruit covered with sharp thorns slapped the moist earth. Paco stopped halfway down the bank, turned the keg on its bottom and sat on it, watching the show. "Be careful," he called out. "They'll poop on you!"

The monkey who'd stolen my pack catapulted through the branches, threading through explosions of flowering bromeliads and epiphytes. He swung upside down from his tail, figure-eighting a landing on a thick branch, where he sat on his haunches. I grabbed one of the fruits from the ground—thorns stabbing my palm—and chucked it, missing him. He hooted at me, blowing out his cheeks with mirth. With perfect dexterity, he clutched the pack between the palms of his feet and used his arms and tail to climb higher to another favorite perch. Settling there, he grabbed the cord for the main compartment of the bag with one finger and unzipped it. Smirking down at me, he flipped the bag over and shook it out.

Tumbling down through the branches came . . . everything I owned. *Charlotte's Web* seemed to toss and roll in slow motion into the waiting hands of another monkey, who fanned out the pages and, finding this hilarious, let out a series of raucous barks before ripping them out. They drifted down, most of them catching on the tangled vines and thick vegetation. My mom's and foster mom's photos fell next; glittering like precious leaves. One of the monkeys snatched up the bigger one—my real mom's photo, my only photo of her—and I swear he looked at that thing like he was *looking* at something, like that was my *mom* looking back at him and he knew it. Eyeing me the whole time, he gave it a few cautious licks before stuffing it in his mouth and swallowing it.

Other stuff rained down: my only other pair of underwear; my jeans and T-shirt; my comb; toothbrush; a plastic bag with an old doughnut another monkey ate whole, including the ziplock bag. Along with everything else, a couple of Kotex I'd stolen from the Versailles in Cochabamba caught and hung in the branches like bizarre Christmas ornaments. Looping the pack over a branch by its remaining unbroken strap, the howler swung from it, braying, his magnificent ruff shaking, until he launched himself a full flip in the air, landing perfectly among his friends, who howled their approval of the show before leaping en masse and vanishing into the riotous mid-story. Torn open, empty, one strap totally gone, my backpack swayed a hundred feet up in the hot breeze, forever a part of the random insanity of the jungle.

I spun around, searching for help, for someone to give a shit. My hands bled from the thorny fruit; the bellowing of the monkeys rang in my ears, their calls still clear, though they were probably already a few kilometers away. I felt slightly deaf, heatstroked, a little bit out of my mind.

Beyond Paco, up the hill, stood the old woman I'd seen with the lepers that morning that felt so long ago. Beya. She leaned on her cane, contemplating me. At her feet sat a small cloth bag that moved slightly, as if whatever was inside was trying to get out, or was fighting with another occupant. Mouth grim and straight, ears bright with feathers, she stared at me with a mix of curiosity and sadness. How long had she been standing there, watching this circus? A chill bloomed in the base of my spine, even in all the mind-bending heat.

Suddenly dizzy, I braced my hands on my knees and closed my eyes for a few seconds, before slowly opening them. Her gaze intensified. I took a step back. The electric buzz of insects whined louder. She seemed to shimmer under the diamond sun, come into focus, then vanish into the pattern of branches and leaves behind her. A palpable, pulsating energy flowed between her and the forest, a buzzing, unbroken loop. I blinked again, trying to shake off the white noise that crashed inside my ears.

I heard her voice—*it had to be her*—whisper in Spanish, as clearly as if she were standing next to me, "WHY ARE YOU HERE? THIS IS NOT YOUR FOREST."

Her lips had not moved.

The voice trailed away in my head, like the rasping of leaves on a fall night. She had spoken without making a sound; that or I was losing my mind. She dropped her eyes, picked up her bag, turned, and made her way up the hill.

Paco pushed himself off his seat on the keg and walked down to the bank where I stood, dumbstruck from the theft and from the woman's voice in my head. He wrapped his sticky little hand around my finger. I yanked him around to face me. "Did you hear that?" I hissed.

He looked at me as if trying to figure out what I wanted to hear, what would make me happy. "I just hear monkeys."

I wiped the sweat off my forehead with the back of my hand. "She spoke to me."

"Was it out loud, or in your head?"

"In my head."

"Was it something nice?"

"Not really."

Paco watched me thoughtfully as I gazed up at everything I owned besides the clothes on my back, hanging among the leaves and branches above us.

"Come with me. I'll make you a comb," Paco said very seriously.

Gesturing at me to follow him, he walked toward a low-lying palm plant, its slender fronds picking up the morning light with a greasy sheen. With a stubby-handled knife, he sliced off a thick, waxy branch, and with quick, practiced movements snapped out every other frond, creating a bright green comb.

He patted the ground and said, "Sit."

"I don't want to sit, Paco, okay? There's spiders in there and—"

"Sit!" he commanded.

So I sat down, very slowly and carefully. No spiders this time. Paco stepped behind me. Laying one hand on my shoulder as if to steady me, he reached up with the other to gather a section of my snarled, filthy hair. I closed my eyes and listened to the receding roars of the monkeys.

I didn't have a clue then, but it wasn't the pain of him wrestling out the knots in my rat's-nest hair with the palm-frond comb that made me cry my fucking eyes out, it was the fact that someone was actually bothering to take care of me.

SIXTEEN

From where I hung like a fleshy chrysalis in my hammock, I woke to a little piglet screaming in my face. Her snout quivered and glistened; morning sun set her pink ears aglow. Suddenly she stopped and sat back on her ass, stumpy hind legs splayed out, front hooves planted into the soft wood, and stared at me agape, like I had been the one braying at her.

I reached out and scratched the top of her head. The hair was softer than I thought it would be, still tufty baby hair. She grunted and snuffled, her eyes squeezing shut in ridiculous pleasure. I took one of her front hooves with my other hand and held it for a second, shaking it like you would a dog's; she seemed to like this, too, but soon she pulled away and moved her head under my hand, as if she preferred the scratching to anything else. I took one of her velvety ears between thumb and forefinger and leaned into it, whispering, "I'm going to call you Charlotte." The pig's name in the story was Wilbur, but this pig seemed much more like a Charlotte to me.

Around me drifted the soft sounds of people waking up, speaking in hushed tones, the dull scraping of utensils as breakfast was prepared. The pig and I held each other's gaze. I missed my backpack like a phantom limb. After years of rambling with it on my back, I felt deeply unmoored without it, as if I might float up and away. At last I placed my unease: I had finally unpacked, and it took a howler monkey to do it.

"Hey, Meessis *Gringa*, let's go, time to get up," Doña Antonia muttered with a little swat of her straw broom at my hammock. "You're going to wash clothes with the other women, okay? Enough of this sleeping all day like a queen."

Like that was possible with the jungle already ricocheting with the calls of monkeys, parrots, frogs, all going at it molto vivace, shrieking and squawking as if the world were waking up in pain, the jungle giving birth to itself each morning. I untangled myself from the hammock and netting and got to my feet. Charlotte blinked up at me. I finally recognized her as the same piglet the woman had held to her breast. A dark line of fur encircled one eye; another seemed drawn on one pink flank, like a bull's-eye.

"What happened to that woman who was nursing her?" I asked Doña Antonia, who stood waiting for me, hands on hips.

She waved me away like it wasn't worth her breath to discuss it. "Angelina? She's away. She's gone."

"Where did she go?"

"Why? She's a friend of yours?"

"No, I just—"

"Now *you* want to give milk to the pig?" She grabbed her saggy tit and squeezed, cackling.

"I just want to know—"

"Forget it, okay? Everything's okay."

"Is she dead?"

She turned to me, took stock of me. "You really want to know, American girl? Okay, so listen. Two days ago, she took off her clothes and ran into the jungle naked. So she's dead. The jungle ate her. Okay?"

"No one tried to find her?"

"Some of the men went looking, but—she was nowhere. After two days, we stop. We call it off. That's the rule."

"But that's—"

"Come on, come with me." She handed me some hot cooked yucca wrapped in a banana leaf—my to-go breakfast. I followed her down the stairs, out of the longhouse, and—despite my horror as I imagined what might have happened to Angelina—took tentative bites of the food, fingers burning, craving a bit of salt, some flavor, something I could recognize.

Squealing and making an insane racket considering no one was interfering with her in any way, Charlotte followed at my heels, scruffling across the floor and falling down the stairs, one by one, each step a little calamity and cause for more complaining.

We followed Doña Antonia through the village to a chicken coop where a few dozen scrawny chickens in a wire cage pecked at dried corn. "Every morning and every night you feed them, got it? You take their eggs and you bring them to me. You keep this rooster over here, by himself, away from his women, or he'll eat them, okay? He's crazy." She shook her head. "We need a new mister. This one has run out of brains." She laughed at her joke as she looped the gate shut behind her with a length of wire. "And this is always closed, okay? Always, always. Or no more chickens, understand?"

I nodded, encouraged in a small way by being given some responsibility, and followed her back to the longhouse. A few of the women, tall woven baskets on their backs held in place by leather straps across their foreheads, were already making their way to the river. Two baskets sat waiting for us, both nearly as tall as Doña Antonia, whose gray head came only to my shoulder. She stood in front of hers, turned, knelt a bit, positioned the strap across her forehead, and stood up, lifting the basket off the ground with ease. She gestured at me and the one that remained.

It looked so easy. I did what she did: faced it, turned, knelt, adjusted the strap across my forehead, and tried to stand. It was like lifting a building. I tried again, straining with everything I had: impossible. I sat on my ass, the strap loose around my knees. A half-dozen spider monkeys watched from their perch in the canopy before screeching some sort of signal to one another; they dropped to the earth and coursed around me in a wave of chattering gray fur like I was a stone in a river. Charlotte was unfazed.

Doña Antonia, halfway down the hill, turned and squinted up at me. I got to my feet, mugging my inability to lift the basket with a lame smile and shrug. With a look of disgust, she turned back toward the river, machete swinging from one hand, her wide-hipped, pigeon-toed walk flinging out her loose skirt from side to side. A couple of bright-eyed little girls sat down next to me with a bunch of green bananas, chattering too fast for me to understand a word. I got that they were asking me questions, but when I couldn't answer, they grew sullen and silent. They opened the tough peels of the bananas with their teeth, making their way steadily through the fruit.

I turned again and faced the basket—my new enemy—bent down, wrapped my arms around it and did a dead lift, pitching backward so hard I almost lost my footing, but turned toward the river, determined. Staring into the thatch, I blindly made my way down to the shore. Charlotte followed me so closely I kicked her now and then; she squealed with indignation but never left my side.

Already most of the women had waded into the river up to their thighs. They rubbed pieces of clothing, mostly *cushma*—the sack-like dresses several women and many men wore—over slabs of rock, dousing them in the water to rinse them. A few sat near the shore, one arm around their tiny babies as they worked the clothes with the other. Everyone spoke nonstop and too fast for me to grasp what they said, but at least they seemed to be looking at me with something like curiosity—as in: *How's the* gringa *going to handle this? Will she be able to hack it?*

Several yards away, Beya stood hip-deep in the water with her own armful of washing, skirt hiked up high and tucked under her belt, her painfully thin brown thighs parting the thick warm water in slow, thoughtful steps. She seemed in her own world, gazing down into the murky depths as if we didn't exist.

I stole glances at the brilliant red, turquoise, and yellow macaw feathers that sprung back from her earlobes; the tattooed lines, swirls, and dots on her face; her narrow, sun-bronzed chest, breasts flattened to nothing by the years under the ragged man's cotton shirt she wore. A beat-up derby hat perched high on her forehead, her long braid glowed silver down her back in the sunlight. She stood near the fish gate, a semicircular stretch of fine mesh wire sheeting that reached from the silty bottom of the river—weighted by stones—to about a foot above, circumscribing a twenty-five-foot stretch of beach where we did all our washing of clothes, bathing, and gathering water for cooking and to boil for drinking.

I stood ankle-deep in the amber-colored water, my arms piled high with clothes, wishing I could wash my own, but they were all I had. Charlotte sat at the shore, her front hooves just touching the water. Warily, I watched the fish gate.

Rubbing the slab of hard yellow soap Doña Antonia had given me into the almost colorless cloth, it hit me that no one was punishing me. The women were just doing what needed to be done: the clothes were dirty and needed washing, and all the women were pitching in. Heartened to be included, I worked as hard as I could, as long as I could, until I had washed all the clothes assigned to me and dropped them back in my basket, which sat in knee-deep water next to me.

Just as I turned back to shore, a wave of pain lashed across my forehead, the light of day suddenly so unbearably bright I closed my eyes and covered them with one hand, the other resting on the rim of the basket.

Moaning, I heard the words "DO NOT MOVE" whispered inside my head.

Nausea flooded me, then passed. I opened my eyes, shielding them from the glare off the water, my headache fading with the echo of the words in my brain.

I knew who had spoken to me.

Void of expression, Beya held my gaze. She stood knee-deep in the river just a couple of yards from me, the basket of soaked clothes balanced against her hip dripping steadily into the still water.

I heard her murmur, "DO NOT MOVE. DO NOT LOOK DOWN. LOOK AT ME."

I obeyed. The words hummed in my head, repeating over and over and over, "DO NOT MOVE DO NOT LOOK DOWN LOOK AT ME, DO NOT MOVE DO NOT LOOK DOWN LOOK AT ME," a one-note song sung in basso profundo. Thirty seconds passed like this, a minute; then a pause—it was as if I was waiting for her to "say" something else. Had I invented this whole thing? The longer we looked at each other, the more convinced I became that I was losing my mind, yet I was riveted, enthralled. A buzzing circle of energy coursed between us, binding us; her eyes burning black.

A child shrieked up on the hill, only in play, but we both looked away from each other, severing our communication, if it had happened at all. I gathered my thoughts, brought myself back to where I was and what I was doing, what was expected of me. The sounds of talking and laughter between the women, the whine of insects, began to leak back into my awareness.

That's when I noticed the top section of the fish gate, maybe two yards from me, jerking side to side, before it began to sink—bit by bit—as if something were pulling it, until it sank completely, dragged under the silty brown water.

Her voice in my head whispered, "DON'T MOVE. DON'T SCREAM."

My head whipped back to focus on her face as if she had physically forced me to do so.

"STAY CALM. LISTEN TO MY VOICE."

All the women shouted at once. They abandoned their baskets and splashed toward the bank, snatching their children from the shallows as they ran barefoot across the dark sand, the thumping of their footsteps loud in my ears as I searched Beya's face.

"Electric eel! Everybody out! Go! *Go!* The fish gate is torn!"

My heart pounded at the cage of my body, the terror in their voices and Beya's words planting me where I was. Only she and I remained in the water.

I looked down.

A dark purple eel, man-length, thick as a car tire, quivered as it circled my laundry basket, its warty flesh rubbery and cold looking. Part snake, part catfish, its wall-eyed stare seemed to see nothing as it banged its head over and over against the weave. I stood an arm's length from it, the water lapping just above my kneecaps. I forced myself to be still, to remember what Omar had told me about these creatures; their vision was bad, but their touch could stun and kill a horse; they were attracted to a heartbeat, to movement of any kind. In a distant part of my awareness, the women called to one another, pointing at me as they ran up and down the shore. I pictured my legs as two stone pillars, the blood in my veins thick and unmoving, a cold sludge. I slowed my breathing, made my heart a dull, muffled clock. Still the thing circled the basket, as if it felt something were alive inside of it, and was trying to figure a way in. My bare feet sank deeper into the silt.

"Stay where you are, Lily!" Anna's voice, like a balm over me. Moving slower now, quivering, every cell of its flesh listening for life, the eel still looped itself around the basket, its paddle-like tail nearly touching its pocked face. Two tiny fins like ears on either side of its flat head shuddered and waved in the murk as if listening closer, as if it knew something living was within striking distance. I forced myself to look up and toward the bank. Anna stood at the water's edge, her beautiful face creased with fright.

"Lily, don't move, okay? Just look at me. Come on, look at me, Lily."

Tears leaked out of the sides of my eyes. Her face smeared until I blinked them away.

Several of the women reached into the pockets of their dresses and pulled out stones, which they hurled into the water, crying, "Come on! Come on, eel, come over here!"

Anna held out her arms as if she could lift me up and out of the nightmare soup I stood in. "You're already on the shore with us, Lily, okay? You're already here . . . just look at me, please, now don't stop . . ."

Doña Antonia came thundering down the shore carrying a foot-long live sunfish. A liana cord was tied around its wide middle, the other end wrapped securely around her wrist. Panting, she whipped it out underhand. The fish flew high up, twisting against the hot blue sky before splashing down into the water several yards to one side of me. It jumped into the air a few times, eyes popping, as if it knew what was in store, before Doña Antonia dragged it back, looping the cord in efficient circles around her elbow and the heel of her hand.

A whoosh of cold water stroked the flesh of my calves. Something had changed. My eyelids fluttered closed, and I prayed to any gods who might have been listening. Anna kept calling out to me to look at her, but I couldn't anymore. I had to know. Forcing the rest of my body to remain still, my neck almost too stiff to move, I lowered my chin in the smallest increments of movement I could summon—just enough to let myself look down—and opened my eyes.

The eel had completely lost interest in the basket and was swimming between my legs.

A few of the women splashed up to their ankles in the shallow section. Jumping and screaming, they smacked at the water with their hands, with pots, pans, gourds, anything they could find.

I dropped my eyes again.

The eel continued to figure-eight around and between my legs and the basket.

With a howl, Doña Antonia tossed out the still-live fish on the cord; this time it plunged into the water next to me, its saucer eye bulging with panic. In a surge of dark purple rage, the eel burst out of the water inches from my elbow and clamped down its prehistoric underbite on the doomed thing. Five feet of eel smashed down as the women grabbed the cord and pulled, screaming at me to run.

After forcing stillness into my legs for so long, it took a few horrid seconds to get them to move again. Abandoning the basket, I lunged toward shore. Dresses glued to their bodies with sweat, Doña Antonia and two other women screamed encouragement to one another as they wrestled with the beast, tug-of-warring it long enough for me to leap onto dry sand. As soon as I did, they let go, falling in an exhausted pile. The eel—released, enraged—leapt up, hanging in midair for several seconds, a demonic black muscle writhing, before it crashed back down into a deep, coffee-colored pool on the other side of the ruined fish gate. In seconds, the water smoothed again, leaving only a soft welt on the surface, perhaps from the last flick of its tail.

Anna hugged me. "Are you all right?"

"I think so," I said in a daze, startled to find myself still alive. As if I were cold, I shook uncontrollably, even my teeth chattered as I took a few steps along the shore, holding my elbows to my gut, trying to coerce my soul back into my body. Facing away from all of us, Beya calmly waded back to shore. Weirdly, I listened for her to "say" something more to me, but only her silence echoed in my head.

Anna watched me with concern.

"Thanks, Anna, for helping me."

"That was the biggest one I've ever seen. So strong!"

As we spoke, a few other women gathered around us, as if Anna had broken through some kind of standoff. I thanked them all profusely. There were some smiles and a few more expressions of concern, even another hug or two. One toothless grandma grinned as she peered at me and patted my arm and said, "You are having a lucky day, *gringa*."

"We fix the gate all the time, but"—Anna shrugged—"you know, we can't always be sure there isn't a tear."

Machete in hand, Doña Antonia brushed by us and splashed into the water. She looped my basket's leather strap around one shoulder and dragged it back to the shore, setting it beside me with a huff. Balancing her own basket of wet clothes on her back, she charged past us, motoring up the hill with shocking energy.

The incident with the eel firmly in the past, the women resigned themselves to lugging the baskets filled with heavy, wet clothes up the hill to the longhouse. With a sinking feeling, I watched them repeat the carry-the-basket routine, this time with a full cargo of sodden clothes. I tried it their way, then mine. No luck. I tried dragging it, but gave up and sat down, Charlotte at my heels the whole time—walking where I walked, sitting where I sat, totally psycho-fixed on me.

Anna watched me and laughed. "Wait here. I'll bring Perla. I use her when I'm too tired or too pregnant."

In minutes, Anna appeared at the top of the hill leading the village donkey, Perla, who honked and brayed as she yanked at her liana leash. Sullenly she picked her way down the slope, her huge belly swaying back and forth under the knotty cord of her spine, big square teeth gnashing, a comical tuft of yellow hair curling over one fly-buzzed eye. Anna tossed my basket's wide leather strap over the donkey's back, trussed it up cleverly on the other side, then hoisted the heavy load off the ground, smacking the donkey's flank as she directed it back up the hill.

The women were stoking a fire, heating irons that had been wedged between hot rocks. Woven mats wrapped around their hands, they picked up the heavy rusted irons and pressed down on the clothes, which were spread out flat on the rocks. Steam rose up carrying the smell of fish, stones, mold, and rotted cloth.

Doña Antonia gestured at an iron heating in the fire, my pile of sopping clothes next to it. At a totally separate fire several yards away, Beya ironed her own clothes.

"Why not just let them dry in the sun?"

Doña Antonia looked at me as if my stupidity would never end. "You think there are only big things that can eat you in the water? These clothes are clean but not safe. There are still bugs, you know. Very, very small ones. We need to kill them, otherwise they'll make your skin white, even more white than you, hah!" She disappeared in a cloud of steam as she pressed down hard on the front panel of a dress. "Also, there's a fungus that can grow if we don't iron. Very, very bad."

I wrapped my hand in the woven mat she gave me, took my own heavy iron and pressed it into the wet clothes, observing her technique as I went. It was tedious, hot, boring work, and she eyed my every move, making sure I'd steamed over every square inch of fabric. Nearby, Beya had finished her ironing and was already heading up the hill, back to the manioc fields. Doña Antonia caught me staring after her.

"You stay away from her, *gringa*. She's no shaman. She's a witch, and she wants you dead."

SEVENTEEN

– JULY –

Though it had only been a couple of weeks, it felt like an eternity since Omar disappeared around the swooning curve of river in the longboat. Since then, the jungle had been seeping into me, changing me, mortifying me. The anti-malarial pills Omar got me in Cochabamba gave me vivid nightmares, each more bizarre, drawn out, and palpably real than the last.

My skin was changing, too, becoming not my own, never dry, always itching, bites infected. Since feeling crappy was familiar to me, I wasn't alarmed. Me and the other fosters were always the ones who needed a bath, their hair combed, the ones with infected cuts or impetigo, but we all survived. I never dreamed something was really wrong with me.

Of all the many things to be afraid of in the jungle, boredom began to creep higher on the list. After all the work was done: the hauling, washing, harvesting, chopping, cooking, and so on, it all became about waiting. Waiting for the men to come back. Waiting for the rain to stop. Waiting to hang out with Anna, who seemed less and less inclined to spend time with me, though I know now I had underestimated her need to be alone in the depth of her grief.

Then there was the waiting laced with fear. Waiting for the poachers to cycle back around, as everyone acknowledged they would, once they'd sold their goods in San Solidad. Waiting to hear Beya's bizarre voice in my head. Waiting for the jaguar to come back and take another hapless child or chicken or pig. The platform was manned sporadically; days went by when no one went up there. One evening I walked under it and heard loud snoring—Panchito was taking a turn. But with the hunters and their helpers gone, we were it: the skeleton crew, those too old or disabled to hunt, pregnant women, children, and me.

With only one set of clothes to wear, I was beginning to feel unbearably foul. No matter how many times I scrubbed myself with the yellow soap, I could smell my own body; this rank pungency; as if all my fat—the little I had—was burning off through my pores, producing a reek I couldn't seem to lose. I wondered what Omar would think of his pretty, sweet-smelling American girl when he came back to her. Even my sneakers were starting to rot.

One morning, I convinced Doña Antonia to lend me a man's shirt. I wore it like a dress as I washed and ironed my remaining T-shirt and shorts and lay them out on a rock. When I returned later with a hot iron to dry them, they were gone. I was floored. Where could the thief wear my stuff, on a night on the town? I thought of all the things I had stolen in my life without a thought. Always this great gaping hole in myself I stuffed with other people's crap, most of it I didn't even want.

So I traipsed around the village repeating my monkey story over and over to anyone who would listen: *a monkey stole my backpack with my extra clothes.* When they stopped laughing, I finally scored a *cushma*, this one from a family whose patriarch had died. In the tradition of wasting nothing in the jungle, the garment was going to be handed over to the family of lepers, but they gave it to me. I washed and ironed that thing till you could almost see through it.

Those early days in Ayachero I felt a part and not a part of anything, tasting a flavor of loneliness quite new for me. In this place, it was clear that everyone needed everyone else. I so desperately wanted to be part of this unbroken circle, yet how could I? I had my foot in this new world, but could not possibly bring the whole of me because I was so very *other*. No matter how much Spanish or Portuguese, Quechua or even Tatinga I learned, I would be this odd one out, this matchstick-colored head walking around in a sea of black ones, thinking different, walking different, dreaming different, being different. Doomed in a way I was sure at the time was unique to me.

But I kept on trying. In late afternoons after siesta, a half dozen villagers would gather around the cooking fires at the longhouse or the Anaconda Bar and drink strong black coffee with lots of molasses-tasting sugar, smoke cigarettes, and tell stories. I'd sit with them and try to understand, even though they never slowed down for me. Paco stayed close by, translating when he was in the mood, but I made sure to laugh when they laughed, or grow serious when they did, to make them think I understood every word, all the slang, every idiom or splash of Tatinga. Mostly the stories were about hunts gone wrong, or soured love affairs, or sometimes about beasts even more fantastical than what already existed: fifty-foot anacondas with horns, five-hundred-pound *pirarucu* that crawled out of the river and sprouted legs and claws, pink river dolphins that turned into beautiful women and seduced men away into the *Encante,* the enchanted underworld in the murky depths of the river—especially during the rainy season when the river rose and flooded the forest.

It was during siesta, that blast furnace time of day when everyone but me—who had never been able to nap—went off to rest or sleep or make love, that I broke my promise to Omar that I would never go into the jungle alone. Beya obsessed me. She was the other odd duck in this place. She didn't seem to fit in anywhere, this person who had bothered to save my life. *Why?* The more people who fielded my questions about her, like she was a source of embarrassment, shame, or fear—maybe all those things—the more fascinated I became. I'd catch myself pausing at odd times of day, grating manioc, ironing clothes, or getting ready for bed, cocking an ear and listening for the thrill of her words in my head, only to hear the snap of insects, or the crash of rain on the roof.

As the village dozed the hot afternoon away, I threaded among the huts to the perimeter of the *chacra*, the small field of plantain and yucca just east of the village. Subtle breaks in the jungle wall marked paths for gathering medicinal herbs or plants, or for a lone hunter to venture out for day hunts that sometimes resulted in the capture of a tapir or paca—a kind of rodent that could grow to thirty pounds—when the wait for the bigger hunts became too long and people were hungry. There was a time when the paths were all the village needed to find game, but the poachers and loggers had changed all that. Now they grew over quickly and had to be cleared by whoever had an interest in traveling on them. Each had a name: Jaguar, Anaconda, Fire Ant, and Caiman; each had several branches, unnamed, that those who traveled evidently knew.

I paused at the entrance to the Anaconda Path where, from the longhouse, I had seen Beya disappear like an apparition, only to appear hours later, a basket on her back overflowing with mysterious plants. As if standing at a great height, I felt equally pulled and repelled by the seething green.

I turned to see if anyone was watching. I was alone; with only the *cor cor cor* sound of the bamboo rats in the fields behind me. A whiff of wood smoke mixed with sage wafted toward me; her camp couldn't be far. Above me, trees tangled riotously, inhaling and exhaling through giant leafy lungs. At that moment I stopped caring about being swallowed by whatever vicious thing wanted me. All the warnings, threats, stories, and myths shrunk to nothing compared to the pull of the forest's wild green heart. I wanted to know this place, however monstrous.

I was going in.

EIGHTEEN

It wasn't like walking into the woods of New England, or anywhere else that I knew. There was no gradual entrance into another world, no piney embrace or chittering of harmless chipmunks underfoot. Three steps in on the narrow trail, and the green curtains closed behind me. Countless plants hung unsupported in breath-warm darkness, leaves and boles and twirling vines, all in air so thick and wet you could cut it. The earth unorganized beneath me; black and green decay mingling with mosses, lichens, fungus. Actual solid ground could have been any distance beneath my feet.

I took a dozen steps toward the smell of the smoke and stopped, listening. A screeching sound; metal on metal. The braying of a donkey. I followed the sounds a hundred yards or so, considering every step. Soon, stabs of golden light filtered through, until I stumbled into an opening where full sun beat down on my head and shoulders.

In the center of a perfectly round clearing, Beya sat hugging her knees on a flat rock, facing in my direction like she'd been expecting me. She was hatless, her iron-gray hair wiry and loose around her shoulders. Her donkey, harness attached to a grindstone by a woven sisal rope, clopped along in a slow circle, lured by a plantain suspended over her nose, tied there by a stick poking out between her ears. Big belly swaying back and forth, she loped in a never-ending circle on the hard clay, turning the heavy stone. Ground up manioc fell from under the flat of the wheel into a metal bucket beneath. Beyond the donkey, sitting on thirty-foot stanchions, Beya's ten-foot-square hut reached up into the mid-story. Half a dozen snake heads hung from the supports under the hut. If a snake was caught in the village, Ayacherans killed them and buried them head down to ward them away; I wondered if this was her version of the custom.

"What are you doing here?" she asked in strained Spanish.

"I smelled smoke and I—"

"No one comes here."

The donkey stopped a moment, wagged her head as if annoyed by the bit in her mouth, and started to trot along again, the lure of the plantain too much to resist.

"I've been wanting to thank you for what you did. Warning me about the eel."

She scowled and spit out a hot brown stream of tobacco. "Maybe I called the eel. Did you ever think of that? Maybe I dreamed his spirit to you."

I looked around. Wicker baskets overflowed with leaves, seeds, dried fruit, flowers, and bark. Old plastic and glass Coke and Fanta bottles full of strange black and brown liquids stood in neat rows on a colorful blanket. "Did you?"

"I could have. I could have had you killed in front of everyone. He would have stung you, then you would be paralyzed and fall in the water and drown. They would have let you drown, too. They are afraid of the eel spirit."

"But you warned me instead."

In my head, I heard her growl the words, "I WAS TESTING YOU."

Her mouth hadn't moved. I shuddered, closing my eyes and shaking my head to clear it.

She pushed herself to her feet, dipped a calabash into a metal pail of water and handed it to me. Desperately thirsty, I drank it all down. As I thanked her, I stared down at her tattooed face, high cheekbones over sunken cheeks, mouth a stern line. I felt a helpless vertigo, as if I were gazing into an abyss of human strangeness I could do nothing to bridge.

"What is the name of your village?" she asked.

"Boston."

"Are you the only shaman in Boston?"

I laughed. "I'm not a shaman."

Her face remained expressionless. "But you heard me speak in the old language. Why didn't you answer me?"

"You mean, speak to you in your head? I can't do that."

"Of course you can. You can hear me, right?"

"Yes."

"So, it's not so hard. Just shine back to me."

I had to laugh. "Boston shamans can't shine."

She gestured to a small thatched stool next to her potions. "Maybe you're tired. Sit. Rest. Eat." She set out a bowl of roasted plantains and a clay pot of dark honey warmed over the fire. After settling herself back on her rock, she watched with strangely hungry, impatient eyes as I dipped the pieces of plantain in the honey with my fingers; never had anything tasted so delicious.

"Now. Try," she said, and closed her eyes.

The forest ticked, looming. I closed my eyes and thought the words, "MY NAME IS LILY. I'M FROM BOSTON, AND I'M NOT A SHAMAN. I WISH I WERE."

She opened one eye. "I don't hear you. Why are you playing this game with me?"

I squeezed my eyes shut, doubled down, and shouted the words in my head. "I'M NOT A SHAMAN AND I NEVER WILL BE! I'M JUST A DUMB AMERICAN KID."

We breathed together under the dripping trees. A little black capuchin monkey with a white face swung down from a lower branch and landed on her shoulder, one arm wrapped around her forehead, a look of *she is mine* in his eyes. Beya got to her feet, shooing away her pet, who chittered up the stairs and into the hut.

"Are you afraid I will steal your spells, your secrets?" She turned to look at me. "I have my own. I don't need your Boston spells."

"I'm trying, I swear. It's just—"

"Were your potions in the bag the howler monkey stole?"

"No, that was just underwear and stuff."

She lifted one gnarled finger. "You're very young. And thin. Your nerves are high. Still, you're hiding your powers from me. You are like the pygmy marmoset, see?" She pointed up to a nearby tree. A squirrel-sized creature with a ruff around its neck like a lion sat at the entrance to a dark hole in the bark, its small hands rubbing nervously together. "He has his own home in the tree, but he never relaxes in his hole. He's always facing out, ready to react to a predator."

"Maybe that's a good idea."

"He never uses the forest to help him. He's always afraid. He will always be afraid."

I squinted up at the nervous little creature at the mouth of his hole. "Aren't you afraid of jaguars out here by yourself?"

She sneered at my question, the macaw feathers in her ears shuddering in the ethereal light. "The poachers took the jaguar, so the jaguar took the child. The jaguar knows I do not hunt him. He leaves me alone. So tell me, when will you die?"

"How would I know that?"

"Don't be ridiculous. Every shaman knows the year of their death. I am sixty-five. I will die at age eighty-three."

"I'm not a shaman."

She waved me away in disgust. "You ask about fear. My only fear is that I will die here, alone in this place. Not with my people. I think you are a message from Boston that this will not come to pass."

"I wish that were true."

"If I show you some of my secrets, will you show me some of yours from the forest of Boston?"

"Yes," I said, wondering what in the world I could show her, and what she would do to me if I showed her nothing.

"Come with me," she said. I followed her down a narrow track of cleared land behind her hut before plunging into the pathless green. I had to run to catch up with her. C shaped, eighty pounds tops—still, she was fast and strong and I had to work to keep her in sight. She stopped short in front of a young ficus tree. A termite nest as big as a duffel bag hung off it like a tumor.

"If you are hungry, you can always eat the queen termite," she said. "These nests are everywhere." With her machete she chopped open the blackened crust; thousands of glittering termites flooded out in panic, soldiers scrambling at the damage. Workers poured down the sides of the tree and circled it in a wave, immediately swarming back up. She held out the machete and pointed at the four-inch-long, white, segmented queen, temporarily abandoned by her workers. "You can eat it raw, or cook it. A few of these will give you strength if you are lost."

Not waiting for comment, she kept walking. We stepped into an opening where a mammoth tree had fallen, taking down half a dozen other behemoths with it. They lay broken across one another in different stages of decay, carpets of verdigris moss melting over hills and valleys of bark and branch. Hundreds of purple butterflies burst from a rotted trunk as we passed, swirling in a violet funnel over our heads. A yards-long spiderweb that draped like lace from branch to branch above us was clotted with the purple wings; a fist-sized spider huddled in a dark corner, waiting.

"I never capture the butterflies, because then the spirit leaves them." She stepped over a few logs, stopping at one as tall on its side as she was standing. Big black ants swarmed a rubber tree sapling that had sprouted up through the rotting log, exposing a V where an abandoned bees' nest still glistened with honey. "But when I see them, I know I'm near my nest of bullet ants. The *isula*. You know this ant?"

I shook my head. I'd never heard of it, but knew that—in this place—if an insect had a name, it was best to stay away from it.

"The bite of this ant is like a bullet. For a whole day, your enemy will be in terrible pain."

She took out a short bamboo tube, flipping the rubber cap free with her tobacco-stained thumb. With a stick, she dabbed honey in the bottom, then lay the tube next to the ants. Dozens crawled in before she kicked the container a short distance away, rolled it under her sandaled foot—crushing the ants that remained on the outside—before snatching it up, snapping the rubber stopper back on, and slipping the tube in her string bag.

"Come on." She led me past the graveyard of fallen giants to one that stood tall, its roots like flying buttresses soaring up and out of sight, its base as wide as a city bus. "This is the lupuna tree. They are sacred. One must never relieve oneself near here. This is where I can hide my soul and keep it safe if some *brujo* or *bruja* is coming after me. Now, look closely here, in these plants that grow near the roots. This is where the poison frogs like to live. See?"

Four jewel-toned orange-and-blue-spotted frogs, each as big as a thumb, hid in bright green nests, bulbous toes gripping the leaves. Black eyes watched our approach; each blink revealing brilliant yellow eyelids. Throat sacs pulsed, skin glistened.

"This one makes poison through the skin, do you see it? How it is shining like that? This one makes enough poison to kill ten men, fifteen men. We use these frogs for arrows, and for darts for the blowguns, to kill. Or we can use a little to make pain go away, to numb. A drop under the skin makes a baby sleep for hours. Four will kill it."

She reached in her string bag and pulled out a small, woven palm box. A frog's little fingers scrabbled at the slits between the fronds. "See? Very useful." She straightened up with a groan. "Do you have these frogs in Boston?"

"No."

"Do you have *isula* ants? Lupuna trees?"

"No."

She shrugged. "How can that be? It must be a very sad place."

"It is."

"Why are you here? Maybe you have insulted your tribe? Have they sent you away, like mine has sent me here?"

"No, and listen, I'm not a shaman—"

Her eyes burned into mine, spirited and alive in her brown, lined face. "No one has heard me speak the old language since I was a young girl. Do you know what that means?" She put a hand on the small of her back, as if it pained her. Her string bag jostled at her waist, the little frog jumping at its cage. "Something is very old in you, a forest spirit, a spirit that can hear. You have traveled from your village, from far, far away, with no weapons, *yet you live*. You stand here in front of me. How is that? Don't you wonder? Maybe you are a young, silly shaman who doesn't know anything yet, but that is what you are."

I stood in my sack dress in the green bath of jungle light, wanting to cry. "If you're right, how can I be less silly, be more like what you say I am?"

"Come and visit me when you're ready to share your Boston secrets. Keep calling me with your mind."

"I will," I said.

"Now leave me," she said gruffly, turning back to her camp, our visit obviously over.

My mind roiled as I set foot on the path toward Ayachero. I had no Boston secrets—but clearly she thought I was holding back from her. What did she really want from me? *What if I could never speak to her as she assumed I could?* What would be the price of that? No more warnings about electric eels or other deadly creatures? Or maybe she'd conjure something much more subtle and menacing, something I would never see coming.

NINETEEN

On my fifteenth evening alone, I sat in my hiding place in the longhouse: on a low shelf in my favorite storeroom, sandwiched between rubberized sacks of rice and farina, a Spanish-to-English dictionary—the only book I had—cradled in my arms. Next to me, lying on her back, her belly full of grubs, Charlotte snored, snuffling each time I reached down to scratch her shell-pink belly.

I raised my head. A voice, a laugh, a certain kind of music I hadn't heard in what felt like months came tripping in through the window, just an open square in the wall of thatch. I jumped to my feet, kicking Charlotte awake and sending the book skittering across the sawdust. A rush of nausea, dizziness, as I got my bearings, took a spare second to wonder again what was wrong with me, before shelving that thought and bursting out of the storeroom, flying down the longhouse stairs three at a time. The entire village had turned out down by the shore, surrounding the hunters in a joyous circle. Chests puffed out, the men gestured at the river, the sky, each other, fighting for the chance to spout some choice tale about the hunt to the rapt crowd. The women who had gone with them to skin game and cook were greeted with less fanfare; they dragged the gear off the boats and gathered the dogs, who wandered famished and skittish along the shoreline.

I saw Omar before he saw me. Suspended between his and another man's shoulder was a thick bamboo pole from which hung a dead juvenile tapir, lashed there by its strange three-toed hooves, head dangling from its broken neck, cropped elephantine nose hanging down. Three four-foot black caiman clamped fierce jaws around the center of the pole as if they were still alive and fighting, but the loose, boneless way their bodies and limbs swayed told a different story. At the end of the pole, just before Omar's bronze shoulders, hung a couple of dead spider monkeys tied in two furry balls, heads tucked under arms, knees bent and stored up under their chins, tails trussed around them, as if they were sleeping. I wondered: Omar had told me once that Ayacherans never ate monkey—only the tribes "stooped" to that sort of thing—but obviously desperation had come into play. Eyes on the ground and bent under his load, Omar, smiling and joking, carried the game to the already blazing fires near the longhouse.

I ran up to him, tasted the sweetness of his name in my mouth as I said it. He took me in his arms as soon as he was able to lay down his load. I went to kiss him, but he took me firmly by the shoulders, held me away from him, and took a good look at me.

"Why are you wearing that?"

"Someone stole my clothes." I became conscious of my uncombed hair, my now chronic sense of uncleanliness, hideous sack dress, legs and arms covered with welts. "A monkey stole my backpack."

His face broke open in a smile. "My poor Lily. The jungle's treating you badly, I think, because it doesn't know you yet." He smoothed my hair from my eyes, kissed me quickly and drily on the lips. "Are you sick, Lily?"

"It's this food. I can't get used to it."

Torchlight leapt up into the evening sky on either end of the Anaconda Bar. A party was revving up on the hill, Bolivian pop tunes blaring. Over the river, remnants of daylight backlit the darkening clouds in brilliant orange, as if a fire burned somewhere beyond the hanging green. Among the trees, light tightened in the way it always did before a jungle night.

His hands dropped from my shoulders; I felt bereft of his touch.

"I brought you a present." From a leather sack he carefully lifted out two turquoise-and-yellow fist-sized balls of fluff with tiny black beaks and spiky green tails: baby macaws. He tumbled them into my palms. They squawked and blinked and bit at my fingers as I petted them with my thumbs.

His face grew serious. "Fat Carlos and Dutchie and his men. We got to their camp just after they left. They were too lazy to climb the trees, so they cut them down and left the babies to die up by the river cliffs. By the ironwood trees where they nest. We couldn't save all of them." He shook his head. "I had to choose. There were yellow ones, green ones, purple, red . . . we got to these before the snakes, or the other birds. But we had to leave most of them."

"What do they eat?"

"Seeds, nuts, fruits, leaves, things like that. Easy to find."

The men called to Omar. Held up full glasses of pale yellow liquid. He took me by the elbow. "Come on, let's get something to eat. Then I have another surprise for you."

I followed him up the hill, carrying the little macaw babies. Thick slabs of freshly butchered tapir dropped fat into the bonfire; nearby, its head boiled in a cauldron to harvest every ounce of meat. A few more fires sprang to life; smoking racks were erected in minutes. The dogs circled them, yipping at one another.

Every seat at the Anaconda Bar was taken, filled with men drinking a sugarcane brandy saved for just this occasion. Some of the bigger kids had started up a betting game with a foot-long bamboo rat they'd caught in the manioc fields. They'd built three tiny little houses out of thatch, each with an opening on one side, each with a different colored splash of paint on its roof, and put the whole miniature village under a big wire cage with a hole on top. People would bet on which color hut the rat would choose, once dropped through the hole: pink, green, or yellow. Soon the adults joined in; losers had to buy the other a drink or cigarettes.

Couples began to dance, throwing themselves around on the hard earth, pressing close to each other, a hundred voices raising up to the night sky, the jungle echoing back its own insanity: shrieks, howls, hoots. But all this joy felt forced and hollow and slightly hysterical. Even as drinks were raised and toasts made, everyone complained that the haul was not enough, the poachers were taking all the game and destroying the forest; the hunters would have to go out again, soon, travel farther, stay away longer, and what sort of life was that?

After nestling the little birds in a bed of corn silk in an old rice sack in the storeroom, I sat on the longhouse stairs near the bar, watching Omar drink with the men, downing my own glass of brandy until it started to taste good and even the fastest conversations translated effortlessly in my mind. Still, the scene felt out of balance, tipped toward mania, dangerous. I got up and made my way through the crowd, looking for something to eat.

Franz ran by me, sweating, frantic looking. "Have you seen Anna?"

"Not since this morning."

Barely listening, he tore off to the longhouse and up the stairs. I ran between the huts, calling for her, even went down to the beach where the black river rolled by ominously. My heart pounded as I recalled the way Anna had been avoiding everyone, doing her washing or ironing off by herself, then disappearing into her hut, face drawn and closed.

Others took up calling for her, until everyone had set aside their celebrating. The dancing stopped; partners separated, breathless, to watch the show, canned music still jangling up into the night. Beyond the village lights, unseen creatures slithered, crept, stalked, forni-cated, glowed with chemical life.

Finally I remembered the place she always went when she couldn't bear it anymore.

"*Anna!*" Franz's voice thundered from the longhouse.

I stood at the base of the tree where the jaguar platform shad-owed the moonlight from the Anaconda Bar. A sob filtered down from high up in the branches. "Anna!" I called. "Are you okay?"

"No. I'm not okay," she cried pitifully. "I'm never going to be okay."

Franz sprinted down the stairs and to the rope ladder. "Anna, come down. Please."

She stood, smoothing her dress over her body. Lit from beneath by torchlight, her pregnant belly nearly obscured her tearstained face. "No! You come up here."

The crowd quieted. Waiting. Only the clink of glasses on the bar. Franz looked at the ground, placed one foot on the ladder's first rung.

"You need to come up here right now," she said wretchedly. "This is where you should have been for the past two weeks. Hunting the jaguar that killed our child, Franz, *our child*, do you hear me?" Her voice broke. Someone snapped off the radio. The jungle shuddered and hissed.

"Just come down from there. It's dangerous, Anna, come on." His face beet red, never looking back at the ogling crowd, he stayed on the ground.

She threw down a heavy, overripe sugar apple that splatted to bits near his foot. "I will never come down until I kill this thing. Do you understand? Now come up here and help me do it."

"Anna, you've been drinking."

"Yes, I've been drinking—"

"Calm down and get—"

"If you were any sort of man, you'd come up here and get me."

He put his other foot on the first rung, hauled himself up, and hung there, swinging, head drooping forward. The crowd watched. He took another step up, then one more, heaving his body up as if its weight were unbearable. He stopped at the fifth rung, eight, ten feet in the air, swaying, ropes creaking.

"You can't do it. Even now." She threw another piece of fruit at him; it smashed wetly on his shoulder; pulp rolled down his back. He didn't react, only stayed where he was, head down. She huffed a shotgun higher up on her shoulder. Disappeared from view.

Franz jumped down, ran a short distance away, and vomited. Omar ran to put his arm around his brother; they went into a huddle. Soon the crowd lost interest in the drama and picked up the pace; the dancing, bragging, laughing, and betting all started up again. Doña Antonia, obviously enjoying her aguardiente, gave me the slightest half smile as she passed by with a large plate of grilled meat.

The hardest part about climbing the thirty-foot rope ladder was the way it kept swaying with my weight. I found Anna crouched on the far side of the platform, pointing her gun down into a nest of leaves.

"He's afraid of heights," she said. "And of planes—flying, I mean. That's why he didn't go to Cochabamba to find Omar."

"I'm sorry."

"Panchito had to do it," she continued. "And then I had to worry if he was just going to stay in the city and drink and chase women and never come back." She dropped her head in her hands. "Sometimes I wish I could be Angelina. Just go crazy and run off naked into the forest—" She paused, wiping her reddened eyes. "I mean, why not, you know? Why not go crazy? What a relief it would be. Wouldn't we all love to go crazy? But I couldn't do that to Franz, or Claudia, or this baby."

She looked at me, considered me, her face still lovely, even puffy and tearstained. "What's it like, being the only white woman here?" Legs dangling over the side of the platform, she stroked her voluminous belly. "You must miss all your big cars and houses, your pretty clothes and diamonds."

"I never had those things."

She squinted at me like I was lying. "You've lost your *gringa* treasures. I'm sorry for you."

I shrugged.

"We all thought you'd leave after the first week. But you didn't. Doesn't your family in America miss you?"

"Omar is my only family."

"I wish you'd met Benicio. You would have loved him. He was such a funny kid. Always making everyone laugh, always a smile on his face. Always bringing me little presents. He must have been so terrified. I can't sleep thinking about it. I can't eat, nothing."

All I could think was, *What have I lost?* At that moment my sorrows felt like nothing compared to Anna's.

"I think Beya called down the jaguar." She paused to wipe the tears from her face. "Or if she didn't, she could have kept him away. She could do that for us, if she wanted to."

"Doesn't she help people here, cure them with plants?"

"She helped deliver Benicio and Claudia, with FrannyB. Lots of other babies, too. But we haven't been very nice to her. So we always wonder. Maybe she cures people when she feels like it, you know?" She shrugged. "And besides, she's Tatinga."

"What do you mean?"

A sigh of frustration. "You've seen them. They think flashlights are captured moonbeams. That radios have little people inside of them. That the big airplanes flying high up are carrying the spirits of their ancestors to the land of the dead on invisible roads in the sky. And the small ones that drop supplies? They think they're alive, that they're big birds taking shits."

"But if you've never seen a machine, how would you know it wasn't alive?"

"Because I would just know such a thing," she said dismissively.

"Do you want to go to America someday?"

"It would scare me too much to go to a place without a jungle. San Solidad is bad enough. I went there once. It's filthy and full of factories that poison the air. I miss the days when more people lived here in Ayachero, you know? When we had enough men to scare off the poachers. Nobody got in each other's way. Plenty of game for everyone. Hunts were one, two days. Now we're alone too much, all of us. The men are, too, out there for days without a kill. Us back here, waiting, worrying."

"Have you ever killed a jaguar?"

"No, but I've seen a puma. A huge one. Sleeping in a tree down by the Tortoise Beach, back when I was a little girl."

"Were you scared?"

She laughed. "Well, I didn't wait around till he woke up. But he was really passed out, he had a bellyful of tortoise eggs, so I just snuck away."

"What are puma like?"

"Puma smell you and circle around behind you, and you're dead. They'll kill you just to kill you. Jaguars don't make the effort unless they're hungry. But the one that took my boy is different. This one is angry." She wiped her eyes and squinted into the velvet, wet darkness. "This one's going to come back."

TWENTY

"You never told me you were a shaman," Omar said, grinning. Taped-together glasses halfway down his nose, he sat cross-legged between the grain sacks on the shelf in the storeroom, his Spanish-to-English workbook open on his lap, the baby macaws snuffling and chirping in their burlap bed. After sleeping in neighboring hammocks in the longhouse the last several nights, we'd agreed the storeroom was the best place—temporarily—to have privacy together.

I sat across from him on a bag of rice, the morning sun already baking us through the open window. "You never asked."

"Okay, what am I thinking?" Still smiling, he closed his eyes.

"Knock it off, Ohms."

His eyes popped open. "I was thinking how much I missed you out there. How much you would have loved it. Parts of it, anyway."

"You don't believe me. About Beya."

He took off his glasses and rubbed his eyes, looked out the window. "First of all, Lily, I'm trying not to be furious that you went in the jungle by yourself. You promised me you'd never—"

"Sorry. I wanted to thank her, and I could hear her donkey braying, and smell her sage burning and her cooking fire—"

He held up one hand. "So I'm going to ask you again. I don't care how bored you get. How badly you want something out there. Will you please, God, never, *never*—"

I got up and paced the room. "Okay, all right." Charlotte opened one eye and got up to trail my every step, clomping along behind me on the creaking plywood floor. She'd already grown out of the piglet stage: I fed her well.

"And second of all, sure, I believe Beya spoke inside your mind. It's called shining. It's the *vieja lengua*, the old language. You've got a dozen tribes in a twenty-kilometer range, all speaking different languages. So that's how they communicated, sometimes just with images—about predators, poachers, what fruits are in bloom and where, everything. Now only a shaman can do it, but not every shaman remembers. Lily, it's an honor."

"Why me, though?"

"Maybe she's lonely. She doesn't want anything to do with us anymore. We've all let her down. Her brother, Splitfoot, let her down. You were open to it, somehow. Anything is possible in this place."

I pictured Beya stewing over my holding back all my "Boston secrets" and shivered. Was I letting her down, too? "So, why is her brother called Splitfoot?"

"Fishing accident when he was a kid. He got too relaxed with a big *pirarucu* he caught, just threw it in the bottom of the boat. Bad idea. They have teeth. Look, Lily, you have to promise me—"

"What now?"

"You have to keep this to yourself." He closed the workbook, the only other book besides my dictionary we'd had the forethought to bring to the jungle. "You're having a hard enough time with these women, some of them. They can be tough. You don't need to be making anyone jealous, or concerned."

"I don't know who I would tell. Anna, maybe—"

"Nobody except me. You can tell me anything. I can tell you anything. That's how it is. That's how we are. And you must honor

Beya. She's the soul of the Tatinga. Splitfoot was never as powerful as his sister. I think it drives him crazy." He gazed out the window as the sun sizzled the morning dew off waxy green leaves.

With a sigh, I went to sit with him; his closeness put my body and mind at peace.

He put his arm around me. "Listen, For God's Sake got here late last night. He's going to take us to the Frannies. I've got a surprise for you there."

"What is it? How do you see through these lenses?" Taking his glasses, I busied myself trying to clean them on the hem of my none-too-clean dress.

He smiled. "Lily Bushwold, you have no—"

"Patience, okay, okay. A surprise, I'm psyched." I carefully slid the glasses back on his face.

"The catch is, you need to give me my next assignment."

I sat back against the wall and gazed at the trees out the window. "Tell me all about the mahogany grove. It sounds like a sacred place."

There wasn't much logic in this, but just the words *mahogany grove* called up the image of where Tia's ashes were buried: an elegant grove of white birches that overlooked the Quabbin Reservoir; to her that was a holy place, and I could feel her there every time I wandered among those trees.

"When's it due?" His eyes magnified behind his lenses, he lifted his pencil over his workbook. I adored him more than I could bear.

"As soon as possible."

"Thank you. I love the homework," he said in English. He shut the notebook and slipped off the shelf to his feet. "Now, show me where the monkey took your backpack."

I led him to the towering trees near the bank, their crowns tangling and blocking the sun. Underneath our footsteps, the ground steamed softly, as if cooling on some new primeval morning. A tiny triangle of bright orange canvas glinted like a lone flower in the tapestry of every kind of green; a frayed brown strap hung down, forlorn. My underpants, jeans, and T-shirt were nowhere in sight. Omar cut a length of liana with a swipe of his machete, tied the ends together, and looped the circle of vine around both ankles. His bare feet bound by the coil, he jumped onto the base of the tree that held my bag prisoner. It offered no hand- or toeholds, but the liana created a band of friction from which he stood, nose to bark. Bracing his feet around the tree, he reached up and grabbed at a section a bit higher up, hung on as he jumped and braced himself still higher on the trunk. Like a human inchworm, he lifted his body up and up using the strength of his arms and legs and gut. In under a minute he vanished into the mid-story, around fifteen yards up. I waited, never believing he could climb high enough. Suddenly the orange triangle shuddered, disappeared, then hurtled from the branches. My backpack, empty of my treasures, torn and ragged and howler-monkey shit-stained, but so beautiful to me, came tumbling down at my feet.

He shunted himself down quickly; leaping soundlessly to the hard mud. I thanked him so much he burst out laughing, wrapping his arm around my waist as we walked down to the shore to rinse the bag clean.

Doña Antonia looped the rope leash Omar had fashioned for Charlotte around the center pole of the longhouse. "You know what they call you in the village? *Señora de Cerdo*." *The pig lady.*

"Fine. They can call me anything they like," I said. "Will you watch her, please?"

"Of course."

"Maybe take her down with you when you do the washing, or to the *chacra*?"

She grunted her assent, already on to some other task. I'd been setting aside a lot of my food for Charlotte, until I figured out she'd eat absolutely anything, any gross thing at all she could root up with her snout: worms, bugs, larva, rotten fruit, frogs, and so on. She even ate some dried pig some kids tossed at her. Still, I left her a bowl of yucca peels just before I left, if only to distract her from my departure and spare myself the resulting hysteria when she realized I was gone.

I ran to the chicken coop, flinging the door wide and throwing down some feed for the birds. The wire door slammed behind me. Feet loose in my decaying sneakers, I hustled to meet Omar and For God's Sake at the mouth of the Fire Ant Path, our agreed-upon meeting place to bring supplies to the Frannies, a half day's journey through the jungle.

Omar's face was serious and purposeful, For God's Sake smiling as always. "I'll be in the lead. Then Perla, then you, Lily. For God's Sake will be last. Lily, don't fall behind. Don't speak unless you have to."

"Why can't I talk? What if I have a question?"

"Later for questions. Talk if you have an emergency, or if we've all decided to stop and talk. I need to listen to the jungle, understand?"

"Whatever."

"Not 'whatever,' Lily. Do you understand or not?"

"Okay. I understand."

"But if you see something, of course tell us," For God's Sake added. "Like a snake, or a snakeskin, over."

"Why a snakeskin?"

"It's protein. It gets eaten right away," Omar said. "If the skin is still there, it means the snake has shed it minutes ago, seconds ago maybe, and it's still close by, *claro*?"

I nodded.

"We stay close together when we walk. Tell us if you have to pee. Don't fall back, don't wander away, even a little, even to look at something. Don't lean on anything, don't touch anything. There are poison ants everywhere, wasps, spiny plants, okay? Do what we tell you," Omar said sternly before turning and plunging through a mat of hanging vines.

Perla stood planted with her rump toward me, furry triangle ears rotated toward the jungle, her soft nose already snuffling at the subtle parting Omar had left in the curtain of vines. She brayed and stamped, rectangular yellow teeth gnashing, her heartbreakingly bony ribs quaking. Smart girl, she had no interest in entering that place, but For God's Sake smacked her hard on her fly-bitten flank, and she hazarded a few steps in. Resigned, she dropped her head and kept on walking.

I followed just behind her. There was so much in front of me, it took a while to see it. Woody vines wound themselves around trees; plants with spines as long as fingers lined the path. Was that a snake looping down? Not this time; just another liana thick as a man's arm coiling from the dimness, unspooling across our path.

Unseen parrots squawked as they flew above us, battling something out. Tree frogs tocked in ditches, as eerie warbling cries filtered through the green corridors. Boulders emitted a sweetish mildew smell. Mushrooms like champagne flutes brimmed with recent rain. Occasionally a shadow flickered above us, but what sunlight filtered through was tinted an emerald green, as if it came through water.

Perla made a tinkling sound as she ambled along, loaded down as she was with bags of hand mirrors, knives, little flashlights, and other trinkets—gifts the Frannies offered the Tatinga in exchange for their allegiance to Jesus Christ. Other supplies had been strapped to her sides: sacks of yucca, rice, onions; cans of strange things you'd never think of in a can like tins of honey or boiled pickled eggs; rubberized packages of dehydrated potatoes; and several bottles of rum. I felt a growing thirst, but it wasn't bad enough yet to halt this odd, clanking parade. Ahead of Perla, Omar chopped with loud *thwock*s at hanging vines that obscured our path.

I found myself not wanting to talk, a rare state for me. A strange, calm alertness buzzed through my limbs; it felt beautiful, grounding. In my nineteen years I had never felt anything like it. I was walking through another world with its own complex systems that had nothing to do with me; it freed me in a way. As brutal as this place was, I didn't have to cheat or steal or lie or run away to survive. Instead I had to pay attention, learn, shut up, accept, keep going.

An hour drifted by, maybe two. There was nothing to indicate time, no slant of sun, no change of vista, just a chronic twilight, Perla's shuddering flanks, and the occasional grassy turd escaping between swishes of her tail.

We began to climb. I watched where Perla placed her hooves, and put my feet there, hoping for safety. Sweat erupted from me, copious. I didn't think it was possible to sweat this much, the rubber grip of my machete slippery in my hand. My thirst went from mild to overwhelming—my head pounded with it.

A sudden eruption of rain burst through the canopy without warning, as if someone had overturned a vast bucket. Our daily deluge. So much rain dumped down, and so fast, that a small stream bubbled up next to us in a foot-wide, shallow ditch; in it, button-sized orange frogs leapt up in joy. A slender, yellow-headed snake burst up, its throat distended by a still-live frog, the impression of its three-toed feet clear from inside the thin skin; then the snake flopped down, disappearing into a tangle of black roots.

In seconds, the rain stopped. The jungle steamed with hot fog. My hair was plastered to my head, my dress to my body. Embarrassed, I plucked it away from my skin, but we were all soaked. Perla shook herself, stomped in the muck, snorted.

"Is there any water?" I thought about the rum, but it was water I wanted.

"Water's everywhere in the jungle, Lily, you just need to get to it," Omar said. We walked down to a swampy area where a grove of twenty-foot-tall bamboo towered above us. Dozens of segmented stalks shot straight up, perfectly parallel to each other. Arrow-shaped leaves drooped from the prehistoric-looking grasses. Omar lopped off a piece stacked like three tallboy beer cans, then handed the heavy column to me. For God's Sake nodded sagely, as if he approved of whatever game Omar was playing. He leaned on Perla, took out one of the matchsticks he kept in his shirt pocket, and chewed on it thoughtfully.

Omar cut off another section at the joint and placed it in my other hand. "You look at these. Tell me how they're different."

I turned the tubes over in my hands. They both sloshed with liquid; otherwise they looked the same to me. I was hot, mosquito ravaged, miserable, in no mood for lessons.

"I'm not getting what you're saying to me."

"Look closer, Lily Bushwold."

A smattering of light had worked its way through the leaves and shown like lace on the ground. I went to it, holding the two stalks under the delicate rays. I turned them, peering closely. Thin gold striations shone down the sides of one of them, so subtle you couldn't see them unless you rotated the stalk with great patience; the lines glittered a bit in the light. The other stalk stayed solid green when I turned it. "I see it!" I said. "I see the difference."

Omar gestured for me to hand him back the stalks. Holding the plain one at arm's length, he neatly chopped off the top and took a long, slow drink from the natural wooden cup, then handed it to me, nodding. Not taking my eyes off his, I tipped the stalk to my lips and took a sip. It was warm but fresh tasting, like diluted green tea. He took it from me, tore off a giant rubbery leaf from a low plant, and poured the rest of the liquid into the leaf for Perla, who lapped it up with enthusiasm, farting and snorting, the supplies clanking together on her back.

He held up the striated one and—lopping off the top—poured the liquid out onto the leaf litter beneath our feet.

"But I'm still thirsty."

"No you aren't," he said, shaking his head. "Why? Because *this one*? The one with the gold lines? That one will kill you in half an hour. And you don't have to drink much, maybe a couple of swallows. It tastes the same, but it'll burn out your insides until you're hollow as the plant, understand?"

I nodded.

"So now *you* go, Lily, with your machete, and you cut down the good kind and bring it to me. Like you're alone and need to survive, okay? We'll be here, waiting. There's no rush."

"Yes, Miss Lily, we will be here wanting to know your decision, over," For God's Sake said.

The bamboo garden bathed me in golden green light. The stalks seemed to vibrate as I studied them. Standing vertically as they were, it was impossible for me to see the striations—*were they there or not?*

I took a whack at a stalk. Like trying to break a stone. I put my shoulder into it. Finally, I freed up a two-foot-long segment. Holding it inches from my eyes under the dim patch of light, I turned it, searching for the glittering strings of gold. But there was nothing. Just smooth, green flesh.

"I think this is the good kind."

"Okay," Omar said, walking toward me. He took the section of bamboo, held it in front of his face, gave it a quick turn, and handed it back. "Go ahead. Drink it."

After cutting off the top as he had, I brought the strange container to my lips. Hesitated. "Are you sure?" He hadn't really looked at it in the light, as far as I could tell.

"No. That's not going to work. Are *you* sure? I'm not here, okay? For God's Sake isn't here. You're all alone. Only you and the jungle.

And you're very thirsty, you've been walking for miles, you're *dying*, and you must drink. Show me what you do."

I walked around with the stalk, in a strange, dull panic, my heart beating fast and light. I held it up in every kind of light I could find, which wasn't much: a little dim, dimmer, full shadow. I saw no glittering gold stripes, but still . . .

"What do you think? Is it the good kind?" he said.

I nodded, suddenly nauseous with fear.

"Then drink."

I glared at him, my lover, the dearest person in the world to me, my only real connection to this foreign wilderness. What if I was wrong? Why didn't he look at it in the light and make sure? What game was this, really? But, good Lord, I needed water, even my cells were thirsty.

I held the hard, smooth plant to my lips and drank every last drop.

TWENTY-ONE

"She wouldn't go by 'Francie,'" FrannyB said. The big woman gestured at the gaunt figure of FrannyA, who sat bent over her intricate task, squinting through smudged granny glasses. "*Way* too stubborn for that."

At an antique children's chair and desk joined by rusted metal workings, FrannyA stitched the words to a psalm into a burlap place mat. Thin gray wisps escaped her tight, small bun and stuck to her damp neck. The palm thatch chapel where she sat was open to the jungle on three sides; a crotched sapling supporting its eave pole, from which FrannyA's wooden Christ statue hung motionless. A black chalkboard made up its one wall, the alphabet neatly written across the top in capital letters, small ones just below. Another half dozen torn-up chairs and desks faced the board. Perched on a lectern, a two-foot-tall parrot missing most of the feathers on its chest clutched a six-volt battery in one talon, its gray, trapezoidal tongue nudging off the white corrosive powder as it tried to take a bite out of the silver metal.

"But we couldn't both be Frances. Lord knows these Indians are confused enough."

Seated high on a tall stool that looked too spidery for her weight, FrannyB tapped off a thick length of cigar ash before drawing and holding in another lungful. A few more cigars, courtesy of For God's

Sake, poked out of her shirt pocket. Her pale green eyes squinted, assessing me.

"But really, I ask you, what are the chances? Two missionaries named Frances, one from Massachusetts, one from Georgia—that would be me, as if you couldn't tell—" She poured on an extra syrupy drawl here. "Both decide to spread the Lord's word in the middle of this godforsaken devil's workshop—this end-of-the-world snake pit . . ." She gestured at their tiny homestead, the spare church, the vines I could almost watch growing around Christ's scrawny hips.

"Think on it: two puny one-engine Cessnas flying low over the jungle, going on twelve years ago now, *on the very same week*, both of us spreading the word of God over a loudspeaker from our planes, *as if they could understand us*! Both of us dropping gifts from the sky—mirrors, silverware, and so on—on the heads of these heathen Tatinga . . ." She shook her head and spat out a piece of tobacco, grinning at some being just beyond my head, as if to meet my eye would have admitted some small defeat. "I have to laugh sometimes at the mysterious ways He works. And to think we—*she* mostly—refused to meet at first, both of us being so dang bullheaded. Like there weren't enough godless ones to spread the word of God *to*. Like there wasn't enough of God's work for a hundred of us—for thousands! We had to crash into each other, isn't that right, A?"

FrannyA ignored her, sweating over her task, fingers shaking with effort at the detailed work. I noticed a faint trail of scars on the back of her neck near the trace bumps of her spine, and wondered. FrannyB let out a belly laugh. "Did I ever tell you about that crash, For God's Sake?"

He laughed in a mirthless way. "A few times, over," he said, busying himself with the task of unstrapping the heavy bags from Perla's back; she shuddered with relief and flicked her rough tail as the weight fell off her. He and Omar lugged the supplies to the door of a small brick house, a perfect replica of a two-story New England home, except the windows were just empty squares, the roof toggled together with baked clay tile, and the shutters—for effect only—cut from stained balsa wood. At only about seven feet tall, it wasn't big enough for two floors. It gave off the feel of a creepy dollhouse, where giant dolls lived. The Frannies' simple camp was a brief, oblong area of cleared jungle a couple of hundred feet above sea level, the highest land for miles.

FrannyB continued, "Her pilot was high on ayahuasca. He slammed into us at a thousand feet. Clipped a wingtip clean off. We both lived, as you can see, only my pilot didn't. Didn't get out of the plane in time . . ." She shook her head, remembering. "But hers? Walked out of the wreck just fine. Wandered around talking about some dragon lifting us into the serpent's mouth to the star of the beginning, some hooey like that. A, you remember that, right?"

No answer.

"You alive over there, A?"

"It's not something I dwell on, B. More pleasant thoughts fill my mind."

FrannyB guffawed. "Pleasant thoughts! Well, let's not interrupt those, right, For God's Sake? And speaking of pleasant thoughts, did you happen to remember—" Without making eye contact, he handed her a slim bottle of rum before returning to his work. "Oh, bless you," she said with a satisfied sigh, as she dragged two chairs close to a clay oven and gestured for me to join her.

"Looks like you've been suffering some of the jungle's delights," she said, gesturing at me.

"What do you mean?"

"Your skin. All those bites. Hold on." She disappeared into her strange home, then reappeared with a small glass bottle. "Iodine. It'll set you straight."

"Thanks," I said, accepting the bottle and a plastic pouch of cotton. "So how did you come to live out here?"

"Just trying to be closer to the Tatinga. But once a week or so, me and A come down to Ayachero to teach and preach, as we call it, sew up whoever needs to be sewn up, help with the babies, whatever's needed, so count on us, okay? I'm a physician, she's a trauma nurse. For God's Sake here keeps us flush with supplies."

With an affectionate slap on Omar's back as he walked by with a sack of yucca, FrannyB continued, "So *this* man was practically Tatinga when I knew him. Spent more time with the savages than he did with the Ayacherans. Jaguar hunting with Splitfoot and so on." She gestured at me with the sloshing bottle. "But you, my new friend. What are you, twenty-two?"

"I'm nineteen."

"Hoo, Omar! Got yourself a young one, didn't ya!" He ignored her. She offered me the bottle. I took a good swig.

"Tell me your story. You're American?"

"Yes."

"And . . . that's it? Omar bought you in a market in La Paz?" She chuckled at her own joke. "How'd you end up here?" She eyed me like no matter what I said, she'd guess the truth.

"I was living in Cochabamba and met Omar, and we fell in love."

She burped softly. "'Fell in love'? Haven't heard that expression in quite some time."

"Stop your nosiness, B," FrannyA said.

FrannyB ignored her. "Why didn't you stay in Cocha? It's a nice town. There's electricity, roads, civilization. In a manner of speaking. What's here for you, in this . . . this accursed paradise?"

"Omar."

She leaned forward in her chair, jabbing at the air near me with her cigar. "Lily, do you have any idea where you are?" She glanced around like there was someone else listening to us besides the men and possibly FrannyA. "You're in the land of Satan, that's where you are."

"What are you talking about?"

She got up and paced around her chair. "Have a look around, Lily. God is here—He's everywhere—but especially here, the highest point for miles and that much closer to Him, but so is the devil." She shook the bottle at me, her eyes watery and red. "I've seen him here more than anywhere. It's the shamans. They've got a direct line to Lucifer himself, almost like I do to God. And these wild ones, these Indians running around naked and fornicating with their brothers and sisters and shooting their curare arrows and eating their dead— yes, they do that, as a matter of *respect*, if you can imagine—these Tatinga are turned to the dark side, even though they'll show up for a sermon and a free cooking pot and a bag of salt. After a dozen years, we still don't have them." She leaned in to me, offered me another drink; I took it.

"Do you know, we're not even the first to try to spread the word of God here? There was a man before us. Pastor from Nashville. Came by himself. He showed them a photo of a peccary. They'd never seen a photo in their lives. Turned it over, no peccary. So they called *him* a devil, can you *imagine*? Eight spears through his heart. He's buried behind the chapel here. For them it's all about their shamans and their dark work. And you know, wherever you put your energy, to the dark or to the light, that's what grows. I'm telling you, the things I've seen . . ." She shook her head, reminiscing with an awestruck horror not devoid of rapture. "They would scare you to death."

"What have you seen?" I flashed to the Tatinga men emerging from the forest at Benicio's funeral, the snake heads hanging down from beneath Beya's hut, the poison frog battling in its tiny cage—all frightening things on the surface, but each so much more than what they seemed. I wondered what FrannyB really wanted from me.

She got up and rummaged around in one of the bags, poured some rice into a pot full of water and placed it on an iron grate over smoking coals. "Their animism, their devil worshipping—"

Omar broke in, to my relief. "I wanted to make you an offer on your sewing machine."

FrannyB busied herself with the rice. "What are you talking about, young man?"

"Lily's a seamstress. She can sew anything. She can be a real help in the village. She'll sew anything you need, for either of you. Right, Lily?"

A sewing machine! Something to do besides wash clothes and feed chickens and grate yucca. "Of course. Whatever you need."

FrannyB wiped the sweat off her forehead with the back of her hand. "Problem is, Omar, you've got nothing to give me for it, am I right?"

"What do you want?"

"That *you* could give me?" She shook her head.

"I can bring you guns."

"We've got guns."

"What about game? Smoked fish?"

FrannyB reached into a little sack of salt, tossed some in the boiling water. "You really like this girl, don't you?"

Omar's face hardened. "Franz and Panchito and me cleared this land. We built this camp, this house, to remind FrannyA of hers in America. Isn't that worth something?"

"Then you left us. Just like that." She snapped her fingers. "You started the whole thing, leaving Ayachero. Gave people ideas. All the sudden everybody needed Nike shoes, TVs, computers. Poachers got bolder. Tatinga retreated. You know the rest."

FrannyA looked up from her mat and turned, as bantam and sinewy as FrannyB was towering and blocky. "It's half mine, you know, B."

"So sell him your half," FrannyB snapped as she stirred the rice with a tin spoon. "You're the one who uses it, A. I'm just looking out for you."

"She can have it, as far as I'm concerned."

FrannyB shook out her shoulders and fed thick fingers through her hair. "Well, all right, then. But we could really use some more game up here, Omar, some dried fish. Some tapir if you can get it, paca, even, whatever you can manage. But on a regular basis. Fat Carlos, Dutchie, they're looting all our traps, or the game has moved on. That's possible, that's what everyone's saying. Anyway. Sick to death of living on fruit and starch."

"It's no problem," Omar said.

"I can bring you meat," For God's Sake said. "Every trip I will bring you whatever we can spare. I will make sure, over."

FrannyB shrugged and looked me in the eye. "Well, come on, then. I'll give you the nickel tour, and you can have the beast, if you can carry it home."

An old-fashioned sewing machine, the kind attached to a desk and operated by a foot pedal, sat just inside their door. Rag in hand, FrannyB squeezed herself between the desk and chair. She wiped off the greenish coat of dust and mold, revealing the shining black metal, then spent the next ten minutes proudly demonstrating the basics of the 1908 Singer machine; how to load the thread and bobbin, where and how often to oil it, its quirks and foibles. I fell in love with the thing right away.

Tucked next to a shortwave radio was a tiny alcove housing a set of spindly bookshelves. A little library. Piles of books, mostly atlases, dictionaries, and Bibles, but also rows of *National Geographic*s, hundreds of them dating back to the '70s, all in clear plastic bags. Even so, they were termite-eaten, the color drained right out of them. Still, I wanted to pore over each of them. I did my best to act casual.

"I've got some novels, too, if you're bored," she said with a little smile, pushing herself free of the sewing machine table and sorting through the stacks. "The classics, mostly."

I nearly grabbed the books out of her hands—my attempt at indifference a failure. Actual novels! Who cared which ones? I was dying for any sort of distraction from Ayachero, if only for a few hours. She handed me *Wuthering Heights* by Emily Brontë, *Pride and Prejudice*, *Sense and Sensibility*, and *Mansfield Park* by Jane Austen.

"A's a big fan of that Victorian stuff. A bunch of twaddle, if you ask me," FrannyB said, not meeting my eye. "But she's a bit of a romantic, so . . ." She thoughtfully turned the books over, smoothing them in their plastic wrappers as she skimmed the back cover copy. "Guess it breaks up translating the Old Testament into Tatinga."

"Would she mind if I borrowed them? I'm a fast reader, I'll return them—"

She waved me away. "You kidding? She's got 'em memorized. Guess we all need our vices."

"Have you read them?"

"Sure. Just to see where her head's at. The woman barely speaks, I'm sure you've noticed that much." She gathered the books in a little stack, a quizzical look on her face as she handed them over. "So, you're pretty good at languages? Pick them up pretty fast?"

"I'm okay, I guess."

"What about Portuguese?"

I shook my head.

"Quechua? Tatinga? Anything?"

"Just Spanish. English. That's it."

"Have you accepted Jesus Christ as your personal savior?"

I swallowed hard, wondering if my answer would cost me the sewing machine, maybe the books and magazines, too. I clutched the little pile on my lap, my palms sticking to the plastic as I stole a glance through the open window. FrannyA knelt at the periphery of the campsite. She seemed to be working something free from a trap—I couldn't see much more than that. With an earsplitting squawk, the parrot hopped onto Jesus's shoulder, lifted its scarlet-and-turquoise fanned tail, and let loose a white stream down his back.

"No."

FrannyB turned her head, adjusting her neck with a dull snap.

She puffed herself out, then sighed mightily, touching the cigars in her shirt pocket as if counting the few pleasures that awaited her. "Well then, we have work to do, which is okay, it's just fine," she said, adding a Bible to my stack. "For God's Sake was lost, too, when I first met him, an unbeliever for sure, but he's come around to be my right-hand man, going on eleven years now, isn't that right, my friend?" she called through the open window.

He didn't answer, though he must have heard her; he stood with Omar at the edge of the camp near the gift rack, smoking and talking. All manner of trinkets: spoons, hand mirrors, a pair of sunglasses, an empty plastic water bottle, and cigarette lighters dangled from a fifteen-foot-long liana strung waist-high between two trees like a clothesline.

"Of course his *name* is unfortunate—forces me and everybody else to take the name of the Lord in vain every time it's said—and believe me, I've *tried* talking him out of using it, but you know . . ." Here, she let her hand rest on the radio dial; it spun uselessly. "None of these people—in any of the tribes around here—will tell you their real name. It's a quirk of theirs we just have to live with." For God's Sake remained mum, stringing up a few small flashlights before pausing to take a swig of rum from a flask in his pocket. "But For God's Sake loves Jesus, don't you?" she called out to him.

"I love Jesus, over," he said, facing the tangled mask of forest.

"See that? It took a while, but now—well, I don't know what I'd do without him. He's my mouthpiece to his people, even though we haven't quite broken through yet. But that's our work." I followed her out of the house. She fingered the hanging gifts strung out along the line, squinting into the malingering green. "That's why we get up in the morning, and it's a blessing to have a reason, so who are we to complain, right, A?"

FrannyA laid down a capybara, a jungle rodent as big as a small dog, on the beaten earth, its face in a death rictus, distended belly about to pop. She took a step back from it. The smell was overpowering. "Don't know how we missed this, B. Looks like it's been here a while."

Suddenly my head swam with bright, sick color. I stumbled to the boundary of the compound near the gift rack, just before falling to my knees and throwing up. In a moment, Omar's hand rested on my back, but I pushed him away. My ears buzzed; the heat of the afternoon threatened to shut me down completely. All I wanted was to curl up in my hideaway in the storeroom away from everyone.

"Let's get the sewing machine loaded up," Omar said, helping me to my feet. "We have to get moving. We can't lose the light."

It took all five of us to deadlift the sewing machine desk onto Perla's back and strap it on tight. We tried to balance out the weight by loading a bag of books and magazines on her other flank. She didn't seem to mind the clumsy, heavy load at first, but when we got walking, she began to snort and whinny, especially as she navigated under, around, and over the drooping vines. All three of us worked our machetes hard to make the path wider for her; my hands chafed and bled with the effort. When we saw that her fur was being rubbed off in places by the machine, Omar took off his shirt and tucked it between her and the sharp-cornered desk. Mosquitos and flies swarmed him, but he brushed them off and kept going, his face steadfast.

As we made our way through the choking green, I couldn't help recalling Doña Antonia's threats to kill Perla for meat. She really was achingly slow, and ate a lot for her size, and tended to get in trouble: sticking her big nose into people's stores of corn or rice, knocking over piles of wood, braying in the middle of the night just to hear her own voice. I'd lay there smiling as I listened to her, happy to hear a friend in the darkness. But the truth was, I badly needed her to carry the wet laundry up the hill, which she did without complaint; I was lost without her. After my close call, I'd begun washing clothes in a big shallow tin pan Anna lent me; still, I couldn't keep Perla from lollygagging in the shallows nearby, cooling off, grinning with pleasure. I was terrified the eels would get her, or piranha. I loved that fucking donkey.

The sewing machine clanking and squeaking, we slogged another hour on the narrow path until pale stabs of evening light cut through the dense green: we were almost to the village. Perla stopped short, her wide body swaying before it stilled. For God's Sake landed his machete in the base of a tree with a sharp crack before racing past me. Ahead of us on the trail tumbled a mass of fur, fluff, and feathers, a muffled, high-pitched screaming coming from it. It looked like two puppies rolling around in a ball, playing, but there are no puppies in the jungle.

"What *is* that?"

"It's okay, Lily, stay calm," Omar said.

"A wolf spider," For God's Sake said. "Eating a chicken baby, over."

The pitiful keening stopped, the chicken's life over, but the frantic rolling continued, now with a snapping and hissing. "I was wrong. Two wolf spiders, fighting for the chicken baby, over."

Perla whinnied, wagging her head in fear, the whites of her eyes big, mouth frothing as she attempted to rear back on her hind legs, but the weight of the sewing machine kept her solidly on the ground. I stroked her tangled, rough mane and cooed to her, but she was shaking and refused to take another step forward. The three of us spoke to her in low tones as the ball of furry legs and bobbing abdomens as big as fists entwined, eventually rolling off the path into the forest. In moments Perla settled, perhaps forgetting she'd seen anything at all, and followed her nose to the light.

TWENTY-TWO

That evening, For God's Sake offered us his hut to give us a break from the longhouse. In fact, he said we were welcome to it as long as we wanted, since he was leaving for San Solidad soon anyway and a hammock in the longhouse would suit him just fine. Grateful and exhausted, Omar and I settled into his small but well-kept hut. I decided to wait till the next morning to deal with Charlotte and the birds.

Under a tattered, moldy poster of the Virgin Mary, we woke the next morning on a thin straw mat under wilted mosquito netting. As he dozed, arms around me, I turned the moisture-swollen pages of my battered copy of *Pride and Prejudice*, mesmerized. My head swam with elegant balls, where glorious food was served and uptight white people who never said exactly what they meant swirled in bodice-cinching gowns on a marble dance floor, holding each other at arm's length while staring meaningfully into each other's eyes.

Omar stirred; he rested both hands on my belly, as if weighing me, assessing me. "Lily," he said. "Put the book down. Look at me."

All I wanted to do was read, but something in his voice was so serious that I slipped a piece of straw between the pages and turned toward him. A window-shaped square of yellow sunlight burned into the far side of the hut, but we lay in shadow.

He gently traced the contours of my face. On his—an expression of wonder, of rapture, all mixed with a trace of confusion. It frightened me. I thought, *What have I done wrong now?* He said, "Why didn't you tell me you're going to have our child?"

"*What?* What are you talking about? I'm not—"

But I couldn't finish my sentence because I had to run down the stairs and hurl. I stayed on my hands and knees like an animal, eyes closed, breathing the smell of jungle rot and half-digested banana as I finally let myself listen to what my body had been screaming for months: you are not just yourself anymore; your body has said yes to Omar in every possible way; you have another life growing inside of you that will do what it needs to survive—make you puke, make you exhausted, make you swell, make you cry at nothing, make you a mother.

Oh sweet Jesus, Omar was right.

I wiped my mouth, spat, sat back on my haunches and laughed a short, rueful laugh: *Ignore what's happening to you, Lily, that will make it go away.* All my life I was so busy protecting myself emotionally; my strategy with my physical body was to pretend it didn't exist. Menstrual pain? What's that? I barely had my period anyway; sometimes I didn't get it for months at a time. Besides, what a luxury to piss and moan about some fucking cramps. I felt nothing, thank you. It was amazing what I could tune out. But look where it had gotten me . . .

Omar helped me to my feet. Held me while I cried, said, "Lily, why are you sad? This is our child—"

I pushed him away. Stood in my sack dress, filthy, frightened, the sun already beating me senseless. *How did I get here?* A year ago I was in Boston, sleeping in church basements, skimming singles at my cashier job to save for a flight to South America. "I don't want to have a kid. Are you crazy? This is nuts." I gestured helplessly at my belly. "I'm a freaking teenager. I can't take care of anything."

"You take care of Charlotte, and those macaws."

"I don't even like kids."

The rapture left his face, and I was ashamed. "Yes you do."

"What are you talking about?"

"Paco loves you."

A sweetish mealy smell drifted by. A pot of farina boiled on a nearby stove. My stomach heaved again, then settled for the moment.

"What happened to his parents?"

"His mother died in childbirth. His father drank himself to death. His face—no one will take him in like a son. They say he has the mark of the devil."

"When you say stuff like that, I think Ayacherans are no better than the Tatinga, even though they act like they are. Didn't the Tatinga kick out For God's Sake because of his leg?"

His shoulders slumped. "Old ways of thinking die hard."

With the first consciousness of something growing inside me, I touched my belly with trembling hands and a squeamish fascination. It was no longer flat, but rounded, the flesh firm, as if my body already knew to protect its precious cargo. But how big was it? Like a peanut? All curled up like a little shrimp?

"Omar, we met at the end of March. It's July. Think about it—I could be three, maybe four months along. Oh my God, I'm so stupid."

He put his arms around me. "It's going to be okay, Lily. I love you. I don't say it very much, but I do. I'll always take care of you and the baby, always protect you."

"Who's going to deliver it?"

"FrannyB's delivered hundreds of babies. Beya has, too. All the women help. For God's Sake brings all the medicines we need. But if there are any concerns, the women go to San Solidad."

"How did we get here, Omar?"

He laughed and drew me to him. "Well, we haven't been careful. What'd you expect, Liliana? I had this idea it was this unspoken thing between us, that we wanted a family. That of course a child would come from our love for each other, as a natural thing. And that's what happened."

"You make it sound so nice." I began to cry. "So normal."

"Come on, Lily. You'll be the most beautiful mother. I can't wait to see you with our child in your arms."

We sat close to each other on a bench under the hut, crying and laughing together, watching the women of Ayachero go about their morning duties: lighting the ovens, chopping vegetables, combing their children's hair. My feelings flipped from excitement to terror and back again as I watched the visibly pregnant ones go about their tasks. Soon, the smell of cooking gruel was eclipsed by that of grilled meat, which for the first time in memory smelled wonderful. I was dizzy with hunger. "Can you bring me some of that?"

"You want *meat*?"

"Maybe I won't throw it up."

In minutes he returned with two bowls of meat cut up into strips. He used a banana leaf to eat his, but I couldn't even stomach the smell of that, so I ate with my hands from the ceramic bowl. It was the most delicious thing I'd ever tasted; smoky and crisp and charred on the outside, barely pink on the inside. I felt much better afterward and headed up to the longhouse. It was past time to check on Charlotte and the baby macaws.

Just as I started up the hill, the sky—which had turned a murky green—opened up. A steady deluge transformed the earth under my feet into streaming mud that gushed past my ankles. Soaked to the skin, I charged up the steps of the longhouse, past several hunters sleeping off their sugarcane brandy in the slowly swaying hammocks, past Doña Antonia carving more meat at the fire. She didn't raise her head to look at me.

My baby macaws nestled in their corn silk pillow in the store-room. They squeaked when they saw me, flapping their little turquoise wings. Blue tufts fluffed off and floated in the heavy humid air as their beaks yawned open in a parody of hunger. I scrambled in my wet pockets to extract the handful of black *aguaje* seeds, their favorite. They ate every last kernel and clearly would have downed more if I had them. I tore a banana leaf from a heavy branch that grew near the window, filled it with rainwater, and dripped it into their mouths until they seemed to not want any more. That was when I noticed Charlotte's leash lying on the floor, but no Charlotte. I examined the braided rope. The loop that had encircled her neck had been sliced open.

My hands trembled with rage. I gathered up the little birds—still begging for food in their sweetly pitiful way—grabbed the liana, and marched out to the main room of the longhouse. A few of the men had begun to stir, lured by the platter of the grilled meat.

Doña Antonia sat on a low stool, tending the meat with great attention. Breathless, I stood over her, dripping onto the thin plywood floor. "Where is she?"

She turned to me, wiped her greasy hands on her skirt. Steam sprung silver coils along her hairline, her thick braid a long, tight snake twisting to the floor.

I lay the birds next to my feet and thrust the liana leash under her nose. "Tell me where she is."

Doña Antonia glanced down at the leash, then gave me a look I will never forget. A mix of pity, compassion, even the beginnings of a strangled affection. Finally she said, very gently, "Oh no, Lily. Charlotte is right here." She gestured at the platter of meat by her side, then at the big iron pot where we cooked the food for the dogs.

"What have you done?"

She picked at a back molar with a stubby forefinger, gazing out into the wall of gray water falling just yards away. "Do you know, Lily, that twin baby girls were born here last night?"

"What does that have to do with me?" I gaped in horror now

at the grilled strips of meat that I had so enjoyed barely an hour ago. At the velvety pink pig ears sizzling and spitting in a shallow pan of fat.

"What does that have to do with *you*, Miss America?" The compassionate look was gone, replaced by the usual ornery, impatient one. "It means," she said, rubbing her thumb and forefinger together as if they held some sort of currency, "there are *two more hungry mouths* in this village, okay? Two more empty bellies to fill every day. *Every day*. Now, do you think I make some magic to get the food, the meat?"

"You killed my pig!"

The men looked up from their seats around the fire, clearly enjoying the show.

"It is not your pig. *It's everyone's pig*." She turned and stooped, flipping the meat on the hot coals.

I went to slap her, but she whipped around like she had eyes in the back of her head and caught my wrist midair. I let out a whimper. The men stiffened, exchanged glances, weighed the cost of getting involved, and kept eating.

"You didn't lock the gate. All the chickens escaped. Are you trying to call the jaguar down to eat us all?"

I gasped as I flashed on the chicken rolling around in the jaws of the wolf spider. All those chickens to be devoured by the jungle's countless ravenous open mouths. My fault.

"I give you one job—*one single job*—and you're too good to do it! Too *good*!" She spat with rage, goiter bobbing.

"I'm sorry," I choked out.

She drew me closer and held me fast; her meaty breath hot on my face, her sunbaked skin the color of clay, her eyes searing into me. "Does sorry fill my belly? *Twenty-five chickens* into the jungle, hunted down by eagles, or jaguar, or anaconda, or wolf spider, you think that is *nice* for them? You think that's a happy way to die?"

I shook my head.

"Look around. You think maybe somebody here wanted to eat the chickens? These men here, their wives and children?"

I nodded, my arm stinging in her grip.

"Now—no eggs for two weeks, until For God's Sake comes back. No, four! He has to go get them and bring them back." She threw my wrist back at me; I clutched it. "And who has to pay for the new chickens? Your man has to pay. You cannot pay. You're a useless girl." She jabbed her finger up in the air toward my face.

"That's not true," I said. "I've done everything you've asked me to do. All the washing and ironing, gutting the fish, and—"

"You don't clean game! The women clean game, but you are too high-and-mighty—"

"I don't know how to do that. No one's ever shown me—"

"You got my best son, woman. The best of the three. You need to be worthy of him."

I bent down to gather up the baby macaws, but mostly to avoid her gaze.

Doña Antonia's voice softened. "Besides," she said. "The tapir was all eaten, and pregnant women need meat."

I sprinted down the stairs with the birds and scrambled under the longhouse, stowing them next to one of the wooden pillars. I put my fingers down my throat. Nothing came up. Horrendous. I'd been puking steadily for three months and now I eat my own pet and I can't get her out of me. I gave up, sat back on my haunches, eyes squeezed shut as I pictured Charlotte becoming part of me, my own flesh, my own child.

Cradling the two twirls of turquoise and yellow in my arms, I ran out into the deluge toward where I remembered our new hut to be, unable to catch my breath as the rain pummeled me, beating at the top of my head, my back and shoulders; I couldn't see two yards in front of me. Each step became a slide until I skied down a valley of greasy mud, the birds flying from my arms. I howled into the thundering rain; it erased my voice. My body, hair, face slathered with mud, I scrambled on my hands and knees until I found one little bird, pitifully muddy and wet, mouth still open, then the other. I gathered them into the front of my dress. I kneeled like that, watching.

In seconds, the basket I had made with my dress filled with water, and the little birds began to float, drenched wings weighing them down, little heads dropping back and sinking until just their yawning pink beaks showed above the surface. In a state of fear and fury at every way I felt I'd been wronged in my life, Charlotte's death stoking the fires of my self-pity, loneliness, and desperation, I watched them begin to drown. My teen brain screamed *the world is turned against me, me, me, always and forever.* I wanted to see those little birds die, to have some power over something, take revenge on something, get as used to death as everyone else seemed to be. Soon the water hammered at their squeezed-shut eyes and filled their diamond-shaped mouths, and they disappeared beneath the surface.

Seconds passed. The water churned in my lap as they tried to beat their way to the top, tiny sharp claws scraping and grabbing at the flesh of my thighs through the thin fabric.

For those few moments, I loved watching them die. I was God, kneeling there in my shit dress, knees sinking in the mud, belly full of my beloved pig.

But then something flipped inside me. Only rage had fueled me, and rages pass. I squeezed my eyes shut and saw Omar's face turning hard, slack with disappointment, knowing I was lying when I told him the birds drowned by accident, because he saw through all my lies.

I stood. A gallon of water flushed from my lap, along with the birds, weak but still moving. Filled with a bottomless remorse, a gutting shame, I bent down to catch them, for the first time feeling the tender swell of my own belly.

TWENTY-THREE

– AUGUST –

The morning Omar and Franz and the others left to hunt, just three weeks later, the heat came early, at sunrise, weighing down over the village like a sodden blanket. Rain leadened the air, but never arrived. The jungle drooped over the village like a thousand giants leaning over, their tangled green hair hanging down, heavy with secrets and sorrows. Overnight, the jungle felt closer. Ferns covered a path cleared just days before, plants sprouted around the huts. Only the daily clearing of new growth kept the area we called the village a village—a crescent of beaten earth that allowed the longhouse and the huts, the manioc fields, the lone barn, with our lone cow, to exist. At night I lay listening to the jungle advance: a squeaking sound, as green burst from more green.

As a surprise, Omar built me a little bookshelf made of chonta wood, a hard, durable palm with a beautiful gold-and-molasses-colored grain. It was there I kept my tiny collection of novels, dictionaries, and *National Geographic*s. His small gift, and those from the Frannies, gave me more comfort than I thought possible; they were the tiny glimmerings of a home of my own creation. As mosquitos buzzed around my head, I drank down the warm, sweet glass of papaya juice he had made especially for me, thinking, *How is it possible for a place to be both heaven and hell?*

As he sorted supplies for his hunt into a string bag, I sat cross-legged on our thin mattress, flipping through his latest English assignment. "Come on. I want to hear you read this."

He fished out his glasses from a straw basket, got comfortable across from me, and read in English.

"'The Grove. I am twelve years old. For God's Sake leaves the Tatinga and lives now in Ayachero with us. He is sixteen. Very sad, very angry. Nobody wants him here. As you say, the Tatinga push out the ones with deformity, just like Ayachero people. But I like him and want to learn from him. He says, if you take care of me, you bring me food, let me live with you, I show you a secret. Such a big secret, that if you know it, people respect you, they think you are some sort of God. We are young, and that is how we believe. That information is always good to have.

"'Then, Beya goes on all the hunts with the Tatinga. She can find game very fast, she can call the game sometimes. She says to us, she wants to teach us a lesson. Like I say, we are only young boys. She is showing us a magic place, but it is created from greed and pain.

"'For three days and nights we travel. Four other young Tatinga men, Beya, For God's Sake, sometimes on a donkey because of his leg, and me. She wants to show us how men become monsters. She wants to warn us. On the morning of day number four we come to a row of rubber trees. We see them before, but never in a row. They are planted. All of their bark is cut in the V shape. That means rubber tappers are there, many years ago, that tribes are made slaves to tap the rubber. Murder and torture and enslave to gather rubber for the barons. A hundred years ago. But the rubber trees still have scars. They remember the torture. The trees bleed out all of their white tears and they are empty. The rubber tappers say no one is allowed to speak your tribe's language, your tribe's language is against the law. This is when people begin to shine to each other, to speak in the old language, the language Beya uses with you.

"'Behind the wall of rubber trees grows the grove of mahogany. Three kilometers by three kilometers, thousands of trees so close it is like night in there all the time. Beya says the men that plant the rubber, the barons, have despair because that trade dies, so they cut down the forest and plant mahogany. The grove grows for many, many years. Generations of men kill each other for the secret, until only the Tatinga know where it is. Lots of people say the grove is a myth, but I know the truth.'"

Omar took his glasses off and rubbed his eyes. "How'm I doing?"

"You get an A."

"Your turn. A secret about you."

I nodded, pushing myself to my feet. "It's not a secret, more of a request. I want to go on a hunt with you." I couldn't get Doña Antonia's words out of my head: *you never prepare the game*. She was right. I couldn't bring myself to do it, yet by now I ate meat every chance I got—animals that others risked their lives to hunt or spent their time dressing. Perhaps it was also boredom with the other "women's work." The biggest draw: a hunt would mean more time with Omar, in a world that he knew like no other.

"You're pregnant—"

"The other women go with you, and some of them have been pregnant, too—"

"It's too hard, Lily. They clean the game, they build the shelters. Lots of bugs, you wouldn't like it." He got up and brushed himself off, as in: case closed.

"You don't know that."

"So now you want to kill the animals, too?"

"Maybe I'll feel better about eating them. I don't know. I want to be with you, to learn what you know."

"You need to be able to run, Lily."

"I can run."

"If you can't, I'm going to have to leave you behind. We can't lose the game, waiting for you."

"I can run," I said, scampering out after him into the blaze of sun as if to demonstrate, all the way down the hill to the waiting boats and men, their women packing the second sloop with supplies.

He threw his gear in the boat, joked with the men for a time, then turned back to me, pulled me aside. "You know, Liliana, if we decide to stay here that long, you're going to have our baby in the rainy season. It's a very hard time, very dangerous." I rubbed my belly, picturing the flooded forest, snakes floating up to the windowsills, manatees drifting under the huts like dark clouds. "Everyone has to work together, the men, the women, children. Everybody. So talk to the women more. A lot of them still don't know you."

"I will, I will."

"I'll tell For God's Sake to show you how to use a pistol. Are you ready to do that?"

"Anytime."

"It's really that important to you, Lily, to go on a hunt?"

"It is, just once."

"If you can shoot, I'll bring you next time. That'll cure you of ever wanting to go again." He sighed and glanced at the heavy sky that still held the rain in check. "So tell me, what's my next assignment?"

"Tell me why you love me. This one is due as soon as possible."

He gave me a wry smile but kissed me full on the mouth in front of all the men and women before he turned to the boats. We both watched each other as long as we could—me from shore, him from his boat—before the jungle swallowed him up.

Before a rapt audience of wide-eyed children who sat in a semicircle around me in the main room of the longhouse, I fed two scraps of a burlap sack under the oscillating needle of the sewing machine, foot working the treadle hard. Sweat dripped into my eyes as the incessant mosquitos buzzed at my ears. Slap and sew, slap and sew, slap and sew. Dark purple iodine stains blotched my legs, arms, neck, and face like birthmarks.

I finished joining the two pieces and offered the now towel-long remnant to the children; they snatched it out of my hands and—one holding each end—twirled in a circle as if to test the strength of the stitching. They'd collected a pile of things for me to sew together: torn dresses and shirts, ripped dolls, even palm fronds. I welcomed all requests, thrilled to be useful.

Bent over with the strain, a line of half a dozen women dragged a trail of fine wire mesh behind them up the hill: the fish gate. So as not to tear it any further, they carried it all the way up the stairs and unfurled it in front of me, Paco bringing up the tattered ends. There were enormous rips in every ten-foot section. The women had been sewing it by hand when they could, but keeping up with the repairs had become impossible. We'd been going out there with no protection at all. For God's Sake had slipped me some nylon thread, but I had no idea if the hundred-year-old machine would hold up.

In the middle of a long seam, the machine screeched to a halt, its gears grinding together, desperate to be oiled. Marietta, a sweet but somber prepubescent twelve-year-old who was fascinated by the machine and who sat on a stool next to me, trying to learn every step, nearly burst into tears when it stopped. The line of villagers with torn clothing looked at me expectantly as the women holding the fish net sighed and looked away, well acquainted with the lack of supplies in Ayachero, as well as the way humidity destroyed the innards of machinery.

"I think some oil or grease would get this thing going again," I said to Marietta, who disappeared into the storeroom, sprinting back with a short length of bamboo tube filled with cooking oil and sealed with rubber on both ends.

Marietta worked the treadle and I worked to spread out the netting, while Paco helped to feed the material under the needle and gather it up once a panel was finished. I was relieved and surprised every time the thick, old iron needle neither broke nor tore the netting as it pulled the nylon thread smoothly through the mesh. Soon I left Marietta to take over the machine—never saw her so excited—to help Paco fold and stack the finished sections. I couldn't remember having a more joyous day in Ayachero.

Just before siesta, Anna climbed the stairs of the longhouse. Claudia in her arms, she handed me a few of her and Franz's clothes that needed repair, insisting there was no rush. Her face still held her terrible grief, but I'd caught her smiling a few times in the last several days. Having Omar gone was frightening and exhausting for me, but she seemed almost relieved when the men were out hunting for weeks at a time, happier and more relaxed. The jaguar platform had been all but abandoned; it seemed its best purpose now was to shade the Anaconda Bar.

She eyed my ever-present backpack. "Lily, I was hoping we could do an exchange. I like your bag very much. May I look at it?"

I took it off slowly, as if shedding a second skin. In doing so, I pulled down the strap of my dress. I hurried to yank it back up, but Anna stayed my hand.

"Wait. Your skin."

I felt her lift my hair from my shoulders, followed by the dry whisper of her fingers across my shoulder blade. I winced—I knew my bites were infected; that sort of pain was familiar to me. But ever since I was a little kid, all my infected cuts and scrapes had eventually healed, hadn't they? I couldn't waste my time worrying about it.

"Wow, lots of bites here." She shook her head. "A bunch together. They look pretty bad. Do they hurt?"

"I'm fine."

I flushed out my bottle of iodine. "Can you put some of this on?" I handed her a piece of cloth from the pile next to the sewing machine.

"Did you know, they are calling you *Chica Púrpura*," she said softly. "Purple Girl." My third nickname. *Maybe I'm growing on them*, I thought as her small fingers dabbed at me. It hurt more than it should have, but I felt sure the iodine could take care of everything. Besides, FrannyB, a real doctor, had given it to me.

Beaming, Anna slipped on my backpack and adjusted the straps. "I feel like a real American now. May we put two holes in the bottom? That way, I can carry Claudia in the *chacra*. It'll be so much safer for her that way, and my hands will be free to work."

I thought of her, eight months pregnant, child on her back, digging yucca out of the hard earth. "Okay."

She laughed. "Your face! You look so sad! It's just a bag. Don't worry. For God's Sake told me he's going to bring us yards and yards of pretty fabric. We'll make party dresses for everyone."

I had to laugh. I took my precious bag back from her and with my switchblade cut two holes for the baby's legs to go through. She put on the backpack and I slipped Claudia in, facing away from her mother, her sweet face smiling up at me. It was as if the bag were made for the task.

Anna said, "So, are you still throwing up?"

"Not as much anymore."

She handed me a bowl of gray-green mush; a wooden spoon stood straight up in the middle. "It's grubs mashed with special leaves. Eat it every morning. I'll bring you a fresh bowl every day."

"Thank you," I said, taking the bowl.

"Give it a try," she said with an encouraging smile.

Not taking my eyes off her face, I dipped in the spoon, scooped out a tiny amount, and ate it. Sweet, meaty, grassy. Horrific. I took another small mouthful and set the bowl down.

"Delicious, right?"

I nodded.

"I knew you would love it. This is your first baby?"

"Yes."

"Ah, careful. No sitting on hot rocks. If you do, the baby will come too early. And stay inside when there's a full moon. That's really bad for the baby. Paco was born on a full moon."

I set the bowl down. "Paco's not such a bad kid, you know. Why won't anyone take him in?" Of course, I knew why, I just wanted her to tell me to my face.

"Well, his face, he's marked . . ."

"You think he's evil, or something? Has he ever done anything bad?"

"Not yet." She looked uncomfortable.

"He was just born like that," I said. "Like you were born with a beautiful face. Like I was born with red hair."

She shrugged and smiled as if what I'd said was true on the surface, but I was still missing the point: the kid was damaged goods. "You can take him in, then, since you like him so much."

"Or maybe you and Franz could do it."

"Franz would never . . . we have enough mouths to feed!"

I shrugged. "Everyone shares the food. I mean, he's the only little kid in the longhouse. It's pretty sad. Doesn't seem fair."

"He seems used to it." She huffed Claudia up higher on her shoulders. "Besides, maybe you better worry about other things. Having your first baby is a big deal."

She quickly thanked me for the bag—discussion over—and set off down the stairs to her hut. It made me sad, but maybe Anna was right. In a few short months, I'd have a child of my own to take care of, be expected to love. That alone felt impossible.

New requests poured in: the tongue of the giant anaconda over the Anaconda Bar had fallen out of its mouth. Reattach it. For that, I stood on a stool and used the big hand-sewing needle Anna lent me. It was like sewing two leather handbags together.

For protection in the jungle, the hunters wanted long sleeves added to short- or no-sleeved shirts, or long pants made from short ones for the same reason. The material was always weird: cotton/ poly blends—heavy on the poly—often with weird stripes or patterns: floral, polka dots, plaids, or sometimes prints with the Little Mermaid, Aladdin, or Beauty and the Beast. I thought the men would hate these fabrics, but the favorite turned out to be the Little Mermaid flannel, which For God's Sake was instructed to bring back as much of as he could find.

One afternoon, exhausted but happy after a day of sewing, I took my time on the steep stairs to our hut, bringing in Anna's daily present of mashed grubs and leaves that she'd left on the first step. Just inside the door, I turned around and saw them.

My clothes.

My only T-shirt and pair of shorts, still ripped and wrecked, but washed and carefully ironed, were folded in a neat pile on the mattress. I picked them up, smelled them: they still held the odor of hot stones. I ran outside and a short way up the hill, a shout stuck in my throat. I turned in a slow circle: there was no one around. Smoked meat hung motionless from a metal rod over a fire, the knotted spine of a capybara glistened like a row of crude pearls in the haze of the afternoon. One of the dogs, her back leg ripped open by a wild boar during the last hunt and pieced together courtesy of FrannyB, lay resting in the shade, ignoring the flies that sucked at the corners of her eyes. Only the still, fetid heat greeted me.

I climbed the stairs back to the hut. Tenting the mosquito netting around me, I crawled onto the mattress, dragging the small pile of clothes under the net next to me. I held the little bundle close to my chest, like I was hugging a piece of my old self, my child self, someone I was starting to forget, or let go of. Still, I wondered: *Who had done this? Was it Anna? Doña Antonia? One of the other women? And why?* And just as mysterious, if not more so: *Why did I have no desire to put these clothes on?* I liked the weird dress I'd sewn out of burlap lentil sacks and odd polka-dot linen. I thought about what Anna said, about all my *gringa* treasures, and it hit me that she was right; I could leave, I had a country to go back to—an immense, beautiful country with seasons and laws and ribbons of highway, libraries and museums, restaurants and ice cream and colleges—*but I didn't want to go.*

Because I had Ayachero treasures, too—Omar, of course. And now, the women expected me to join them in the morning to do what needed to be done, and they were grateful for my sewing. Beya's belief that I was a shaman was laughable to me, but the delusion felt magical, like anything was possible, and always, the jungle enthralled as much as it repelled.

I was still lost—in countless ways I didn't know what I was doing—but I was beginning to be found, too.

TWENTY-FOUR

S quinting at a purple orchid several yards away in the mid-story, arms out straight, I tried to steady the pistol with both hands. For God's Sake stood just behind me, observing my technique. We'd been practicing all morning at the Tortoise Beach and I was yet to hit anything remotely close to a target.

"Can I rest my hands on a tree stump or something so I can aim a little better?"

"Will a tree stump be ready and waiting for you when a jaguar is coming at you, over?"

"Okay, okay." I took a wider stance, aimed a little higher than the target as instructed, and fired, the gun knocking back hard into my bruised hand. The orchid trembled but remained pristine.

"Are you exhaling before you pull the trigger? Or are you holding your breath? We talked about this, over."

"I'm exhaling, I'm telling you," I said, frustrated.

"I don't know, Lily my friend. I think you are maybe a little afraid to be good at firing a gun. Maybe you don't really want to hunt down the animals." He leaned thoughtfully on his cane. "There are three more bullets only, over."

Fuck afraid. I turned back to the target—determined—and fired. The cluster of flowers exploded into a purple cloud.

For God's Sake pointed to a clump of white mushrooms at the base of a rotting log—I missed them entirely—then a paprika plant, its fist-sized fruit dotting the tree. I took a bead on a big fat one and pulled the trigger. Its rich red seeds plumed over the lush green leaves.

"All right, Miss Lily. Excellent work, and it is only your first time trying this difficult thing. Now come with me to the longhouse where I must prepare for my trip to San Solidad, over."

On the way back to the village, we discussed the kind of suit I was to make for him someday: dark purple silk with black velvet collar and cuffs. He'd seen it worn by a man named Prince in an old American magazine.

We settled in the storeroom next to a towering pile of empty burlap sacks.

"One more very important thing. You must show me how you load the bullets. We have to pretend, because we don't have any more of them, but show me, over."

I took off my new backpack, one I'd sewn out of old farina bags with woven sisal straps, and took out a short length of bamboo.

"I'll keep my bullets in this tube, and load the gun like this." I unlocked the chamber of the gun, pretended to load in the bullets, then snapped it shut.

"Where did you get this, your bamboo, over?"

"The men tore down that bamboo hut Omar and I stayed in when we first got here. Everybody was taking pieces of it."

"Did you check for tarantulas, over?" He laughed and took the gun from me, storing it in a side holster he wore loosely around his waist, the whole setup invisible under his capacious Hawaiian shirt. "You will be the best hunter of all. The jungle should be very afraid of you, Miss Lily. I wish I could go with you, over."

"When will you be back?"

Suddenly looking older, more fragile, he rested his cane against one wall and took a seat on the bench between the rubberized sacks of grain and salt, a place I'd found solace for hundreds of hours by now. "The most important question is, *will* I be back, over?" His hands fell loosely in his lap, fingers like knotted leather. Big smile gone, his face turned ashen, slack and defeated looking.

"What's wrong?"

"You know, sometimes I feel like I am the devil to wear four faces. A face for the Frannies, a face for *civilizado*, a face for Ayachero village people, a face for the Tatinga, over."

He began to cry. I'd seen so few men cry, it terrified and confused me.

"You know, Lily, I am afraid I will die this way, a man who does not honor his own *ca'ah*. I am feeling the biggest, loneliest weight in my heart and I cannot lift it. The weight of a thousand ceiba trees. I am too many things, so I am nothing, over."

"But you have to come back to us. We need you, and I'll make your suit . . ."

For God's Sake pulled a knife from his belt, reached up to his neck, and sliced off the leather cord that held the cumbersome tin cross. He tossed it out the open window. "I am tired of this dead white man, Jesus Christ. He means nothing to me. He is not the spirits of the plants, of the river, of the trees, of the four corners of the earth. He is someone else's God. It's okay to bring the Frannies the cans of beans, of pickled eggs, of coffee, but they want my soul, too. They want the souls of my family, the souls of the Tatinga, to have the souls of all the tribal people would be just fine with them, and why should that be?" He paused, a look of disgust passing over his face. "But For God's Sake says *yes, okay, I will do it*, For God's Sake always says yes. I bring the shiny toys and pretty things, so they give me money for my family to live, over."

"I would do the same thing."

"Well, you are just a young girl who thinks childish thoughts, but I am a grown man who will one day go to my own gods, and what will I say to them, over?" He wiped his eyes and continued. "A while ago, before you came, there was a young Tatinga boy at the Frances camp. He was twelve, or maybe thirteen, and he was trying make a fire to smoke some fish for the Frannies. He was doing it the way of the Tatinga and all the tribes: two sticks with a rock under a pile of kapok fibers, and he was rubbing and rubbing. For a lot of minutes. There was a little smoke, even, the fire was going to come, but I became my impatient self, and took out a match and struck it and lit up the little pile of seed pod fluff. And then do you wonder what happened after that, over?"

"Yes . . ."

"The boy became full of shame. He took the matches from me and kicked away his little pile of sticks and rocks, and swore he would never light a fire in that way again. He said he would rather starve, for the shame of doing things the old way when the new is so much better. So much faster! And he took that seed of shame back with him to the Tatinga, among all the other seeds of shame. Here is a poison that spreads, and soon no one remembers anything. No one remembers the plant that cures a stomachache, or fever, or joint pains, or the vine that cures grief. He will not teach his son how to light a fire the old way, or his son's son, and it all dies. No one can do anything without a match. The jungle becomes useless, over."

"But For God's Sake, everybody here loves you. Omar loves you like a brother."

"One day you will understand, over."

I sat next to him on the platform. His face was creased with anguish. "What's your real name? Your Tatinga name?"

"I'm sorry, Lily, to say that I cannot answer you. It is the only thing that is mine, over."

I nodded, wondering what was truly mine. I knew it was nothing I could touch.

Suddenly all business, he pushed himself to his feet, grabbed the empty sacks, and threw them over his shoulder. I followed him all the way down to the bank of the river, a hollowness banging in my gut. It felt like a father was leaving me, and there was nothing I could do to stop him.

He tossed the empty bags into the belly of the boat and climbed in. One hand on the tiller, he yanked at the motor's rusty chain before settling himself on his well-worn seat. It rumbled to life on the first pull; water churned and smoked under the turning blades. Jamming his ancient golf cap down over red-rimmed eyes, he cast a lingering look over the village that steamed in the early-morning mist.

"Lily, are you happy here? Because I have enough room here, in the boat today, with empty bags and no supplies, to take you to San Solidad, over."

I burst out, "How can you even ask me that? I can't leave Omar."

Part of me wanted to fall to my knees, moaning with desire for refrigeration, electricity, movies, sherbet, Snickers bars, roads, malls; the heartbreaking miracle of the familiar. I stroked my belly through my gunnysack dress, the memory of the gun still shaping my hand, the taste of Omar's kiss on my mouth, his dear voice reading his assignments playing in my head. Howler monkeys called in the distance, a sound that always presaged a soaking rain.

For God's Sake waited patiently. I thought, *I'm going to stay. I'm going to survive this place.*

"You don't have to say yes to my idea, young Lily. I remember how it was with my wife in the earliest days. In fact, I would be so surprised if you said yes and climbed into this boat right now. No one would be more surprised. But you are not too young to think about your own *ca'ah*. Maybe it's good to actually choose this place, to choose any place, over."

TWENTY-FIVE

– SEPTEMBER –

We cut the motor, the air hot as breath. Under high, dark passages, past trees wreathed with strangler figs, a swift current swept us along a slender vein of water. Omar crouched at the bow of the boat, his body bent in a C of concentration as he read the secrets in the channels of brown and black water beneath us, of the strange whirlpools and eddies, the spinning logs that looked like animals that sank and mysteriously rose some distance away. Nuts and rotting fruits floated swiftly by. A three-foot ashen tube—an abandoned wasps' nest—bobbed past. Every now and then, Omar stood, gazing out into the maelstrom of thickened fleshy leaves at the shoreline; just the subtle shift of his weight steering the canoe into a slightly different slipstream before he squatted again, pulling the soft water behind him with a leaf-shaped palm-wood paddle.

We had veered from the main river long ago, choosing a mind-numbing series of tributaries, each more narrow than the last. All of them looked the same to me: just brown water creeks walled in by chattering green jungle. Ferns unfurled toward us; flesh-eating flowers oozed their oils in the sun, luring insects to sticky deaths. Orchids steamed like giant dozing ears in the boughs of trees. Every now and then we'd all sprawl facedown or flat on our backs in the boats to pass under fallen trees that hovered just feet from the surface, or skid over logs, propeller yanked from the water. We plunged deeper and deeper into the green.

"You smell them?" Omar said under his breath to Franz and the three other hunters in our boat. "Maybe thirty, forty."

We had been tracking a herd of white-lipped peccary since early that morning. Franz squinted up into hulking branches above us, on constant lookout for snakes lounging there. We drifted in the narrowest channel yet—just five feet across—its water black with sediment but glowing an eerie gold where the sun filtered through.

I sat behind Omar, revolver tucked into a holster looped over my belt. Franz and the other men sat behind me. It was a position I'd fought bitterly for, to sit in the hunting canoe with the rest of the men. At five months pregnant, I felt strong. I wore a dress I had pieced and sewn together from two rice sacks, complete with sleeves to help protect myself from the bugs.

A boat carrying three women and five dogs kept nose to stern behind us. The women watched me with blank, hard faces: all three were older, maybe in their forties, with grown children. Unlike the younger women, these three had never warmed to me anyway, so I didn't take to heart what I read as resentment for traveling and hunting with the men.

We swung around a hairpin curve; the creek joined another, widening into a pond. Six eight-foot black caiman basked on the far bank, sunning themselves. One of them lay with its head in the water, mouth open wide as if to eat anything that might float by; along the row of ceramic-green bumps on its snout a handful of bright orange butterflies balanced, fluttering delicately. At our approach, the biggest one rose on its short legs. Carrying its belly just clear of the ground, it hurtled headlong and with a thrash of its armored tail it disappeared, leaving a soft swirl of bubbles on the water. Every log was a caiman unless it proved itself otherwise.

Omar stood as he gondola-ed us to the opposite beach; the other canoe followed swiftly behind. Dozens of Morpho butterflies—each as big as a child's hand—danced along the bank, turquoise-and-black wings glowing like stained glass. Our boats nosing onto shore spun them into brilliant blue vortexes before they settled on the sand just yards away. The dogs leapt from the boat, eager to be free from its confines, but wary of the snapping jungle, sniffing at the ground and keening at our sides. The men mumbled excitedly to one another; there was an electricity among them. The water smelled putrescent, steaming with its myriad biological transactions; beyond us, the forest shimmered with midday heat.

Omar said to me, "Lots of peccaries were here. Recently. The butterflies are eating the salt in the urine, see?"

The men gathered at the mouth of the jungle; dogs circling. This would be our camp, where the rest of the women would stay until we returned. A few of us ventured several yards in, hacking at branches and vines with our machetes to gather wood for the night's fire; others cut lengths of palm frond to build a shelter.

Our movements freed up a couple of Brazil nuts—as big as small melons—that rolled by my feet, nestling against each other with soft knocks. With a rock, I broke open the hard, woody seed pods; brown segments the shape of orange sections scattered; I hammered at those to reach the sweet white meat of the nut. Everyone gathered and took several pieces; I even got a few muttered thank-yous from the women. They each wished us luck on the hunt, and we turned to leave.

I followed Omar and the rest of the men into the forest. His sure feet glided with assurance along the rich, sweetish loam of the jungle floor. Torso bent forward, progress smooth and economical, he moved with an awareness and anticipation of what was three, five, ten steps ahead of him, whereas my stiff, clunky body strained forward, at odds with everything, stalling at this pile of logs, that protruding root, battling curtains of lianas. I stopped, started, and hesitated while his rapid trot never slowed.

The men followed me in silence. Roped together, the dogs huffed at our sides, whining and yipping with their sensory overload. My skin shone with sweat, my hair dripped from the mist that drifted among us, an earthbound cloud. Occasionally the men paused, consulted in Quechua or Spanish spoken too quickly for me to understand; possibly on purpose. All I could think about was Omar asking me back in the village if I could run. As I walked I felt my belly, a hard, swollen ball, push against the rough fabric of my dress. Somehow I hadn't been afraid in the canoe as we traveled to this hunting ground, but now I silently apologized to my baby for my foolhardiness, my youth and stupidity.

Omar held up one hand; we all stopped short, our breath ragged in the heavy air. We'd all heard it: a strangled cry of pain, almost human. The dogs lunged forward, slavering and yelping; the men restrained them, but they leapt again, wild for the hunt. We crept toward the pitiful sound.

A big black howler monkey lay on its back on the forest floor between two intertwined roots, its head and neck held flush to the ground by a metallic snare loop. Another, smaller snare lay empty nearby. Listlessly, it reached over and snatched up its dismembered foot, the toes long and furred and strangely graceful; it sniffed and rubbed the foot against its face, then threw it at us as we approached. Eyes bulging from their sockets, it struggled against the cruel wire, making a good show before howling weakly. Its head fell back among the lush moss in momentary defeat, black nostrils flared wide; flies already landing, beetles, too, all the carrion eaters whispering to one another and gathering from every corner of land and sky.

Franz nudged Omar; they consulted briefly. "They want you to shoot it, Lily," Omar said.

"*Me?* Why?"

"Because you say you're a hunter. Do it, Lily. It's suffering."

The monkey lunged again, the ring of metal cutting deeper into its neck; black blood coursing onto waxy green leaves. Up on one elbow like a man in bed, it looked at me, its big, noble head and thick black ruff shuddering as it opened its mouth again, letting loose a weak, guttural moan. *Okay*, I said silently to the creature, *I'm coming.* My limbs moved as if underwater. I took a step toward it, shifting the stock down and the muzzle forward, its coldness, heaviness still foreign to me as I lifted it toward the ridge of flesh between the creature's eyes.

I can't do this, I thought. *There is just no way . . .*

Omar fell to one knee, pulling me down next to him and encircling my hands with his, wedging the barrel under the monkey's chin and forcing his head back.

"*Now*, Lily."

I looked for the pain in the monkey's eyes, pictured it gone, and pulled the trigger.

The shot traveled up through the monkey's jaw and out the top of his cranium in a fountain of pink. With badly shaking hands, I slid the gun back into the leather holster at my waist. *Forgive yourself*, I thought, *he was going to die anyway. You are only following the rules in this wild place.*

"Good," Omar said, briefly kissing my forehead. "You freed him."

The rest of the men dropped down over the creature, cutting it free from the poacher's trap. Franz flung it over his back, holding it by its yard-long tail.

In less than an hour, light poked through the jungle and we burst through to another tributary, this one twenty or so feet across. The tightly coiled river had doubled back on itself. The men groaned, annoyed to be slowed down by this impasse. The water was murky toward the shore, but black at the middle, much slower moving than the water we had just left, its depth impossible to gauge. The dogs paced at the bank, noses twitching toward the other side; I caught a whiff of something skunky: the herd was close.

"Let's cross," Franz said, standing ankle-deep in the tannin water. The other men mumbled in agreement. Omar squatted just where the water touched the sand, dipped in his finger, tasted it, peered into its opaque depths. He looked up at Franz and said, "Give me the monkey."

Franz snorted and shook his head. "Why?"

Omar got to his feet, tension vibrating his limbs. He was so much smaller than Franz, but so agile he could have probably leapt over him cold from the ground. "Come on, Franz, give me the fucking monkey."

Franz shifted his weight; as he did so black blood rained down from the creature's wounds and sizzled into the sand. The monkey's head hung heavily down, hands at the ends of furred arms almost touching, as if he were diving toward the center of the earth. Across the short stretch of water, a flicker of movement through dense green; shadows passing quickly.

"I'm going to cross." Franz turned toward the water and hiked the monkey higher on his wide shoulders. "We're losing them."

Omar leapt at Franz. He wrenched the monkey by its tail from Franz's grip and spun in a circle, launching the poor creature across the water to its very center, the darkest part. Before Franz could acknowledge this offense, the water began to boil, the piranha so thick they leapt out of the water and banged into each other before falling back in, pieces of monkey flesh in their sawlike teeth. Bits of fur popped to the surface, floating with the current; soon the skull rose white, grinning and bobbing.

In minutes, the men had cut down two trees, each only a few inches in diameter, and laid them across the river. Franz crossed first;

the dogs skittered along behind him. The rest of the men casually forded the narrow bridge, all the while joking about what would happen if they fell; their balance remarkable. I hazarded a few steps out in my rotting sneakers, froze, swaying, my body heavy in all sorts of new places. The men shook their heads, impatient; not only a woman on the hunt, but a pregnant one, holding up everything. I turned back to the shore.

Omar cut down another tree, laid it between the two, then cut down two more slender ones, sharpening the ends to use as walking sticks. He walked back to me on the sapling bridge, demonstrating their use. For each step, he methodically stabbed one down to the muddy bottom while pulling the other free, till he reached me.

"I can't do it, Omar. I just can't." Sweat dripped down my shoulder and spine, burning into the bites that never seemed to heal. Of course I couldn't go back into the jungle by myself, but I also couldn't go forward.

He said, "Lily, you need to get down on your hands and knees. Go as slow as you need to. Don't listen to the men. They're being idiots. Listen to me. Listen to your strong self, the one who's gotten you this far, the one who's not afraid of this place. I'll be right here in front of you. I won't let you fall. Understand?"

I nodded. Quaking, I got down to my hands and knees, centering my body weight in the middle of the bridge. Clutching the slender trees, knees aching, I crawled toward him inches at a time, never taking my eyes off the water that still churned beneath us with snapping silver fish that moved as if shot from a gun, wild with the taste of blood.

TWENTY-SIX

We stepped back into the steaming jungle. The reek of peccary all around us, a skunky musk. The strongest dog of the pack, who had to have some husky in her of all things, sprung into the air, straining her lead, finally snapping it. After a moment of confusion, the dog's eyes wild—*how could freedom be suddenly possible?*—she bounded off. The others, still tethered to each other, followed in an ecstasy of liberation. The men, all except Omar, turned and ran after them.

Omar grabbed my arm. "Come on, Lily, run!"

I froze in place, caught in a paralyzing cycle of fear and hesitation. His body was taut with readiness, trembling with the cool heat of the hunt. In microseconds, we exchanged an understanding of promises kept and broken, my good intentions colliding with our physical realities.

"Stay here. I'll come back for you."

The ground shook. Squeals, clicking teeth, barrel-chested grunts filled the air. I gathered myself to run, strapping my gun tighter to my side, but Omar gave me no second chances. He turned and flew, he and the other men out of sight before I'd taken my first step. Still, I ran toward the chaos of noise and confusion, chasing after the snorts and barking, the calls of the men to each other, the stink of the animals, until the sounds became distant, muted. With my machete I sliced my way through nests of vines woven into vast mats that tented the forest floor, pulling my feet out of swamp mud that sucked me down to my shins. I'd long stopped paying attention to what I was stepping on or over or around, ignoring the rules Omar had pounded into me: don't touch anything, don't lean on anything, fire ants or worse are everywhere, if you look up into the canopy and see nothing *don't believe your eyes*, because a thousand things are looking back at you. Bats are hidden in the leaves. Goliath tarantulas are burrowed in nests in the ground. Scorpions that look like bark are watching you.

This is a battlefield.

His voice in my head: *Think, concentrate, wait, look.*

Open your third eye to see what is really there.

Be where you are.

I slowed to a fast walk, still determined to catch up with them. Their shouts and calls barely audible now; the funky smell dissipated. I stumbled into a small clearing where thin arrows of light striped across the remains of palm nuts ground up by peccaries in their search for tubers and roots.

Second by second, my breath roaring in my ears, I began to accept that I could not catch up with the men. I was a foolish, arrogant, pregnant teenager wandering through the rain forest alone. I bent over, rested my hands on my knees, panting. Breasts aching, belly bulging, energy gone. I found myself wishing for a compass, then recalled Omar telling me that the iron and other properties in Amazonian trees rendered them worthless. As if the jungle had reached into modernity and had a good laugh. It made a strange kind of sense.

I straightened up, turning in a tight circle in the sweltering green bowl; all around me things slithered, crawled, flew, all in agreement that I was the food. No need to manufacture my own chaos like I did back home; it was all around me. I was up against something I couldn't lie to or manipulate, something I couldn't run away from; the way I had survived my entire life.

Nothing like that worked here.

I had to pay attention; I had to adapt; I had to stay.

I began walking again, with every step guiltily recalling Omar's admonishment to stay where I was. Though staying put freaked me out even more, I made myself stop next to a lupuna tree, its voluminous roots soaring skyward. I thought of that Ayacheran rule of the jungle: when you're lost, they only look for you for two days.

I screamed Omar's name once, twice.

The looming green tunnel submerged my voice. From what seemed a great distance, as in a dream, I heard my name. Faintly, in all the wildness and from so far away. *Lily* . . . It was eerie; was I imagining it? Was it Omar? A muted gunshot, and another, dull pops, the muffled clattering of hooves.

Under my sodden sneakers, the earth seemed to buzz. Omar called my name; clearly now. I called out to him as the men's shouts and the yips of the dogs grew louder and louder. Now the ground shook with the drumming of hooves; the peccaries were coming toward me. Screams from the men, shouts from Omar. Unintelligible.

Again, a paralysis stilled my limbs, but there were only moments to think. I had to move, now. I scrambled around the base of the enormous tree, listening. The hoofbeats rumbled louder and louder— how many were there, dozens? From what direction? Where were the dogs? The men? I had to hide—*where?*—in seconds the peccaries would crush me to death. I ducked down in the hollow of a curved root, covered my head, spoke to my baby, said, *I will protect you, sweet thing, little thing, helpless thing*.

Screaming bloody murder, dozens of black pigs roared by on either side of the tree, flattening everything, fury or fear or both sending them plummeting into the jungle beyond. In seconds, three dogs bulleted by, mouths frothing with rage. A brief lull, then Omar and Franz and the other men hurtled by, all of them yelling so loudly at each other and the dogs that they didn't hear my shouts.

I ran toward the sounds of their voices, the yelps of the dogs. In minutes I realized where we were headed: back to the river we'd just crossed on the sapling bridge. The dogs—out of control—were instinctively rounding the game and trying to herd them back to where they knew we had left the boats.

At the bank of the river, two dogs cornered half a dozen eighty-pound pigs, nipping at them and jumping back, nipping and jumping back. The pigs squealed, edging toward the water but never touching it, as if they knew what awaited them there. Franz and Omar and the other men scrambled a dozen feet up into some strangler fig branches that overhung the bank, firing. I called out Omar's name and he turned to me with a look I'll never forget: surprise, fury, terror.

"Get up in that tree, Lily!" He gestured at the one closest to me.

I climbed as high as I could, only six or seven feet, since the branches higher than that were too slim to hold me. The husky—still with her three-foot lead thrashing about—leapt at the throat of one of the pigs, killing it just as the other pigs turned on her and piled on, tearing her to bits. The other dog ran yelping into the forest. The only sound was of the pigs grunting, devouring what was left of the husky.

Franz trained his gun and shot one of the pigs dead; it looked like a juvenile. Except for the biggest one, who must have weighed over a hundred pounds, they all scattered to the forest, leaving the dog's corpse. But the big one stayed. It circled my tree, eyeing me like I was the one who'd shot her kid. She snuffled around the base of the tree where I crouched, her gray tail whipping back and forth at her wire-haired rump.

"Shoot it, Lily, *shoot it*!" the men yelled, firing off shots, but the creature had migrated to the other side of the tree, all the wrong angles for them to hit it. She peered up at me, her long snout reaching, huge freckled nostrils opening to taste the air around me. Her powerful shoulders rippled, the skunk stink fouling the air.

Omar called out, "It can't climb, but you have to shoot it!"

I stiffened as I reached for my gun, my weight firmly back in the crotch of the tree, both hands on the pistol, an extension of my hands, finger on the trigger. But the pig wouldn't stop moving, circling my little tree. Omar shot again and missed. Snarling, it ran around to the other side—far from the men and out of their range. It started to dig frantically into the thick mud at the trunk of the tree with its powerful hooves. I leaned down, training the gun on the top of its head—*just shoot the thing; why can't I pull the trigger?*—but I missed the moment. The creature shifted a bit to the left and began burrowing again. I hadn't understood what its plan was until it dropped its block of a head and rammed it again and again against the base of the tree, shaking my whole body with each strike. It snarled up into the barrel of my gun with a loathing that felt personal. Weakening at its base, the tree juddered and swayed. I adjusted my weight against the new equilibrium, bark scraping at my arms, the gun slick with sweat in my hand.

"Lily, *shoot!*"

The pig, on a mission, ran back around to dig some more, ripping at the roots and spitting them aside. It dropped its square, iron-gray head and rammed.

I swayed, found my balance. One more hit and I'd be on the ground. Feet jammed in the notches of the tree, I rested my forearms on my pregnant belly and pulled the trigger three times. Her head opened and she fell flat, arms and legs splayed onto the mud and ripped-up roots. The taste of gunmetal flooded my mouth as the tree finally gave way, and I jumped to the earth.

TWENTY-SEVEN

Nobody talked much on the way back. Though the men seemed grateful to go home with any game at all rather than an empty boat, they were sobered by the loss of four of five hunting dogs—the husky especially; clearly she was Franz's favorite, though he would have never admitted it. Omar assured me that sometimes trips went bad like this, that losing dogs was terrible, but everyone was alive, not even injured. The husky dog breaking free from the others caused the whole plan to go out of control. The men had only been able to cut another dog free; the rest were corralled together and attacked, helpless. All I felt was lucky to have survived.

The evening sky over the river was streaked purple as we rounded the bend to Ayachero, lulled by the rhythmic splash of the paddles in the chocolate-brown water. The canoes nudged into the soft mud, and we gathered ourselves to empty the boats. I couldn't understand why no one had come down to greet us, until we saw the torches burning in the clinic.

Doña Antonia came running down the hill, her face in the throes of the closest thing to joy I'd ever seen. "Franz, my son! Come and see. You're a father again." Franz tossed aside the paddles he was unloading and raced up the hill.

———

After Franz and Omar had their turn, Anna let me hold her. There was nothing like it for me before, a baby just hours old in my arms, purplish and not totally cleaned up, but perfect in every detail, her head resting in my palm, all trust, the tiny fingernails, perfect lips in a sweet pucker, eyelashes like insect wings. Women crammed the small space, cleaning up, talking, laughing, their warmth to me now doing wonderful things for my heart.

I knelt down next to Anna and gave her back her little girl. "How was it?" I said, not sure how to phrase the question.

She sat up a little. "It started at dinner last night. FrannyB said it was a breeze. I don't know if it was *that*," she said with a laugh. "But it's my third, so maybe easier, a little. She says I'm a natural mother."

I passed my hand over my bulging belly and thought, *Am I a natural mother? Not very likely.* The hut we called a clinic—meaning the usual one-room dwelling, this one featuring a lone shelf with bandages, splints, iodine, aspirin—was hot and smelled like blood and vaguely of shit. Doña Antonia gathered a pile of bloody cloths and assigned the washing to Marietta and some of the younger girls, who dutifully left with armfuls of it.

"Where's FrannyB?"

"Napping in the longhouse. She'll go back to her camp in the morning."

The other women took turns holding the baby, each of them seemingly overjoyed about the new addition to Ayachero. All I could do was wonder, *Would it be like this for me? Would people here greet our child like this? And what if something happened during childbirth that FrannyB or Beya couldn't handle?*

I promised myself I would not give birth in this place.

By the light of a bonfire, a few of the men helped me unhook the pig's hooves that had been lashed to its carrying pole. We laid it on its back; its four legs fell open, exposing an ash-colored abdomen. Determined to gut and skin it myself, I forced myself to concentrate on the steps I'd learned by watching the others: come down hard and swift with my machete so the head is removed from the body in one stroke. Hold the point of my switchblade just so between skin, fat, and muscle. Get help to gather the viscera, cut it free, picturing the dogs eating their well-earned meals. I remember the moment my perception went from gore and sadness for a life taken to *food*; in a way it was like holding the newborn—it was a revelation, a new understanding of life and death that stayed with me forever.

I brought a few cuts of meat to Doña Antonia, who nodded approvingly; big love from her. She'd been right about everything.

Two weeks later, in late September, it was time for Omar to leave again. That morning, I sat down on a bench near our oven to recover from my sense of dread at his departure. Catching a glimpse of my reflection in the big tin pot we used to boil cassava, I didn't recognize myself. Except for my huge belly, the rest of me was thin, my face gaunt, hair lank. I'd been losing weight, not gaining it; dismissing the whispered comments of the women: *she's sick, something's wrong with her*. I ignored them—as well as the persistent painful itch near my shoulder blade—and listened only to Anna, who prepared special herbs for my appetite that seemed to work pretty well. She and Claudia and the new baby seemed healthy, so I took everything she gave me. I made my way back upstairs.

"Come on, Lily," Omar said softly, setting a piece of tapir skin on the floor in front of me. We were both sluggish that morning, reluctant to move, sick of saying goodbye. "Stand on this. You can't go around barefoot." My sneakers were being held together with rubber strips cut from the supply bags.

I took a wide stance. He nicked into the leather with his short-handled knife the outlines of the soles of my feet, placing a gentle hand around my calves one at a time.

"I'll punch the holes, and you'll sew these sandals, so I can see my wife wearing something new when I get home."

I peered over my big belly at the muscles in his shoulders working as he measured. "What about your assignment?" I asked, unable to resist running my hands through his shining black hair.

"About my love for you? I thought you'd forget," he said with a grin, peering up at me. Crossing our hut, he shyly pulled a piece of paper wedged between *Pride and Prejudice* and *Sense and Sensibility*.

"I know your next assignment," I said. "A letter to our unborn child. What do you think?"

"I like it very much," he said in English. Cross-legged on the floor, next to our window, which rang with early-morning bird and monkey song, he read this to me:

Why I Love Lily Bushwold, by Omar Mathias Alvarez

I love that you are different from me. Your red hair, your pale skin warm me. Who can help but love the sun shining down?

You do not judge me, and I thank you. In my culture I am only the things I have done in my past, and I am behind that black curtain. You see me, Omar. You throw away the curtains and see my heart. And it is a good heart, it is not a perfect heart, but it is trying. You see that I am trying. I see that you are trying. I see the little flame in you. The little flame that makes you take a peccary life when he wants to take yours. I even like the little flame in you that makes you say: "Fuck this, and fuck that. I will do it my Lily way." It doesn't bother me. But when I say listen, or when I say slow down, or, be quiet to hear the jungle animals, you honor me. I love that flame.

You are kind with my mother. My mother is not sweet. She had only boys, so she does not understand girls. She lost me to you. I am the favorite boy, and I come back with you, a white girl, so she thinks of poachers, she thinks of loggers, of a big country up north full of ice and hungry for drugs.

We will not live here forever. Ayachero has problems, more problems than I can solve. I made a promise to you, I remember it well.

Maybe someday you say why you love me. This is an assignment for you.

TWENTY-EIGHT

– OCTOBER –

Their fluffiness leaving them, my two little macaws hopped in their basket. With their technicolor feathers sprouting, gorgeous tails longer day by day, each day I wondered, *Were they ready to fly?* If I put the basket on the window, would something swoop from the sky or slither up the sill and make a meal of them before they had the chance to try their wings?

With trembling hands I lifted the nest to the long wooden plank. The birds strutted around, jabbing at the seeds at their feet, gnawing on the rim of the basket.

I looked up. Shouting came from beyond the longhouse, calls for help spiked over the early-morning birdsong. Heart pounding, I left the birds on the sill and raced down the stairs as quickly as my big belly would allow.

The main room of the longhouse was deserted. Hammocks hung empty, a few still swaying as if vacated in a hurry, cooking fires still smoked. Hurrying down the hall past the storage rooms to the far east end of the building, I saw a crowd had gathered near the opening of the Fire Ant Path.

More shouts, cries. I made my way down the long set of stairs to the hard earth and took off toward the cropland. Paco ran to meet me, grabbed my hand, and pulled me along through the crowd of families and children.

FrannyB staggered along, one arm around FrannyA's waist as she half carried, half dragged her down the narrow path along the manioc gardens. Exhausted, she lurched a few more steps forward, then dropped to her knees; FrannyA's limp form tumbling into the sharp grasses of the field. By the time I reached them, one of the men had picked her up and was running with her to the clinic, followed by the buzzing crowd.

FrannyB spoke to anyone who would listen. "She got so sick, so fast! I didn't think we'd make it. I had nothing to give her . . ." She covered her mouth, didn't recognize me. *Did I look that different?* "Lily," she finally said, "have you seen For God's Sake?"

"No."

Wild-eyed, she turned to Doña Antonia, who hurried ahead toward the clinic carrying a bucket of water. "Forget about him," she said, face set.

"*Forget about him?* What's going on?"

"We sent Panchito to find him. We haven't heard anything. What difference does it make? Is he here now to help us?"

I stood in the shadows of the clinic, filled with dread at the scene unfolding before me. Two small fans, motors whining, clipped at the dull hot air. After the batteries inside died, there would be no more.

Her face naked-looking without her spectacles, FrannyA lay on her back on a thin straw mat on the floor, her arms secured to her body with lengths of liana, her bare feet tied snugly to two stubby poles the men had pounded into the soft wood. After their task, they stood around looking awkward, arms looped loosely behind their backs.

"Get out of here," FrannyB barked, sending a few young boys out for more water. "And bring clean cloth, as much as you can find. *Go!*"

FrannyA moaned, her head rolling back and forth on the meager pillow, spittle dribbling from the corners of her mouth. She struggled weakly at her ropes as she tried to lift her arms, turn from side to side, or bend her knees. Sweat greased her face and drenched her thin gray hair, soaking the drab cotton sheet she lay on. Doña Antonia busied herself loosening the cords while still keeping her immobile, all the while making small sounds of comfort, sounds I hadn't known she was capable of.

Eyes swimming in reddened sockets, FrannyA turned to me, looking me up and down, my gaunt face, my big belly, my sack dress, and purple-stained skin. "You are going to have a bastard child. You are not married in the eyes of God. I'm dying, Lily, but I'm going to a beautiful place—"

"Shut up, A," FrannyB said. "You're not dying. We're going to get this all cleared up." Kneeling, she held her friend's fine-boned hand with her ham-fisted one, gazing at her with so much love I had to look away. Doña Antonia handed me some folded-up sections of cloth, motioning to place them under the ties, which were already cutting into the thin skin of the sick missionary's scrawny ankles.

"Oh, B," FrannyA said. "You know and I know. You can't do this thing . . ."

A few young boys entered the hut, eyes downcast, hushed by the thin veil that hung between life and death. They carried tin pails of water and armfuls of cotton cloth and burlap scraps, all ironed to board-like stiffness. Anna knelt at FrannyA's head, cooling her forehead with a damp cloth.

FrannyB spread out one of the lengths of cotton next to FrannyA's tortured body. When she knew FrannyA couldn't see her face, she let her own terror show; the skin ashen, taut over her sharp chin and cheekbones. Out of a lumpy canvas bag, she removed and arranged on the cloth: a slender silver surgical-looking knife, a small pair of scissors, tweezers, a sewing needle, a bundle of waxy-looking black string, and a label-less bottle of pills. Water boiled in a pot on a brick stove nearby. She lay the sharp ends of the tools in the hot water, then held three white pills and a brimming tin cup of cool water to FrannyA's lips.

"Why are you bothering with me?" FrannyA said, turning her head away.

"Take the fucking pills."

FrannyA shut her eyes, a wave of pain rolling across her features, her face whitening. "If it will make you happy, my dear." She opened her eyes, focusing first on the clipping fans, then on all the faces staring down. "But you know we've failed, don't you? You know we haven't made one bit of difference—"

FrannyB pushed a pill in her mouth, spilling water down A's pointed chin; she gulped it all back, coughing, blinking, then opened her mouth like a little bird and accepted the rest, bony throat bulging. FrannyB exhaled heavily before pushing herself to her knees to free a hip flask from the pocket of her camo pants. She unscrewed the top, held the flask to FrannyA's mouth, and tipped it.

"If you waste a drop of this, I'll kill you myself."

But the missionary, chastened, eyes never leaving FrannyB's, was now accepting any and all liquids.

FrannyB turned to me. "Go find Beya. Now."

Holding my belly, I marched off to the manioc fields, to the cow barn, to the huts where the lepers lived. Machetes strapped to abbreviated limbs, the group of four adults worked the fields in the oppressive sun.

"Have you seen Beya?" Faces obscured by straw hats, a couple of them looked back at me. They shook their heads and returned to their work.

Panting and sweating, I made my way to the far perimeter of the fields, to the mouth of the Anaconda Path. In the trees above, six king vultures peered out from under orange wattles with white-ringed, bottomless black eyes. All patience, all waiting. As long as death existed, so would they.

Under the vultures' dull, hungry glare, I planted my tapir-clad feet wide. Cradling my belly with both hands, I shut my eyes, all energy focused on silencing my noisy mind—full of the usual deafening chatter: fear, worry, doubt, longings—until, for a few precious moments: silence, as after a heavy snowfall. In my mind, I heard myself say in Spanish:

"BEYA, WE NEED YOUR HELP. FRANNY-A IS SICK. SHE'S DYING. WE ARE IN THE CLINIC. PLEASE COME."

As I spoke the words in my head, a buzzing sensation traveled through my teeth and jaw, down my neck to my shoulders, arms, fingers. I knew I had done it—even if she hadn't heard me, even if she wasn't listening or chose to ignore me—I *knew* I had spoken to her.

The sun beat at my face, the vicious jungle air seared my throat. "ANSWER ME . . ."

I made my mind an empty thing, a blank canvas on which she could paint her words back to me, send a picture, an emotion, anything.

Silence. Emptiness.

One of the vultures spread its enormous black-and-white wings as if to dry them in the sultry air; the others did the same, like a wave, one after the other, till the first one flapped his closed and the others followed suit, all one vulture mind.

I squeezed my eyes shut and silenced my clamorous mind for a second time. Waited for the delicious hush, the lull, the pulsing calm. In my mind's eye I saw my open mouth, heard myself calling to her in English, then Spanish, then English again. I called up the image of FrannyA lying prone, suffering; I showed her the woman's blank face staring at the ceiling of the hut, the way her ankles were tied and bleeding. I showed her FrannyB's face in devastation; held all this in my mind's eye until I couldn't anymore and shards of the picture broke away into the smudgy blue and black shapes behind my eyes. Exhaustion and dizziness flooded me.

I opened my eyes.

Just the dusty path before me, the unforgiving sky above. Tapping one last dram of energy, I sent one more message: "WELL, FUCK YOU, THEN." In defeat, I turned back to the clinic. I'd taken only a few steps before I heard the whoosh of a machete clearing a path. Bit by bit, as the vines and branches fell, Beya emerged from the matted tangle of forest.

TWENTY-NINE

Without a word to each other, we took slow steps up the ladder to the clinic. My body felt heavy, legs swollen, my shoulder blades burning, as if my bug bites had gathered together in one large wound.

The air in the hut was thick with heat. Rough cloth squares had been nailed over the windows. A half dozen votive candles flickered close to FrannyA, who had stopped fighting her bonds and lay muttering to herself. Her shirt had been unbuttoned to just under her breastbone and her belly lay exposed, the rest of her draped with the stiff cuts of cloth, modesty intact. Her rib cage rose sharply like two bony hands meeting; her belly concave, breaths quick and shallow.

Beya made her way to the sick woman's feet. Candlelight sparked in each eye. Bright yellow feathers sprung back from her ears like canaries in a cage of blackness. Her net bag hung from a belt around her waist; the material jerking this way and that.

"Are we ready?" FrannyB said, her voice gravelly and low.

FrannyA's eyes opened, widened. "Get that devil away from me!" she called out hoarsely, neck cording as she lifted her head.

Pressing the flask to her mouth, FrannyB forced more cane alcohol down her throat. "Relax, you fool. She's here to help us."

The ill missionary's head dropped back to the pillow as she laughed maniacally, belched, then returned to her nonsense mumbling, eyes fixed on the dark conical ceiling, sooty from countless fires. Shafts of sunlight cut through the split bamboo walls, striping her stricken face.

Snapping on a pair of bright blue latex gloves, FrannyB opened a bottle of iodine and swabbed a purple circle on her belly with a piece of cotton from a decaying plastic pouch.

"This is going to hurt, for just a little bit," FrannyB said.

"Ha ha ha, that's okay," FrannyA said, now in deep communion with the ceiling.

A couple of women who had been standing by with pails of water or cloths parted so Beya could walk around to FrannyA's exposed belly. The old woman got to her knees. FrannyA panted, spilling non-sense words at the ceiling, or at her God, impossible to tell. Beya loosened her string bag and withdrew a fist-sized woven-palm box. A brilliant turquoise-and-yellow frog jumped within, its rubbery fingers probing the interlaced leaves, a black eye bulging now and again at an opening. From another, much smaller leather bag, Beya withdrew a long tobacco-leaf-wrapped package. Ceremoniously, she unwrapped it and arranged a few dozen needle-fine palm spines on FrannyB's cloth.

The sick missionary turned to Beya, eyes narrowing. "Don't let her touch me! *B!*" Fat tears rolled out of her eyes, darkening the thin cotton of the pillow.

FrannyB grabbed her by the chin and turned A's face toward her own. "You just pay attention to me, okay? You watch my face. Every second."

"But *B*—"

"We talked about this. You agreed, remember? You're not going to leave me."

"But she's going to kill me, B. She's going to—"

"Do I have to strap your head down? Because I will."

FrannyA's eyes squeezed shut; her eyeballs danced furiously under the thin skin.

FrannyB nodded at Beya.

The shaman drew hard on a hand-rolled cigar of wild tobacco she'd lit at the fire, forcing the air out with strenuous coughs before filling her lungs again. Clouds of musty smoke fogged the hut, swirling up into the shadows. Barefoot, Beya slowly walked around the prostrate woman, blowing smoke over her body and chanting nonstop, a song with no more than three distinct notes but a clear, syncopated rhythm. Finally she stopped where she'd begun, at FrannyA's side.

She got to her knees and slid a palm-spine needle into the box, scraping quickly along the shining flesh of the frog. Placing one gnarled brown hand flat against FrannyA's stomach—FrannyA jumped slightly at the contact but held steady—Beya slipped the needle at an angle into FrannyA's taut little belly, entering a throbbing vein near her groin. FrannyA stiffened and cried out, thighs quaking under her rough black skirt.

"Hold her down," FrannyB barked at me. I kneeled and dropped down over her, holding her shoulders to the mat, while Doña Antonia pinned her down at her hips. Anna sat at her feet, pressing them down and together. Strange but somehow right, the three of us joined in this task. "Don't let go until I say so, no matter what happens. Got it?"

I nodded yes, my full weight pressing down on FrannyA's shoulders, her sickness-fouled breath in my face, her pale blue eyes gazing through me.

"And don't look at what I'm doing, all right? Keep your focus on her."

I said nothing.

"Answer me, Lily."

"Okay, all right."

But I kept glancing down anyway. I couldn't help myself. With a dozen swift, small jabs, Beya pricked the skin just below FrannyA's rib cage; she winced but made no sound. Dosing the other palm spines briefly and lightly against the frog, Beya slid them in again and again on opposite sides of the tiny missionary's gut, circumscribing a circle on the pale skin.

FrannyB palpated the shivering iodine-stained skin under her hands. "Do you feel that? Do you feel anything?"

"Just pressure."

"Okay, that's good. Really good."

"I love you, B." A few more tears rolled down the sides of her face, pooling in her ears.

"I love you too, A," FrannyB said quietly, a note of embarrassment in her voice. She nodded at Doña Antonia, who with bamboo tongs fished the knife, tweezers, sewing needle, and scissors from the bubbling water and spread them out on the cloth.

FrannyB began her incision at the top left side of her abdomen, just below the rib cage, and continued in the shape of a smile down below her belly button and back up the other side. With a scrap of cloth, Doña Antonia soaked up the line of blood at the cut. A few of the young girls who had brought water waved palm fronds over the wound, whisking away the gathering flies.

As she lifted the flap of skin, FrannyB snipped at a thin membrane of white tissue. A firm nest of intestines lay glistening in the candlelight.

"Now, Beya. Call them."

Beya's mouth dropped open. A bass rumble rolled out of her, the lowest sound I'd ever heard emanate from a human being. Only when she paused for breath did the pain in my eardrums ease. I felt it in my bowel; my teeth thrummed with it. The floor of the hut vibrated beneath my knees where I crouched, my face inches from the sick missionary's. But the part of her that could speak up and object was gone: oblivious, she'd switched back to humming, even singing snatches of hymns.

The thrumming noise deepened in round bellows, booming out

of the shaman's chest, a living instrument. The sound came from above me, beneath me, from inside me. Forehead pearled with sweat, FrannyB never took her eyes off the opened gut as her bloodied gloves—knife in one hand, scissors in the other—hovered over the coiled purplish ropes.

"The Lord is my shepherd," came FrannyA's thin voice, her eyes unseeing. "I shall not want, he makes me lie down in green pastures—"

"A, be quiet. Shush."

"He leads me beside quiet waters, even though I walk through the darkest valley, I will fear no evil . . ."

Her voice drowned under Beya's booming song. Every corner of the hut had filled with a sickly sweet haze, as if the cigar was smoking itself in its terra-cotta dish; the air shimmered with heat and closeness, sickness and sound, the smell of hot blood like iron in my mouth. Beya dropped her face closer to FrannyA's open abdomen, calling and calling; all the while FrannyB's hands trembled, waiting. Time stopped, taffied out, stalled again.

Two tiny white dots poked through a thick intestine that descended her left side. In seconds the dots turned into knobby, wormlike protrusions with their own tiny sucking mouths, their tube-like bodies stretching, then wriggling out. They waved their blind heads in the smoky air, reaching toward the sound of Beya's voice. FrannyB cut into a rope of intestine just next to them; a fistful of parasites burst to the surface, waving and twisting. My own gut heaved—I couldn't look away—but FrannyB had long since stopped caring about what I did. Beya dropped her head still lower, her face just above FrannyA's open abdomen, her voice pulsing in punishing beats. Stars burst inside my head. The big missionary pulled out the horrid things and put them on a cloth; dozens of them. She cut the length of blackened intestine where the creatures had emerged, a foot or more of it, and lay that out on the cloth as well. Beya kept calling, hoarse now, sweat rolling down her face and neck, drenching her cotton shirt, her necklace of jaguar teeth clacking, eyes swimming to the back of her head; she was only sound, only calling, until she suddenly stopped, threw her head back and gasped for air. With infinite gentleness, FrannyB drew the two ends of intestine together and began to sew, joining them with tiny stitches as FrannyA hummed a tuneless tune.

It was dawn when I finally descended the hill to our hut. Soon after FrannyB had sewn her up, FrannyA had gotten hold of my hand and wouldn't let go, so I stayed with her while she slept. Bleary-eyed, I peered into my oven, despairing over how to get it lit. The night's drenching rain had seeped into the main compartment, soaking the coals. I pushed the sodden burnt wood out the back, sweeping the damp inner walls as dry as I could with a straw broom.

Out of the corner of my eye, Doña Antonia appeared on the hill. I watched her side-to-side, bowlegged gait as she made her way—I realized with a sigh—in my direction. She carried something with both hands. Smoke escaped from its center. All I could think was, *What fresh hell is this?* I wanted to run away, but she had already seen me, and there was, of course, nowhere to run.

"*Buenos días,*" she said, two words she'd never before uttered to me. Still, she didn't meet my eye.

"*Hola,*" I said, pushing myself to my feet.

"This is for you." With great ceremony, she placed a shallow stone bowl filled with red embers on the flat oven top.

"Thanks," I said. "My fire was out."

She finally looked at me, her expression set, determined, but I also caught a trace of fear. "You know what this is—the *jenecherú*? Do you understand what I'm giving you?"

"Fire?"

"The fire of the hearth. The *jenecherú*. It's something offered to a new family member," she said, kneeling, her face hidden now as she scraped out with my broom what wet wood remained from the belly of the oven. "It's sacred."

"I've lived here six months. What took you so long?"

"You speak to Beya. She does what you ask. I don't know why."

"She does what she wants."

She pushed herself to her feet with a groan and faced me. "You don't know what she's capable of. The men have never been gone this long. The women are afraid she's done something. Will you protect us from her?"

"What . . . would she do?" I touched my belly protectively, instinctively.

"You think she's so kind, always there to help. You weren't here years ago when she let babies die, babies we needed her powers to save, or when she cursed the river. For months, no one caught a fish."

We stared at each other for several moments until she broke away and poked at the fire; the coals sputtered the dry wood alive. "So don't forget, you're with us now, okay? You are Ayacheran. And you can never let this fire go out, understand? It lasts your whole life."

"Then you'll have to help me fix the cracks in the top of this thing. Otherwise"—I shrugged—"the sacred fire will go out the next time it rains."

She cocked her head at me as if to say, *Are you fucking with me?*, then bent down and peered at the slab of clay as she ran her rough brown hands along it, frowning at the cracks and chips. With a grunt, she lifted off the heavy top, tucked it under one arm, and started up the hill. "Come on," she called back. "I'll show you how to fix it."

Weeks later, my fire still burned, as if Doña Antonia's assignation of its sacredness were real and the coals would burn for Omar and me forever.

THIRTY

The next day, I sat with Doña Antonia, Paco, Anna, Claudia and her new baby sister, and a few of the other women at the shore, preparing a dozen small piranha for dinner. The amount of meat was tiny and a lot of work to get to, but it was a delicious fish. Alberto, a sweet, quiet twelve-year-old—too young to go hunting with the men and never happy about it—had taken his small dugout to the Tortoise Beach that morning and speared a big catfish along with the piranha. We'd completely run out of peccary, even smoked meat, so everyone was grateful. FrannyA remained in the clinic, sleeping, FrannyB at her side. She'd been in pain when she awoke, but Beya had left her a small dose of the toxin and that seemed to help and set her back to dozing.

Sultry waves of ever-hotter air swept in that afternoon; even the animals and insects stayed eerily quiet, and there was a feeling of anticipation in every breath we took. The children entertained themselves somberly at the bank, the boys playing a desultory game of soccer with a deflated rubber ball, the girls quietly building little huts for their rag dolls with clay and palm fronds. No one talked about the hunters, as if to talk about their absence would extend it even further. We were a village of women and children who watched; watched for the men to come sweeping around the bend, watched the banks of the river for jaguar tracks, watched the food supplies dwindle, the balance of everything off at a profound level.

Anna and Doña Antonia looked up from their work, eyes widening. Then I heard it, too. Metal on rusted metal; the grind of a motor close by. The stench of diesel. A dredge chugged around the bend in the river, the Mad-Max-on-the-Amazon contraption that was Fat Carlos's boat. It swung wide, carving a perfect V in the thick brown water of its wake. Seven men draped themselves at various aspects of the boat. Three hunched over the side, carbines held loosely in their arms. On the roof, two men leaned against a ragtag stovepipe, ratty baseball hats pulled low over their eyes. At the bow, Fat Carlos and Dutchie sat side by side in lawn chairs wired to the cabin, stogies in one hand, flasks in the other.

I'd barely rinsed the scales off my hands when the clanking rig rammed aground, motor running full speed into the red clay bank, the thick mud churning. I gathered up a few pieces of fish with a banana leaf and handed it to Paco. "Why don't you take this up, throw these on the fire for the Frannies. I bet they could use some lunch." Clutching the leaf, he reluctantly made his way up the hill.

The women swiftly gathered their own children, ordering them to drop their toys and stop their games, and herded them up the hill toward the longhouse.

The men grinned, clearly amused at the reaction their arrival had caused. The ones on the roof dropped down to the deck, eyeing the women as they lifted their skirts above their knees to move faster up the bank. Muscles pumped from working the logging camps, they shared a squinty-eyed malignance, like a pack of dogs goaded by cane alcohol. All except Fat Carlos and Dutchie leapt onto the damp sand. They swaggered up the hill toward the longhouse, their attitudes relaxed, celebratory, dangerous; their acrid sweat filling my nose as they passed by.

Doña Antonia pushed herself to her feet, hands trembling slightly as she pushed her braids back. Alberto stood his ground next to us, doing his best to push out his bony chest.

From his lawn-chair post, Carlos tipped the brim of his disintegrating sisal hat, its vestiges held tight to one of his chins by a rawhide strap. "Ladies. Gentlemen. How are you this fine afternoon?"

No one said a word.

"Pretty well, pretty well, thanks for asking," Fat Carlos said, leaning forward in his creaking chair. "But I have to tell you, since you're so curious, that today, well, *today* I woke up tired. You see, I spent the night dreaming of mahogany trees. Acres and acres of them. And in my dream, I laughed!—did you know you can laugh in a dream? I can. I was laughing because I was wandering around in pure cash. I could smell it. I could taste it. But the bummer was, I didn't know where the fuck I was, so I woke up just plain tuckered out, and frankly, a little frustrated."

He paused to puff on his cigar, popping out a few smoke rings in the still air. "Ever feel that way, like maybe you're just working, working, all the time working, never getting ahead? Just treading water to pay the bills?"

Doña Antonia shifted slightly, her hand gravitating toward the flensing knife she wore tucked in the folds of her skirt.

"Maybe it's just me, but I'm tired of working so hard just to keep these men fed, their *families* fed, tromping around in these godforsaken forests killing anything we can get our hands on, getting bitten and dirty and sick, when just the *simplest* little bit of information would set us all straight. We'd never have to hunt again, isn't that right, Dutch?"

The skinny man howled and stomped his foot and cried, "Nowheeeee!!! We'd be all set, right, Carlos? All done with this place."

His friend smiled. "We could just sit around and drink all day. Someplace posh, like New York or Paris. Dutchie here could get fat,

I could get even fatter. Buy us summa the finest poon-tang on God's green earth."

"Dis-ease *free*!"

"You're readin' me, Dutch." He stubbed out his cigar under a rubber boot. "*You are reading me.* Now, young miss Lily, why don't you tell me where your husband's hiding, so we can settle this?"

"All the men are hunting," Doña Antonia said. "There's nothing for you here."

"Been gone awhile, have they? Tough stuff. Maybe that's why you're cooking up all that trash fish, is that right?" He levered his girth off the sagging seat and climbed down the rusty ladder to the bank, canteen, sunglasses, bullet pouch, and hunting knife swinging and clanking from the loops on his belt. Dutchie followed, cinching his own belt tighter on his emaciated frame.

The big poacher peered in all directions, his bushy mustache twitching, then fired his gun into the trees. A family of vultures burst like demons into the sultry blue sky.

"Where is *Omar*!" he shouted to the shuddering forest. He whipped around to face us. "You know, I've known him since he was a boy. I'm not going to hurt him if I don't have to. I'm not like that."

"You can see the boats are gone," I said.

"Indeed they are." The men's boots clomped up the stairs of the longhouse. Doors banged open; rifle butts pounded on wood. The men leaned over the railing on the deck, shook their heads.

"Fine," he said petulantly, turning in a slow circle as he gazed up at the answerless sky. "*Fine.* Then we need that lame Tatinga river driver. For Shit's Sake. For Fuck's Sake. Whatever he's called. When's he coming?"

Our shoulders sagged.

"You just missed him," Doña Antonia said. "We won't see him for weeks now."

"I see. Well, that leaves that witch, I'm afraid. Now where does Beya keep herself?"

Doña Antonia glanced at me; I looked away, my mind buzzing.

He wiped his brow with a filthy rag, then pointed his gun first at young Alberto. "You know, I'm in no mood. So someone"—then at Doña Antonia—"*someone* is going to tell me." He swung the gun toward me. "In fact, someone's going to escort me there. Now."

He shot at the dirt at Alberto's feet. A crater bloomed in the bank. Like a spring, the young boy leapt in the air and tore up the hillside.

"Anybody?" he said. Seconds passed; nobody moved. "No? Then this won't end well." He trained his gun on Anna's mother halfway up the hill, who, mostly deaf, bent over her oven tending her vegetables, oblivious. The oven exploded in a cloud of red clay. One of the shards impaled her calf, she limped up the hill, screaming.

"I'll take you there," I said.

Carlos glared at me with red-rimmed eyes. "So the *gringa* and the shaman are besties, huh? I bet that's not going over very well here." Not waiting for a word from me, he whistled to his men. Ragged, shuffling limbs gone clumsy with booze, they made their way toward us.

His face gone sour, Dutchie turned with a huff and climbed up the ladder to the boat. He planted himself back down in his lawn chair, dropping his mirror shades down over his eyes.

Carlos took a slow turn toward him. "What's the matter, Dutch, forget your tampons?"

The blond man folded thin arms over his birdcage of a chest. "Fuck you. I don't play with no witches."

"Get down here."

"You got enough guys. You don't need me."

"We're a team. Get your fuckin' ass—"

"No way. *No way!*" He got up and paced the tiny bow of the boat. "I do everything. I cook. I clean. I handle the men when they get fucked-up. All the shit work. Since the *beginning* I been with you, Carlos, since *Panama*, man. Twenty years! Never mind all the times I saved your skin. Never mind you pay me the same as every other asshole, even if they been with you five minutes. All I've ever asked for is one thing. *No witches. No shamans.*"

The entire crew held its breath, waiting for the fallout. Carlos took stock of his gathered men, red eyed, raw skinned, waiting. "Get your wimpy white ass off the boat."

Dutchie looked near tears. His voice thickened. "It's like this, I don't know. What *am* I to you, man? Friend, business partner, both, neither, *what?*" He turned in a tense arc, hands on narrow hips. "Fuck, I could never be like you; you're this poet. The way you talk. People are like, drugged when they listen to you, they do whatever you say. Any crazy, mean, piece-of-shit thing you ask them to do, they don't think twice, they just do it—"

Fat Carlos shot the tip of Dutchie's left ear off. He dropped to his knees, clutching his head and howling, blood spurting through his fingers. Carlos holstered his gun and said, "My apologies for the domestic disturbance. Men! Get him cleaned up. We're going to see the witch."

Carlos, Dutchie, and their posse at my heels, I tried to shine to Beya as I walked past the huts, along the manioc fields, past the barn, all the time warning her, pleading with her to listen. There was no response.

The men paused at the entrance to the Anaconda Path, grumbling about entering the jungle or really just where I was taking them like: *Is this a setup?* Dutchie, bleeding through his bandages, leaned on his gun, rage and sorrow plain on his ravaged face. I stole those few seconds as they debated, closed my eyes and sent her a mental picture: Fat Carlos and Dutchie, guns in hand.

She was squatting on the large flat stone in the center of her homestead, bare feet splayed, calmly smoking a bamboo pipe. Behind her, water boiled vigorously in an iron pot over her fire. Carlos, Dutchie, and the men stumbled out from behind me into the clearing, a little at a loss, turning and squinting into the green-tinted air, sensing something they maybe shouldn't fuck with. A few whispered to each other in Portuguese; others spat, adjusted their weapons on their belts. One wandered off to take a piss.

"Wow," Carlos said. "Looks like they don't want much to do with you in the village, you living way out here."

"I live where I wish to live," she said coolly.

"Still, it must be lonely, living far away from your people and all."

She tapped out some ashes from her pipe. "What do you want?"

"Oh, I think you know. How many years we've been playing this game? A dozen? I need that grove. Now."

"This knowledge is sacred to the people of the forest. It cannot be shared."

Carlos unhooked his gun from his holster. "Fuck your sacred nonsense." He cocked the gun and pointed it at her head. "You, you crazy old bat, are going to take us to the grove. Now get up."

Beya pushed herself off the stone and rose to her full crooked height. She raised her face to him, the tattooed whiskers blacker and deeper in the rich afternoon light. She opened her mouth and let loose an unearthly cry of desolation and loneliness, like a creature calling for the last of its kind in a final bid for companionship.

"What the fuck are you doing?" Carlos said, stealing glances at the shimmering green and black of the forest. "Knock it off."

She staggered backward slightly with her efforts, but regained her balance fast.

"I told you," Dutchie muttered. "She's—"

"Shut up."

The man who was taking a piss hurriedly zipped up; otherwise no one moved.

She filled her lungs and unleashed the same heart-wrenching call; her head fell back as if to make room for the otherworldly sound.

Above us, an identical cry rang out; an answering call, followed by a rush of wind as the biggest eagle I'd ever seen barreled down through the canopy, claws open and hurtling down at the big poacher's face, its red-rimmed eyes enraged. Yelping, Carlos disappeared under an eight-foot wingspan of furious raptor, an explosion of black-and-white feathers obscuring his prone body. The men grappled for their weapons but didn't shoot.

A ripping sound, of tendon from bone. An agonized shriek under the powerful shoulders of the bird. With two or three powerful flaps of its massive wings, the harpy eagle lifted itself off the poacher, one of his blue eyes and part of his cheek in its talons. It thumped and heaved itself through the cleared circle skyward, stringy red and yellow pieces of flesh hanging down, headed—I imagined—straight toward its canopy-top nest, where its naked, screeching young demanded to be fed.

Beya and I were forgotten as the men circled the howling, sobbing Fat Carlos. They lifted and carried him away. By nighttime, their boat was gone. I thought, *Ayachero is safe, the grove is safe. I will never see these men again.*

How wrong I was.

THIRTY-ONE

– NOVEMBER –

The voices of the hunters woke me at dawn, Omar's among them. I threw aside my mosquito netting and sat up, listening for a while, letting myself cry with relief.

After nearly three weeks, Omar and the men had come home.

From the top of the stairs, I watched the entire population of the village pour from their huts and gather at the beach. Under a sky laden with clouds, the last two boats swung around the elbow of the river, jutting into the soft sand. The hunters and their helpers leapt from the boats, hurrying into their families' embrace.

A massive bull tapir weighed down the center of one of the boats; it looked to be two or even three hundred pounds. It was flanked by a couple of brocket deer: small, delicate-boned Bambis that to me seemed the strangest animal of all to call the jungle home: What defense did they have except perhaps speed? Trussed to a bamboo carrying pole by its giant ham hocks, the tapir took four men, including Omar, to lift onto shore and carry up the bank.

In no time, the bonfire blazed and the singing, drinking, and dancing had begun. There were no more batteries to play the radios, so a couple of the men brought out beat-up guitars and rapped on empty jerry cans for percussion as they gathered around the fire.

Step-by-step, I made my way to Omar; at eight months along, running was a thing of the past.

After unloading the enormous catch, Omar turned toward me. He looked thinner, exhausted, but all in one piece.

He put his arms around me and must have said something, but a hush of sound in my head blocked it all out.

Suddenly feverish and weak, I pushed him away, our baby in me kicking and turning, my swollen breasts aching with every step. I remember saying something about wanting to lie down for a few minutes in the longhouse. I staggered away, reaching for the smooth handrail, making it up three steps before a drunken sort of dizziness hit me. My grip weakened as my legs jellied at the knees; black curtains drew closed on both sides of my vision.

I woke to Paco's little face hovering above mine. With great concentration, he spooned a kind of gelatin out of a clay saucer and held it to my mouth. It was steamy hot and cinnamon smelling, so much like America and diners and Cinnabon I wanted to cry. I swallowed some. It was sweet and warm and so fucking delicious.

"What is this?"

"A dessert. From the feet of the cow. Pregnant women like it."

"The cow is dead?"

"Sí."

Framed by our hut's open door, Omar stood facing us. Evening light filtered in through the dark green pulsing rectangle. *How long had I been sleeping?*

"She got out," Omar said. "Something got to her in the field. We think a fer-de-lance. Everybody ran to help her but it was too late. The women are working on her now. We'll have to smoke the meat all night. I have to go help soon."

In this place, you never named something that you would one

day eat, but privately I called her Bella. It was true, giving her a name made her loss harder to bear. I pictured her sweet, dopey face, long lashes shading big brown eyes. As I pushed myself to a seated position, I noticed my dress had been lifted up to just above my knee, revealing an infected mosquito bite. But I knew then that it was something worse than that. The bite had craterized, widened, formed a crust around the edges. The itch was gone, replaced by a pulsing pain that reached deep into my flesh.

Omar pulled a stool close to me and sat by my side, his face stricken in a way I had never seen before. All the light gone from it, his lips a colorless line. Cavernous shadows dwelled under his eyes. He looked like an old man.

He gently touched the circle of redness that radiated out around the bite, the skin still purple from iodine. "How long have you had this one? This wasn't here when I left."

I pulled the cloth down to cover myself. "I don't know."

"Paco, leave us awhile, okay?"

Paco looked to me; I nodded in agreement with Omar. His little face drawn, he took his time gathering himself to leave.

"Listen to me, Lily. FrannyB was here. She looked at this."

"While I was *asleep*?"

"Do you have any more of these on your body anywhere?"

Of course I did. The gloomy walls of the hut closed in. Something rustled in the thatched roof.

"What difference does it make? I'm taking care of them with the iodine, like FrannyB told me to."

"Turn around and show me your back. I don't like the way the skin looks by your neck. Pull your dress down and let me see." His voice boomed; I felt his fierce strength above me, my complete helplessness.

He reached up toward the ties at the neck of my dress. I pushed his hand away. Realized: I and only I had gotten myself in this deep.

In the silence that followed his command, I began to acknowledge the strange, faint voice that had been telling me something was terribly wrong with my skin, and had been for a while. "I need to see you," he said more softly this time.

"I ran out of iodine," I said sheepishly.

"Why didn't you tell me?" he said.

"You've been gone for three weeks. How could I?"

"Take this dress off. I want to see."

With great effort, I pushed myself up to my elbows and dropped my head forward. It felt weighted, like a sack of marbles. Omar loosened the string tie at my neck and gently drew back the rough material from my shoulder, drawing my arm out of the sleeve. He let out a low whistle. I watched his face as his eyes grew wet.

"Liliana, *cariño*." *My darling*.

Fear at the possibility of being sick and shame about showing any weakness suffused me. Blowing the whistle about physical infirmity had never helped me before, so it hadn't occurred to me to do it then, even though in some deep, inchoate part of me I knew how bad it was, knew I had been putting my head in the sand. The stupid truth was that my whole life I was used to feeling crappy, undernourished, vaguely sick, but had prided myself on toughing it out. Dukes up, ready to fight, my soft humanity a fiction I could rewrite.

But this time it was different; all I had to do was look at his face. In his eyes, I saw that *I could end*. And for the first time this possibility meant something to someone.

THIRTY-TWO

I lay on my side as FrannyB examined my shoulders and the backs of my legs, the whisper of air on my wounds like small daggers. She pushed herself to her feet with a sigh. From my mattress on the low platform bed, I watched her pace the hut, the rickety plywood floor creaking under her heavy steps, her face tacky with sweat. Omar stood silent, leaning against the open door. Our little lamp, a tin container filled with kerosene, a strip of wool stuck in the top for a wick, gave only a spark of light, lending a ghostly gloom to the hut and dousing it with smoke. Outside hung the noxious green flesh and weight of the jungle. A steady rain hammered the thatched roof. Night and all its terrors.

"She has it, Omar." She folded her husky arms. "It's a textbook case."

"So we leave for San Solidad now," he said. "We have enough gas."

"You know that's five days if you're lucky. Could be six—more, with all this rain . . ." She didn't, wouldn't, look at me. Her voice dropped. "She doesn't have five days, Omar. Take a look at the back of her leg—"

"What the hell do I have, can someone please tell me?" My intention was to sound sarcastic, strong, but my voice came out breathy and weak.

FrannyB dragged one of our two stools closer to the bed and sat. "You have leishmaniasis. Tropical misery. You get it from a sandfly. They're tiny, smaller than a mosquito. They can get through this cheap netting. It's a skin disease, a bad one, a microscopic parasite that can also get in your organs. Judging by your fever and a few other telltale signs, it looks like it has."

I flashed on Angelina, the woman who'd walked naked into the jungle at night. In my mind I watched its monstrous green arms close around her tender flesh.

"I'm sorry, Lily. God loves you," the missionary said without conviction.

The air thickened and stilled with a new presence. Beya stood in the doorway, soaked through her dun-colored dress, her long gray braid heavy and wet over one shoulder. Steam rose from her body.

"Why are you here?" I asked.

"She came to my camp," Beya said, nodding to FrannyB. "She told me about you."

I closed my eyes, wishing everything and everyone away. "Why is everybody making such a big deal out of this?"

Omar pulled a stool next to our bed. "Let her look at you. She won't even touch you."

Beya took a step into the hut. Rainwater dripped off her derby hat, puddling on the floor.

"Look," I said. "I just need some sleep. Which I can't get with all of you poking at me all the time."

"You've been sleeping for two days," FrannyB said.

Beya came closer.

"Show her, Lily," Omar said. "We have no choice."

I turned away from everyone, staring into the black corners of the hut. In full teenager mode, I hissed, "Everyone needs to leave *right now*."

Pain bolted across my skull. This time, there were no words or whispers, only an image of myself, naked, gray-fleshed, huge-bellied, pocked with disease. Stiff and prone on the mattress, lifeless. Flies landed on my still-open eyes.

With a sharp cry, I shook my head and forced the image from my mind. I held myself, felt my belly, felt my baby shift under my skin, convinced myself I hadn't seen anything, until the image returned, clearer and sharper than before.

"Stop it, Beya," I whispered. "Please just stop."

The picture blurred, but remained, an afterimage.

Omar touched my back; his gentleness astounding to me. Why did it still bring tears to my eyes? I knew—my cells knew—that Omar was right. That if I wanted to live, I had to cooperate. I had to show Beya my devastated flesh. I drew in a deep breath, turned back around to the sputtering lamp and three hovering faces.

"Okay," I said. "But let me do it." Fingers quaking, I untied the string that cinched the neckline of my dress and rolled back the mud-colored fabric, turning my shoulder toward the light. Beya held the hissing lantern close to my flesh; its heat seemed to set my wound on fire.

"You need the sacred plant, Lily," she said. "Don't wait. You must go in person, otherwise they won't give it to you."

FrannyB gently covered me again. I searched her face, but it was unreadable. Beya and Omar stood at the doorway for several more minutes, speaking in low tones. Without a backward glance, Beya climbed down the steps in the rain. A minute later, FrannyB gathered herself to leave; I listened to her goodbye—low, dire, more warnings whispered urgently—before the squeak of her sneakers on the stairs as she left the hut.

Omar took both of my hands in his, his skin rough and dry. "Lily, listen to me, this is what we have to do. There's a plant that grows on the land where the Tatinga live. A day downriver, then a day's walk. It *only* grows there. We'll make a poultice from the leaves, put it on your skin. It'll take care of this, fast."

"What's wrong with San Solidad? That clinic—"

"There's no time."

"That's crazy," I said, as the words *there's no time* slammed me deep in my gut. "Listen, Ohms, I'm not going, okay?" I closed my eyes against the memory of the vision. "Why don't you go and bring it back for me?"

"You heard Beya. Splitfoot won't just give it to me. The Tatinga aren't like that. They need to understand who they're helping, and why. Besides, that would mean four days before I got back to you, maybe longer."

"Can't FrannyB get it from them?"

He shook his head in exasperation. "The tribes only tolerate the missionaries. They like the gifts, otherwise they think they're complete fools. We leave in the morning."

I pushed myself to my feet, in defiance of my weakness, fever, the stabbing pain of the lesions. "I'm staying here."

Rage contorted his face. "This isn't a game, Lily. You think you'll get better by doing nothing? You don't care about our baby?"

I eased myself onto a stool. "Why would the Tatinga give us the plant? Give *me* the plant?"

For the first time, I saw fear creep into his face, a tightening around his eyes, helplessness in the cast of his shoulders.

"So what are you *not* telling me now? What are you leaving out, Omar?"

"I'm telling you what you need to know."

"They might kill us, right? They might kill me . . ."

"We're going to get you this plant, *cariño*. You'll be cured, and I won't have to hunt for weeks, we've got so much meat. We'll leave this place soon. We can have our baby in the city if you like. We can stay there for a while before we decide what to do next. The men are better hunters now, and it looks like the jaguar's moved on. Even if it hasn't, we've done everything we can for this place. For God's Sake has abandoned us, but Panchito will be back soon, I know it. He's a good man. Even with his leg, he'd be an excellent river driver, if he can ease up on the booze. And Beya's frightened off Fat Carlos and his gang. I think Ayachero's going to be okay."

He looked close to tears. I reached out and touched the contour of his cheek. "You can't save everybody, Omar, you know."

"Maybe not. But I can save you and our child."

I nodded, but had no energy to speak after that. With great effort, my body slow, heavy, and awkward, I lay back down, closed my eyes, and watched the image of my dead self fade into tatters.

Dawn arrived full of fog and ghosts. Omar, his arm around my waist, half carried me down to one of the longboats, which he'd packed with all the supplies Ayachero could spare. It wasn't much. A small bag of farina, a few strips of dried meat, torn cloths for bandages, a half canister of gas to get us back upriver.

Anna stepped away from her fire where she was making manioc cakes, her new baby girl snug in my old backpack, little Claudia clinging to her skirts. "Take this," she said, pulling a black-and-red beaded bracelet off her own wrist. "It's Tatinga-style. It'll bring you good luck." Around her eyes lingered traces of the grief I thought had eased. With a jolt, I realized hers was the face of someone saying goodbye forever. We hugged and held each other for a few extra seconds before she quickly turned back to her morning duties.

A little brown streak tore down the hill. Paco jumped in the water and flipped into the boat like a fish, settling himself down as if this was the plan. He carried his slingshot and a small canvas bag I'd sewn for him to hold his few belongings; he stashed everything at his feet in the bottom of the boat.

"Hey, stowaway," Omar said sternly. "You're not going any-where." A couple of dogs skittered along the sand and jumped into the boat—ready for a hunt—he slapped them on their rangy flanks and they leapt out again.

"I speak Tatinga," Paco said.

"Out of the boat!" Omar pointed to the shore.

Little shoulders slumped, Paco slipped his slingshot across his back and reached for his bag. He dropped into the water off the lip of the boat, waded to shore and trudged along the bank, watching as Omar lifted and carried me to a thatch-roofed section of the canoe, under which he'd spread some rough blankets. I felt ridiculous, an invalid. I could have walked into the water and climbed into the canoe, but he insisted I keep my skin as dry as possible.

Paco splashed back in the water and handed me his slingshot, his most prized possession. I'll never forget the look on his face, of love, of desolation. I told him no, I didn't even know how to use it, but he pressed it into my hand anyway, before turning and running off, lost among the families cooking breakfast at their smoking ovens.

THIRTY-THREE

Clouds hung in a thick cottony mat over our heads. From where I lay: on my side, curled on top of the pile of thin woven blankets under the palm-frond roof, I watched Omar's lean brown legs as he stood at the prow, guiding us through the strong currents with a leaf-shaped paddle. The banks of the river were soft brown clay, pitted with holes the size of softballs where armored catfish lay their eggs. Rain fell steadily, beating at the roof and coloring the air green, as though we were at the bottom of the ocean. Big blue kingfishers dashed at the water's dimpled surface, emerging with wriggling fish. On a black shoal, an alabaster egret balanced on spindle legs. In waves from the river walls came the dense, half-rotted, half-sweet smell of flowers.

My baby was due in the next few weeks—that was FrannyB's best guess—but Anna thought my baby would come late because of the shape of my belly. Though I'd felt glimmers of excitement and anticipation for this new life, my sickness had become inextricable from my pregnancy; both meshed into mere helplessness. Still, I conjured mental images of myself alive, the baby alive, all of us alive.

Omar called down to me. "Are you watching where we're going?"

"No."

"Sit up and watch."

"I can't."

He lay down his paddle, crawled under the roof, and squatted next to me. "Are you hungry? Why are you crying?"

I didn't know I had been. "What do you want to name the baby?"

Rainwater dripped off his raven-black hair, ran down his handsome face. "We can talk about that later."

"Are you excited?"

"Of course I am, *cariño*." He stared at me a good, long time. "In fact, I've already started my assignment, my letter to the baby. But now, Lily, you need to sit up."

Something in his voice compelled me to push myself at least to my elbows, where I could watch both sides of the jungle slip past. Now the rain came down softly but steadily, as if the air had always been suffused with water that way.

"There are two sorts of rain," he said. "Men's rain and women's rain. Men's rain comes down fast and hard and it's over quick, like their anger, or their sadness. Women's rain falls all day, into the night, it just goes and goes, because women cry so much, for so long."

From the river rose the sad, beseeching limbs of submerged trees. Rain pocked the surface evenly, constantly. Definitely women's rain. "So that's why I'm sitting up? To look at rain?"

"You need to watch, Lily. Listen. Think. Look around. Up, down, everywhere. Do you know how many turns we've taken since we left? And which way?"

"No."

"We've taken two left turns. How much time has passed?"

"I wasn't really—"

"Three hours."

He took my hand and helped me stand in the canoe. I clutched the palm roof for balance, the taste of the rain electric on my tongue. With his paddle he pushed deep into the belly of the river as we swung around a bend into an oxbow lake, a vast area where the river had doubled back on itself. The water lost its urgency, spread out, stilled.

"Lily, listen. I know you don't feel well. I'm sorry. But you don't wake up alive in the jungle because you were smarter or trickier. You stay alive here because you paid attention."

THIRTY-FOUR

The night falls very fast, the last birds scolding the day. We sleep in the canoe, his body wrapped around mine, the velvet sky beating with stars, constellations doubling in the river. My eardrums vibrate with stuttering volleys and cries too deranged to sort out. *Bird? Mammal? Insect?* Unknowable. Rough cawing, angry barks, the stone-on-stone grind of cicadas. Millions of mist particles sparkle in the light of our torch lashed to the prow of the canoe. Bats swoop from their roosts, haunting the faint light left in the sky. Hawk moths bigger than my hand skim the water, hunting for insects and small fish.

All around us, in the darkness, caiman watch from the shore or the water, their eyes red orbs. Omar tells me that every animal's eye-shine in the night is different: cats' eyes—jaguars'—are bluish green when a light is shone on them. Fish eyes glow orange or silver, neon green for snakes, and they never blink. Spiders' eyes flash as they skitter across the water, tiny white orbs. Nestled in the branches above, three owl monkeys observe us with orange eye-shine; I can make out their round bodies, white-and-gray faces, all hugging one another, bushy tails intertwined, a family.

Omar tells me that in the jungle you need to be in a state of chronic watchfulness as well as readiness. Both are necessary to stay

alive. Every tribe has their own word for how the jungle can mes-
merize, or put you in a trance of watchfulness only, a dangerous
state. In Tatinga, the word is *umahtar*, pronounced *oo-mah-tahr*. It's
easy for the jungle to *umahtar* you into a state of watchfulness only,
forgetting readiness.

The moon's face looks down on us, dour, asks why we are there.
I stare at my hands: otherworldly white, wrinkled skin that never
seems to dry. My back aches with the weight of the baby. Omar
covers me the best he can with what mosquito netting we have, but
mosquitos land and bite anyway. All around us the river curls and
rumbles, wrapping itself around the boat, pulling, eager to wear
away the lianas that tether us to an overhanging branch. When full
dark hits, Omar leaves me and stands at the prow, watching for
snakes, listening for jaguars huffing at the bank. Because he sits in
readiness, I let myself doze, holding every detail of his graceful form
in my mind's eye.

THIRTY-FIVE

The next morning, Omar hid the boat, disappearing it completely along the bank under vegetation that he marked with a few subtly crossed branches. He stepped into dense forest with no hesitation. Turning back to me, he offered his outstretched hand, whatever anxieties he felt hidden behind a determined expression. Behind us, the splash of a fish left a soft scar on the water. My baby kicked up under my rib cage, more interested in living than I was at that point. Finally, I took Omar's hand and pushed myself through the pulsing, ticking green.

We walked for hours, stopping only to drink from plants or vines. Even though he made a few forays to search out my favorite fruit, a kind of apple called *annona*, by the time he was done cutting and peeling some sweet sections, I had no appetite, for that or for the dried tapir meat. I told him I craved peppermint, so he climbed a small tree that bent with his weight and broke off some leaves that tasted strongly of mint. Though dizzy with the stabbing pain in my skin, I hadn't let myself look at the lesions that morning: it would have given the microscopic demons more power. Instead, I chewed leaf after leaf, breathing peppermint air as I trailed just behind him, his lean back shining with sweat as he hacked through the vines, machete flashing in the wan light.

Early afternoon, after we crossed a stream by way of a massive downed tree, Omar stopped short and raised a hand for silence. He pointed at the ground; to my eyes only the usual snarl of vines, tangled roots, and leaf litter. The air shuddered with the call of parakeets.

He picked up a sapling that had been bent into an L shape and laid across the path. "They know we're here."

"It's just a—"

Again he silenced me. Why that branch looked special to him, among all the other bent branches, remains a mystery to me. I tried to read his face; I saw no fear, but knew how well he masked his own trepidation, knowing if I saw a shred of it, I would be too terrified to go on. We walked another couple of hours through claustrophobic tunnels of towering saw grass and hanging vines, through the constant twilight.

At the foot of a rubber tree, he turned and held his finger to his lips—even though I hadn't uttered a word for hours—held his other hand out to stop me, then pointed up. Just above his head, a tapir skull—two feet long, black with age, molars yellow—sat wedged in the crotch of a tree. A column of black ants trekked along its cranium, vanishing in the hollow of a gaping eye.

"What does it mean?" I whispered.

"It's a sign. It means go away."

"They're going to kill us, aren't they?"

"They would have done it by now."

He slapped a hand over my mouth just as a cry escaped my throat. My cheeks burned under his cool, dry fingers. Even now his face read blank to me; could it be he felt this insane plan might work? I had no such confidence. I blinked tears out of my eyes, dropped my head back in his arms, sent prayers to the impenetrable canopy as he slowly, carefully took his hand away. A leaf dripped its sweat onto my forehead.

"We have to go back, Omar, please, what good is it—"

"Come on." He disappeared into a thicket of tree ferns dozens of feet tall. I followed the hard whack of his machete as he slashed our way to a small clearing, where a stream burbled among the immense roots of a ficus tree. White, disc-like fungus, like plates, clutched at various intervals at the base and lower branches. On one of them something steamed with a corporal energy. A pile of entrails had been placed neatly in its center.

"Another sign?"

He motioned for me to be quiet. The shrieks of spider monkeys shattered the silence. I looked up. The trees hung with a terrible stillness.

"Where are the monkeys?" I whispered.

"Those aren't monkeys."

The calls grew louder, closer. Directly overhead, all around us. A shrill note of fear in them now. I turned in a circle, peering up, hugging my filthy burlap dress to my ravaged skin. Nothing but the canopy, unmoving.

"The Tatinga are mimicking the monkeys. They're hunting them. Making the calls of distressed infants. Come on, we can't stop here."

High-pitched chittering cries grew piercingly loud until dozens of monkeys exploded into view, swinging and leaping over our heads, slender branches bending and swaying, some snapping under their weight. Small fruits and nuts rained down. Screaming in panic as they searched for their imperiled infants, they vaulted from perch to perch above us, long muscular torsos stretched out in the air, faces distorted with terror. Just under their calls, a subtler sound, like puffs of air. A dozen two-foot-long blowgun darts shot up into the canopy; the monkeys screeched and soared in search of cover. One of them catapulted over us, acrobatic, its tail twice, three times as long as its body, an arrow impaled just at the center of its taut red chest; yet it kept flying, arms still reaching for a branch it would never grasp—

so graceful I thought it might outwit its own death—until gravity caught it and sent it crashing to the forest floor. The sounds of the monkeys echoed beyond us now, retreating.

A rustling just beyond where we stood. A presence. Omar clutched my arm with a death grip.

I gazed into the green puzzle before me. Patterns of colors: bright orange, yellow, black. I don't know how long I stared before I finally understood that I was looking at a human face.

THIRTY-SIX

Six men, none over five feet tall, melted into view all around us. Blowguns—held ramrod straight and perfectly still by their sides—towered a foot or more above each of their heads. Bright red tattooed lines zigzagged from mouths to earlobes; six-inch porcupine quills bristled on either side of their full lips; macaw-feather earrings dashed back from stretched earlobes. Six flat, wide, staring faces scanned us from head to toe, blue-black bowl-cut hair stark against the gleaming foliage behind them. They were naked except for braided fibers wrapped around their waist.

The first impression was of sinewy muscle tensed and ready, of violence only casually held back, perhaps by curiosity alone.

One of them stepped forward. A squat man with a powerful head and jaw, his calves bulging from the strain of the ligatures of palm fiber tied just under his knees. Twin quivers holding smaller blowgun darts crossed his chest. Over his shoulder, the slain spider monkey hung limp, its hands and feet already trussed. Another man—slightly taller than the rest—carried a giant tortoise on his back, held in place by a leather strap across his forehead, its prehistoric head and neck stretching down past his knees.

They gaped at us, at me especially, with an unguarded mix of fascination, lust, and revulsion. A wave of language rippled through the group.

Face lit by an eerie column of yellowish-green light that seeped through the canopy, the squat man took another step toward Omar, chest puffed out, tightly sprung. A bone curled through his septum; in his left earlobe he wore a 35mm film canister. Fierce brown eyes peered out from under a heavy brow. In the middle of his forehead was a depression as big as a small saucer, as if someone or something had bashed in his skull and he had lived.

Through the mesh of greenery, the tips of three more arrows emerged, pointing from various angles toward us. Three more men stepped out from the vegetation.

The hunter opened his mouth to speak to Omar; I tried not to gasp. Each of his teeth had been sharpened to a point; several were pitch-black, others a dark yellow. Out came a blur of language, highly articulated, completely incomprehensible to my ears. Omar answered slowly, repeating his own name a few times. The men visibly recoiled to hear their language coming from this non-Tatinga, his enormously pregnant *gringa* at his side. As he spoke, Omar made eye contact with each man, before at last turning back to their leader.

"*Pacchu*," the man said. The whites of his eyes shown as they widened in their background of black-and-red-stained skin.

"It means 'Possum Face,'" Omar said. "My Tatinga name." The men flashed each other angry looks, pointing at my belly, my hair. "Lily, this is MiddleEye, Splitfoot's son. I won't say his Tatinga name, understand?"

I nodded, not a drop of saliva in my mouth available to speak.

MiddleEye scowled, barked some sort of joke at the men; they laughed and took a step forward, shoulders relaxed, emboldened, many of them gesturing at me.

"They think you're a missionary. They're asking for gifts," Omar said, never taking his eyes off the men. Black blood dripped from the spider monkey onto a wide, waxy leaf beneath him.

The taller hunter with the tortoise pointed at Omar's machete and smirked, inspiring another escalating volley of Tatinga before Omar handed it over, along with his gun and another knife. They took turns running their fingers along the machete's blade, nodding appreciatively before turning to me.

The chirring of insects throbbed in my ears; my arms trembled at my sides. I could feel myself being chewed away from the inside. The eyes of the men bored through me.

"Do you have anything?" Omar said.

"My knife, that's all."

"Give it to me."

"But it's—"

"Give me the goddamned knife."

My hands shook so hard I almost couldn't free my switchblade from my belt. Never thought I'd feel nostalgia for a knife, but it was one of the few things I'd managed to hold on to, and by then I'd skinned and cleaned countless animals with it and never went anywhere without it. The last weapon between us, gone.

MiddleEye accepted the present from Omar, turned it over a few times, sneered, and handed it back to one of the men, who took it and tucked it in his liana belt. He took a step toward me; his rank breath steaming up at me, a smell of rancid fat emanating from him, pointy teeth glimmering obsidian in the weak light. He reached up seemingly to touch my hair; I bent my head slightly so he could do it and be done with it.

He touched it gently at first, then grabbed a handful and yanked hard, pulling out a few long scraggly red hairs and holding them up like a prize. Omar took a step forward but didn't stop him. Sweat pouring down his chest, he stood close, his eyes begging me to keep my wits about me. The men laughed, relaxing now as they threw strands of my hair up into the tea-colored light, warming to the afternoon's entertainment. Smirking, MiddleEye put his hand flat on my belly and said something I sensed wasn't a compliment. Omar stiffened, took another step, almost between us now, but the hunter grinned with his row of cat teeth and moved his hand, slowly, tauntingly, up toward my breast. Omar smacked his hand away. A moment later; a solid thud. An arrow pierced the top of Omar's foot, pinning him to the ground, the shaft humming in the dim light.

He howled, dropping to the earth in a crouch just as the hunter who'd shot him dropped noiselessly from the trees above us, landing with another arrow already drawn and trained at Omar's heart.

I knelt down beside him, my face inches from his. In his, agony, but also a command: *Do not fall apart. Keep your cool.*

Omar snapped the arrow close to the top of his foot and tossed away the shaft. Lifting his foot from the ground, he reached under it and pulled out the arrow from the other side, then threw it at the men's feet. Something about this seemed to change the power dynamic among the men. A smaller hunter with close-set eyes and a shaved head began to argue with MiddleEye, jabbing his finger in the air at me, then Omar, then me again. MiddleEye bickered back at him, but it seemed like a draw, and in moments they turned, vanishing in an ocean of waving ferns.

Limping, Omar leapt after them. I froze in place, immobile with fear until the tribesman who had shot him through the foot screamed in my ear and I broke into a stumbling run, the hunter on my heels.

THIRTY-SEVEN

Zigzagging behind the hunters, Omar left bloody tracks on a path less than six inches wide. The Tatinga walked in silence, dodging evil pools and stepping over fallen logs swiftly and without pause. Every now and then I caught a glimpse of the spider monkey's dangling arms bouncing against a slender back, or a warrior's wide leathery foot padding along, their shoulders and arms just brushing the narrow confines of a path only they knew. Their brown legs were thin but sinewy, their chests concave, shoulder blades wide and sharp, flashing in the many-hued shade. Not a sign of fatigue even from those carrying thirty-, forty-pound animals on their backs. Hesitant light sifted through the understory, sizzling the moisture on the sweating plants.

Pain glowed brightly from deep inside my blighted skin; the suffocating heat of the afternoon intensified. My vision blurred with exhaustion. I wasn't walking, I was falling forward with each step. We passed a tripped snare, a lethal contraption of fire-hardened bamboo spears balanced under a rock. The hunters paused to free a trapped howler monkey, its neck broken, before tossing the animal across their backs and pushing on.

Glimmers of light poked through the wall of trees in front of us. A clearing. As we approached, I hallucinated an ocean beach opening up before us, choppy blue waves full of sailboats, happy families swimming and picnicking on the sand.

The jungle expelled us onto the cleared area. Instead of dozens of huts and a longhouse, here, a moat of hard mud surrounded one fifty-foot oval roundhouse—I saw no other structures. Palm thatch sun-bleached to a silver gray stretched from the ground all the way to a thirty-foot peak. Full sunlight drenched us before we passed through a low entryway into the huge open plaza in the middle of the structure, the roof cut away from its perimeter to let in the sky. The clearing was littered with small fires, palm-leaf baskets, and a couple of old dugout canoes used as troughs. Young children, naked except for adornments like the red-and-black beaded bracelet Anna had given me, ran through the center, young boys with child-sized versions of their fathers' bows and arrows or blowguns taking aim at small lizards. Odors of grilling meat, burning cecropia wood, the dense smell of humans in close proximity overwhelmed me. Dogs yelped, pet macaws screeched, a baby sloth wrapped itself around a young girl who wore it like a shawl as she dropped still-moving larva from a palm leaf into her mouth.

The hunters dropped their game to the dusty earth; monkeys, the tortoise, a bagful of birds blow-gunned through the eyes. Two pre-pubescent girls grabbed the howler monkey, which still had life in it and started to claw at them. Without a second's hesitation—as the smaller girl stood by with a thorn-studded club—the taller of the girls snatched it by its snare-tied legs and swung it hard against a pole that supported the roundhouse until its limbs hung loose. In no time the creature lay facedown over a sizzling grate. So much death, but just as in Ayachero, no one blinked an eye.

As word of our arrival spread, tides of people spilled out from every part of the roundhouse, even from the roof. Small, powerfully built bodies sprinted in our direction before stopping just yards from us, as if this was an agreed-upon distance. Everyone wore the jaguar whiskers: long quills were embedded in the solemn faces of the adults; on children, short palm shoots. Even babies were painted with dark blue lines from their mouths to their ears, exactly like Beya. I wondered if she'd removed her quills in an attempt to conform to Ayacheran life.

Naked except for the occasional red breechcloth and countless strands of black, brown, and red beads around their necks, wrists, and ankles, the women wore their hair long with straight-cut bangs. Cooking pots hung suspended from poles around small fires; other trinkets: small mirrors, flashlights, combs, sunglasses—gifts from the Frannies, I assumed—had been thrown in careless piles in the gloom of the roundhouse.

Everyone began talking at once. MiddleEye, clearly unhinged— even the Tatinga cut him a wide berth—strutted back and forth, jabbering and gesturing back at us, fury animating his movements. At intervals, he took off and swaggered around the entire perimeter, calling to those who remained in the shadows. Most of the men smiled at his ranting, which slightly lessened their threatening look; only on the very young children did the cat quills look innocent.

"He's bragging about how he found us," Omar said under his breath. "Telling people I fought and lost. He's never been right in the head."

MiddleEye, hearing Omar consult with me, whipped his head around and glared at us. Roaring, he charged full speed at Omar, stopping with his face an inch from his, white froth rimming his mouth. The anger was real, but also certainly for show; still, my heart beat out of my chest. Omar stayed immobile, expressionless, my hand nearly crushed in his.

Breaking the face-off, a chubby middle-aged woman snatched a pair of aviator sunglasses from a pile of gifts, jammed them on her face and ran up to me, long breasts swinging, hair flying back in twisted ropes dyed dark purple and deep red. In the reflective lenses my filthy, pale face twisted in fear as the woman—chattering away—palpated my breasts as if she were assessing fruit at the market. Everyone seemed amused. Omar did nothing.

Long seconds passed until I couldn't take it anymore. My arm lifted up to smack her away, but Omar caught it and forced it down. "Let her," he hissed.

"What is she asking me?"

"If you have milk."

Laughing uproariously, she pressed her palms down hard all over my enormous belly, breaking her merriment only to bust out into a staccato burst of words. Finally she walked away, smiling and clapping her hands.

"What did she say?" I whispered.

"She said it's a boy."

Only later did I learn that if she had thought my child was a girl, chances were they would have gotten it out of me and kept it, since the tribe had too many boys and men, and not enough girls to keep their numbers steady.

A wide-eyed young woman, black lines staining her face in an intricate mazelike design, hands dyed deep blue and just showing her own pregnancy, handed me a calabash of water with a shy smile. Freshly cut cicatrizations, tiny ritual scars, oozed red on either side of her navel. I took a long drink, the light glowing amber through the skin of the womb-shaped gourd. Behind my closed eyes, my baby boy floated, waiting. I called to him for strength, told him I wasn't going to fuck this up, that we were going to live. He nodded with his closed, swollen eyes, his Mona Lisa smile, amniotic. It was the first time I can remember feeling something like love for him, a budding devotion.

The young girl took my hand and pulled. We followed her. MiddleEye stalked darkly behind us along with several of the other hunters. Omar asked the young girl something; she nodded solemnly. We entered the welcome shade of the roundhouse. Hammocks, drying vines, and tobacco leaves hung from the rafters. Woven baskets brimmed with grinning monkey heads, turtle eggs, water gourds, green bananas, baked white bones, and explosions of brilliant bird feathers.

From behind a bamboo screen, a high-pitched screeching, metal on metal. Seated in a wheelchair rusted to a crusty flaking orange, a man wheeled himself out from his sanctuary. He wore a headdress of black-and-white harpy eagle feathers, the bodies of multicolored macaws sewn by their beaks between the larger feathers. An old Timex watch with no hands hung loosely on his wrist, the metal band stretched out. His shoulders and midsection were wiry and strong, rippling with muscle, but his legs were atrophied, thin as a girl's. His wide, flat feet—one of them split halfway up the middle— were planted firmly on the footrests. Along with half a dozen quills, scraggly silver hair sprouted from his face. Large hands—nails dark and chipped—came to rest on his lap where a bone needle, ball of palm-fiber thread, perforated nuts, and hawk feathers lay, a project we had interrupted with our visit. He studied us with deep-set, weary eyes.

Swollen with his news, MiddleEye rushed toward his father and barked out the story again, brandishing his knife, pointing at Omar, at me, at the forest beyond the walls of the roundhouse.

Omar approached the man in the wheelchair, dropping his eyes as MiddleEye rattled on in Tatinga. Color drained from his face, from pain or fear or shame or some combination, I couldn't be sure, I only knew his knack for hiding emotion seemed to be failing him. Finally, MiddleEye wrapped up, struck a wide stance, and folded his arms.

"Keep your eyes on the ground, Lily," Omar said.

In low tones, Omar spoke in Spanish to the man in the wheelchair, who responded in kind. "Splitfoot, I am here with my wife, Lily."

His rheumy eyes rested first on Omar, then me. Fresh sweat beaded out all over my body.

The old man's Spanish came out slow and stilted, as if he hadn't spoken it in a while. "My sister is dead?"

"Beya lives."

"Your father? My old friend?"

Omar said, "He died in Cochabamba."

"He was a good hunter. But a greedy man. Selfish. Your brothers?"

"Panchito is well. Franz and Anna still mourn Benicio."

He nodded. "We know this jaguar. We hear her at night, but she's smart, she knows where the traps are, no matter how many times we move them. We think she's the spirit of our ancestors, angry at us for how far we have fallen from the people we used to be."

"What happened to you?" Omar gestured at the wheelchair.

Splitfoot turned away to gaze out at the children playing in the sunshine. "A few years ago, I fell from a tree while gathering honey. Perhaps it was Beya who pushed me, or perhaps the spirits of the bees took their vengeance." He tossed up his hands. "Either way, now I am half a man."

"I remember you as a great hunter."

He shifted in his chair, opened his mouth in a grin, but his eyes stayed hard. Ebony teeth, shaved to points, gleamed in the dim light. "You visit to tell me your childhood memories?"

"We need your help." Omar touched the small of my back. "Turn around," he said to me. "Pull your dress down in the back. Show him your shoulder. Show him your skin."

I shuffled in a slow arc to face a scattering of low-slung hammocks filled with men resting or women breast-feeding their babies, all eyes on us. I focused on the gray earth, my feet in their muddy tapir sandals. Hands shaking, I reached back and loosened the tie at my neck. Fabric sticking here and there to the festering skin, the strap finally dropped from my arm and shoulder, revealing my back to the men in a whoosh of searing air. Clutching the front of my dress tight to my chest, I took short bites of air through my mouth in an effort to not smell myself; to not think about the fact that I was rotting from the inside.

THIRTY-EIGHT

"My wife is dying," Omar said. "The plant that can cure her is on your land. We need your help."

Splitfoot jettisoned a stream of brown tobacco juice through his sharpened teeth onto the ground inches from Omar's bloody foot. "There is no plant for her."

Pain snapped across my belly. Another "false contraction," at least that's what FrannyB had called them a few days ago. I fell forward onto my knees, shuddering to think what the real ones felt like. Brown limbs moved in my peripheral vision; I inhaled the grassy, acrid smell of crowding bodies as the Tatinga stood nearby, curious, close. *Will the red-haired* gringa *give birth here, now, in front of us?* Mouth dry as sand, I pushed myself to my feet, whispering to Omar, "I need to walk, or I'm going to faint."

"Okay," he said, eyeing Splitfoot. "Walk around the oven here. I'll explain to him what you're doing."

Clutching my belly, I stumbled forward, walking in slow circles around the low grate, on which spat and sizzled a set of monkey arms. Omar's and Splitfoot's voices rose and fell, a blend of Tatinga and Spanish. I stroked my belly, spoke in soft tones to the child who slept under the harsh fabric of my dress, my stretched skin; whispered to him the story of Wilbur the pig and Charlotte, the brave spider who stood up for him; he was going to be courageous like that one day, too.

Screaming in Tatinga, MiddleEye jumped in front of me, jaw thrust out, porcupine quills twitching. I halted midstride and sucked in a lungful of air, tried to put my heart back in my body. Rivulets of sweat ran down his face, black eyes swam in yellow pools.

"Lily, stop!" Omar hissed.

Slowly, I turned toward him.

"He thinks you're putting a hex on the village."

MiddleEye shouted at me again; my head whipped back to face him. Spittle foamed in the corners of his mouth, dragon teeth clicked. With exaggerated goose steps he marched the opposite way that I had walked around the fire, calling out what sounded like numbers . . . had he been counting how many laps I'd taken around the oven? Nine times he circled it; each time he came to face me, glowering, rattling his chonta knife, the long muscle of his torso tightening like a chord. Every third word was "Beya." I felt a hand take mine; the young woman who had given me the calabash of water chattered in Tatinga as she led me to an empty hammock. I melted into it.

Night had fallen, the blackest I'd ever seen. Around me, vague shapes weighted down hammocks, while several men leaned against the poles, smoking and gazing out at the night.

Omar rushed to my side. "Listen, Lily. Splitfoot said MiddleEye is going to ask the spirits of the plants if you're worthy of being cured. That's the way he put it."

"But MiddleEye's not a shaman."

"Splitfoot refuses to do it. He says his son can ask just as well as he can."

"He's out of his mind. He won't—"

"Come on, they're making a meal for us. We need to be there."

"I don't want any—"

"Let's *go*, Lily."

I tried to move. Shock waves of agony rippled deep in the mar-row of my shoulder, the backs of my legs. I could barely unwrap my body from the clutches of the hammock, heavy against the knotted palm twine.

He reached under the hammock and lifted me until I could stand; half carried me outside and sat me down at a long, rough table, just a pitted slab of wood laid across two stumps, where men and women sat eating bowls of some kind of soup. A woman with a baby at her breast handed me a deep clay bowl filled to the brim with steaming liquid. A monkey arm was sticking out of it, resting against the edge. Its little hand hung limply down from the wrist, fully articulated, creased palms, fingernails, everything. It looked like a child's hand.

"Omar, I can't eat this," I said softly.

The villagers watched, solemn, cheeks bulging, chewing their food with great energy. On wide clay plates, fish pounded into a gray paste and spread on mashed, fried manioc was folded into a kind of pan-cake. Youngsters leaned over and tore off pieces of it, cramming it into their mouths, while older women sat with their own share, flac-cid breasts pointing straight down, jaws pumping. Bowls of the soup were being passed around as well; only Splitfoot also had a monkey paw. He picked it up and chewed it with his mouth open, obviously relishing its crunch. He never took his eyes off me.

Omar leaned into me and whispered, "They gave you what they consider the best part. Eat it."

The flames of the cooking fire danced on the circle of warm flesh. Masato was passed around in rough bowls; at the time I only knew the smell—pickles, cloves—turned my stomach. Later I learned the drink was made by women chewing yucca and spitting it out into a trough, where it fermented. Everyone drank it, even the children; my portion sat festering and popping next to my monkey soup. Omar drank his, wiping the stringy remains from his mouth; his bowl was quickly refilled, which for some reason gave me hope—*was this all for us?*—until I realized this meal was in celebration of the fact that their hunters had returned alive, and with game, just as we celebrated when the same thing happened in Ayachero. We were a diversion, but nothing to celebrate, nothing compared to food.

MiddleEye finished his meal and went to sit opposite another hunter by the fire. Cross-legged, he picked up a three-foot section of bamboo and stuffed it with something from a pouch before settling the tube in his mouth. Just as the other man lifted the pipe's opposite end and rested it against his nostril, MiddleEye took a breath and blew hard. The man snorted and fell back with a groan, which seemed theatrical but perhaps wasn't; recovered, he packed the pipe with powder, and did MiddleEye the same favor. Mouth open and panting noisily, MiddleEye got to his feet and began to dance and spin, shooting looks at me with eyes like dark, empty tunnels.

Half a dozen men got to their feet. They snaked around the fire in a halting dance, taking two steps forward, one jump back; three steps forward, two jumps back. Some wore breechcloths, some belts made from the skins of small spotted cats—ocelot or margay. Countless seed necklaces clattered together at their necks and chests, intertwined with hand mirrors and nail files and other small gifts from the Frannies. Some wore fantastic harpy eagle headdresses over four feet high. Young boys pounded drums covered with the skins of giant leopard frogs. I felt caught in prehistory, before speech or time.

I turned to Splitfoot and asked in Spanish, "Why don't you ask spirits of the plants?"

His eyes burned into me, at the monkey's hand I couldn't bring myself to touch. "Because they will not answer me."

He put down his bowl of masato and continued. "There was a time when the plants and animals of the forest were at my command and did my bidding. My potions cured my people. My enemies grew sick and died from my word alone. At night, I made love to the spirit of the river, who waited for me with open arms like a woman starved. But when the Frannies gave me this wheelchair in exchange for my promise to throw my healing stone into the river, my powers left me completely. They said the stone was blasphemy. The spirits of the plants and animals stopped speaking to me. I have never been so lonely. My family is silent, my family shuns me. I hate myself for this bargain I made."

For some reason, his story made me remember how, when I was a kid, I'd made friends with kids I didn't even like, knowing they always had food on their dinner tables, which is when I would conveniently appear. It didn't matter what they dished up. I ate it. I felt Splitfoot's sad, intense gaze on me and on the bowl of soup, as if perhaps he would have enjoyed the opportunity for seconds.

I took a sip of masato before picking up the monkey arm by its tiny wrist. Turning the fingers away from me, I raised it to my mouth.

THIRTY-NINE

MiddleEye spun like a top, around and around us as we ate, eyes rolling in the back of his head, sweat flying and staining the dusty earth. He pounded his chest, gurgling out bizarre groans and whimpers. Dropping to the ground, he rolled in the dirt, quivering as if electrified, before jumping up to resume his furious dance.

He grabbed me by the wrists and yanked me from the table. I stood, swaying, as he ran in circles around me, shaking his head, eyes jangling. I sought out Omar; his face said, *Stay calm*. MiddleEye fell to his knees and pounded the ground near my ankles, where he crawled, raving, possessed. Once again on his feet, he jumped from side to side as if on hot coals as he made his way to Splitfoot. Pointing at me, he whispered in the chief's ear, then sprinted from him, drunk with his own madness.

Splitfoot turned to Omar. "The spirit of the plant has spoken. The woman is not worth saving."

Omar got to his feet and towered over the old shaman, a picture of youth and strength next to the shriveled man in the chair. "MiddleEye is no medicine man. The plants have never spoken to him. You know this," he hissed.

The shaman shrugged, drank his masato, and rubbed his small, tight belly before continuing his meal.

My skin crawled with sickness and fever. Omar stood closer to the old man, put a hand on the desiccated leather armrest of his chair. They locked eyes.

"What do you want from me?" Splitfoot gestured at Omar with the remains of his monkey paw before tossing the twisted thing into the flames, where it popped and sizzled to nothingness. "The plants have spoken."

MiddleEye whooped his encouragement, spinning around Omar and clacking his teeth like a Halloween skull. The shaman watched from his rusted throne with a sort of rapture like, *He may be crazy, but he's my only son.*

"You owe this to me," Omar sputtered. "This small thing."

The chieftain smiled; a hundred lines gathered at his mouth and eyes. "Why?" His hunters, sensing tension, took their places around him.

"We were like family once."

"She is *one white woman*. She means nothing to me."

Omar reached out to strike him. Lightning fast, the hunters grabbed his arms and smacked him to the ground. He fell down on all fours, breathing hard.

Splitfoot screeched his wheelchair toward him and dropped his head close to Omar's. "Beya does not answer when I shine to her. This is an unforgiveable insult." He glanced around, as if to see who was listening, some element of his pride on the line. "She was our most powerful shaman, and she chooses to stay in Ayachero. This has weakened us. We have not recovered."

"She wants to come back."

Splitfoot lifted his chin. "My sister can speak for herself. I hear only the wind when I call to her."

"She will come—"

"Your father settled Ayachero," he hissed. "Too many people came. We were forced deeper into the jungle, farther and farther from game.

Now poachers—*white poachers*—come looking for mahogany, now come roads, planes. The spirits leave when the land is cleared. The trees are crying, just as we cry. Can you hear them anymore? You used to."

Omar pushed himself to his feet, the warriors eyeing his every move. "When I was a boy, we walked together. I helped you gather the sacred plants. Do you remember, Splitfoot?"

The chief waved him away with a smirk. "That was before you became a white man, as far as I can tell. Listen to me: we can feel the change coming. If we don't move soon, from this camp, we'll all die here. And there will never be any rest. We need to keep moving, until we have fallen off the edge of the earth."

"I'm sorry."

"You're sorry—"

"My wife has done nothing wrong."

"You ask me to save this white woman?" Splitfoot said with an exasperated sigh. "Why? How will she help us?"

"She will—"

"I have suffered, Omar. The Tatinga have suffered. Our sister tribes have all suffered. How will you suffer for me, Omar?"

Omar dropped his head in what I read as shame; perhaps it was only respect.

"Answer me!" he roared. "How will you suffer for me? What will you give me?"

Omar gestured at me. "Here is my suffering, in the body of my wife."

Splitfoot's chair squealed as he whipped around toward me, glowering with rage. "How have *you* suffered?"

"I—"

"Don't show me the wounds on your body. I am not interested. Show me your dead babies, your family starving because there is no game. Show me your empty forests, your poisoned rivers. Your dead spirit."

It hit me then, even lost as I was in the cage of my own agony, that I didn't have a corner on suffering or despair. Here, now, it was time to justify my existence with some sort of rationale that had nothing to do with my own misery.

"*Who are you?*" Splitfoot spat out. "Why should I let you live? Tell me."

"In my country," I said, "I am a shaman."

Splitfoot snorted his derision. He wrenched his wheelchair around and began to screech his way back into the shadowy rooms, ropey arms pumping. A night bird called mournfully as it soared across the vast black sky.

I stumbled toward him, trying to cancel out the noise around me. Just before he vanished into his lair, I called out to him in my head, "IN MY COUNTRY, I AM A SHAMAN."

He turned, his expression layered in fear, curiosity, and wonder. He said, "Who do you hunt with at night?"

I dropped my head in my hands, conjuring the whispering diamond scales and hot breath of the female anaconda that had visited me in my dreams while Omar was hunting, the one seeking revenge for his killing its mate. "MY SPIRIT HUNTS WITH THE ANACONDA."

Slowly, Splitfoot turned his wheelchair toward me. "I have seen you in my dreams," he said. "I have seen you by the Black Lake."

"If you help me," I said, "if you let me live, I will help the Tatinga. I promise you."

He glared at me without expression. After a full minute, he gave me the slightest of nods before wheeling himself out of sight into the gloom of the roundhouse.

FORTY

They didn't wait until morning, Omar made sure of it, his haste heightening my fear. The women who had at first run from me because they believed—according to Omar—the tale that white-skinned people strip the flesh of Indians to make fuel to fly to the moon, spread out into the night jungle with torches and gathered the plant, armfuls of an unremarkable-looking pale-green fern. They boiled down a dozen bushels into a mush, mixing it with animal fat to make a paste. While Omar slept in a nearby hammock, three Tatinga women led me to a firelit area in the roundhouse made private by two screens of split bamboo.

Chattering softly, they helped me peel off my dress in the smoke-filled room. It dropped to the hard dirt at my feet, a little pile of unthinkably filthy burlap. In their eyes, I saw just how bad I looked, and as they spoke, I hallucinated that I understood every word. There was kindness and maybe a little fear in their faces, voices, hands. They helped me get down to my knees and lie down on my side on a mat of woven palm fibers. The sound of their necklaces of heavy beads and small shells clacking together calmed me, their whiskered faces hovering over mine like curious human cats. One kept touching my hair, but I'd stopped caring about that. Buzzing all around me, they placed flat, wide clay basins at my shoulders and hips, layering the warm poultice thickly on my skin. Wherever it touched my lesions, the pain was indescribable. A rich green smell, like basil mixed with grassy dung, filled my lungs and brain.

In a lilting call-and-response pattern, the women sang and chanted as they worked; the rhythm soothing, a narcotic. Every now and then, one of their children would run in, their eyes wide with an instinctual fear of sickness. The women would turn them, nudging them toward the main living area where another adult would scoop them up and take them away, cooing.

As the poultice dried, it hardened like clay. The women pressed down gently, snapping off sections, then brushing off the remainder with their hands. Piles of green flakes surrounded me. The second they were done with one round, they applied another wet layer, each time singing and chanting over that area, blowing smoke at me from a banana-leaf cigar. Each time a fresh layer was ladled over me, tiny daggers stabbed deeper, battling their cellular war. I shut my eyes picturing this, trying to rally my own weakened defenses. I don't remember making a sound.

In a few days, I was able to get up and walk around a little bit; the pregnant teenager who was so fond of my hair—the one who brought me the calabash of water that first day—constantly at my side. Bright crimson stained her face from ear to ear; an iridescent beetle-wing bracelet shone on her small wrist. Her name sounded like Pulia; Omar said it meant "Sprouting Leaf."

She brought me water to bathe in, took my dress away, washed and boiled it, then brought it back decorated with a circle of kapok fluff the women had sewn in around the neckline; they believed the spirits of the tree would help protect me.

Omar and Splitfoot talked late into the evenings, cooking fires popping and smoking all around them. Among the gentle chatter of the women as they peeled manioc and nursed babies, the soft thud of their bare feet as they swept the hard dirt floors, men smoking and repairing weapons, I felt—for those few days—immersed in a cocoon of humanity I never felt in Ayachero, or really anywhere I had ever been before or since. I felt like an infant; in fact, the part of me that remained infantile took note, soaked it all in, let myself be healed in all sorts of ways. Mostly I lay on my mat, my fever spiking then easing with each application of the poultice, the women tirelessly applying it to the places on my body I couldn't reach, or making sure the dry patches were brushed off and fresh salve applied. I was grateful for the agony each dosing brought; I could feel the battle tilting my way. *It's going to be okay*, I told my baby, *you're going to be welcomed into the world, you're going to be loved.*

I listened to the creak of the hammocks as the men slept in shifts; for safety reasons, at no time was the entire village asleep. Sprouting Leaf was always at my side when I woke, either sleeping next to me or tending to my lesions. Omar taught me a few words of Tatinga, translating Sprouting Leaf's endless stream of chatter. She said that the plants wouldn't work unless I had a good heart; since she could see I was healing, the women were happy to help. Mostly she talked about wanting to be a shaman, but that she had a lot of training to do and was looking for a teacher. She told us that Beya had eased a terrible fever her father had suffered, with a tincture made from a certain kind of bark, and asked us countless questions we couldn't answer about whether she might return.

On the evening before we left, Sprouting Leaf watched me admire the young boys practicing their blowguns. They could nail a butterfly jig-jagging in the air or a lizard zipping across the dirt. With a few words in Tatinga, I commented on their uncanny aim. She ran off to her family's area of the roundhouse and returned with a foot-long child-sized blowgun, a bamboo container filled with five palm spikes—darts—and a much smaller section of bamboo sealed with rubber and filled with curare, the poison to dip the darts in. Smiling, Omar translated that she was afraid I would stab myself with the darts, so that's why she kept the toxin separate.

"She wants to make a trade," he said. "She says the blowgun is for our little boy, if she can have some of your hair."

"What do you think?"

"Just say yes," he said. "Always say yes here."

Drink the masato. Eat the monkey arm. Let the women coat you in green mud. Give Sprouting Leaf a lock of your hair; yes, yes, yes.

That evening, "some" of my hair quickly turned into all of my hair when the women sat me by the fire. Singing the whole time, they shaved my head with a set of piranha jaws. Sprouting Leaf did her work with such care I barely felt it, not once nicking my scalp; in half an hour I was a bald, green-fleshed, hugely pregnant *gringa*. Afterward, she took me aside and showed me how to use the blowgun, demonstrating how to sight my target through a V created by two paca teeth set inside the pipe, and how to lay each dart along a nest of kapok fluff to steady it. She gestured for me to practice, the hollow eyes of a monkey skull grinning from the rafters my target.

Omar and I left at dawn on the sixth day. Mist boiled over the roundhouse, the desolate cries of the piha bird announcing the new morning. Wearing a liana belt and several bracelets shot through with the shining copper of my own hair, Sprouting Leaf stood under the palm eave of the main entrance to the roundhouse. Her goodbye was just a solemn nod, but I had to remind myself that hugging and smiling and expressing big emotions wasn't something that happened in this place. I slung a string bag over my shoulder, another gift she had made for me out of woven chambira fronds; she swore it was strong enough to hold a hundred-pound peccary. Now it contained the blowgun, darts, and curare. I touched the bag and nodded back at her before turning away from the roundhouse and the people who had saved my life, following Omar and a few Tatinga hunters into the green morass.

MiddleEye blasted along the jungle path, two more hunters behind him, all of them carrying leather bags on their backs filled with the heavy plaster. I carried a much lighter bag packed full of the leaves, as did Omar. These we could mix with fat in Ayachero. Chunks of the green clay flaked off my arms and legs as I walked, the edges of the lesions crusted over but still weeping. Twice I doubled over with shooting pains in my belly and back; this time the ache radiated down my legs. *Were these real contractions?* All Omar could do was help me to my feet again. There was no time for discussion: the hunters never slowed down, and we would have been utterly lost without them.

The boat was where we'd left it. In just six days, a dozen vines had grown around it in tight loops and had it on lockdown. Once the men chopped the boat free, Omar dumped it over, releasing into the river a family of small green snakes coiled into a cozy pile in the bottom.

MiddleEye and the men dropped the bags of poultice into the boat and left without ceremony of any kind, not a goodbye, not even a backward glance. The jungle closed behind them as if the entire experience had all been a dream.

The river coursed swollen along the bank, stronger and higher by several feet than when we arrived. Omar made a bed out of the soft bags of leaves under the thatch awning that tented one end of the canoe and settled me there.

"Take off your dress, Lily."

"Really?" I considered begging him to give me a few hours' break. Each treatment was like painting on misery.

"Come on. You need this stuff on you all the time."

With a sigh, I peeled off my dress and tried to get comfortable on the bags; the hot breath of the river prickling my skin. Stained in lighter and darker patches of sage by the poultice, my skin looked like beech bark.

Omar kissed my bald head, dipped his hand in one of the bags, and spread green goop across my shoulders. Tears seeped from my eyes.

"Your skin is looking better," he said.

I didn't care if he was making it up. The words comforted me and I loved him for saying them. He rinsed his hands in the river and pulled out a beat-up sheet of notebook paper from his back pocket. His capital-lettered sentences filled the pages.

"I finished this while you were sleeping," he said, sitting on the gunwale, bare feet touching my swollen belly. "You know you slept for almost two days, right?"

I smiled. "You did your *assignment*?" I felt like a wet grub, shivering under cool, green mud.

He cupped my cheek, kissing me tenderly before he cleared his throat and read:

"'Dear Baby Boy,

"'I am your proud father, a native Amazonian. Your mother is a beautiful American seamstress who loves the jungle life.'" (A little smile to me here.) "'I am learning English for you, because your parents want to give you knowledge, to make you understand what choices are in your life, because the world is different from when I am a baby boy. I know that with my strength, and the soul and kindness and magic of your mother, you grow to a man who can survive any world, the jungle world, the *civilizado* world, the Ayachero world, and the world of any tribe in Bolivia, even the ones who kill on sight. They do not kill you, because you are high up in the trees as they pass under, you hide in holes only you know exist, your arrows fly sooner than theirs, you run faster, the anaconda dies from your machete before he can close his jaws on your flesh, and always, dear one, your stomach is full from your own cleverness—'"

The sound of a gun cocking stopped him cold. Dutchie emerged from a thatch of tall ferns near the bank. He walked quickly toward us, carbine lifted.

Omar sprung to his feet, the tattered paper flying out of his hands as he reached for his knife, the only weapon the Tatinga had let us keep. I went from mesmerized by Omar's beautiful letter to a ball of terror in the pit of the boat, snatching at my dress to cover myself.

"I like it, Omar," he said, smiling his snaggle-toothed smile, eyes arctic blue under stringy-blond bangs, sweat-soaked bandana tied around his forehead and half-an-ear. A threadbare shirt and rope-belted shorts hung off his gaunt frame. "I think I'll call you Shakespeare from now on. Carlos'd hate that. Cuz *he's* the bard, see?"

I slipped my dress over my body, my string bag over my shoulder.

"Problem is, the stupid fucker isn't here to piss off. Nahh, he'd *never* believe ol' Dutchie took control for once, which is why he's going to lose, lose, lose—"

"Where is he?" Omar said, stepping out of the boat. He coolly took a few steps toward the poacher, blocking me.

"In Ayachero, looking for you. All the guys are there, waiting. Getting bored, drinking, screwing all your women." He grinned at the thought of this. "I'll have my turn, but first things first. You," he said to me. "Get out of the boat."

"My wife is ill—"

"And ready to pop one out I guess!" He gestured with the gun. "Get the fuck out of the boat."

Steadying myself with the seat, I stepped out onto the wet sand.

"Give me all your weapons."

Omar tossed the knife a few feet from Dutchie, who scrambled for it and tucked it in his belt.

"You. Give me that bag. Toss it over here."

I did what he asked. He dumped the contents out on the ground: blowgun, darts, curare. In despair I gazed at our only remaining weapons scattered on the sand.

"What is this, *Tatinga* shit?" He gave the blowgun a swift kick; it flew off into the vegetation nearby. "Where're your *guns*?"

"The Tatinga took them."

He walked a slow circle around Omar. "Take off your shirt. Turn around. Empty your pockets."

He did as he was asked, slowly, deliberately.

Dutchie lowered his gun and shot just inches from my right foot, blowing a hole in the sand. I jumped two feet to the left, my heart slamming in my chest.

"You better not be fucking lying to me." He swung the gun first at me, then Omar, then back at me—at my belly. "You. Get over here."

Omar gave me a small nod. Head down, I walked past him, feeling his warm breath on my neck. The moment I was in reach, Dutchie seized me around the shoulders, slammed me against his hard breastbone, and jammed the cold muzzle of the gun against the skin just above my left ear. I imagined my brains exploding out the other side.

"You're taking me to the grove, or she dies."

"The grove is days away," Omar said. "Two upriver, two on foot."

Out of the corner of my eye I watched Dutchie's face screw up; maybe he hadn't counted on this. *Maybe he'd realized his miscalculation and would let us go.* His stinking breath filled my nose as he ground the O of metal harder into my flesh; I heard the subtle flicking of his finger against the trigger, an unscratchable itch. He gripped me tighter, I could barely get enough air, the tang of his sweat searing my lungs.

"Fine," he said. "Get in the boat, both of you."

Omar shifted his weight to his other foot. I prayed he wasn't planning on rushing him. "I have to bring those bags of leaves with us. Otherwise she'll die."

"Get the fuck in the boat." The muzzle drilled deeper into my forehead.

"Not without the bags."

"*Get the fuck in the boat.*"

"I'll—" I sputtered.

"Stay where you are, Lily," Omar said with unimaginable calm.

A troop of spider monkeys rattled the branches above us; nuts and small branches rained down. Dutchie jerked me harder to him; my collarbone bending under his vise grip. "You think I'm kidding?" he growled. "*I don't need her*, understand?"

"This ends here without those bags."

"Oh yeah? Oh *yeah*?" Dutchie shifted his weight, and I helplessly shifted with him. "Who's the boss here? You forgettin' already? Old Dutchie. At the reins. And I *will* kill her."

"I don't believe you."

He sputtered out a laugh, releasing me, before he wound up and clocked me over the head with the butt of the gun. I fell forward onto the sand, blood dripping from a gash on my forehead. Dazed, I looked up at Omar. His eyes pleaded with me to stay where I was.

"We need the bags. Then we'll go."

"You son of a bitch." Dutchie head-gestured toward our boat. "Wasting my fucking time. Put the shit in the canoe. Make it fast."

Dutchie followed Omar to our canoe, shadowing him closely. I stayed crouched on the sand, watching, head throbbing from my wound. Omar slipped me the subtlest glance before bending over and rummaging among the bags.

"Quit screwing around or your bald green bitch is history."

"Two seconds, man."

Sweat dripped into my eyes. *What in hell was he doing?*

"Come on, *come on*—" Dutchie whined.

In one shockingly swift movement, Omar pivoted, torquing the biggest, heaviest bag in a low arc, slamming it into Dutchie's gut and sending him sprawling toward the river. Firing willy-nilly, Dutchie landed on his back in the water, where he flailed, momentarily stunned.

Omar had been blown back, a hole in his stomach and shoulder. Roaring to his feet, he leapt at Dutchie, landing on top of him in the river. He held the man's head and chest underwater, the poacher's skinny legs in decayed rubber boots kicking up on either side of him. I splashed into the river. Grimacing, Omar strained to keep his grip on Dutchie's shoulders as the poacher tried to wrestle him down. His bandana floated away, the lobe—what was left of his injured ear—bobbling against his head in the current, the unfairness of his whole life legible in his face full of rage and surprise. Dutchie's mouth opened and closed as if pleading for his life, his ice-blue eyes still lasering up through the murk. Blood poured from Omar's wounds. Crying, I gripped his shoulders, which felt like rocks until, slowly, they softened, muscles slackening, his grip weakening on Dutchie until he collapsed on top of him. The current lifted him, rolling him away toward the bank.

For long seconds I stared down into Dutchie's greenish-white face, his hair floating out like a blond medusa, his expression one of disappointment, betrayal, his mouth open, still.

Are you dead? Are you dead? *Are you dead?*

He had to be! His eyes looked into mine but were motionless, his face several inches from the surface of the water, his bony chest still as clay under his unbuttoned shirt. I lunged toward Omar, but Dutchie's hand leapt out of the water, grabbed the fabric of my dress, and wrenched me down to him.

He pulled me underwater, clutched me tight to his chest, so close we could have kissed, his rubbery flesh touching mine, the whites of his eyes filled with madness and panic. I put one hand on each of his skinny shoulders and pushed down with all my strength, my head flying out of the water as I gasped for air. Still his big-knuckled hand gripped my dress. *Why don't you die?* Wailing, I held him down until his fingers loosened. They scrabbled at the fabric of my dress until his hand fell away. After long moments, his legs stopped churning and his face relaxed and smoothed out, all his problems over as his eyes glazed like milk on a china plate, gazing up at the brooding sky above me.

FORTY-ONE

Sobbing, I pushed myself away from Dutchie's body and stumbled to where Omar lay facedown in a shallow eddy. I turned him over and held him in my arms, the river lapping gently at my back. His open eyes saw nothing. I screamed his name, screamed for my heart, my love, till my voice was gone.

Only the sullen silence of the jungle answered me, the patter of the rain on my head and shoulders, women's rain, the kind that never ends.

I dropped my head down on his motionless chest, pulled his body close, as part of me fell away. I ached to go wherever he had gone, thought, *I can't live through this.*

I'm not sure how much time passed.

Cradling him, I walked toward shore. Grappling with him by his armpits, I dragged his body up on the wet sand, stopping to rest, cry, look at him; to give up, start over, and give up again, finally getting all of him out of the water and laying him down on his back. As if I were getting into bed with him, I got my own cumbersome body down on the wet sand, fitting myself next to him on my side. I inhaled his gorgeous Omar smell, present even in the early minutes of death. I traced the contours of his face, felt the subtle cleft of bone under his handsome cheeks. I muttered words of love, shutting each eye before combing his hair back from his forehead with my fingers.

The baby's foot kicked near my heart, as if he was trying to resuscitate me.

A bird shrieked in the high green clerestory above me. I pushed myself to one elbow, all awareness, every cell firing. Dutchie's gun lay nearby; I scrambled over to it and flipped open the magazine; all bullets fired. I blinked back nausea, dizziness.

There was nothing of use in Dutchie's canoe. I peered out over the churning brown water. His body had caught in a bony snag of fallen logs several yards away in waist-high water, one arm and leg lifted up against it and held there by the current, as if he were trying to climb over it. I waded out to him. Tried to shut out the ridiculous idea that he might still be alive. Squeezing my eyes shut, I felt along his back for his belt. The second my hand landed on Omar's knife, I grabbed it and launched myself away from him.

On shore, I rescued Omar's assignment from a thicket of ferns where it had landed, and read the last few lines:

. . . *your stomach is full from your own cleverness. Learn every day. No knowledge is beneath you. Respect your elders. Hold on to your little flame of self, because the world wants to blow it out, my beloved son.* With a sharp cry I fell to my knees, tucking the note to my chest.

Acknowledging that it would be close to impossible to keep the paper dry, I wrapped it in a palm leaf and put in my string bag. The jungle would come for Omar no matter what I did, but it crushed me to leave him on the sand. It took all my strength to drag his body to Dutchie's canoe. I gathered a few dozen big leaves, heliconia flowers, and some giant white lilies floating near the bank, creating a soft, fragrant bed in the canoe. Bit by bit, I rolled his body in, the jungle above me a cathedral of sorrow. I took his glasses from his back pocket, wrapped his fingers around them. I kissed him one last time, lips already cold, then covered him with the rest of the palms and flowers, trying to remember what the Tatinga had placed in their death canoe for Benicio. Plants, flowers, his slingshot and toys, and a set of his little clothes. I had no such talismans for the father of my child. I told him that I was sorry, that I would have to keep his knife, and my blowgun and darts, and smiled to myself as I imagined him saying, *Don't be a fool. Take everything you need to survive; I'm already in another jungle . . .*

Parting wheel-sized water plants, I waded out waist-deep with the canoe. Before I let myself think, I let go of the battered gunwale. The river took him with a kind of elegance, turning him just once, as if granting a benediction, then carried him off so fast I couldn't bear it. I hadn't said enough goodbyes, as if there is ever enough time to say all there is to say to someone we love.

Standing in our canoe, I yanked at the rusted chain attached to the nine-horsepower motor; a feat of contorted gymnastics as I tried to avoid smacking my bulging belly. Nothing. I sat a moment, attempted to gather my wits. Got up and tried again. The motor farted gray smoke, sputtered to silence. I cursed a bloody streak of loathing at the thing. *Was I flooding it? What would Omar do?* I eased myself back down on the seat, closed my eyes and saw—without Beya's assistance this time—my own death; a green, swollen body under circling vultures. Got up and tried again, harder, wrenching a muscle in my shoulder. Still nothing, the jungle eerily quiet, as if mocking me. It finally occurred to me to check the gas. *A third full, was that enough?* Fourth try, I jerked the thing harder than I thought possible. It caught with a snorting sort of rumble—such a beautiful sound, such an intoxicating smell. The muddy brown water foamed at the bow as I nosed out into the flow, passing Dutchie's body still held fast against the snarl of river detritus.

The boat began to turn in sickening circles. I reached back and grabbed the till as I'd seen Omar do—he'd used the motor as a rudder—and lay back against the damp leather bags. Eyes shut tight, I breathed the peaty smell of the leaves, asking them to heal my heart as well as my skin; where was my strength, where was my bravery, where was my *self*? How could I survive this? As I inhaled the sickly jungle-sweet air, a thousand images flashed by, a gallery of scenes from my short, strange life: the cameo-sized photo of my foster mother Tia at her sewing machine, smiling up at me from her kaleidoscopic nest of threads and bobbins; of a hundred doors slamming behind me as I ran from group homes, into rain, into snow, into blazing sun, on buses, on trains, on foot, away from what was never good enough; I sat laughing and drinking with Britta and Molly at the bar in Cochabamba; I followed Omar under the string of Christmas lights as he led me to the smiling sloth; I watched Paco make me a comb out of palm fronds; there was Anna swirling in the new burlap dress I'd sewn her; Doña Antonia handing me the sacred fire, the small nod of Splitfoot's head telling me *I believe you are a shaman*, or *I believe you enough to give you this plant that might save you, so that you will do something good for our tribe.*

An hour passed, maybe two, as I hugged the bank, where the current was weaker, to make the most of what diesel remained. My eyes rested on the shore and the wall of jungle passing by, all that sameness along with the sound of the motor chugging along lulling me into a torpor. One hand on the tiller, I lay on my side tasting the breath of a billion plants exhaling. Above me, the great heavy sky passed sullenly, crossed by barbets, tanagers, and jacamars—small birds—all of them bright, quick flashes of color. Much higher up, dun-colored raptors floated, their claws weighted with prey. A pair of vultures threaded in lazy figure eights through the canopy; I would not let myself think what had brought them there. The death of Omar was just a shadow passing, met with a sigh of apathy from the jungle, meaningless to everything here but myself.

With a jolt, I remembered what he had said to me just days before. *You don't wake up alive in the jungle because you were smarter or trickier. You stay alive here because you paid attention.*

I pushed myself up to my elbows, as close to a seated position as I could manage. In those hours of nonfunctional grief, I had veered out toward the center of the river, where the current was strongest. My progress was pitiful. I watched the shape of the bank closely; I was bumping along at a standstill. Leaning on the rudder—the force of the river resisting my every move—I aimed the bow of the canoe toward shore.

Too fast. I fishtailed; the boat spun. Jumping a sunken tree, the stern yawed into the current, slamming me into a tangled mass of broken tree limbs, sluicing me with a soaking spray. I cut the motor. Chastened, determined, I spent several minutes pushing myself away from the outcropping.

Free of the bony snag, I yanked on the motor's chain, dizzy with relief when it caught and rumbled to life on the first try. My arm ached from the pull of the rudder as I forced the boat to follow the contours of the bank. Behind thin clouds, the sun grew swollen and turned sickly white, burning through the haze and baking my head and shoulders. The poultice dried and flaked off in chunks that fell in the river and were swept swiftly away behind me.

Think, I told myself. *What was the route we had taken?*

From Ayachero, Omar had veered off into two different channels to arrive at the river I motored on now. I had a memory of always turning right, but that had been from my position lying down in the boat, facing . . . *which way?* I mentally lay down, head under the thatch. Saw Omar's intense face as he leaned down to me, saying, *Sit up, Lily, pay attention . . .*

It was a right. It had to be. I had to make two right turns. And I would not stop to sleep.

A glowering red sun dropped behind the wall of green as macaws, paired by color—turquoise, crimson, yellow—soared high above, squawking at one another like old married couples. Banks of pink mimosa and purple tonka bean throbbed with a chorus of frogs. Now and then, to either side of the boat, a gulping sound, as a whiskered rubbery mouth popped to the surface, then disappeared. Both hands clutching the tiller, I puttered along into the night river, knowing the moment I ran out of diesel would be the end of everything.

Darkness closed like a door, the trees looming ogres, their big faces gaping down. I held on to the putt-putt of the motor like it was Omar's heartbeat, Omar's love for me, carrying me home. Feathery clouds drifted across a fingernail of moon. Mist spiraled off the river in fairy twists. A large fish jumped out of the water and came belly-flopping down. I motored on, my skin dry and pinching. Chambers of cool, wet air wafted by me, through me.

A warm wetness spread out beneath me, soaking my dress. Had I peed? I reached down over my belly and felt myself, smelled my hand; no urine smell. More liquid gushed out of me. My water had broken.

The baby was coming.

FORTY-TWO

A spitting mist accompanied vague, ominous dawn light. From high in the canopy, a howler monkey roared his loneliness. As I rounded a bend, the river split into three different branches. Nothing looked familiar. In despair, I chose a hard right, when really it could have been any of them. I hugged the shore, one hand on the tiller, the other across my belly, my guts twisting and pulling. The weight of my body shifted, gathering and dropping down hard between my legs.

Fat droplets became a steady gray wall of water. Men's rain. I strained to keep the shore in sight. Steering around islands of fallen trees forced me out to rain-strengthened currents that bested the puny strength of the motor. I passed under a hulking set of tree limbs that reached out like a claw. It hooked under the thatched roof, tearing it completely from the boat with a racketing boom like a gun going off.

Instantly drenched, I struggled to see more than two feet in front of me. My belly convulsed in vicious, pulsing waves as if it had a will separate from my own. Fresh pain felled me back onto the soaked bags; another entity seemed bent on drilling into the base of my spine. I screamed into the rain, gulping it down with a bottomless thirst, blinded as I bellowed into the blank face of the sky. Big logs rolled past, freed by the deluge.

Rain pooled in the boat, quickly puddling in the center and rising; small tributaries formed around the hard leather bags of leaves. Water pounded at the thick sludge on my body, washing whatever poultice remained cleanly away and leaving only the green stains and healing lesions. I jammed my cold white feet in the tapir sandals between the supplies; they looked like someone else's feet: swollen, bruised, cut, filthy. The thought that I had to bail the boat and had nothing to bail it with was torpedoed out of my mind by a whip crack of agony; a burning.

I was splitting open.

Gasping for air, I swallowed more water instead, gagging and coughing. But I had to know what was happening. To feel it, because I couldn't see it. My hand traveled over the moonscape of my belly, down and down. It shook so hard, I had to press it against the quivering flesh of my thigh to steady it. The water rose all around me, my body an archipelago. Haltingly, my fingers cold as death, I worked my hand down past the folds of my sex until I felt the top of his head.

For a full minute I rested my fingers there, pain dulled by wonder, by the knowledge of him; the insanity of where I was and what I was doing forced from my consciousness by his physical reality, the hot rain pounding down like I was with him in his water, too. We were all in water together. I ran my jittery fingers along the tiny section of his hard and soft skull, felt Omar's thick hair, tangled, matted, wet. I closed my eyes and listened to my baby's desire to be born, no matter what; on a beach, in a plane, in a hut in a jungle village, in a dugout canoe, and I loved him for making his fierce claim on the world.

Water climbed all around me where I lay on the bags; it surged into channels and inlets around my breasts and shoulders, crept up to my knees, lapped at the curve of my hip, licked at my chin. I pictured him coming out of me, facedown, drowning; Dutchie's dead visage flashed by. I scrambled higher up onto the bags of leaves to elevate myself, which bought me a minute, less. The rain came down harder as if enraged. The bags sank under my weight. Blood turned in S shapes in the rainwater at my hips; the little lake in the boat swirled with sticks and leaves as the water lapped over the sides. I had been torn; I knew it.

My hand left his head, which had lodged in me as if it might never move—a thought that filled me with a new level of horror. Wailing, I kicked at one of the leather bags of poultice, wedged it under my heel, and dragged it to my hand. Groaning with its weight, I dumped the sludgy green contents over the side of the boat. One hand still on the tiller, I bailed water with the empty leather bag. Ridiculous. I couldn't keep up. In agony, I dragged the other bags under me, lifting my pelvis higher than the gunwale, but could no longer bail from this position. Water poured into my mouth, ears, nose, eyes; the sky pummeled me with its hard water fists, my hips ached and split, I was giving birth into a vast vault of clouds.

I had to let go of the tiller. This boy wanted all of me. Any second he would be born head down into the brown lake that lapped at the sides of the canoe. But to lose the tiller meant we would go spinning into madness, we would lose the bank and any sense of where we were, any hope of getting home. Knees bent, heels jammed under the bags, I held my hand at his crown and bit at tiny sips of air, refusing to push, though every cell in my body screamed *get him out get him out get him out!* I kicked the last bag under my pelvis, gaining two inches and just a few seconds more. Lianas dragged across my convulsing body from overhanging trees. I tried to time it. Between contractions, I lifted my arm and dragged my hand across the curtain of green ropes. I yanked one of them free, wound it around the stuttering motor, then lashed it to the seat, anchoring the tiller in place. The boat jigged and jagged, but stayed steady in the current as it made its miserable progress forward.

My guts twisted, wringing themselves out like a dishrag. No force on earth would stop him now, no filling boat, no will of mine, nothing. Bands of muscle in my gut cinched and relaxed in one final wave, pain a white devil in my head. I felt the box of my pelvis drop open, my bones soften and separate. My body was turning itself inside out. Gulping equal parts air and water, I dropped my head back on the bag of green sludge and cried out for Omar, knowing we might both be with him soon. My eyes bugged in my head; I saw nothing but a green ocean in the sky. The water between my legs gushed red. I reached down with both hands to catch him just as the liana stretched and snapped, freeing the tiller. The boat turned in a wide, slow circle. I rode a fresh wave of torment, my screams joining with the riotous songs of morning, the spider monkeys, the macaws shrieking their loathing of the day, as he gushed out of me crying his first tears, slippery and warm and covered with my blood.

FORTY-THREE

I held him—purple umbilical cord still joining us—just above the flooded canoe. Rudderless, we drifted from the main current to the shallows, where the canoe beached sideways, gently, onto a narrow strip of hard mud, feet from an edifice of jungle that rose up thickly, shadowing us. Still the rain came down.

I rocked him in my arms as he cried, stuck to each other by our secretions, mud, and filth. After working my quaking hand down to the knife tied into my string bag, I doubled the warm fleshy cord and sliced it through, tying it in a big ugly knot, terrified that he would bleed to death. The placenta gushed out of me like some wanton sea creature, a bruise-colored slab of meat, the final statement of my helpless, terrifying biology. Baby Omar in my arms, I scrabbled away from it, kicking it into the river where it sank down into the harrowing depths, no doubt to be devoured.

I carried him to the shallowest section and dipped him in, pouring handfuls of river water over his head. Though his eyes were squeezed shut, his father was written across his face—Omar in miniature—in the shape of his mouth and eyes, his olive skin, the little whorls of hair at the crown of his head; the slightest wave in the wisps at his neck the only trace of me I could find. I cupped his head to my breast and—after a bit—he settled there.

A whiff of sage woke me from my trance. I stiffened. *How do I know that smell?* I knew it had to do with wonder, but how? Beya's camp. She burned sage constantly. I had to be close by, which meant Ayachero was just upriver, or a few minutes' walk through the jungle.

That's when I heard the screaming. Thin sounds of terror from the direction of the village, then nothing, until the tinny, familiar, distant sounds of Bolivian pop music started up. I got to my feet, dizzy with pain as blood dripped down the insides of my legs.

Holding baby Omar to me, I gathered with one hand everything of use from the canoe: my string bag, the blowgun, and the quiver of darts. The little bamboo tube of curare had washed away entirely. I stepped into the forest, following the scent of sage as the heat of the day began to build.

I crouched behind a scrim of leaves at the perimeter of Beya's camp. Signs of a quick departure were everywhere. Her metal tub of water boiled over into the flames of her open pit fire; next to it, a freshly killed paca lay belly up on a flat piece of slate, ready to be disemboweled. Beya's donkey stood attached by her pole to the grindstone, motionless except for her tail swishing across shuddering flanks.

"Beya," I whispered. "*Beya.*"

A distant howl and whoop from the direction of Ayachero. I held little Omar tighter; he squirmed and let out a plaintive whimper.

Gnashing her blocky yellow teeth together, the donkey swung her big head toward me, blinked, then turned back away, pawing at the dusty ground with her front hoof.

I took a few slow breaths, calming myself before conjuring Beya's bright eyes that missed nothing. In my head, I spoke the words loudly and clearly, "WHERE ARE YOU?"

Seconds later, I heard her as if she were standing next to me, as if I was leaning down to better hear her whisper: "THEY HAVE TAKEN ME. I HAVE HIDDEN MY SPIRIT IN THE LUPUNA TREE."

I stepped out onto her camp's circle of hard dirt. Beya's string bag, the one in which she carried the poison frog and who knew what else, lay abandoned by the fire, unmoving. Still, I gave it a little shove with my toe before picking it up and making sure it was empty. Whatever had been in there had escaped. I slipped the bag over one shoulder. Carefully, I dragged the pot of water off the grate and onto the ground, so it could cool enough to clean myself and the baby.

My tiny boy filled his lungs and let fly, filling the air with piercing cries as I paced the camp. I tried to comfort him in the limited ways I knew, but he didn't want my milk, and nothing seemed to calm him. From the direction of Ayachero, a scream so chilling even the baby paused his wail. It sounded like Anna, but I couldn't be sure. I was desperate to run to her, my dearest friend in this place. *What were they doing to her?* I clutched my screaming baby to my chest; he must have heard my pounding heart and felt my own terror because he wailed even more pitifully, like he knew better than I that this was the end of us. A gunshot ricocheted among the treetops. Baby Omar paused for breath, or to register the sound, before opening his mouth again.

To save my life, I had to somehow quiet my baby boy.

I climbed the stairs to her hut. Under yellowed mosquito netting, a hammock hung motionless in the still air. Neat piles of plants marched along every wall. Dozens of old plastic and glass soda bottles filled with black or green sticky-looking liquids stood in rows on a colorful woven mat on the floor. Under the one open-air window, a well-used mortar and pestle and a half dozen empty bamboo containers sat on a simple wooden table. Tied to the sill by a jute cord, a small palm-frond box moved ever so slightly. A turquoise frog splotched with brilliant orange peeked from between the fronds. It lifted its head at my approach, throat pulsing, flesh glistening. It pushed itself up on its front legs and seemed to taste the air, blinked.

Another gunshot, far off, absorbed by the jungle.

I stared at the little frog, but what I saw was Omar's body floating down the river in the bed of the canoe, its living wonder gone forever. I thought how he was no longer himself, just a meal for the fish and birds and river otters; this day—this jungle—was a nightmare I couldn't stop dreaming, wide awake.

Again I tried to quiet my baby, but he wasn't having it. I kissed him on his forehead and lay him down in the hammock, praying I could muster the strength to do what had to be done.

The frog's bulbous four-fingered hands scrabbled between the fronds, its orange blotches glowing in the tannin shadows of the hut. I pulled out a dart from my quiver, slipped the flat, sharp edge between the fronds and scraped it along the length of the frog. It squeaked in terror and leapt at its enclosure, flattening itself against one side of the box.

A drop under the skin makes a baby sleep for hours. Four will kill it.

One drop of clear secretion trembled on the edge of the dart.

I turned to the hammock. In one swift movement—just as he drew in another breath to cry—I slipped the tip of the dart into the tender flesh of his elbow. Immediately he closed his mouth and went limp. With a stifled cry of my own, I snatched him close to my chest and listened for a heartbeat, holding his face against mine to feel for his breath. Both were there, faint, fluttery, hummingbird fast. He lay silent and slack in my arms, his body pale and already cooler to the touch, even though I spoke to him and rubbed his little limbs.

I felt a hundred years old. Exhausted, beat-up. Part of me wanted to give up so badly: *What in hell was I supposed to do now?* But I knew what Omar would say: *Everything you will ever need is right in front of you. Use what you have.*

From a basket suspended by sisal rope from the ceiling of the hut, I scouted out a few pieces of genipap fruit, cut them in half, took out the seeds and mashed them with the mortar and pestle, the black dye of the seeds exploding in the pulp. Sprouting Leaf had shown me this trick when I'd asked her how she made the dye for her face. Now I coated my face and neck with it, even my scalp.

Another wail from the direction of the village.

Adrenaline charged through me as, one by one, I scraped each of the five blowdarts alongside the frog, air-drying them before tucking them back into their hard leather quiver. I loosened my string bag, laid it out flat on the floor of the hut. After wrapping Omar in a small woven blanket I took from Beya's hammock, I tucked him in the bag and slipped it over my shoulders; his tiny body now nestled against my back. In Beya's bag, which I wore over one shoulder so it hung in front, I stored the blowgun and darts. Got up to leave and took a final look around. Well-worn but clean-looking shirts were folded in a basket—I took two. From Beya's table I chose a bamboo container, tested the seals on both ends, and made my way down the stairs.

After taking a few minutes to wash myself in the pot of now warm water, I tore up the shirts into strips and wrapped them around my waist and between my legs, mentally apologizing to Beya for ruining her clothes. My bleeding had slowed, but fatigue ground every sensation to a fine point. I made my way past the sprawling base of the lupuna tree, to where the young rubber sapling burst through the pile of rotted logs. Globs of dark honey still stuck to the abandoned bees nest. Bullet ants swarmed it as they carted off small amber chunks, carrying them aloft in their pincers.

Crouching in the humid green cave, I dug out some honey with a stick and poked gobs of it into the tube. Picturing Beya in my mind's eye, I laid it on a patch of moss near a line of ants. Immediately, dozens branched from the throng and filled the tube to overflowing. With the stick I nudged it away from the nest; it fell to my feet. As she had done, I stepped on the tube, rolling it back and forth under my sandaled foot to kill all the ants on the outside. Snapping on the rubber cap, I slipped the bamboo tube into my shoulder bag along with the blowgun and darts.

I fed Beya's donkey a couple of armfuls of hay that had been just out of her reach, walking past the dead paca before it occurred to me that I might be able to use it. I wrapped the already stiffening, twenty-pound rodent in palm leaves and fit it into my shoulder bag.

At dusk, in the jungle, there is this moment of stillness, of heightened awareness by all creatures, during this palpable shift to night. You know that this is the moment you need to get home, or make sure your shelter is built. This was the time of day that I left for Ayachero.

Sleeping newborn on my back, dead paca and supplies in front, I took a few moments to find my equilibrium with all this strange cargo before turning toward the darkening path.

I shined to Beya, "I'M COMING."

There was no answer.

FORTY-FOUR

Never leaving the cover of the jungle, I crept along the boundary of the village, past the now-empty barn and the manioc fields, the plants shirring against one another in a light evening breeze from the river. I concentrated on silence in every step, searching out any variation in the darkness to light my way: glowing mosses, lichens dotted with bioluminescence, giant buzzing insects with blinking tails; beyond these, the flicker of the torches from the longhouse and Anaconda Bar guided me forward. Occasionally I stopped—unwilling to take one more step until I felt him breathe against me.

Sparks shot up into the night. Over the blare of the radio, more whoops, a shriek. Barking male laughter up the hill, full of cruelty. A sulfur smell.

The thumping sound of two people running full speed across the hard earth of the settlement.

"Get her get her *get her*!" Another round of laughter, gunshots.

Marietta tore across an arc of land toward the longhouse, pursued by a poacher in ragged shorts; he caught her easily and dragged her to the ground. She screamed as he pawed at her, twisted in his grip, got up and ran again; he let her get away like a cat might play with a mouse before finally ending the game at its leisure. He got up, dusted himself off, and followed her.

I peered out from under the longhouse. Torches blazed from all four corners of the Anaconda Bar. Poachers—I stopped counting at twenty—danced with reluctant Ayacheran women, throwing them around or grappling them tight into an unwanted embrace. Fat Carlos, in a sweat-stained undershirt and filthy khaki pants, a purple kerchief tied across his missing eye under his frayed sisal hat, sat at the bar holding court, clutching a woman I was too far away to recognize. A small figure lay trussed and gagged on the ground, motionless.

I had mere seconds to do what I had to do. Breathing hard against cramps that would have felled me at any other time, I pulled the dead paca by its back legs from my shoulder bag, laid the rigid body on the ground in front of me. In the darkness my fingers found his little sternum and rib cage. I slipped my knife into his fur and flesh and drew it to his pelvic bone, gutting him. I parted the skin and scooped out the still-warm entrails with my hand, cutting around with the other to free them. Making sure no one was watching, I darted out to the bald earth of the village between the bar and the longhouse, lay the hot pile on the ground, and disappeared back into the forest.

Second by second, I drew closer to the Anaconda Bar behind my shroud of jungle. The trussed, gagged body was Beya; she lay motionless on her side in a circle of jumping torchlight. Carlos held Anna on his lap, his hands traveling where they wished, tossing her back and forth like a doll. I spotted Doña Antonia, Paco, the other women and children, a few elderly men including Anna's father, and all the hunters except for Franz. Huddled half in, half out of the light, most of Ayachero was patrolled by a couple dozen poachers who corralled them into a tight circle, barking at them nonstop like they were hopped-up on something, occasionally shooting near their feet or into the black clouds above.

I huddled in the shadows just feet from the rope ladder to the jaguar platform.

"You're a gorgeous little thing," Fat Carlos said, holding Anna tight. "Maybe I'll take you with me, would you like that? Wouldn't you like to be rich and fat, traipsing down the streets of gay Pareee, farting through silk?"

She turned her face away from him, but kept her body limp. A shout came from up the hill. The man who had been groping Marietta thundered down the slope to the bar.

"The Tatinga are here!" he said, his face tight with dread.

Carlos shifted Anna to his other knee, knocking back a glass of brandy as he did so. "What the fuck are you saying?"

"There's a pile of guts on the ground!" the man said, breathless.

"So we cleaned a few jungle turkeys, so what?"

"We threw those guts in the river. These are fresh! These weren't here a few minutes ago, boss, I swear to God."

Fat Carlos pushed Anna off his lap. She stumbled away, a sharp cry escaping her throat. I wondered where her infant was, where Claudia was, then pushed the thought away. "This better be worth my time."

"I swear—"

"Show me."

Cursing, Carlos began to stroll across the shadowy hill, led by the clearly rattled poacher as well as a couple of his men; the rest of his gang kept watch over the terrified villagers.

I crept onto the first rung of the rope ladder, which creaked as it swayed, the sound muffled by the jangling radio. Pain bit through the flesh of my shoulders and back, my illness still alive in me apparently, but shooting cramps in my pelvis made each step a little journey through hell. My breath ragged in my lungs, I pictured myself on the top of the platform, telling myself I would not stop. I pushed myself up a few more rungs, praying for the strength to climb the twenty-five feet that remained.

Fat Carlos stopped dead just where I had dropped the pile of paca innards.

"It's the Tatinga," the poacher said, hand on his gun, bronze face shining with sweat. "It's a warning, boss. Come on, let's get out of here."

"Tatinga, my ass," Carlos said, turning in a slow circle as he addressed the gaping jungle. "*Dutchie!* You stupid little traitorous *bastard!*" He fired a shot into the treetops. "I'll fuck you up, do you hear me?"

The jungle answered with the sonorous buzz of night insects.

"I know you're out there, you little prick, so just come on out and show yourself. Nobody buys your asinine tricks."

The high-pitched scream of a night bird rent the air. Afterward, silence.

Carlos shook his head and looked down, jowls shuddering, then raised his head in resolve. "*You*," he said, jabbing his finger toward the three men who stood over the pile of guts. "Check the longhouse, tear apart this whole shithole town. Find him."

One man took off for the longhouse while the other two—though they seemed to be following orders—were clearly spooked by the poacher's fear, and scattered helter-skelter in the village, a whiff of mutiny in the air. I was two-thirds up the ladder when Carlos turned back toward the Anaconda Bar. I simply couldn't climb any faster, I was so depleted.

As if enduring a change of heart, Carlos suddenly turned and yelled back. "I skim off a little ear. What's the big deal? Just trying to scare some balls in you." He blinked his one good eye into the velvet blackness. "Twenty years I've been keeping your skinny ass fed, keeping you in pussy, cutting snakebites outta you, dragging you down this godforsaken river—and you betray me like *this*?"

The jungle snapped and whined, a round of locusts joined the symphony.

"I'm giving you a chance here." He huffed as if the one-way conversation was exhausting him, placed his hands on his knees, and squinted at the shadows under the longhouse where I'd hidden just minutes ago. "Not a lot of men would do that. It's time to stop playing games, wouldn't you say? Just show your face and all is forgiven, okay, man? Just show your fucking loser face."

He yanked his hat tighter on his head, adjusting the purple eye patch as he peered with his one good eye at the yawning dark, at a million different things that could kill him. Arms folded over his belly, he stood a full minute, mumbling elaborate curses, listing all the many favors he'd granted Dutchie over the years, finally declaring in conclusion that as of this moment he wasn't worth the shit on his heel. I scrambled higher and higher. The fat man turned back toward the bar, shoulders drooping in defeat.

"Well fuck you then, you little pissant," he said, his voice empty of bravado.

With a stifled gasp, I reached the platform. I dragged myself up on it, bellying forward on my elbows, inch by inch, to the edge that overlooked the bar.

Carlos paused at the dancing light and shadow thrown by the torch next to Beya's still form. He crouched down next to her, said something inaudible, then got to his feet again.

"It wasn't you, was it, you nasty old witch?" He gave her a swift kick in the gut. She didn't move. "You're not trying to fool old Carlos, are you?" He gave her one more vicious kick and strolled toward the bar.

Never taking my eyes from the scene beneath me, I reached for Beya's string bag. With badly shaking fingers, I wriggled the first dart out of the quiver and placed it—in total darkness—as I had been taught, alongside the soft kapok fluff inside the gun. Beneath me, the big poacher's hat bobbed as he took a long drink, settled himself down again among half a dozen of the men who had gathered for their meal—it looked as if they were eating in shifts in order to keep guard on the villagers. Carlos accepted a plate of food from one of the men, laughing at something I couldn't hear. His shoulder was in my sights, and on this windless night, was perhaps beefy enough that I could hit it, even from thirty feet away.

The men spoke in low tones, clearly sobered by the incident. They gathered around plates of roasted plantains. A large slab of tapir cooked on a wide metal grill over a fire.

I looked for the stillness inside myself, for hope and confidence, for the opposite of everything that I had ever felt. I let out all the air from my lungs till I thought I would pass out, drew in a long, silent breath, and blew.

Nothing.

His big shoulder shone with sweat by the firelight, flexed as he kept on eating, chatting with the men.

The dart landed a good five feet behind him, quite close to the forest wall; it looked like a stiff blade of black grass in the dirt, not remarkable at all unless you were looking for it. I crawled across the platform to the other side, just five feet from where I shot the first dart, before loading the second one. Drew my long, slow inhale.

The moment I let it go, Carlos reached out to accept a tapir shank offered to him; the dart landed exactly where his shoulder had been, sticking out of the ground just where the leg of the bar was stuck into the dirt. Fuck.

Sweat dripped into my hands as I held my head, trying to hold back a flood of dread. My pelvis pounded, screaming at me to stop, rest. Could not. Would not. Three more darts.

Anything, everything could go wrong.

Hands slippery and trembling, I quickly loaded the third dart. Blew it out of the gun without taking the time to completely fill my lungs. God knows where that one landed. A completely useless panic shot. Heads down into their meals, the men spoke in tones too low for me to hear, snorting at their own jokes and wiping greasy fingers on their many-pocketed pants.

Chastising myself, I slowly, methodically began to load the fourth dart, breathing little prayers into the hollow tube. The baby stirred on my back. Just the smallest, smallest movement. It might have even been a little hiccup. My hands froze in place, one finger on the soft kapok, the other making sure the business end of the dart faced downward and away. With terrible slowness, I set the blowgun down on the thin, uneven planks. I closed my eyes and took shallow breaths, my body tense as wood, a lightning rod, listening, blanking out pain so I could feel for any movement or sound.

For long seconds he stayed where he was; I exhaled—it had been a burp, or some dream. *Good boy, Omar*, I thought, *good boy*. The moment I reached for the blowgun, his little knee jammed into my spine. I felt him struggling to turn, tiny fingers grappling for purchase against my back. Thankful for the radio, I pushed myself from my stomach to hands and knees to a seated position, got my legs under me, and—every movement considered—slipped the strap of the string bag off one shoulder as Omar squirmed.

I lifted him off my back and tucked him in my lap. His little blanket fell open. With one hand I stroked his head and chest, he felt slightly feverish, his skin like silk. I felt my way down from his shoulder to the crook of his left elbow, to the place that still held the indentation from my first injection. He panted into my fingers, his lips mouthing my flesh as he sought to suckle, limbs moving slowly as if he were treading water.

Holding him still, I felt my way past the kapok fluff and withdrew the dart. I dabbed the very tip of the poison dart in the still open wound, all the time telling myself it could not have been more than one drop seeping into him, likely much less. His head dropped back in the crook of my elbow and his little arms and legs fell open and back. Stifling a cry that had leapt up into my throat, I rocked him in my arms, shining to him, "I'M SORRY, I'M SORRY." I wrapped his slack body in the blanket, tucked him carefully back in the bag, and looped the straps back over my shoulders.

I took out the fifth and final dart, loaded it, got back down on my stomach and leaned over the edge. Numerous bare male shoulders gleamed up at me from below.

Giving up on Fat Carlos, I aimed at the poacher directly beneath me, took the deepest breath of my life, and blew, imagining Omar's steadying hand on my shoulder.

He leapt to his feet, food flipped over, screaming as he wrenched the dart out of the meat of his shoulder. "Something hit me! *Fuck!*" He hurled the dart to the ground, took a few stumbling steps, then swung his gun toward the platform.

Quickly, I pushed myself to my knees and stood, the plywood groaning under my feet. Struggling for balance, arms out, I backed up to the tree and—in total blackness—turned and wrapped my arms around the smooth bark. There was just enough space for my feet on the tiny lip of wood that—doughnut-like—encircled the far side of the tree. A few drops of blood dripped down my inner thigh; I squeezed my sweating eyelids shut as I pictured what the odor might attract, as I imagined my baby dangling helplessly in the string bag on my back among the coiling vines and creepers. An insect walked across my forearm; I let it. Another clicked and snapped near my ear. I didn't move.

Fat Carlos jumped to his feet, threw down his food and barked, "Turn off the fucking radio!"

The far end of the platform—the precise spot where I'd been lying seconds ago—disintegrated as bullets blasted up through the thin wood into the branches above. Methodically, shot after shot obliterated bits of the scaffold, shards of wood flying out to all sides, the air sawdust. In seconds there was nothing left to the structure except for the narrow, back-facing rim I stood on and the ladder attached to one of the stronger tree branches.

The radio clicked off.

Animated with fury, Carlos strutted around to Beya. He bent down, picked her up by the shoulders, and shook her viciously; she hung loose as a rag doll. "You called them, didn't you?" he spat in her ear. "If I didn't need you, I'd kill you now, so slowly you'd beg for me to hurry the fuck up."

The men, losing their nerve, fired off their guns haphazardly into the jungle, their unseen enemy more terrible by the second.

Carlos dropped Beya and slammed the butt of his gun down on the bar. "Everybody calm down. *Calm the fuck down.* Somebody's up there, but they're not Tatinga. We'd all be dead by now."

The man who'd been hit by my dart staggered off, fell to his knees and vomited repeatedly, pushed himself to his feet, then lurched into the shadows and threw up again.

"You." He gestured at one of the men. "Get up there. Now."

One arm still hugging the tree, I loosened Beya's string pouch and withdrew the tube of ants. Directly beneath me, the man who'd been given the order leapt onto the ladder, climbing two, three rungs at a time. Bit by bit, I eased myself down to a squatting position, a fantastically painful maneuver.

I lay the tube just where the ladder met the edge of the platform, only a foot from me, and flipped off the rubber cap. It fell silently into a mat of leaves below.

Dozens of ants exploded out of it, most of them crawling down the ladder, but three or four made their way onto my sandal and up my leg. I straightened, flicking them off with my free hand, dancing on them, crushing them, as the man flew up the ladder like a monkey.

In seconds he began to howl. At twenty feet up the ladder, he launched himself off it, falling to the hard ground, where he cried out, rolling to one side as he favored what might have been a broken arm.

"Men!" Fat Carlos's voice boomed. "Pick up the witch and get on the boat. We're leaving."

Chatter, whoops, scattered nervous laughter as the poachers mustered themselves, the one hit by the dart clasping his arm and staggering along with them. Balancing on my narrow foothold, still hugging the tree, I waited for my heart to stop slamming its way out of my chest. Bit by bit I squatted, squinting at the first few rungs of the ladder, searching out any black ants that remained on the white sisal rope.

Seeing none, I started my descent, stopping at three or four rungs down. My view was the entire village lit by scattered fires and torchlight, even as far as the beach and the roiling black river. For the first time that night I saw Franz. Crouching on the dock, he uncoiled the last ropes that tethered the poachers' barge, vanishing for a moment as he dropped down into the shallows, head bobbing as he pushed the monstrosity into the current. In seconds, the river took it. *How had he escaped the poachers? Had he hidden himself before I arrived on the scene?*

In seconds, my elation—as well as pride in what Franz had done, however he'd done it!—turned to horror. A gruff panting sound from near the longhouse. A flash of yellow and black, a liquid movement. I forced back a scream as my hands whitened on the rope. The men hadn't seen it yet, but an enormous jaguar was circling the pile of innards in the middle of the village. Ears back, her gold-and-onyx patterned coat rippled as she walked, all power and grace, her mouth open as she huffed every living thing in miles, including me, a dangling sack of flesh on a rope. Briefly she lay next to the pile of guts, tail languidly switching back and forth, sending up little puffs of earth at every slap.

The man who'd been hit by my dart was in the lead, walking in the direction of the beach, but faced back toward his friends, making fun of himself, laughing as he mimicked his own puking. Mouth stretched open wide, far exceeding the width of the man's head, the jaguar left the ground as if gravity did not concern her. Her yellow fangs gleamed as she flew toward the man's bare neck. He must have died instantly, he made no noise. His limbs flopped back and forth as the animal shook him like a toy, not pausing before dragging him toward the jungle.

All the men raised their weapons at once—even the man who carried Beya let her roll out of his arms as he snatched at his gun and trained it at the quickly disappearing beast.

But none of the men got to have their shot. One by one, their bodies stiffened and froze, guns tumbled out of their hands. They fell forward onto their knees as one, two, and in some cases half a dozen yard-long blowdarts porcupined their chests, as an army of Tatinga men stepped out of the forest from the dark perimeter of the village.

Fat Carlos turned in a slow beat, watching the last man fall, before raising up his hand as if beseeching the stars and sharp sickle moon to stop the swift dart from flying through his trembling throat.

FORTY-FIVE

On my last night in Ayachero, just one week later, the rain fell in torrents, beating down the banana leaves that draped themselves over the railing of the longhouse. No more fifteen-minute downpours; men's rain now lasted hours at a time. The river rose daily by half a foot or more, steadily erasing the beach.

Enveloped by the familiar smells of grilling meat and boiled yucca, the air clouded with tobacco, I watched electric-blue lightning flash in the canopy, obliterating for seconds at a time the darkness that reigned in the understory. I lay in a hammock listening to For God's Sake spin tales about his month away. He'd come back just in time, bringing, among other things, antibiotics that FrannyA desperately needed to beat back a secondary infection.

He sat on a stool next to me, wringing his hands as he gazed at the glowing coals in the oven. "My wife was very sick, you know, and I couldn't leave her. My three children had no one to take care of them and so I became the mother, you know?" he said with a little laugh. "I put on an apron like a woman and cooked the meals and washed the clothes and took them to school so she could rest, and I see, wow, this being a mother is very hard work, and I look at my wife with new eyes now, over."

Grinning as he listened, Franz crouched on a section of palm-thatch roofing he was repairing. "Sounds like they miss you a lot back home."

"Yes, or I should probably say, maybe. I know that when I'm gone my wife is so happy because I'm not there talking to her nonstop all day long and getting in the way. But I am happy to be back. I miss my important job here. I miss the river and I miss being the best river driver and supplier for Ayachero. It is my destiny, over."

Under his continual chatter, I heard some other truth, something I was too tired that night to really get at. Nestled in the crook of my elbow, my baby boy slept, his hot, dense warmth fitting to my side, key to a lock. I drew back a thin cloth to look at him; he wore a little shawl and a cotton diaper knotted at his tiny hips. Anna had let me borrow a dress I'd sewn for her, the one she loved best, with the pattern of smiling, dancing coffee beans in little black and red hats. I peeled back the fabric from my arm, forcing myself to look at my skin. Even by flickering torchlight, it was clear the lesions had shrunk to less than half their original size, retreating like islands being devoured by the rising tide of healthy skin around them. The last bag of poultice—Panchito had retrieved it for me—sat at my feet.

We were all relieved to learn that Marietta had escaped the poacher by hiding under a pile of empty food sacks in one of the storerooms. Now she sat at the sewing machine, struggling to repair the tiny sleeve of a child's shirt. Though—in my mind—the machine really belonged to Ayachero, I told her that if she promised to take care of it, she could call herself the village seamstress. She was thrilled with the idea.

"Lily," she blurted in frustration. "Can you help me with this?"

"Be right there." Every move a negotiation with my aching body, I swung my legs over the side of the hammock, cradling the baby along one arm.

As I sat at the sewing table, I felt a hand on my back. Anna, her infant tucked in my old backpack, Claudia and Paco by her side, pulled up a bench next to us and sat. She hugged me and said, "So how are you feeling? Are you ready for tomorrow?"

"As ready as I can be, I guess," I said. "But I can't tell you how much I'll miss everyone here." It was impossible to express my mixture of bottomless grief for Omar, sadness—and relief—about leaving Ayachero, and angst-filled anticipation for a future back home with a newborn, alone. Every time panic overcame me, I conjured Omar telling me there was no problem I couldn't solve, no jungle so dark and deep and dangerous I couldn't find my way through.

"No one's claimed my magazines or books," I said. "Do you want them, for when you learn English?" My passport, tucked securely in the back pages of *Pride and Prejudice* these many months, was now in a small pocket I'd sewn into my dress.

"Of course." She laughed. "Thank you. For now, I'll enjoy the pictures."

Paco dragged the heavy leather bag of poultice closer to me. "I can put this mud on you."

"Will you, Paco? Just here, on the back of my shoulder where I can't reach."

Paco scooped up a handful of the green mud, applying it so gently I cried a little bit, thinking of Omar's touch, something I would never feel again. As he worked on my back, I spread the salve on all the places I could reach; in moments came the familiar stab of healing pain.

"We've decided to say yes to your wish," Anna said, her hand resting on Paco's shoulder as he did his work. "He'll live with us. From now on, he'll be our son."

I turned to him, scooped him in my arms, and kissed him.

He looked abashed, crestfallen. "I wish you were my mother. I still wish it."

"You love Anna, I know you do."

"But I love you best." He patted his salve-sticky hands at the peach-fuzz growth on my scalp. "I'll grow to be a great man, and you'll come back for me."

"You'll grow to be a great man, and always keep me in your heart, Paco, promise? Just like you'll always be in mine."

"Okay," he said, embracing me before returning to the bag of poultice. "Okay."

The next morning, as I gathered Omar to bathe him in a freshly boiled and cooled pot of water, Doña Antonia gruffly set down a plate of meat on a stool next to me. She sat on a neighboring one, grimacing as if her joints pained her, shoulders slumped. In the bitter set of her mouth and eyes I read her grief for her favorite son, the one who was supposed to save Ayachero.

"He's the only one who cared for me, you know. Really cared for me. He always sent me anything he could spare. Money, food, supplies."

"I'm sorry."

Omar yawned, never opening his eyes, his tiny toothless mouth pink and sweet.

"You're going to take my only grandson away to America?"

"Everyone's been so kind to me here, but my home was with Omar." The truth of that statement gutted me, as did the irony that I would be taking Omar's child from his only other family: grandmother, aunt, uncles, cousins.

"People shoot each other for nothing in your country. I've heard of great storms that kill thousands. Ice everywhere. I'm afraid he'll die there."

"I'll protect him, I swear. He'll have the best life I can give him."

"All right," she said, giving me a nod. "As long as you can promise me that." She pushed herself to her feet and cleared away a few empty plates. "Welcome to this loco world, baby Omar."

She turned away, seemed to struggle with some decision, then pivoted back to me. "I should have been nicer to you. Now it's too late—"

"It's okay. I learned a lot from you."

She pulled her favorite knife from the folds of her apron, blunt handled, chipped and dull. It had seemed part of her hand whenever she used it. "You can use this to clean the animals in Boston, now that you've become so good at it, okay?"

"But this is your best knife—"

"It's just a knife. For God's Sake will bring me another when he comes back." Without another word, she picked up the pot of dirty dishes and brought it downstairs so the rain could wash the plates clean.

The rest of my goodbyes took all morning. People surprised me with their warmth; some were tearful, and soon I was, too. Each farewell gift moved me in its own way: Franz's jaguar-tooth necklace Omar had made for him when they were children; Panchito's little flask of pisco "for the flight home"; the Frannies' heartfelt hugs and benedictions; Anna's set of three smaller-to-larger calabashes carved with beautiful images of anaconda, pink dolphin, and jaguar. She told me all the women had had a hand in making them, all sent their best wishes.

By late morning, it was time to meet For God's Sake at the dock. He made sure baby Omar and I were settled comfortably under the palm canopy that tented his well-loved dugout canoe for the journey to San Solidad. As I watched the last hut disappear behind the towering wall of trees, a wave of loss crashed over me—for Omar, for the people who had cared for me, for the child-self I would never be again. My face must have said it all: For God's Sake kept quiet as we chugged our way upriver.

Finally I said, "What's the real reason you came back?"

He laughed and took off his scratched aviator sunglasses. "Well, you know, Lily, *ca'ah* is not a simple thing. I am making peace with complicated *ca'ah*. Do you know what I'm talking about? How that is? How sometimes you think you know something, and you are quite sure it is the truth, and there is only one truth, but then, the next day even, you wake up and realize, *How can I be so stupid?* You say, what about this, or what about that, over?"

I had to laugh at that, at my own shifting beliefs about what was true and what wasn't.

"I said to myself, okay, For God's Sake, this is not your God, this skinny man on a cross, but I can still help, you know, I can still bring the people of Ayachero foods and medicines, I can still be on this river and be Tatinga in my heart, and that will have to be enough for me. But also I was afraid, Lily. I will tell you that truth. Those men the Tatinga killed would have killed me to know about the grove. And it's not over, this bad story no one can get away from. There will be other poachers. This is not the end of those bad men, of these terrible times. So I am sorry to be a coward, I'm ashamed to be a coward, and I am sorry about Omar, because I loved him like my own brother, over."

"I know you did."

"But there is also the good things, too, you know? We forget those things. We are in a big rush to go on to the next thing that makes us afraid, that makes us sad. Beya is with the Tatinga again. She is home. After all these years, Tatinga saying no, Ayachero people being afraid of her, but then accepting her gifts when she gave them. That is all over. And the Tatinga have killed the jaguar. She was a man eater, there was no doubt. They will use every part, nothing goes to waste. That is how it is there, over."

He paused as he paddled hard now, urging the dugout toward the black waters of a much wider tributary, so much larger in volume than any part of the Amazon I'd ever seen. This was the mighty river itself—no strangled creek—its far bank just a watercolor smudge of green and brown in the distance.

"So I'm back now, you see. I'm not going to run away again, no matter how afraid I get, because now at least I know that much about my *ca'ah*, that this place is part of me, over."

"It's part of me, too, For God's Sake."

A surge of cold air dropped down over us then, something I had never experienced in ten months in the jungle. It smelled of peat, of ever faster cycles of death and rebirth; it felt strange and foreign and foreboding.

The rainy season had begun.

EPILOGUE

O mar was nine when he really asked me about my scars, like he wanted to know the story and was ready to hear it. He'd taken them for granted before. Saw them as just part of his mom, instead of an actual piece of my history, our history, written on my skin.

I suggested we take a walk in the woods near our home in Western Massachusetts, something he loved to do. It was a beautiful fall day, the air dry, fresh and cool, the kind of day I had craved in the jungle. We stopped to sit at a wooden bench overlooking a pond where an orderly row of three painted turtles sunned themselves on a fallen log near the shore. He listened with rapt attention to my stories: meeting his father in Cochabamba, Ayachero and the villagers, Beya, Fat Carlos and Dutchie, our journey to the Tatinga, his birth in the boat, and the jaguar—probably an overwhelming first installment for him, but the floodgates had opened.

His first question was, "So, do you hear her anymore?"

"Beya?" I laughed. "Not for years."

"Yeah, but have you tried?"

"Plenty of times."

"Try now, with me."

We sat cross-legged on the bench, facing each other. He closed his eyes. "Okay, Mom, concentrate." He didn't just look like his father, he shared his calmness, unflappability, a serene confidence. None of that had come from me.

"I'm not hearing anything, Mom." He opened his eyes.

"Could be I'm a little rusty." I caught a whiff of sage: faint, swift, passing. *Was it the memory of the scent or the thing itself?* Then— another jolt of it—stronger this time.

"Omar, do you smell that?"

"Smell what?"

"It's okay, never mind."

He turned back toward the lake, swinging his legs back and forth under the bench. "So, Mom, what did you do for the Tatinga? You made that promise, right?"

I draped my arm over his small shoulders. "When the tropical disease specialists in America examined me, back when you were still a baby, they asked about the plant. Where it grew. They'd never seen anyone so sick with the disease who'd lived to tell about it. It was a hard decision, Omar. Even though I knew I'd be helping a lot of sick people by telling the doctors where the plant grew, I also knew the Tatinga's land would be destroyed if I told them the truth."

"So you lied?"

"Yes."

"What else have you done for them, the Tatinga?"

I looked at him. "I've been busy with you."

"Is Ayachero still there?"

"Not like when I was there. The grove was found, a road was built." I'd been following this for years on the internet. It felt devastating, yet inevitable. "Ayachero looks a lot like San Solidad now. The Tatinga have moved even deeper into the jungle."

"Tell me about my dad's letter to me again."

Countless times I'd recited to him the parts I could remember. He leaned into me and closed his eyes. "The other tribes cannot kill you, because you are high up in the trees as they pass under. You hide in holes only you know exist. Your arrows fly sooner than theirs. The anaconda—he dies from your machete before he can close his jaws on your flesh, and always, dear one, your stomach is full from your own cleverness. Hold on to your little flame of self, because the world wants to blow it out, my beloved son."

"So he was badass, huh."

"Yes. Like you."

He turned to look up at me, took my hand, and traced a scar on my forearm. "Do they still hurt?"

"Not anymore."

Worry lines creased his brow. "So what's my ca'ah, Mom? I don't think I want to be a hunter."

"You have plenty of time to figure that out."

He jumped to his feet, excited now. "Maybe there's something we can do together. We could, you know, put our ca'ahs together."

"Okay, how?"

"Try to save the jungle like Dad wanted to. Save the animals and birds and land. Help the Tatinga. I want to meet Beya and see a jaguar. Drink a beer at the Anaconda Bar. We can wait till when I'm older. Do you want to go back there with me?"

I laughed. "Yes, honey." I stroked his shining black hair, hot in the sunshine. "I do."

That evening, I sat by candlelight at the window of our small but cozy third-floor walk-up, closing for the moment my college textbook on invertebrate zoology. Thrillingly, I was just one semester from my undergraduate degree in biology.

I let my robe slip from my thighs. Pushed up my sleeves. The scars looked like shallow pocked lakes where the parasites had eaten their fill, or smooth and taut, like a burn. I hadn't been quite truthful with Omar: the scars still ached, as if the muscles beneath held tight to the memories, the loss. But there was a sweetness in the pain: a reminder of a world that felt not of this one in its astounding beauty and strangeness.

I understand now that I will always be creating and re-creating my family; actually, I prefer it that way. Omar is keen eyed, sharp eared, curious, and kind; ready to spring forward into the future and explore all of life's steaming jungles. We're both determined to do something good for the world.

And we're just getting started.

ACKNOWLEDGMENTS

I am indebted to the entire team at Simon & Schuster for making *Into the Jungle* a reality, especially to Jennifer Bergstrom for believing in me once again, and to my gifted, cheerful, and unbelievably patient editor, Kate Dresser, who with her unerring editorial eye macheted her way through some pretty gnarly early drafts. You slapped me silly but scared me straight. I owe you a thousand drinks. To my wonderful agent and champion, Erin Harris at Folio Literary Management, immense gratitude for your dedication to the success of this book: I am so lucky I found you.

Big thanks to everyone at Gallery and Scout who accomplish so much, and always with kindness, warmth, and enthusiasm. A no-doubt incomplete list includes: Molly Gregory, Meagan Harris, Jennifer Robinson, Abby Zidle, Mackenzie Hickey, Diana Velasquez, Anabel Jimenez, Wendy Sheanin, Lisa Litwack, Christine Masters, and Stacey Sakal.

I love you, Pamela Rickenbach, executive director of Blue Star Equiculture, for inspiring me with your own adventure in the Amazon. Huge gratitude to Dr. Paul Beaver and Dolly Beaver, owners and founders of Amazonia Expeditions and of the nonprofit group Angels of the Amazon, who welcomed me to the Tahuayo Lodge deep in the Peruvian Amazon on the Tahuayo River, my base camp for conducting research. Thank you to the shaman Adolfo, who gave me hours of his precious time, sharing priceless knowledge about his life and work. To my (truly) fearless and knowledgeable guide, Adrian Gomez Villacorta, thank you for making me touch that foot-long caterpillar when all I wanted to do was run screaming back to my cabin.

For guidance, advice, insight, and information, big thanks to Jonathan Quint, Ned Strong, Dr. Biorn Maybury-Lewis, Michael E. Pereira, and Dr. Theodore Macdonald. For their inspiring, brave, and beautiful books, thank you to the authors Sy Montgomery, Lily King, Ann Patchett, Peter Matthiessen, Barbara Kingsolver, Joe Kane, Douglas Preston, David Grann, Dr. Paul Beaver, Candice Millard, Paul Rosolie, Scott Wallace, Buddy Levy, Chris Feliciano Arnold, Eugene Linden, Holly Fitzgerald, Edward Docx, Ed Stafford, Andrés Ruzo, Dr. Mark J. Plotkin, Petru Popescu, Yossi Ghinsberg, and Pablo Amaringo.

For guidance on the manuscript, cheering me on, putting up with my surliness when asked, *How's the book coming?*, or all three: Nan Kellett, Lira Kanaan, Stephanie Schorow, Andy Mozina, Mary E. Mitchell, Betsy Fitzgerald-Campbell, Ray Bachand, Jude Roth, Jac-Lynn Stark, Nina Huber, Anne B. McGrail, Mary McGrail, Ruth Blomquist, George Ferencik, Katrin Schumann, Holli Andrews, Charles Andrews, Valerie Spain, Portland Helmich, Sandra Miller, Bill Nelson, CeCe Hansen, Drew Pearlman, Phillippa Benson and family, Cheryl Umana, Shannon Rano, Judy Quint, Tatiane Hatchoua, Monica DeOliveira, Amy Karibian, and Leah Parker-Moldover.

Special thanks to Linda Werbner, who read so many drafts with so much loving attention we both lost count.

Gratitude to the Amazon and all its inhabitants, its miraculous plants and creatures of the land, sky, and waters, which fill me with never-ending wonder. Apologies for the many liberties I took in the interest of writing this story.

I am forever grateful to my family for your love, patience, and encouragement: Alaska Grey Ferencik, Jessica Ferencik, Michael and Rebecca Ferencik, and the bravest man of all, my husband, George, who encourages me to venture into the vast unknown, trusting I will always make it back to him in one piece.

INTO

THE

JUNGLE

ERICA FERENCIK

This reader's guide for Into the Jungle *includes an introduction, discussion questions, and ideas for enhancing your book club. The suggested questions are intended to help your reading group find new and interesting angles and topics for your discussion. We hope that these ideas will enrich your conversation and increase your enjoyment of the book.*

Introduction

Lily Bushwold thought she'd found the antidote to endless foster care and group homes: a teaching job in Cochabamba, Bolivia. As soon as she could steal enough cash for the plane, she was on it.

But when the gig falls through and Lily stays in Bolivia, she finds bonding with other broke, rudderless girls at the local hostel isn't the life she wants either. Tired of hustling and already world-weary, crazy love finds her in the form she least expects: Omar, a savvy, handsome local man who's abandoned his life as a hunter in Ayachero—a remote jungle village—to try his hand at city life.

When Omar learns that a jaguar has killed his four-year-old nephew in Ayachero and decides to go back, love-struck Lily goes along, following Omar into a ruthless new world of lawless poachers, bullheaded missionaries, and desperate indigenous tribes driven to the brink of extinction. To survive, Lily must navigate the jungle—its wonders as well as its terrors—using only her wits and resilience.

Topics & Questions for Discussion

1. At the beginning of *Into the Jungle*, Lily describes herself as "a half-starved, high-strung wild child" (page 7). What were your initial impressions of Lily? Did you like her? Why or why not? What factors contributed to Lily's wild nature?

2. Discuss the epigraph that begins *Into the Jungle*. Why do you think Ferencik chose to include it? How does it frame your understanding of the narrative? Who were the shamans that you encountered in *Into the Jungle*? How did they use their powers? What do you think makes a shaman worthy of the title?

3. Describe Omar. Would you have responded to his initial overture? Why does Lily? When Omar shows up at the Versailles the day after meeting Lily as promised, Lily says that it was "just a simple promise kept, but it gleamed and sparkled" (page 27). Explain her reaction. Even though Omar has shown himself to be trustworthy, Lily initially lies to him about her background. Why do you think she does so? What did you think of her lies?

4. Although Lily has been told that life in the jungle is hard and unforgiving, she "had begun to conjure some fairy-tale magical life under the stars in 'nature,' away from the filth and noise of the city" (page 43). Compare Lily's imaginings of life in the jungle with the reality. How does she first react to life in Ayachero? What is her day-to-day life like and what challenges does she face? Why does she decide to go despite the warnings that she receives? What would you do if you were in her position?

5. Early in the novel, Lily muses, "Sex was nothing, or it was a violence, a currency; love a ruse" (page 31). What did you think of Lily's views of love? Do her thoughts on sex and love evolve throughout the novel? If so, how and why?

6. When Lily first sees the Frannies, she is "struck by how American [their wave] looked and felt" (page 83) and wonders whether she is as brash and loud as she finds them. Were you surprised by Lily's reaction to them? Why or why not? Who are the Frannies and what are they doing in the jungle? FrannyB describes the jungle as a "brutal place" (page 84). Compare her view of the jungle to that of Lily and Omar. How and why do their perspectives differ?

7. Omar questions Lily's desire to know "everything," saying, "You think knowing everything is good, Lily. Is that an American thing?" (page 97). How does Omar's view on knowledge vary from Lily's? Why does Omar see withholding information as an act of protection? Do you agree with his perspective? Why or why not? Are there other notable cultural differences between the two of them? What do the people of Ayachero initially think of Lily?

8. Lily describes putting on her backpack as "a move that always comforted me" (page 76). Why does this action give her a sense of security? How does her backpack serve as a talisman? Do you have any objects in your life that provide you with a sense of comfort? What are they and why?

9. For God's Sake plays an important role in the lives of many in the jungle. Who is he and how did he come to receive his name? For God's Sake tells Lily, "sometimes I feel like I am the devil to wear four faces" (page 197). What are those "four faces" and why does For God's Sake feel he needs to occupy each of the roles? How do each of the different groups he interacts with view him? What did you think of him and why?

10. Many of the inhabitants of Ayachero fear Beya. Discuss some of the stories that they share about her. Why is she shrouded in so much mystery? What did you think of Beya when you first encountered her? How did the mythology surrounding the woman compare with the reality of who she was? Lily confesses that "Beya obsessed me" (page 138). Why is she fascinated with Beya? Can you think of any similarities between the two women? Did you agree with Lily's decision to go into the jungle to seek her out? Explain your answer.

11. Lily says, "I couldn't remember having a more joyous day in Ayachero" (page 190) when recounting the afternoon that she spent working with many of the villagers to repair netting with her newly acquired sewing machine. What makes the day so special to Lily? Why do you think that Lily derives so much pleasure from working? Describe the ways in which her views on work evolve throughout the novel.

12. Omar writes that, although it may sound contradictory, he "believe[s] the only way to save the jungle is bringing people from all over the world to see it" (page 36). What threats does the jungle face? Why does Omar think that showing the jungle to outsiders may encourage more conservation? What do you think? How would you go about raising awareness for the need to conserve the jungle?

13. After Lily has lived in Ayachero for six months, Dona Antonia gives her a bowl of embers, explaining that it is "the fire of the hearth. The *jenecherú*. It's something offered to a new family member" (pages 228–29). What prompts Dona Antonia to give this gift to Lily when she does? Describe Dona Antonia's treatment of Lily when the two women first meet. What reasons does Dona Antonia have for being distrustful of Lily? Did you think that Dona Antonia's treatment of Lily was fair? Why or why not?

14. When Omar first attempts to appeal to Splitfoot, the chief of the Tatinga tribe, using their shared history, Splitfoot dismisses him, saying, "That was before you became a white man, as far as I can tell" (page 275). Explain Splitfoot's statement. Why does he view Omar's time outside the jungle negatively? What are some of the views that Splitfoot and the rest of his tribe hold? How do the Ayachero villagers view them?

Enhance Your Book Club

1. One of the items that Lily carries in the backpack that she takes everywhere is a worn-out copy of *Charlotte's Web* that she stole from her last group home. She says, "I had no explanation for why this little pig's life saved by the efforts of the spider who really loved him tore my guts out. I only knew that the story had gotten to me . . . but also gave me hope that I could—someday—overcome my wordless sorrow" (page 12). If you haven't read *Charlotte's Web*, do so and discuss it with your book club. Why do you think the book resonated with Lily? Are there any books from your childhood that have stuck with you? If so, tell your book club about them and consider having a childhood classic–themed book club meeting.

2. While waiting for Omar in the jungle heat, Lily "thought of the parts of America I missed: Dairy Queen, the movies, candy bars, Cheerios, malls, scented soap, libraries, fall leaves, snow; things Omar had never seen, had no interest in seeing" (page 2). Have you ever been far away from your native home? Did you miss

anything specific? If you haven't, are there particular parts of your home that you love and think you would be nostalgic for? What are they? Share some of your favorite things about your birthplace with your book club. What is it about these things that you love?

3. When Lily visits the Frannies, FrannyB offers Lily her copies of books by Jane Austen and Charlotte Brontë. FrannyB explains that "A's a big fan of that Victorian stuff . . . she's a bit of a romantic, so . . ." (page 173). Why do you think FrannyA took those particular books with her? If you were moving to a distant location and could only take three or four books, what would you take with you and why?

4. To learn more about Erica Ferencik, request that she visit your book club, read about her other writings, and more, visit her official site at EricaFerencik.com.